HOT WATER

"HOT WATER"

DON WALLACE

SOHO

The author gratefully acknowledges a grant from James A. Michener and the Copernicus Society of America. He especially thanks K.F. and J.P. for the loan of a room—with a view—without which this book could not have been written.

Published by Soho Press, Inc.
853 Broadway
New York, NY 10003

Library of Congress Cataloging-in-Publication Data
Wallace, Don, 1952–
Hot water / by Don Wallace.
p.   cm.
ISBN 0-939149-44-3 : (hc : acidfree)
I. Title.
PS3573.A425646H68 1991
813'.54—dc20   90-49802
                                                    CIP

Book design and composition by The Sarabande Press

To Mindy

HOT WATER

I was laying on my belly in a loblolly deadfall, a great tangle of sand clods and hair roots and gnarly tap roots as big around as my thigh. It was a good place to hide: dark, with plenty of holes to look out of. I peered through the black *V* of my gunsight and waited for some kind of sign.

On the other side of the war zone was a rude parish church, just across the creek in a cornfield. A woman seated on the porch steps had been combing her hair there for the last half hour. She had her head tilted over, as if she had one ear to the ground and was listening to the earth her long, red hair almost touched. She ran the comb through it in lazy strokes. Behind her was the gray pine shanty; it had a disused look. The cross was a television aerial painted gold.

"Jayssuss . . ." she sang. "Jayssuss . . ." It was pure as well water, that voice. I knew right away she was a gospel singer. "Be mah friend . . ." Her voice fell like a ray of light on the cornfield, as the clouds parted overhead.

I took my mind off the gap between the forest and the riverbottom thicket of green willow and blue cottonwood. I let my eye drift across the stubble of the disked-off corn that looked like a GI's first haircut, and I wished I wasn't lying here in a cold, muddy hollow between the fire ants and the black widows, in camouflage from head to foot, my face painted in green and brown streaks, and a tan watch cap pulled over my stinking hair. The silly things a man will do to fill the hours of his life. Here I was, suffering, when I could have been bass fishing.

The gospel singer sat on the steps and put her hands on her knees, threw back her head and whooped it up, testing those pipes. It shamed me just to listen. She was having a grand time. Letting it out. Toying with the gift He gave her. And where was I and my gift? In the mud. Playing soldier.

Run-through or not, the gospel singer could have had my bottom dollar if the collection plate was to come gliding up over the cornfield, across the river and into the war zone. It wouldn't even have to be lit by a ray of love, or escorted by white doves of peace.

I had as much as decided to end my piece of the war. Then a slight rustle in the brambles on the other side of the loblolly caught my ear. The brambles were swaying. Yes, some fool was sneaking along the trunk of the fallen tree, creeping like a serpent, gun out and hopes high for a kill. It was in the cards, one of us had to go, so I scrunched up to give a smaller target and stretched out my pistol. I was going to blow that sucker away.

Splat—my forehead burned. My neck went rubbery. I dropped my gun and put the back of my hand to my head. I brought it down slowly, afraid to look.

It was red, all right. I was dead.

A shrub stood up and walked across the clearing on the other side, between the forest and the riverbottom. It was a good-sized shrub, about five-foot-five. A juniper around the head and shoulders, it became a silvery clump of willow leaves from the waist down. Blue-gray eyes stared out from a face all green and brown, like mine.

"Nice shot," I said. When I touched my forehead, I felt the beginnings of a welt.

"I knew I had you when that woman started to sing."

"Virginia Roy, is that you?" I got to my feet and stared at the shrub. She'd done a good job—it figures that a woman would have a way with camouflage—but I was still surprised not to recognize my own wife under all the botanical garb.

She raised her pistol up and cocked it by pulling back the slide. "You know what this means, don't you?" she asked.

"I guess I'm the one to save us a table at the barbecue. You going to win this thing, or what?"

She shrugged. The weekend skirmish had been her idea. When we arrived Friday night for the briefing, all I was good for was a beer and bed. Virginia Roy not only went to the briefing but came back with maps and rules that she studied on the motel room floor. I would wake up and see her there, making marks on the terrain with orange grease pencil.

"Well, I'm off," she said, waving the barrel of the pistol. "Save me some of that barbecue. This war is *work*."

"Sure thing. Good luck, honeybunch." We looked each other over, trying to see where we should attempt to plant a kiss. She wasn't showing a bit of cheek.

Someone cleared his throat. "Ahem."

I jumped straight up. Virginia Roy whipped around and almost got her pistol level, but not before she caught a bullet in the belly. A safe shot—not a pretty kill like the head shot on me. But she was dead and she knew it.

I felt a little better: there *had* been someone creeping along on the other side of the tree trunk, after all.

"Darn it." She reached up and ripped off the juniper bush covering her head. "Darn, darn, darn!"

We both turned to see who had lucked out. The brambles shook slightly. "It would be the polite thing," said Virginia Roy, "to introduce yourself."

Something black, white, and shiny flipped out of the bushes, over the fallen tree, and landed at my feet. I picked it up. An ace of spades.

The bushes rustled again as the ambusher pressed on. "Okay, wise guy. Enjoy your war!" Virginia Roy shouted. I hated it when she lost her temper. Next thing I knew she was off at a trot, and I had to hurry to catch up.

"Listen, V.R., I'm sorry about that."

"My own fat fault. I forgot the rules of war: kill and move on."

"Actually, I was setting up to blindside him when you nailed me."

"It was a trap." She stripped grass and willow switches from her as she walked. Underneath she had on a black leotard that covered every inch from ankle to wrist. It was to help stop chiggers and ticks, but that wasn't all it did. She was starting to look like a woman again.

"It was so obvious," she said.

"How'd you figure?"

"Somebody knew to get me by following you. Well, you live and learn."

"At least we're getting back in time to shower before everyone else at the motel uses up the hot water." I flung an arm around her shoulders and kissed her, camouflage paint and all. "Let me buy you a Coke at the barbecue?"

She squeezed my hand and laid her head on my shoulders, pulling off her hairnet with her other hand and showing off her glossy black curls. My fierce and beautiful wife.

We came around a bend in the creek, opposite the gray parish church. Somebody had put a satellite dish in the stubbled cornfield. The gospel singer was gone. I didn't care.

That was one strange barbecue. There were pork ribs with the meat cooked out of them until gristle was what you got, something called chicken, and a pot of chili beans. But it's not the food I'm talking about. The air did get pretty smoky, but what else is a barbecue for?

It was the people. Oh, everybody mixed it up, there wasn't any prejudice against those of us who'd gotten killed, but you could tell who was who. There were winners and losers. The live ones had a way of walking with their arms out from their sides. That and their stiff backs got to me, and I'm normally quite tolerant, a people person.

I overheard two survivors talking.

"One of my better days," said this guy in a green Special Forces T-shirt, flashing a nice gap-toothed smile. "I got one target by turning within my own circle, then bisecting the hypotenuse. A win-win solution."

"The game was good today," replied the other man, who was dark and had long hair tied in a braid. He wore a down vest over his bare chest. "I felt the spirit of Brother Eagle guiding me as if we really were one."

I must have made a sound, because they both turned and stared at me briefly. It seemed best to move along. Yet everywhere I looked, I saw what appeared to me to be even stranger people. And the T-shirts they wore! "Kill 'em all—let God sort 'em out," read the one on a large, bearded man with small, close-set eyes.

The organizers of Weekend Warrior worked hard to make us feel good about each other. They gave us T-shirts. There was a Hawaiian band. But it was a relief when the festivities began to wind down and the keynote speaker took over the podium from the sad-eyed Hawaiian bandleader.

"My name is Rico Octoponte," the speaker began. He let that sink in, a squat, bearded fellow in fatigues that were as neatly pressed as a suit. "I hope you had fun today—those of you who are here for a first time. Maybe you are a bit tired, yes? Feet sore? Didn't that hot bath feel good? *Ahhh.*"

Rico Octoponte closed his eyes and smiled, stretching out his

7

arms to either side as if he was floating in a tub. I kind of liked him for that.

"Friends, I am here to talk about real war. You *Norte Americanos* are truly under God's wing not to have known war as others have. As I have. Otherwise, friends, I do not think you would enjoy this game. When I first heard of this war game, I thought: What a difference! What a way to spend a weekend. And, I admit this, I laughed. Forgive me for that, please."

The people around me shifted uneasily. The large man with pig's eyes murmured, "Who's the spic?"

As if he'd heard, which was clearly impossible, Rico Octoponte stared directly into the group I was with. "Now I take it all back," he said slowly. "Having seen you today. There is something going on here. It is not just play. I believe you are all here for a purpose. You aren't satisfied with the decadent pleasures of America the Beautiful. You seek truth; what the philosophers call meaning and substance. You sense a danger. You wish to be prepared. And, I think, the danger is real. You are right to be here because your time is going to come, believe me, and the reflexes you have learned today, painful as the lessons may have been, will make a difference. They just may keep you alive."

The crowd had quieted.

"In other places what you were doing today is done for keeps. No pellets. Live ammunition. I, Rico Octoponte, come from such a place. I can't go back there; the Communists killed my family. Today I live on the kindness of strangers here in a foreign land. But I swear to you that I will not rest until the devil is driven from my land, and all lands. And that includes your land."

The large man looked thoughtful. "He's a Cuban, right?" he asked his companion. But his friend disagreed: "No, he's from the other place, Nicaragua."

A Panama hat was making the rounds. By the time it got to me it was pretty full of bills. "Just remember that a 7.65 millimeter bullet costs roughly one dollar," Rico Octoponte was saying. "If there are any philosophers here, that is what I call 'Meaning and Substance'. Seekers of truth, here it is."

He held a shiny brass cartridge up and revolved it in his fingers so it caught the light. "Live ammunition, amigos."

Looking around me at the crowd of faces all turned to the stage, all lit by the same light, here and there I saw a familiar welt on a forehead, like a caste mark on an Indian. Shot in the head, like me. Then I saw Virginia Roy in back helping serve pieces of gummy chess pie on flimsy paper plates, and I wished she didn't have to get into the act so wholeheartedly. This wasn't the USO at Cam Ranh Bay. I needed a break.

There was a side door near the stage and I took it. The building doubled as a VFW lodge, and the room I walked into for a breath of fresh air was, if anything, worse than the hootenanny in the main hall. On the walls there were twenty portraits of old soldiers, boozers in bright Kodak color, their red noses looking tender and their eyes deader than the stuffed deer whose rack was hung with banners and one yellowed brassiere. But there was a soft drink machine, the old kind with the thick glass door.

I got a bracing blast of icy air when I opened the door and grasped the neck of the closest bottle between my knuckles. With my other hand I readied two quarters and looked for the slot.

I did a double take. My heart kind of went out to those VFW guys. Anybody who kept an old nickel Coke machine running got my vote; it even had the rack on one side for the empties, which were all thick glass, six-ounce bottles, of course. Irreplaceable, dark black beauties, the full Cokes waited in the machine, beaded with condensation. I hesitated. This was the real thing. How could I resist?

I used the opener under the coin return and leaned up against the humming metal box. I took a drink. Not a sip, but a sudden tilt of the bottle so the supercarbonated black wave, so sweet and sharp, crashed and foamed in my throat. What a feeling. I groped in my pocket for my notepad with the stubby golf pencil and looked for a distributor's address on the machine. Perhaps he could sell me one, or tell me how he found this one; at any rate, a supply of the old-fashioned glass bottles would be nice. I could see having a private stock at home, for hot nights and dog days.

Those six-ounce bottles are just long enough to feel short. I put it in the rack with true regret, bidding goodbye to an old friend. Then it was time, time to drag Virginia Roy away from the party and head back to Valhalla.

I found her talking to a bald fellow who I recognized as one of the organizers of the weekend. There was another man there, his back to me as I approached; I didn't pay him any mind.

"Virginia Roy, we have a drive ahead of us," I said.

She didn't look up, just scrunched her eyebrows together to show me her attention was somewhere else, and would I mind? Well, I can be as polite as the next man. But then I saw who it was: Rico Octoponte. He saw me, too, and tucked his hairy chin in and looked grave. "I was just congratulating your wife on her shooting. She made many fine kills."

"But she saved the best for me."

Virginia Roy looked pleased and relaxed, a bottle of beer in one hand, the other across her belly, fingers hooked in the belt-loops of her jeans. She threw me a smile. For that, she could stay here as long as she liked.

The organizer said, "Rico here was telling us about the war." Even his bald head was tanned.

"Which war was that?" I asked.

"*Exactamente*. That is my point," Rico Octoponte said. "There is but one war under God on the planet Earth. In every nation, the serpent's tooth is sown. Nobody is immune. When the blood of one freedom fighter is shed, the stain is on all our hands."

"Not when you're using Red Dye Number 2," I said, pointing to my forehead. I'm not usually a wise guy, and a prickle of heat along my neck and ears told me I was in for it. Without even having to look, I knew Virginia Roy was embarrassed.

"Oh, Gar."

The skirmish organizer laughed nervously. "Yes, the dye does wash out — we learned a lesson after the first time. We had some very unhappy people on our hands."

I checked out Octoponte. He was looking at me with a sleepy smile on his face. "Have you got a dollar?" he asked.

I goggled at him. He nodded up and down, slowly. Well, I figured it was better to be the butt of a party trick than to pick a fight with the guest of honor, so I dug in my pants pocket and held out a wadded-up dollar.

But as I put the bill in the palm of his hand, he grabbed my wrist with his other hand and twisted it upside down. It hurt like fire. Yet I could see plainly that he was only holding it by his thumb and forefinger.

He put the dollar in his shirt pocket with his free hand and, taking something out, he put it in my palm, then closed my fist around it. I knew what it was from the size, small for such coldness and heaviness.

I didn't open my fist, didn't look, just put it in my pocket. "You bet," I said.

He nodded. At least he wasn't mad and I hadn't spoiled the party. "I was saying," he went on, with a nod to the others. "We fight a many-headed monster: Communism. It is taught to children in schools, delivered to your doorstep in your newspapers. It runs from your tap water in poison additives that they say cure tooth decay." I chuckled. He balled up one fist and jammed it in his fatigue jacket pocket, stared fiercely at me, not seeing my face at all. I realized he was younger than I'd thought; there were gray bags under his eyes, which were bloodshot.

"*Hasta libertad*," he said, to Virginia Roy, the organizer and, barely, to me. He turned on his heel and walked away fast.

The bald organizer's eyes followed him until he was in the middle of the room, and still he spoke in a whisper: "They say his mother was tortured after his father was taken away, never to be seen or heard from again. By the security forces. . . ."

Virginia Roy patted the organizer on the shoulder and said we had to hit the road.

We'd packed after taking our showers at the motel and the car was in the lot outside the hall. In five minutes we were well out of there and on the highway.

She was driving this leg, from Ofahoma to Jackson, then down to Bogue Chitto. Cities made her nervous, so I would take over again near the suburbs of New Orleans, over Lake Pontchartrain to Gulfport, up US 49 a hitch, then to home. Valhalla, Mississippi.

"Did you have fun?" she asked, one foot propped against the dash.

I made a face.

"Was it that bad?"

"I can think of better things to do, that's all."

"I bet I could've won, too." She sighed, happy.

"Sure. That'll teach you to shoot your husband."

"Well, we gave it a try. I suppose you're going to want to go fishing next weekend?"

"I was thinking of it. If you don't mind."

"I don't mind," she said.

"Welcome to come along."

"No thanks."

"It just makes more sense to me. I mean, instead of playing GI Joe in the mud."

"The point is, we weren't playing. Didn't you hear what Rico was saying? We were training."

"For when the *Communistas* come to call, eh?"

"Stranger things have happened, Garfield Foote."

"Well, Virginia Roy, all I can say is I hope you don't go

gunning for no *Communistas* in that sexy black leotard you was wearing today."

She didn't say anything. Then she began to giggle.

"What's so funny?"

"The look on your face out there in the woods. You looked like you were in church, listening to the angels sing. And then bingo. Bull's-eye. The look on your face."

"It was a good shot, I'll grant you."

"I'm good, aren't I?" She shook her head so that her curls whipped around. "Me, Virginia Roy. The jungle girl."

That's my wife. Feisty and freckled and nobody's fool except mine. All female, no bull. Ever since I've known her she's given her all to everything, whether it's doing the wash or weekend warrior-ing. She even tried bass fishing to please me, but that was one area where the girl had no talent. It didn't stop her from learning everything the sport had to offer from a technical standpoint. She just couldn't catch fish.

"Gar, what was Rico doing when he asked you for a dollar? Did he give you something?"

"Oh, that." I decided not to tell her; I'd already caused enough trouble. "It was a Masonic handshake. Surprised the heck out of me."

"Huh." Just then an eighteen-wheeler, going the other way, hit his brights on and off. She slowed down as we went around the curve. "Where is he? Do you see him?"

I searched the roadside. A side road, a billboard, a dilapidated barn, the boards falling every which way. "Looks clear to me."

"There he is." She unwrapped a finger from around the steering wheel and pointed. I still couldn't see a thing. "Between those two trees," she said, impatiently, and then I saw him, a motorcycle policeman. We eased past at an even forty. At the top of the hill there was a cruiser with its driver's door open and a sheriff leaning out, aiming a radar gun down the way we'd come.

"I hate those traps," Virginia Roy said. "You know, we ought to get ourselves a Fuzzbuster. It just isn't fair otherwise."

"Maybe so." I reached out a hand and stroked her leg. "I notice you got him before he got you."

She grabbed my hand up and kissed it.

A mile later, she said, "I'd like to try a war game—a weekend—again. Just to see how good I could be."

"Sure. Fine." But the thought of going back and crawling in the mud was enough to make me want to take another shower. "Tell you what. I'll sit on the sidelines so you won't have any, you know, conflict of interest."

She nodded absently.

By the time we pulled into the driveway it was midnight. Bats and mosquitos were strafing the lonesome porch light. While Virginia Roy ran herself a bath in the old clawfoot tub, I went for a walk down to the pond. The air was full of steam but there wasn't any rain in it. It was least hot under the big sycamores on our place, as if they'd drawn cool air around themselves. The pine woods, though, tasted hot as frying oil. I stood by the pond, which I'd improved by blasting out some stumps and damming up a tributary so as to be eligible for the state bass stocking program. I let peace come into my bones after the long drive. The pond was tarnished like good silver. The bats dipped low, nipping baby mosquitos. A few ripples broke the surface here and there. Those were my babies. My bass.

My thoughts were melancholy. It only goes to show nothing is ever as you planned. I'd made this pond back when I thought I was going professional. Now I never fished it. It was as though I wanted that pond pure and untouched.

For me, the weekend had been a total wash-out. But not for Virginia Roy. She was feeling pretty good about it. She had a right to her fun. Just as I had to mine—like when I was a bass fisherman and didn't have the time of day for anything else.

My fellow man is not my idea of a good target, dummy bullets or not. It's just a feeling I have. I'm not saying it makes me better, just different. Sure, Virginia Roy will never understand how I feel about bass fishing. That makes us even in what we can't share. But is that the way God planned it?

On my way back to the house I stopped at the garage. The two Yale padlocks and twenty feet of chain were wet with dew. I couldn't help it, I let myself in. I didn't need to turn on the light. The boat was there, eighteen feet long, the gold fleck metal-flake green paint picking up moonbeams and starlight like a galaxy all its own. The big outboard on the stern reared up like a horse's head. I squeezed the tires on the boat trailer and the pressure was good.

Driving to the plant at five-thirty the next morning, I detoured off the main drag to check up on the rest of the gang before they went off to work. At Lucky Bonnard's canalside split-level both cars were gone. He and his wife had probably stayed overnight at the lake. Cecil George was asleep in his little apartment, and his car was tarped. Eddie Bucci's 4×4 was in the driveway and hooked up to his boat. I leaned out the window and took in the damage. His cherry red paint job needed a wax and a buffing, but it would take more than that to fix the scratches along the side. He'd been in the stumps again. Good for Eddie. I bet he had caught bass.

At the plant the night watchman woke when I punched in at the time clock. "Mornin', Boss," he said, rearing up on the cot. I switched on the light and he held a hand over his yellow eyes.

"Git on home. Your working day is done."

"Shore it is. You catch any bass this weekend, Boss?"

"Did something else for a change."

"Why'd you do that? I thought you liked to fish."

"Sometimes you need a little change, Jesse, that's all."

"But you love to fish. You still love to, don't you?"

"I sure do, but even I need a change now and then. All right? Now git along."

"Seems to me a man don't change what he like. I know what I like, and I don't change." He waved a hand at me and picked up his shoes, walking barefoot out the door.

I opened the refrigerator and took out breakfast, a thirty-two-ounce Super-Saver bottle of Coke, and looked at the daylog to remind myself what had to be done. The 64- and the 128-millipore filters needed servicing, which meant shutting down the tank farm pumps, probably half at a time. All the hoses and mixing tanks might as well get a good steam-cleaning, too, but they'd have to be done before 10:00 A.M. There also was a section of bottling track that was due for its thousand-hour checkup. Deliveries were set on the half hour, loadings a quarter to.

I had company. Outside, in the parking lot, a car with a smoker's cough and a horse's whinny pulled up and stopped. A minute passed. The fluorescent tubes jumped on all over the plant. The air conditioning sucked on, the lights flickering off, then on. The reserve generator whomped on and off—just a quick toggle of the switch. Finally, Trank du Lac poked his head in.

Trank has the flattest, shiniest, blackest hair I've ever seen. He had on his white short-sleeve shirt and a black tie, just like mine. Sometimes I wish he wouldn't do that, imitate me, but you can't fault him, he's so sincere. Among Orientals this dressing like the bossman is considered a sign of respect, so I can't very well tell him to knock it off. Even if folks do call us the Bobbsey Twins.

"Good morning, Mr. du Lac."

"Good morning, Mr. Foote," Trank said. "It's to be a great week. Production quotas one hundred percent. No downtime. No on-the-job injury."

"Right you are, Mr. du Lac," I said. A memo from the main office had said I must address all management staff as Mister. It was hard to keep to it, because Trank was all the manager I had, so I generally dispensed with the Mister by mid-morning or earlier. "Care to join me for a Coke?"

"Thank you, Mr. Foote." He brought a white sack out from behind his back. "I am having also Egg McMuffin."

It's a sign of his loyalty that he buys his Cokes. We have a policy that allows each employee one free sixty-four-ounce bottle a day, and a considerable discount on any case purchases, but Trank does his own bit to uphold our market share. You have to respect the guy. When they first sent him, a Vietnamese, I wondered if Atlanta had lost its mind. But you couldn't ask for a more dedicated or loyal bottling-line foreman than Trank du Lac. The man was a tank commander and he had lost everything. He could have lost his respect for the USA along with his home and his family, but Trank is a true believer. Becoming a member of the Coca-Cola family suited him perfectly and he understands, maybe better than anyone in Valhalla, what it means to work for a corporation that carries the flag, so to speak, into every country and nook and cranny around the globe. He feels a responsibility that I wish more Americans did.

Trank and I have this in common. Everyone else think it's because of Vietnam, but they're wrong. After joining the National Guard in college, at Martinsville Trade Technical School, I spent two years driving a bulldozer on my weekends so I could stay close to Virginia Roy. I was kind of surprised to find the war still going strong when I graduated, to tell the truth, but I was game. All I really wanted to do was get my job at Coca-Cola and marry Virginia Roy, but if my country needed me to defend and preserve, I'd do that, too. I soon found myself in Cam Ranh Bay writing invoices and sweating off four forty-eight-ounce bottles of combat-strength Coke a day (they went heavy on the syrup over there for some reason). I got shipped back a year later and that was it for the Vietnam War. So I'm no vet, not hardly. Coca-Cola, not Vietnam, is what holds Trank and me together.

Trank finished his breakfast and left. The punch clock started thumping at about a quarter to. The older employees still find it hard not to come in early, remembering the days when the least little thing could land your butt in the dust. Back then, plenty of folks gave the company fifteen free minutes a day. Twenty years back folks didn't have much choice.

By a quarter after, the punch clock was going like a jackhammer. We're the biggest employer in Valhalla. Then the banging slowed to an occasional backfire, as the late sleepers, the go-slows and the hangovers trickled in. I always give my workers an hour to get into the rhythm before I shift anybody around, so I spent the time making up work details for the week.

There was a knock on the glass panel of my door. "Come in," I said. The door opened and a messenger in a fancy silver jumpsuit looked down at the clipboard in his hand.

"Garfield Foote?"

"That's me." I reached out for the letter he was carrying.

"I'll have to see some proof."

I waved to my nameplate. But that didn't seem to register, so I handed him my wallet. He made me sign a receipt on the clipboard as well.

I've maybe received one registered letter before in my life, back when I won the Mitresboro Bass Bonanza and it seemed for a while that I was on my way to turning professional. This was going that one better; this was an overnight express letter sealed with sticky cellophane. Inside was another envelope, and the return address was from the president of the company! I was shaking a bit by now. I couldn't stop thinking that maybe my balance sheet looked real good over in Atlanta.

But as soon as I opened the letter I knew it wasn't any big deal. It was just an announcement from corporate headquarters. Wasn't even personal. I leaned back, took a pull on my Coke, and cocked my wrist with the letter in it so I had enough light to read by.

> An important moment has arrived . . . there comes a time when changing tastes . . . younger people, brighter people, with new and now life-styles . . . when we say we're chang- ing, too, we mean for the better . . . a better future . . . more in tune with today's youthful style, demand a lighter brighter taste . . . lemony, crisp, with a tingle . . . the same devotion to quality that's always been . . . in the soon-to-be announced near future, get ready for the biggest . . . history of the company . . . brand new Coke . . .

Brand new Coke?
It was such empty-headed nonsense that I skimmed most of it. But this caught my eye, at the bottom:

> Treat this news as classified information. Do not tell anyone—not your wife, not your children, or friends. Re- peat: Do not tell anyone. If you do, and we hear of it, you're fired. Guaranteed. We want complete surprise.

I put the letter down and laughed. Those public relations guys in Atlanta had me going for a moment, but I know a gimmick when I see one. This was a honey. Oh, they'd let everyone get good and worked up. Heck, I'd pay attention, too. But in the end nothing would come of it. Except some good publicity. Those guys, they're sharp.

The rest of the morning we were busy as bees. The lunch bell went off in my empty belly like a gong, so I took my chances with everybody else in the parking lot. It looked like a stock car rally, what with all the dust and skidding cars and pickups. I put my foot down to the floor, heading for the Sizzle Shack.

Even so, half of the gang was already there, taking up two booths and the counter stools facing them, saving room for any latecomers. Monday's only just tolerable if you take lunch at the Sizzle Shack; it's best to get here early, though. They run out of specials.

Lucky Bonnard waved me over. Lucky has a skinny body and a skinny mustache, but his hair makes up for it: black and thick and oiled down so he can comb it out like Elvis's, sprayed so it'll hold in a tornado. Lucky is a realtor, the same as his wife, who also has a major league hairdo, but hers can't hold a candle to his.

"Hot action on the lake, Lucien?" I said.

He planed his flat hand up and away. "Should've been there, buddy."

"Hey, Gar, how was the war?" Eddie Bucci called out, the only one already eating. A Roto-Rooter man, he's always on call with a radio in his truck, and orders and eats fast.

Eddie and I were in the Guard together, so I thought about my answer a bit more than I might've if someone else had asked the same question. "It was interesting in its way, I guess. Kind of hard to get into. Other folks seemed to be having fun and enjoying themselves."

Eddie nodded, mouth full of chicken and cinnamon gravy.

The waitress came up. I pointed at Eddie munching. "Hi, Lurleen, you got any more of that?"

She gave me a smile, but under the white pancake makeup she looked beat. "Only one of him, praise the Lord," she said.

"How the kids?" I asked. Lurleen went to high school same time as us. We used to see something socially of her and her man for a couple of years after. And of course he was a regular here. But when they split up, he had to stop coming to the Sizzle Shack, though sometimes he would pull up in the parking lot and sit in his car, looking at Lurleen with hard, black eyes.

"Not exactly kids anymore, Gar. Coke?" she asked.

"Coke."

After she'd gone, Eddie sighed. "Lurleen tempts me, but then I couldn't eat no lunch with nobody else but her."

Lucky put his arm around Eddie's shoulders. "You sure that Roto-Rootin' doesn't keep you from tootin'?"

Eddie held up a gnawed drumstick. "This is what your pecker'd look like after a weekend of the kind of romance I routinely experience."

Lucky reclined in his chair and stuck out his chin. "That's what my red worm looked like Saturday at the lake." He paused and savored his next words: "After the bassin'."

Well, we all settled down to hear about it. Lucky is a manure artist, but he knows what we like and he can dish it out: bass action, hot and heavy. But first he paints in the scene, the quiet hour of getting the boat out on the road, sipping a mug of coffee, pulling up at the lake. It's high summer, a mist hangs on the water like a steambath. A couple of panfish jump in the shallows, doing silvery figure eights. Maybe an old raccoon slinks out of his way, a crawdad in his teeth. Dead silent. Then he yanks the rope and the big throaty water-boiling outboard splits the morning down the middle, the way his boat's going to fillet the lake's unmarked surface in another second. But before that, Lucky sits still and empties his mind. A shadowy idea forms: he sees a ledge about two miles away, a pile of weed, a swirl of tailfin and a yellow gleam of eye. Only then does Lucien Bonnard shift the V6 two hundred horsepower Johnson into gear.

Bass boats are wide and shallow, with sharp bows and low, sleek lines. Touch the throttle and a bass boat leaps forward, up on plane in an instant. Lucky rides down low, squeezed into a tuck-and-roll upholstered bucket seat, slicing the lake down the middle, leaving a crisp ever-widening V as his signature. He glides along at forty miles an hour; no need to punch it higher, he'll save his head gaskets for tournament action. The shoreline curves in and out, any one of a dozen lucrative pockets to the unaided eye, but Lucky's eye is turned inward—to the console dash instruments. He's reading the lake bottom. A chart is scrolling off the graph depth finder that Lucky prefers to a flasher-type sounder.

He watches the charcoal scratches, looking for bottom structure or, if lucky, an actual school of bass. He's also factoring in the water temperature display and pH level as he nudges into a promising cove. Lucky's a very scientific basser. He'll take home that depth finder chart after a day's fishing and file it away after noting his results in a code only he can decipher. Others, for instance me, use a liquid crystal display that flashes up the information but doesn't mess up your mind with wads of paper. To each his own. Bassers are split down the middle into those who make their own charts, like Lucky, and those of us who use prepared charts and spot-on readings off the flasher. Lucky will always know a lake better than I will, but I'll be fresher, my mind less cluttered, more open to reading a pattern or following a hunch. At least, that's the theory.

"What I saw down there," Lucky drawled, "was confusing, to say the least. It was a square structure, with a thin line three feet above it, like a board, and my graph was showing lots of bogies ducking in and out of that structure. First I covered my hands with crawfish essence and I musked up the lure with Worm Blood."

Eddie pointed a fork. "What lure did you say?"

"I didn't say." Lucky took a small nickel-plated comb out of his shirt pocket and began to run it through his fenders. "I cut the Johnson and switched to my Minn Kota weedless electric trolling unit and walked the boat in quiet, stern-first, and dropped my plug. The structure was a rectangle, so I did a perimeter run, a diagonal, and a deep-sink troll. No luck. So I backed off, changed to a different lure—I don't mind mentioning that it was a golden Rapala with a little Peck'it Potion on it, Eddie, my friend—and then I did a suicide run, dragging it under that thin line that showed above the structure on my graph.

"Right away I took a strike. But then the line went dead, like a weed clump was on, so I reeled her in. And check it out, boys." He reached into his pants pocket and brought out his bony fist, slowly turning it over, opening it. He grinned. In his palm was a pair of black sponge dice with yellow spots, mildewed and pock-marked.

Lucky tossed the dice on the table. "I'd caught me the good-luck charm off a '57 Chevy's rearview mirror. But that ain't all. When I looked over the side to bring in those dice? There was a monster smallmouth just about to take the hook. With a flip of his tail he was gone, all twelve pounds of him."

Eddie was staring into space, lips tight. "Had to be near a road for a car to make it," he mused. He glanced at me. "Gar, it sounds like Purcell Cove to me."

"That, or Tompkins Sawmill." I turned to Lucky. "So, did you go back after that monster?"

"I left him, just like that," he said. "Went across the lake and caught a nice string on my red worm — six fish, eleven pounds, five ounces. I'm saving that monster for the next tournament."

I nodded appreciatively. The whole time he'd been telling us his story, Lucky had been setting us up for a sucker punch. He'd just given us all something to think about the next time we faced him in competition. That was Lucky, the consummate bass strategist.

Eddie belched. He regarded his empty plate. "God, that *was* good, though. You done bullshittin', Bonnard? Then listen to this: I caught and released twenty-two bass yesterday. I figure my best string would've weighed in the neighborhood of fifty pounds."

It was an absurd claim. "Where were you, the Gulf of Mexico?" I asked.

"Ross Barnett Reservoir."

"That's a lot of miles to put on your Sears Diehards."

"I wanted to practice on some tough water, in somebody else's backyard," he said. "Tournament season is upon us."

He had brought us to heel.

"Some big bucks riding on the Classic this year," Lucky said heartily.

"Forget the Classic," Eddie said. "None of us is going to be fishing the Classic unless we win us one of the qualifiers. And to win the qualifiers you got to be ready." Eddie was a guard on the high school football team, and a sergeant in the Guard; it showed. A tough little runt. Snaking that Roto-Rooter coil down the drains of plugged sinks and toilets for twenty-four hours a day, including Sundays, has given him a view of the world that doesn't leave much room for sugar-coated daydreams.

"How many tournaments?" he said. "A hundred and ten. But that only means a hundred and ten ways to lose." Eddie had on a muscle T-shirt, and his short, lifter's torso rose and fell with his words. The logo on the front screamed BASS IRONMAN: 200 HP SAYS I CAN, which he had won by coming in fortieth out of forty at the Lake Eufala Invitational. We know he wears this record of his humiliation like a hair shirt, to remind him how low he can go.

Lucky said, "You only have to get hot once or twice, to qualify."

"Who qualified last year? Tell me that," Eddie sneered.

After a silence, I tried to break the tension. "Since we ain't none of us millionaires, we fish close to home. That should give us an edge, but the fact is, last year it didn't. We were in a rut."

"I wasn't in a rut," Lucky said. "My Mister Twister purple firetail worm was in a rut."

"Maybe we didn't study our home water enough," I suggested. "We thought we had it pat, and the bassologists came in and outfoxed us."

Eddie drummed his fingers on the table. "I think that's all true—even the part about Lucky's Mister Twister. The plastic worms didn't catch fish last year; maybe the dimples were too small to hold air bubbles, something like that. But that's just one bait we're talking about. As for the lake, well, we've got the same instruments the bassologists use."

Eddie's logic can be maddening. I shouldn't even call it logic. He just talks slower than everybody else, and that makes him sound twice as thoughtful. But this time he'd slowed us down at the right time.

I said, "The problem was, we weren't being aggressive enough on our own water." I paused. "The solution is to go on the offensive, I guess."

"We are going to take the war into the enemy's lake." Eddie checked eyes. "We will be where they will *not* expect us to be. And we will be good."

"Sounds promising." Lucky stifled a yawn.

"We will be like commandos," Eddie declared.

"That's us, the Bass Commandos." Even as I spoke, I felt a silence overtake the words — almost before they left my mouth.

There was a stillness in the Sizzle Shack, one of those moments that kill a conversation or, as in this case, make it stand out in time. Then the door to the restaurant opened, its double-dippy bells ringing, and Cecil George, the last of our group, came walking in right on cue. Damn me if he wasn't wearing camouflage pants, a green fatigue shirt and a blue baseball cap with gold embroidery spelling out *USS Coral Sea*, and as he approached, walking easy with his arms swinging at his sides, shoulders thrown back and an unsuspecting smile on his face, I knew that each of us watching was having the same sensation. Our bell was being rung, our numbers were being taken. We were birthing a legend.

3

The rest of the afternoon passed in a haze. I'd be standing with my clipboard, watching the bottles go by on the conveyor belt, half-listening to the *clickety-clack* of the rollers and the *snickety-snick* of the twist-top capper, and I'd think I was counting, or checking fluid levels, or something. But five minutes later I'd be sweating, standing up on the balls of my feet, the muscles in my forearms aching from tension as I fought another bass into the net.

I have no idea if the others noticed. Probably they didn't. I'm the boss, for better or worse, and so what goes on behind my face is presumably of a higher order of thought than any they know. With a clipboard in my hand, and my necktie, I'm miles above them, they think. If only they could read my mind. They'd see a team of guys in fatigues racing across a huge body of still water in a chevron of bass boats, the whole tight formation breaking apart on cue and spreading out to various coves, the Commandos unshipping their rods with military precision and—at exactly the same moment—casting.

If they could read my mind, they'd see the makings of a hot half hour on one of the television sport shows, narrated maybe by

Lorne Greene or else by a country music star, an outlaw type like Waylon Jennings. "The Bass Commandos was brought to you by"—fill in the blank and make the check out to me.

It got so I had to go into my office and close the door. In the bottom drawer of my desk, under the time sheets, in a file marked "Corporate," was last year's copy of *Bass Classic Report*. There they were, the forty men who'd made the cut.

The phone rang. "Valhalla Bottlers."

It was a fuzzy connection. Trucks and cars rumbled in the background. A husky voice drawled: "We're going to kick some tail, ain't we, buddy?"

I smiled into the receiver. "You bet, Cec. What's up?"

"This is one hot idea. I'm too excited to work."

"Know what you mean. I was just checking out the competition myself."

"All for one, one for all." Cecil's next words were swallowed up by a thundering tractor-trailer rig that seemed to take two whole minutes to pass. I turned the pages of the magazine, reading the capsule biographies of each of the contestants, studying their pictures. A lot were what you'd call Hopeful Harrys, just so pleased to be in the Classic that they wouldn't be too much trouble to handle. The big guns—guys like Rick Clunn and Roland Martin—were too smooth to really hate. Heck, you wanted to *be* them. Pulling down the endorsements and the money was gravy on top of the life the big bassers lived, fishing one hundred and fifty days a year, picking and choosing among the tournaments.

"Where are you, Cec?" I asked, when the truck passed.

"On the road. Listen, where'd you get your camouflage outfit from?"

"Virginia Roy found it. I'll ask her tonight. But you've got yours already."

"I know. But don't you think our camouflage should match?"

"I never heard of camouflage matching before, Cec. It's supposed to look like it isn't there."

"Well—" He took a deep breath. "Maybe we can have patches made up."

"Sure we can." It occurred to me that Cecil had been drinking some. "Listen, keep an even keel, you hear?"

"What's that supposed to mean?"

"Easy, now. I'm excited, you're excited. But excited don't catch bass. That's all I'm saying."

"You aren't fixin' to drop anybody if they don't, you know, do real well right off?"

I hunched over the phone. "Cec, you were there, you know what we decided. All of us. A team. Commandos."

"We shook hands on it, Gar," he said with just a little quaver in his voice.

"We did indeed. All for one."

"One for all."

"But," I said, gently, "we need you, Cec, we need you *sharp*. It's okay to celebrate a little, but remember: You're a Commando now."

"Ten-four." Cecil sounded like he'd snapped back. "I gotta go, now. But don't worry about me, Gar. Concentrate on catching your limit."

"Right now I'd better concentrate on bottling my production quota for the day or find another line of work. See you."

I came home with the fire in my belly banked off a bit. Daydreaming will do that to you, I've found. It's a fine line to walk between inspiration and doping off. Talking to Cecil drunk had sobered me up, because if that was how I sounded. . . . It's different for Cecil—he needs something to believe in, has always needed a push, God knows—he's been drifting for much of his life. Drinking a little too often, never quite putting anything together. Working jobs but not finding his life's work. As a basser, he's strictly a streak player.

Our house sits back from the road on a wild acre. The mailbox at the entrance of the gravel road is a steel box bolted to a concrete post chained to a sycamore, because boys here tend to take Daddy's truck out on Saturday night and Daddy's truck has positraction, four-wheel drive and big knobby tires—perfect get-up-and-go for ripping out mailboxes and lawn ornaments. Sunday mornings on the way to church, it's not a rare thing to come across a chain of boxes, post lamps and jockeys of color with rings in their hands.

Our house is a plain one-story with a tall, peaked attic over the original structure. A porch takes off on the left side and wraps around back. Some lawn still manages to carry on year after year, though without my help. Virginia Roy is responsible for the planter box—an old rowboat that was gathering dust in the garage. I needed space when I won that Ranger bass boat of mine, so we made a deal. The rowboat was sawed in half the long way and tipped up and filled with potting soil. The two halves sit to either side of the walk, blooming with yellow roses.

It was dark inside, but there was no need to put on a light. I moved around in the hallway, leafing through the mail on the wobbly oak table, hanging my hat on a peg. The uneven wood floorboards under my feet made me feel I was rocking on a boat somewhere, even though I was standing still. I stared at the lead glass doorknob in front of me and thought over what to say to Virginia Roy.

The kitchen is a bright room with those windows, still filled with handblown glass, catching the late sun and bending it this way and that. Her black nylon sack was on the table beside a string bag of Vidalia onions and three of the yellow roses from out front. I looked out the back window, thinking she might be out walking on the path to the pond, but then noticed the cellar doors open. Getting the wash in, I thought, and instead of waiting on her to come up, I decided to pay a call down below.

She was folding towels with her back to me. "Hello, honey," she said, without turning to see who it was.

I went up and put my arms around her, kissed her neck exactly where her hair was pulled up in a knot. She tasted like raspberry vinegar. Sweet sweat. I hummed into her neck. She just kept on folding towels, flipping them in half, then half again, as regular as a machine. But when she moved I could feel her breasts move up and down, rubbing against my arms, and I thought how that must feel for her. I know how it felt to me.

The last towel went into the plastic basket. She turned, leaning back inside the ring my arms made around her. Her eyes are interesting at any time of the night or day, but now, like this, they were so cool and knowing I could feel the nerves jumping under my skin.

She kissed me and reached behind her back to undo my hands. I felt myself being taken off the way she'd unhook a necklace. "Have a nice day?" she asked.

"Tolerable. How's the prickly porcupine?"

"Not so tolerable." She put her arms around the laundry basket and lifted it easily, moving it to the foot of the stairs, setting it down on the steps, chest-high. Turning around, she nodded over to the laundry table. "Where'd you come by that?"

All I could see was a pile of change, a dollar bill, some scraps of paper, which must have come from the pockets of my pants. I took a step closer, stopped. There it was, standing by itself a little off from the dimes and quarters: a shiny brass cartridge, 7.65 millimeter. Rico's gift.

"Oh, that. It's a bullet."

"I have eyes." She was standing with the bare light bulb between us. All I could see were her jeans and her T-shirt, so she really had me at a disadvantage; with Virginia Roy, you have to be able to read those eyes.

"It was lying in the road. I picked it up. Didn't want any little children playing with it. I know when I was a kid I'd have tried to find some kind of way to set it off. Hit it with a hammer, hit it with a rock. Your brother and I were always — "

"Okay, I believe you," she said abruptly.

"What's eating you, honey?"

She picked up the basket and started up the stairs. I went after her. She made a quick left into the kitchen, dropped the basket right where I'd have to step over it, and reached into her black nylon sack. Out came a long, pink paper with blue carbon copy handwriting all over it. "Since you asked."

I took the paper, read what I could. "Doin' seventy in a thirty-five?"

"I thought I'd shop during my lunch hour and was late getting back. We are definitely getting a Fuzzbuster."

"School zone, too. You don't mess around."

"I don't need any of your preaching, so just shut your mouth up." She stared out the window over the sink. "Leave me alone, please."

"Hey, now — "

"Leave me alone. Go fishing, I don't care. I got dinner to fix already." God, she was fierce. Her black curls were practically bristling, those eyes flashing. "Don't you see how busy I am, how important everything is — the laundry, the shopping, the cooking, the nice touches, like maybe a flower arrangement, that you never ever notice? I've got no time to be depressed."

"Now listen, V.R., don't let a little thing like a speeding ticket put you off your feed. And, talking of important, you know I think highly — "

"Highly?" She clapped her hands together, the sound like a bang. "*You* think *highly?*"

She froze, controlling herself. Slowly turning her head, she faced me with heroic calm. "Go fishing, Gar. I'm sorry to shout. But just go."

I opened my mouth.

"Nothing. Just go. Out to your little pond."

To oblige her seemed the only thing. But I couldn't let her think that I would dream of fishing with her so upset. "I'm going to rake up the yard," I said evenly.

A day without an argument with Virginia Roy is a day without salt, so I wasn't all that upset when I went out the back door. Not that I'm coldhearted. But to be flint to her steel would just set our world on fire. It's happened enough—especially when we were first married—that I don't shed many tears over lost quarrels.

We live on a wild acre, but there is a kind of yard around the house. Actually, it's more of a clearing. I always thought we would raise dogs here. There's a strip of level ground alongside the property line that would be perfect for a kennel and a run. Virginia Roy loves dogs, too. But it didn't work out; there was the business about babies, for one thing, and after that she didn't want it to look as if raising dogs was her idea of a substitute.

I tried to convince her that she could make a go with dogs. It wasn't any use. Then she decided she wanted to open a gift shop at the crossroads of US 49 and Rural Route 1. I had to say no, much as I hated to disappoint her. She didn't like it one bit. Said I cared too much what other people thought. Maybe she's right, but with Coca-Cola you learn to look both ways before you cross the street. Her gift shop would have been in direct competition with the only other gift shop in Valhalla, which belongs to Sally Frears, the wife of our mayor, T.O.M. Frears. You can say what you want about living life the way you think it ought to be led and to hell with what other people say, but how many of us go out and do it? Take a giant step in a town this small and you can end up outside city limits.

In the end, she did the sensible thing. She's an administrative assistant to the assistant dean of curriculum of Palestine Junior College, about twenty miles from here. She really gets to use her telephone and typing skills to the fullest.

I got the rake out. It was a sorry-looking rake, the bamboo teeth all out of plumb, the ones that weren't broken or missing.

Scraping the sycamore leaves and the blown pine needles out of the clumps of grass, I tried to make the best of it by flexing my wrists and forearms as if I were cranking a bait back to the boat. After a few months off, my hands were pretty soft, too. It was instructive.

I began bearing down more on the rake. Lifting it up using only my forearms, pressing it down fast, dragging those teeth in the grass: up, down, drag; up, down, drag. It was tougher than it sounds, because I was doing it without any slack in my muscles, working at it. But something was missing. A weight, a good-sized bass about seven pounds. I cast my eye about me. A tile under the drainpipe gutter seemed about right. With some twine and my Barlow, I snugged it up on the bridge of the rake and let her rip.

This was more like it! I could hardly lift the sucker. I had to dig in my heels and suck in my gut, while the tendons on my elbows tingled with the strain. And the whole time the head of the rake, with that curved tile tied to it, danced and bobbed just like a real fish.

Was I excited? Lord, yes. Up, down, drag. It hurt. Up, down, drag. Feel it in the belly. How many tournaments had I hit a prize patch and had the sensation, reeling in my fifth bass in six minutes, that my arms just couldn't take any more action? First the smooth cranking motion goes, then the rod tip starts to fly around as the arms get stiff. Next thing you know, you lose a fish, or worse, snap the leader. Then, with your fingers trembling with strain and the release, you have to tie on a new lure and leader, with the minutes ticking away and the feeding frenzy tailing off. How many times have I said: Well, look at all the bass I caught. All the time not saying: I wonder how many I could have got?

I was on to something here. Up, down, drag. The early tournaments, nobody is ever really ready. The boats and engines and equipment are all overhauled and raring to go, but the human equipment rarely is. But *we* could be.

"Supper's on, Gar."

I looked up. It had gotten darker. She was standing in the

lighted doorway, a silhouette. Her voice sounded sweet again. "Be right in, honey."

As I bent to untie the tile from the rake, I noticed that the lawn, such as it was, seemed much cleaner than it had been in years. There were definitely no leaves. Hey, maybe I'd killed two birds with one stone—invented a better rake and a bass exerciser all in one. Maybe fame and fortune awaited me around the corner.

4

The bed sank and sprang up, and I opened one eye to see Virginia Roy slipping out into the morning light. It was Tuesday, my day to sleep in because of the Chamber of Commerce breakfast. I closed my eyes and didn't stir until she shouted from the foot of the stairs: "How's pork butt sound for dinner?"

I sat up and looked out our bedroom window at the greeny woods and glimmer of pond. Pork butt smothered in gravy took shape in my mind. She elaborated.

"Cauliflower. Velveeta cheese cauliflower sauce. Snap beans. And, for dessert—"

"Scooter Pies." I grinned.

"No!"

"Yes!"

She sighed, and I heard it all the way upstairs.

I wrapped a towel around me and sat on the bed to trim my toenails. "Don't forget my Black Jack chewing gum." I like to chew a pack of Black Jack and watch the television before turning in.

"Roger that." I could hear her moving around the kitchen, her steps quickening. "Do you think your paycheck cleared?"

"Wouldn't bet on it. Why?" There was no answer, just the sound of a bowl being set down atop the dishes in the sink. It's funny, but that little clink of glass brought her up in my mind just as clear and sharp as a picture on television.

"I'm going. Bye." The screen door creaked open.

"Hey!" I shouted. The screen door slowly creaked closed, but which side was she on? The spring leaves of the branches that fluttered outside the second story could have been my heart. Then footsteps creaked on the stairs. A flush traveled over my skin like warm milk.

She looked in, wearing that long tan skirt with the slit in the front and a green top. A thin brown leather strap crossed diagonally between her breasts to the little purse on her hip.

"What's this squawking all about?"

I dropped the towel.

"I see," she said.

"Come over here."

"Gar, honey, you know I have to run."

I waited till she looked up. "No, you don't." Walking toward her, it was like watching a morning glory close up at sunset, that proud face gradually turning away. I put my hands on her hips. She stayed frozen in profile, smelling of lotion and attar of roses. Loving her is never easy. I began rubbing my hands in a circle, imagining them as chamois muffs you'd use to buff a new paint job: polishing, caressing, bringing out the lost luster, smoothing out the aches and scratches and dings.

"You always wait until I'm dressed."

"Hmmm."

I unhooked the purse and let it fall. She was still as a statue but when she lifted her foot to nudge the purse aside, I knew she was good for it. She had her head turned away. I kissed her neck. She twisted around; I wrapped my arms around her waist. "I love you," I said to the back of her head, breathing in deep. God, I love

Clairol. When she didn't say anything, I removed my arms an inch from her. "Make me your Dixie love slave."

She took each of my hands and pulled them tighter, like a belt cinching up her waist. I molded myself to her from behind and tucked my chin over her shoulder; we rocked like that until she stopped on the half-beat. "This is going to mess up my dress," she said.

"Sounds like fun."

"Wait a second." She took two steps away and commenced to strip. When Virginia Roy makes up her mind, she's a real take-charge person. Her fingers flew down that blouse and she shucked it with a double-jointed elbow flop that looked like a dragonfly popping its glistening green chrysalis. Pinching her fingers at the shoulder points, she lightly hung the blouse on the back of a chair. *Zip* went the zipper on her skirt. She made herself narrow and it dropped like a tube; at the last second she caught it with an upturned toe and one hand, so it never touched the floor and ended up neatly folded on the chair.

With her tanned arms crossed over her alabaster white breasts, she turned to me, giving me the most dark and serious look she had. "You still think I'm sexy?" she asked. It was enough to break your heart or make you lose your erection, and I had a fight on both scores, but then it was all right. The thing is, at times like these I can always see the muddy, gap-toothed, twelve-year-old Virginia Roy with the loud mouth on her, trying to make her brother Jerry—who's a big-shot fugitive in Costa Rica now—and me so mad that we'd turn our bikes around, come back, and give her a licking. She's capable of anything. She'll seem to give in and then pull out the dirtiest trick in the book. Sometimes I wish Jerry could come back from Costa Rica just to thrash her for old time's sake.

"Jungle girl." I advanced on her and she retreated, palms up, fingernails crooked at me. We circled each other. I stepped in and she hooked a foot around my ankle and tried to throw me. I swept her with me and we landed on the bed. She was on top. I raised up and kissed the nipple of her right breast, my thing flopping big as a fish against her buttocks.

"Gar, I want a Fuzzbuster."

"Oh, *come on*, Virginia Roy!" Licking quickly at that rosy red bud, I closed my eyes and listened to my body humming.

"You sure your paycheck won't clear today?"

"Sure." I dragged my tongue down the dry skin of her belly, toppling her slowly onto her back as I rocked up. The blood sloshed through me, filling my thing like a red balloon. For a moment I thought I would lose all control, so I put myself on a lake in the middle of a problem: in murky Ross Barnett Reservoir on a clear day after a lot of rain, what bait's going to work at thirty feet, pH of $+.4$, water temperature: sixty-one degrees. She went totally limp.

"What's the matter?" I asked.

"You smell like fish."

"I do not."

"I swear I smell fish."

"Not on me you don't." I gave her a poke.

"Cut that out. I'm not ready." Her voice was getting tight and anxious.

"*Aaaaooooowwww.*"

"What *are* you doing?"

"Fuzzbusting."

She whacked my kidneys with her bare heel. My hard-on shriveled. She laughed.

"Not funny," I said grimly, keeping my head down. She began to mutter. I couldn't make it out. She began to tighten her thighs together upon my head. Now I couldn't have heard her if she screamed; a roaring filled my ears. Suddenly she lurched. Her stomach muscles quivered. I nosed my way up the little braid of copper-colored hair running from her navel, kissing the silken cord as I went, then launched myself into her with a long, steep, shivering glide from which there was no pulling out.

Afterwards, we were laying there when she said, "Poor Gar." She was flat on her back and staring at the ceiling.

"Why poor?"

"I said a prayer. Did you?"

"I always do." To my ears, my voice sounded thin.

"Then everything will be all right." Her mind sounded made up. She raised both her knees to her chest, rocked upright, and sat with her arms clasped around them. Her back was to me. "I know one day we will be rewarded, if we just keep growing in grace. Otherwise, what's the point?" She took a breath, and the skin over her ribs tightened. I didn't say a thing, rubbing my hand like a chamois over her back.

Then we were both late. As Virginia Roy ran out the back door with her hands behind her buttoning up her blouse, I headed in the opposite direction, shoes in my hands and necktie in my teeth. I was halfway down the steps when I stopped in my tracks. It was our lawn—I mean, there wasn't any. The ground had been scraped clean as the infield of a baseball diamond. The pinkish brown dirt didn't even have any clods in it.

My first thought was vandalism. Over by the woods there was a pile of leaves and dead clumps of grass. It occurred to me that maybe I *had* heard something outside the house last night. Just then there was a screech and a roar and Virginia Roy's red El Camino burst out of the back driveway, rattled up the hill and, without braking, turned onto the road.

The dust settled around me. This was too neat to be vandalism. Some practical joker, Lucky or Cecil, had put my poor, unappreciated lawn out of its misery.

My eye lighted on the piece of curved tile that sits under the drainpipe and deflects the water away from the foundation. And then I remembered raking leaves last night. My bass exerciser.

Well, I thought, as I got in my van and drove off, maybe this

was a sign to take some interest in the place. But not another lawn.
I'd try anything but that: wood chips, white pebbles, anything that
wouldn't require maintenance.

The Chamber convenes over at the Red Lion. I was counting
on sitting with Lucky, the only other Commando who attends
these meets, but I happened to run into Woody Thuper and Villis
Green, our local contractors, and we all squeezed into a booth. I
don't think I've spent an hour with either one since high school, but
all the five- and ten-minute chats do add up over the years. Woody
was wearing a brown corduroy jacket with a leather shooting pad
sewn into the right shoulder that I'm sure had never felt the butt of a
shotgun. He looked to me more like one of the Hattiesburg college
crowd, but that was his business. I knew Woody to be no fool. He
and Villis have taken cotton fields and turned them into whole
neighborhoods, the houses springing up in exactly sixty days.
Their two biggest tracts are Tara Towne and Lafitte Lux, and
while you wouldn't catch me living in either place, in those tall,
narrow plasterboard houses that look like they come out of a kit
and do, the commuting people who've moved in are going to put
new life into Valhalla.

It occurred to me that it wouldn't cost me any skin to ask their
advice: "I'm in a jam." Villis and Woody listened intently while I
explained my lawn predicament.

"Sounds serious, don't it, Woody?" Villis said, with a wink to
me. "I recommend six-inch concrete, all around."

"What kind of soil you got?"

"Mixed clay and sand."

"How deep?"

"Before I hit the greasy stuff, about three feet."

"Some sort of gravel base," Villis said crisply. "Then a layer of
fine white sand, then loam. A mattress of clover on top. You can
play croquet on it the very same day."

This sounded expensive and, anyway, who played croquet? "I
was thinking of something simple, like wood chips."

"Chips just bring down value in a single family dwelling. You want a lawn," Woody said.

"Oh. Well, thanks. Thanks a lot."

Our breakfasts came and we ate. I thought I knew those two pretty well, but I wasn't coming up with anything to say. Then Woody shoved aside his plate. After lighting his Garcia y Vega and laying down some smoke, he said, "Gar, let's talk turkey."

"White or dark meat?"

Villis leaned forward. "All white breast meat, with gravy, oyster stuffin', and all the trimmin's," he said. His eyes, behind the tinted Porsche glasses he wears, to go with his 911-S, held mine. "Just say the word."

I looked down at my plate of eggs and sausage. "Did Thanksgiving come early for somebody?"

"For you, Gar, it just might," said Woody.

They called for order up at the podium, but Woody kept his back turned and his voice down. "We are making what you might call a draft. A group of local business people, a small group, is looking for someone to guide Valhalla these coming years. Mayor Frears won't be around forever, you know."

I had my doubts about that. T. O. M. Frears has the constitution of a cigar store Indian. "I think either one of you boys would be a natural pick to run this town."

Villis laughed, took off his shiny glasses and gave Woody a look. Woody rolled his Garcia y Vega between his thumb and forefinger. "We can't get into politics. It's as simple as that. Too many decisions too close to home."

"Gar," Villis said. "Would you be interested in Mayor Frears' job?"

I picked up my glass but didn't drink. I'd have poured Coke into my nose if I tried. "Me? I've never run for anything, you know that. T. O. M. Frears is a pretty good mayor, too. I wouldn't stand a chance."

"We're not talking about a campaign." Woody paused. "That's

throwing money away and wasting everybody's time. Besides, I happen to agree with you about your chances. The way to get it done—" Woody smiled. "But maybe you can tell us first is, are you interested?"

They both stared into my eyes to see if I'd blink. You get about ten seconds in these situations, unless you can come up with a good stall. So I tightened my face up into a smile. "Yes, I am," I said. Anyway, I was curious.

The Chamber president coughed into the microphone. "Villis and Woody and Gar Foote, we're going to assess a fine here for holding your own private meeting," he said. He raised a fist over his head. "How much of a fine, boys?" He held up one finger. They booed. Two fingers, they booed harder. Three, some clapped. Four was about fifty-fifty. Five they cheered. "Five dollars each, please. Pay up."

We all dug in our pockets and passed the money up front. Immediately Villis turned his back on the podium and said in a casual way, "T. O. M. Frears has gotten himself out of touch with his constituency. This isn't a backwoods town anymore. The mayor should be somebody younger. Somebody who can talk to the governor and the legislature about things that concern us: roads, education, taxes, jobs."

Maybe Woody could see the doubt in my face, because he flashed a reassuring smile. "Don't worry about what you're going to say. We can help you with that. You're a natural leader, you run a successful business. Coke is next to Jesus around here, man. You even got a little following from your fishing days, I understand."

"That's worth about five votes," I said.

"You must have forty employees, though," Woody replied. "And each of them has a family, and each of them has friends, and they all know you. What you got to realize is you already are leading this community. Everybody drinks Coke; most everybody fishes. You have prime leadership qualities that can and must be developed."

"Woody's getting ahead of himself." Villis gave me a look of forebearance. "Gar, the fact is, Old Man Frears wants to unload his farm. He's seen where the money is. He also wants to see his name carried on. Here's the deal: he resigns for reasons of health or whatever, appoints his successor, you, to serve out the two years of his term, and we buy his land."

"And we call it The Estate at Frears Farm," Woody said. "How's that sound?"

I laughed. "Sounds like you have it figured out. It's funny, but my grandaddy used to say it happened like this."

"What do you mean, 'like this'?" Villis asked sharply.

"You know, politics in Valhalla. Grandaddy said it was closer than flies on pies."

Villis stared at me a while before he laughed.

"This is just supposin'," Woody cautioned.

Villis glanced at his partner. "I think Gar knows that, Woody. I think Gar knows where it's at. You think it over some and we'll get together for lunch soon to see if you're still interested."

We went back to pretending to follow the Chamber's plans for the May Day tag sale and catfish fry. Every so often our eyes would meet. Villis and Woody looked like a pair of poker sharps stuck in a small stakes game. Not me. I couldn't get over it—they were serious! I'd actually been approached, just like you read about in the papers. I felt dizzy with excitement, although I didn't enjoy the feeling; I knew this was one sure way to get to the State Farm at Parchman.

As soon as the meeting broke up, I drove to the plant. I don't know why it is, but there are some people, no matter what it is you say to them, you come off feeling small and dumb. That's how I felt. Villis and Woody weren't doing this out of the goodness of their rich little hearts, but even so, some people would say it was a fine chance they were offering me. I wondered what my granddad would have thought of it.

In a way, I was glad I wasn't in a position to be sorely

tempted—this was going to be our year on the bass circuit. The season opened in two weeks at a lake in North Carolina. Nobody would be expecting us up there this early. And if we were ready, if the Commandos fished hard and well in the early tournaments, I might get into the Classic; I could turn pro. And nobody would stand for a mayor who fished one hundred and fifty days a year.

That afternoon a new bottling procedures manual arrived by express mail. The cover letter was brief.

On April 23, there will be a new Coca-Cola. As in the past, the formula will remain a closely-held secret. Our bottlers will be responsible for mixing in the proper ratio of water and sugar. Shipments of the new mixture will arrive in time for you to stop using the old formula, make some equipment changes and perform a general cleaning. A representative from the Atlanta office will be on hand to answer any questions.

April 23 was sixteen days away. They had to be kidding.

I leafed through the manual. Damn me, they were altering the proportions. If I went along with this publicity stunt, it was going to cost me plenty of money and aggravation. If I didn't—well, I don't own this bottling plant. There are those who do, whose grandparents bought a piece of the action when the old man, Mr. Woodruff, took his vision to the world. They can call the shots, those guys. I couldn't.

That's when it hit me: Mr. Woodruff had only died last month. No wonder there was this rush, the secrecy, the feeling I got in the pit of my stomach. The man they called The Boss hadn't even been buried before they set this scheme in motion.

I've been getting these strange feelings about Coke lately; you might call them bad vibrations. It's hard to say when it started. I only know that there are some definite facts to give a person pause. The chairman is a Cuban. The president is Argentinian. The vice president of bottling and marketing is a Mexican. The chief financial officer is Egyptian. The spokesman on television is Bill Cosby. And you wonder why people say these are the Last Days? Coca-Cola would be a hundred years old next year, reason enough to fear any talk of change. Doesn't Atlanta know anything about what Coke means? Well, maybe they don't. Maybe it takes an American to know.

My daddy used to talk about the red barrels of Coke syrup on horsedrawn wagons going out into every rural parish in the land. Now it's tanker trucks, but the product is the same. Coke is Coke. The other side has that preening rock n' roller singing their jingles; fine, let them have him. We don't need anything but a bottling line here in Valhalla. "Put it within an arm's reach of desire," was what The Boss said back before I was born. That other man, the newspaper man from Kansas, he had it right too: "Coca-Cola is the sublimated essence of all that America stands for. A decent thing, honestly made, universally distributed, and conscientiously improved with the years." We know The Boss had that on his wall in the Atlanta office. At bottler's school, we memorized it.

I decided it was time this American tried to put a halt to the foolishness. The minute I made that decision, it was like throwing open the doors in a tobacco barn. I could see again. I was in my office, in my chair, sweat pouring off me, the phone in my hand.

"This is Dr. Purviance."

"Gar Foote, sir. Degree in Bottling Science, Martinsville Trade Tech. I'm down in Valhalla."

"Yes. You're with the company, I take it?" He had one of those Virginia voices, the fat smoked off it.

"I have a formula manual you sent out here, and there's a question or two I'd like to ask."

"Is this a secure line?"

"Beg pardon?"

"Are you calling from your office?" He laughed. "Forget it. The cat's out of the bag anyway."

"It is?"

"Your question, Foote."

"The proportions. If you'll turn to page seven—do you have your manual in front of you?"

"I wrote the manual. Proceed."

"Well, the proportions are wrong, sir."

"How so?"

"Sir, if you remove that much of extract and lower the sugar base just to add more aspartamine, it's going to make Coke strange, real strange. No matter what your new additives are, the ratio is the thing. I'm a bottler, that's my responsibility, you see, it's something I'm familiar with, and I know my ratios. I know it supposedly can't be done, because of quality control and all that, but I can taste the difference in a Coke that's come into the country under license, when I've been on a fishing trip down by the Mexican border. I really can. And while I've never been to Africa, I've heard stories about what happens to Coke there that curls my hair, literally."

"Are you done, Mr. Foote?"

"I'd hate to see that happen here, sir."

"Well, you'd better lay in a supply of hair straightener. Something is going to happen, and soon."

"People are not ready for this. This won't be Coke, sir. It'll be less . . . less big, not as . . . dark—lighter. Sweeter."

And there popped into my mind the image of the other side's jingle-singer, that dancing, prancing, primping boy with the girl's voice. The cloven hoof, all that was missing to complete the picture.

"And don't forget lemony," said Dr. Purviance and I'd swear the sonofabitch was chortling. "Gar, my advice to you is don't worry. This has been researched for years, millions went into creating this new formula. Tests in the South show it's favored over old Coke by a two to one ratio. It's the Real Thing of the future."

. . .

The last clunks of the punch clock had long faded into silence when Trank du Lac opened my door. He pretended to look down at his clipboard, shooting quick glances at me when he thought I wasn't looking.

"What is it?" I asked.

"It is Royal Wingate's birthday tomorrow, Mr. Foote."

"So?"

"If you remember, it is my duty to remind you of birthdays and anniversaries."

"Okay." I didn't show any expression, trying to get Trank to leave. "So, you want to get her a card?"

"Mr. Foote, it is good to offer employees positive reinforcement." He raised up his hand and that was when I saw the magazine.

"Mr. du Lac, have you been reading that tripe again?"

"Management is a science, Boss."

"Well, if the *Harvard Business Review* says so, then it must be the truth. Am I right?" My voice was starting to rise despite my best efforts. "It's what *they* read up in Atlanta, isn't it? And I'm just some hick down in who-cares-ville, so fuck me, yeah, that's right."

Trank kept his eyes on his clipboard, while the hand that gripped the magazine slid slowly to his side.

"Oh, go get Royal her darned card. Here," and I dug in my pants for a dollar bill. "Make it a Hallmark Card and have everybody sign it."

"Thank you, sir," he said, and left.

But he'd broken my trance, and I didn't have the heart to sulk alone anymore, so I locked up and drove slowly home. I took my time. You can see farther into the woods now with the leaves still just bare buds. Later on the new leaves crowd everything out; you can't walk in a straight line in a forest, you're lucky to even take ten steps. Thinking about it made me feel worse somehow. There was so much bothering me, I suddenly ripped off my seat belt, then my necktie. My heart thudded, sounding all out of whack. I was a misery.

You have strayed, Gar Foote, I said to myself. What are you doing with your life? What good is it for a man to profit if he loses his soul in the bargain, pounding a hickory gavel on a table at the high school gym every other Tuesday night, acting like a big shot but having his chain jerked by Villis and Woody whenever they pleased?

Worst of all, I knew that just thinking about this mayor thing, on top of the madness that had overtaken Atlanta, could easily jeopardize my shot at the Bass Classic. You need cool nerves to tournament fish.

I hardly saw the entrance to the drive—scraped the fender on the mailbox—and flew reckless as a flushed pheasant down our steep road. It was like I had the worst tunnel vision, because only at the last moment did I notice Virginia Roy standing on the front steps with both her arms spread wide as if feeling for raindrops.

I turned off the engine and sat there, too bushed to move. "You absolute darling," she said, grinning at me. "You cunning little devil. Come out of there and let me kiss the skin off your face."

Mumbling, I kicked at the door. Naturally, it swung back faster than I could get out and banged my shins. As I was cursing and hopping I felt her hands slide up under my arms. She laid her face against my back. I stopped. I had to. It was either that or buck Virginia Roy off.

"What's got into you?" I asked my shoulder gruffly.

She snuggled into my spine. Well, this must have been what I needed. My eyes seemed to fill with light and I smelled a pungent, earth-is-opening aroma of manure and new grass.

And then I saw the lawn. Thick and perfect. Greener than Eden. Except for the brown stitches where the pieces had been joined, I could have sworn it had been here forever.

Virginia Roy kissed my neck and then stuck her tongue in my

ear. "This is the most romantic surprise I've ever got in my whole life. How *did* you do it — keep it a secret, have it done so fast? Oh, Gar, honey!" She whirled around to face me. She peered into my eyes and something there slowed her some, but she was too happy to question who or why. "Let's take off our shoes and walk on it," she said, shyly.

"Yeah," I said. "What else is a lawn for?"

5

"You can't be uptight and be good."

"You can't be drunk and be good either, Cec."

"This is my life, man." Cecil waved around the smoky, green room. "I'm one hurting dude."

This was his latest apartment, but nothing stood out as different from the last. What I saw first were the bottles, of course. The apartment complex sat in the dirt by the railroad tracks—I've never known Cec to live anywhere but near the tracks—and I climbed up an exterior metal staircase as a hundred empty boxcars rocked by. All along the wall were empty bottles of beer. They were dust-covered and they shook and rattled for another minute after the train passed.

Inside, the lights were off. I saw more bottles. On shelves, on tables, on the floor beside the plaid sofa bed that faced the little television, also on the floor. Some were old and some were alive in a verminous sort of way; it wasn't like Cecil had drunk them all in the past week or even month.

Cec had come out of the bedroom in his underwear. He didn't like me coming here, but he knew better than to show it at first.

A few minutes later he was getting worked up; his boyish, handsomely-square face, red and puffy. "So, what's up, man? Have you seen what you came to see?"

"Yeah. Come on, get your things. I'll drive you to Lucky's and drive you home after."

Cec sat down on the plaid sofa. "Not right now." He stared out at the Formica coffee table like the bottles on it were pieces on a checkerboard. Your move, Gar.

I sat down at the other end of the sofa. "Okay." Looking at the table, what caught my eye weren't the bottles but the space between the bottles. Every bit was taken up by bottle caps. And each bottle cap had this neat grayish black cylinder, about a quarter-inch high, standing up in its center. They looked like funny little hats with upturned brims, like those hats colored people wear in the parishes on the Feast of the Epiphany.

"You know, lay down a conveyor belt and you'd have yourself a nice little bottling line."

Cecil saw the humor in this, barely. He puffed on his unfiltered cigarette, began laughing, choked some, and then hawked—a huge gob from the sound of it—up into his cheeks before swallowing. His idea of manners.

"You're kicking me off the Commandos, huh?"

"How many times do I have to tell you: Nobody gets kicked off the Commandos. We just send a ninja around to strangle you." I jumped up and crossed the room to the window, pretending to have seen something interesting, like the weather, when actually I'd just had a thought about what kind of bugs might be living in Cecil's sofa bed. I knew, from his endless boasting, about the girls he brought here—the seventeen-year-olds he finds at the bus terminal and the Continuing Education classes—that the sofa bed was where he made his move.

My foot kicked a cardboard box, full from the feel of it. "What's this?"

"My old weight set. I'm thinking of getting in shape for fishing, like you said."

"That's what tonight is all about. You about ready to go?"

He sighed. "Yeah." Carefully pinching the butt of his cigarette between thumb and index finger, he positioned it in an empty bottle cap, burning end up. Another funny hat for someone.

As we drove through flat muddy fields of budding cotton plantations set between tall green willow breaks, I listened to Cecil blow on his harmonica. At first it just sounded like slobbering, but then he got a sound going, high, wailing, and before long he was chugging out chords and rocking in the passenger seat of my Ford van. Just like in high school, driving around during lunch hour, aimless, listening to the radio or to Cecil.

That's all right my mama,
That's all right by me.
That's all right my mama
Anyway you do,
'cause that's all right.

"I just know Eddie's going to get on my case," he said, breaking from the song and wiping his harmonica on his sleeve.

"Eddie gets on everybody's case. You ought to know that."

"Yeah, but with me it's different. He pulls that vet crap. It wasn't like he was a Green Beret or a Marine."

"I've never heard of any 'vet crap' before now. He's just Eddie. In high school he was the same."

"Yeah, for you it's different. See, you're a vet, too. He can't do it to you — pull that stuff." Cecil rocked in his seat, staring straight out the window at the road. "Worst decision I ever made, letting the doc declare me 4-F."

Lucky and Yvonne live in a canalside split-level, with a gravel ring drive bordered by flower beds, a walk made of sawed-off telephone poles and a lawn with a bronze statue of Terrible

Terrence, their stud bluetick hound who had finally died a couple of years ago. The burnt wood sign over the door said *Cajun Country - Bon Temps Roulez.*

Yvonne opened the door. "It's Gar and Cecil!"

We kissed cheeks, twice. She's particular about that with me, but I noticed she stayed well back from Cec, just brushing the air near his cheek, and only once at that. "Well, I am just going out, can you believe it?" She winked.

Yvonne is a skinny, dark, feline version of Lucky, with wads of black hair in a bouffant do. She was wearing a long white suit and a white straw hat, and carried a large red purse that looked like it was stuffed with real estate listings.

"Tell Virginia Roy I said hello, will you, Gar?" She paused and, since she'd had the impulse, bent forward. We kissed cheeks twice more, Cec got his almost-kiss again and she blew out the door.

"God, she's adorable, ain't she?" Cec said. "The way she par-lay-voos that fran-say?"

Lucky popped around the corner. "There you are. We'd about given up hope. You sober, Cec?"

"What business is it of yours, you little gran-wee?"

We went on back to Lucky's rec room. It's a man's world there. The wet bar, the forty-inch Sony with VCR, the lamps with pine bark shades, and the coffee table: a massive black oak burl with knots and holes opening out in the rich golden wood grain like whirlpools. Lucky's got portraits of his bluetick studs and bitches on the back wall, and a bonefish he caught off Honduras mounted above the door.

Yvonne had laid out a spread of spicy ham, sliced onions, tomatoes, peppers. I set down my two sixes of Coke beside the beer. Eddie nodded from the easy chair by the picture window that faced the Toll Road. He waved at the food.

"Lucky married a real woman, didn't he?"

Cec bent over the table. "I believe I'll make me a po'boy." His hand closed around a beer.

I cleared my throat. "Let's take care of business before we do any eating or drinking." Cec slid his thumb under the pop-top. "That includes you."

Cec glanced up, looking pained. When he saw us all waiting, his face lost its stubborn cast. "Yeah. Okay."

Lucky rolled a chair out for Cec, who sat down in it without a word. He hunched his thick shoulders and crossed his legs at the ankles. Lucky stepped around the chair until he stood behind him. He put his hands on the back of the seat and, after a short pause, began: "Cecil George, have you accepted the Lord Jesus Christ as your Saviour on earth and in heaven?"

Cec stiffened. His face went pale; his eyes rolled up in his head, stared at me, closed. "Thanks a lot, Gar."

"I'm asking you, brother, as your friend in Jesus." Lucky laid one brown hand on Cec's camouflaged shoulder.

"Just leave me be," he said miserably. His eyes were still closed and his fists clenched.

"I've accepted Jesus Lord," Eddie said. "I have sinned and he has forgiven me all my sins."

"This is really unfair." Cec hugged his arms around his body and shivered.

I said, "The Lord Jesus Christ loves you, Cecil." Cec seemed to withdraw, grow smaller, with my every word, as the Holy Spirit worked its power upon him. "Do you think each of us didn't reject Him, spurning the deep water of His love? I was as blind as the Pharisees. I sinned. I rejoiced in my wickedness. It took the most terrible thing to show me the sorry state I was in."

The room had grown warm, and I could feel the sweat starting to bead up all over my body. I shuffled forward and put my hand on Cec's head. Eddie came over and put a hand on his other shoulder.

Lucky said, "May the Holy Spirit enter this poor sinner, Cecil George, and teach him the error of his ways." He began to sway; the room pitched this way and that with all our slow rocking.

"Lord Jesus—say His name, Cecil—Lord Jesus," and we all began saying His name, rolling it over and over upon our tongues until rapture blossomed in the stone that was our brother's heart. He wept. We all did, for we are all unworthy of such love as we do receive.

After Cecil accepted the Lord, we broke for sandwiches and refreshments. Lucky brought out his VCR and set it up on a tripod in the corner, where it recorded us toasting Cec's going on the wagon with Cokes and the usual horseplay. Then it was time to get down to business.

Lucky, as usual, had come prepared. As a realtor, he's a dynamic salesman. It shows. He set up an easel and began flipping a large pad. One sheet listed the number of possible tournaments to enter, another the number necessary to qualify for the championship rounds. A third broke down the entry fees and other costs such as transportation, food, lodging, and equipment. He had an interesting statistic that showed how strong performances in early tournaments led to momentum down the stretch. Lucky read from the next page: "Cost for a year's quest to reach our lifetime potential as fishermen: $14,488."

"There I go," said Cecil, as calmly as he could.

Eddie seemed stunned. "Isn't there some way we could limit the number of tournaments we enter?"

Lucky ran a hand over the top of his hair to his duck-ass. "That's a minimum figure. I know; it's too high. I couldn't make it, either. I didn't marry Yvonne for her money."

He turned the page. In precise copperplate script, it said: "Projected income from tournament finishes: $78,030."

Lucky stepped back and acknowledged our applause.

Then it was my turn. I was nervous doing it in front of the video camera, but that was part of the deal. We were thinking about down the road, and making our own video. Though it seemed like the last order of business, it was actually the first. I ran through my training methods, and brought out the old baitcasting rod that I'd converted into a bass exerciser. We agreed to break while everybody took a shot at it.

Lucky popped in Clarence "Pretty Big" Floyd's latest bass video about fishing for lunkers. Pretty Big is currently serving out a two-year banishment from tournament fishing. He tried to pad his limit with a bass he'd frozen in a block of ice, then anchored just below the lake surface at a secret spot.

Pink-skinned and unrepentant, Pretty Big stared out at us from Lucky's forty-inch Sony. He sat on the swivel seat of his bass boat, a rig in his hand. He wore a safari vest with all sorts of flaps and pockets, and no shirt. His arms and chest were orange-red and covered with white hairs.

"Look at that ape," Lucky said. "I hear he fishes nekkid."

"Sure was a dumb stunt he pulled." Cec pulled at his Coke.

"The only dumb thing was getting caught."

"Everybody gets caught, Lucky."

They didn't look at me. We've never talked about it, my little experience.

"I only meant that he should've known that they'd have a fisheries biologist there to do tissue analysis." Lucky pulled out his short, chromed comb and began working on his fenders.

"He's a wise, old man of the water, the lunker bass is," Pretty Big said. "What the Indians might call a Spirit Father. He's lived twelve, maybe fourteen years to get up to the ten-pound size. He's a smart 'un. That don't mean he can't be fooled, though."

Pretty Big looked too big for the tiny swivel seat, perched way out on the end of his boat. I said, "They must have sandbags at the other end to keep the thing from tipping over."

"No, just a fishwell full of frozen lunkers." Eddie gave a bitter laugh. "That's some gut, ain't it?"

"Some belt buckle, too." It was a silver cast of a longhorn steer, just the head and the rack. But instead of tucking those long, curved horns in, they'd been made to stand out, as sharp and as nasty as a live steer's. "He's lucky he doesn't gore himself."

"Now when I went to Cuba and caught that seventeen-pounder, I didn't take a whole lot of time to get acquainted with the local cantina girls," said Pretty Big. His wide, fleshy face got a crafty look. "I was too busy courting my one, true love."

"How'd he get into Cuba anyway?" Cec asked.

"Fucker broke the law." Eddie gave the exerciser a twirl.

"I would, too," said Lucky. "Seventeen pounds is a lot of bass. Jesus, I nearly had a heart attack that time I caught my lunker and he was but eight and six."

"Yeah, fuck the law. What I want to know is: How'd he do it?" Cec said.

"He flew to Mexico, didn't he, Eddie?" I asked. Eddie shrugged. "He got a visa and talked some guy into letting him bring his equipment. Didn't he make a video?"

"I never saw it," said Lucky.

"That's one video I'd pay the full eighty-nine, ninety-nine for."

Eddie grimaced and sat up straight on the bar stool, knees high, feet tucked into the rungs. It was just like a bass boat's swivel seat, just like the one Pretty Big's body seemed to have swallowed up so that he looked mounted on a pole. "Customs confiscated it," Eddie said, and grunted.

"That's one lucky agent. You know he's got a bootleg copy that he watches at home."

"Cec, you talk like it's some kind of pornography." Eddie began reeling the brick up and down, up and down. One by one we took turns while Lucky put an egg timer on us. One by one we tried and failed to last the entire five minutes: muscle-bound Eddie; lanky, energetic Lucky; me; Cecil. Surprisingly, Cec did the best. "Jesus is standing behind you," Eddie said with a laugh. But I remembered what Cec had said earlier this afternoon. You can't be uptight and be good.

Eddie had the last word. "Get down on your bellies and give me ten push-ups," he snapped, and dropped to the floor. We gasped and groaned trying to keep up. My lungs were burning and that spicy Cajun ham was rising in my gorge, and we'd only just begun.

Eddie kept on us for forty minutes: sit-ups, push-ups, running in place. We began to sag. I ended up going through the motions. Lucky just plain quit. Panting, he leaned against the wall, pressing his sweaty forehead to the wood paneling.

Eddie shouted: "Keep humping, Lucky!"

"Fuck you, Bucci-balls."

That's how Yvonne found us. She raised her arms up and shook her skinny fingers in the air, the rings and bracelets and bangles clashing like cymbals. "What *is* going on here? Have you all lost your pathetic little minds? Lucky, close those drapes immediately!" She didn't wait to see if he'd obey but marched over to the picture window and yanked them shut herself, first one side, then the other. She stood and faced us, her sharp, beaked nose held high and her snapping black eyes drilling into us. Of course she was laughing, too, but she still managed to sound deeply disappointed. "Do you realize what a spectacle you were from the street? I had to shoo away half the neighborhood!"

The next evening we took our show on the road. I had done some soul searching. There comes a time when you have to let go of the past, and this was one of those times, I decided. After inviting the boys over, I spent the hours before they arrived in violating my private bass pond. It wasn't that I had been saving those little babies for my own pleasure—I'd been saving them, period. But if anything could signify my seriousness, then this was it.

"Nice lawn!" shouted Lucky, getting out of his Toyota Land Cruiser. There were three barking dogs in the wire cage that took up the cargo seat. He stood, hands spread wide and a "not bad" look on his narrow face. "*Very* professional," he said, and bent down on one knee. "This is quality sod. Who did it?"

"Oh, you know, Woody and Villis."

"Woody and Villis?" He clucked his tongue. "I didn't know they contracted out. Did somebody do you a favor?"

"Nothing of the sort," I said firmly.

"Well, *bon chance.* Yvonne and I'd given up hoping that you'd ever show some interest in this place." He put a hand on my shoulder and squeezed. I looked around at the green carpet where once there'd been brown mange; it made the old house seem finer, and yet also magnified her flaws so that I began thinking of slapping a coat of paint on her—maybe Woody and Villis could be of help. It wasn't as if there was any money in being mayor.

A horn blared. Six notes from a tuned car horn—"Wish I Was In Dixie"—followed by a long *aaa-oooo-gaahhh!*

" 'The Talk of the Town'," Lucky said. "I do believe."

Rumbling down the drive came Eddie's van, a streamlined box with a chocolate paint job flecked with orange-blue metal-flake bits. It had blue and white accent lines and a big clef note on the front fender, and a painting on the side of Stone Mountain in Georgia, that world-famous chunk of palest granite with its carving of Robert E. Lee bigger than any of those Mount Rushmore Yankees. The smoked glass porthole in the van opened out of General Lee's hat.

"You know," Lucky said, running a finger along his skinny little moustache, "I could see where, if I was a housewife with a stopped-up sink, I might find Eddie irresistible. That van's a work of art."

Eddie set his parking brake and bailed out. He had on fatigues and was wearing a new hat with "Bass Commando" in gold braid. Waylon Jennings' honky-tonk baritone boomed out of stereo speakers mounted in the door.

"There's one in every crowd, crying out loud—
Why does it always turn out to be me?"

Eddie waved and went around to the back, opened the doors and took out his rig and lure cases. He lugged them over and set them down at our feet. "Cec here yet?" When we shook our heads no, he bent and picked up his cases again. "I say we get cracking. Can't always be waiting on old Cec."

"Go easy there," said Lucky. "You're only here because she made you stop at fixing her sink."

Eddie rubbed his jaw with his hand. "Is that a crack, fluffhead?"

Lucky twisted his butt around and pointed. "No, this is."

I heard a crashing in the woods. Nowhere near the entrance to the drive, Cecil's rusted-out 4×4 bounded over the slope above us, and started plowing down through the underbrush, its high knobby tires riding roughshod over brambles and stickers. He flashed his headlights on and off, then his yellow fog lamps. "Christ Almighty, he's gonna plow up your lawn," shouted Lucky, breaking into a sprint. I'd never seen him move like that.

Cec slammed on his brakes, and the 4×4 went into a short drift, wiping out a clump of blackberries and leaving a red smear of clay before the tires dug in and nearly stood the two-ton beast on its nose. His head popped out of the cab. "I thought I had the wrong address," he said.

"Gar's a born-again homeowner," Lucky said.

"So, anyway, Gar—" Cec dropped to the ground. He had his new fatigues on. His skin looked scrubbed and pink. "Is it God's own truth about changing Coke's formula?"

The air sucked out of me. "What did you say?"

Cec looked mildly surprised. "You mean you didn't know?"

"Well. I knew there was something, I mean, they said—"

"Keeping secrets from your buddies?"

"Where did you hear this?"

Cec shrugged his thick shoulders. "It's in the paper, and I heard it on the radio as I was driving."

"Did they say for sure?"

"Not exactly."

"What, exactly?"

"Oh, just that, you know, nobody will come out and admit it, but . . ."

"Okay," I said, consciously letting the air out and loosening up my posture. "You had me going there, for a moment. I thought maybe it was serious."

"Since when is Coke changing the formula not serious?"

"Since they're not, it's not."

"Say again?"

"I got to admit, there's been talk afoot. Coke is about to launch something that should bury the other side. But change the formula — no. This is just a little deception that got out of hand. They'll never go through with it. So let's work," I said. "We're here to fish."

I led them back to the pond, ducking through the screening pines to the earthen berm that I had bulldozed in front of this little gulch ten years ago, damming a rivulet. We scrambled up the slope. Nobody said a word. Across the pond were three ropes, dividing it into four lanes ten feet across. I'd moored a bunch of Clorox bottles in clumps of five in each lane, to simulate tree stumps, and placed a tangle of dead branches a few feet to either side: an obstacle course. Finally, there was a rope at chest height at the edge of the bank, where four folding chairs were spaced out. That was for sidearm practice.

"I gotta hand it to you, Gar," Lucky said at last. "This must be the world's first crankbait casting range. Too bad it's dark already."

I bent over at the base of the dam, picked up a yellow industrial power cord and plugged the ends together. A string of Christmas lights burst forth all along the perimeter's treetops.

"That's it. That's the right stuff," Eddie said.

"Can't wait to get started myself." Cec bent over his rod case and began to assemble his rig.

I cleared my throat. "Just so you understand. We're all going to meet a minimum of training hours. There'll be a clipboard to sign in and out. Honor system. But I also want us to start meeting every morning. Not here, at the reservoir. We're going to overhaul our engines, test our batteries, practice our backing and maneuvering, and work on electronics and navigation."

"Bye-bye love life," Eddie said, happily.

"Mr. Bonnard?" I asked.

"I can't wait to hear what Yvonne says about this." Lucky tucked his chin to his chest. I watched him closely. Lucky Bonnard isn't a hardcase like Eddie, or a honky-tonker like Cecil. He's a man of many parts, a man with two daughters in high school, a strong and godly wife, a passion for raising dogs. Not least, Lucky is our most scientific basser. We needed his input.

He gazed out across the pond. The red and green and yellow lights winked off and on, shifting the shadows on his meditative face. There was something noble in it: the pursed lips, the beaked Cajun nose, the jet black eyebrows, the deeply wrinkled forehead with that great black wave of hair poised to fall over it.

"Well," he said, and he looked at me. "If you can get this past Virginia Roy, I don't see why I can't do the same with Yvonne."

"Don't worry about Virginia Roy."

"You say that every year." Eddie laughed. "And every year she gets you on some technicality or other."

"Not this year she won't. We have an agreement."

"Agreements don't matter to women. They break 'em where it suits 'em." He shrugged. "That's what Adele did to me."

"I thought she caught you messing with the wrong kind of plumbing," said Cec.

Eddie gave Cecil a long cool look. "The agreement was she wouldn't follow me around. She broke the agreement."

He turned to me. I could tell he was no longer in a kidding mood; he misses his boy now that Adele took him to Galveston to be with her folks.

"I want to hear it from Gar's own mouth. Gar, can you swear that nothing and nobody will stop you from making every tournament we decide to enter?"

"I do."

"This is kinda unfair," Lucky said, "making Gar out to be the only one."

"Gar's the only one married to Virginia Roy." Eddie held up his open hands, lowered his head and shot me a look that was meant to be calming. "Boy, I know you know I know that she's an absolute miracle. But she isn't a Commando. Remember that. This is your year, Gar. The time is now. She'll understand that this is something a man has just got to do."

I sat up, trembling. My mouth was open and I could feel the strain in my throat from shouting, yet all was quiet, only the curtains were stirring over the open window, and my wife was sleeping still. I lay my body back down, but despaired of my mind resting before dawn. The weakness, the feeling unworthy, these were things I knew well, but this voice was new, telling of betrayals and transgressions no one man could ever imagine, let alone overcome.

Perhaps I did doze off. Either that, or The Voice was much nearer now, because this time it filled my head with a clanging, clamorous noise like the smiting of an anvil. Again, the room was silent. The curtains were a shade lighter, fluttering in a faint breeze.

A warm hand entwined its fingers with mine. "Did I wake you?" I asked.

"I don't know anybody who could sleep through that."

"Sorry . . . go back to sleep, I'm fine."

She turned on her side to look at me, letting go of my hand. "Are you?"

"It was just a bad dream."

"Who's dreaming?"

My first thought was: What did *she* have to worry about? But I said, "We've hardly seen each other this week, it seems."

"Is that all this is?"

"Perhaps I ought to tell you; this Coke rumor has put me under some kind of pressure at work."

"Oh, *that's* it. Pressure at work! That's why I'm generally considering walking into the Okatoma River with my pockets full of rocks."

"Do you have to talk that way?"

"Yes, and you're back into bass fishing again like you promised you'd never be."

"Not true. Not the same."

"I can feel it. You're nervous, nervous all the time. You walk into a room and it's like I have to walk out in order to breathe. I can't bear looking at you; you can hardly bear to talk to me for thinking about fishing."

"V.R., let's get this straight. I'm not the same man who made those mistakes years and years ago. You've helped me grow in every way, and you know I'll always be grateful for your forgiveness. You know if you ask for something, it's yours. But at the same time, I do have a certain God-given talent."

"Didn't I have a God-given talent, too?" She burst out angrily. "And look what happened." She took a ragged breath. "I'm sorry," she said, in a harsh, pained way. She went on in a much softer voice, "Maybe I'm just a little jealous of what you have with your friends. I just want something to matter in my life — to belong to something and for that something to be worthwhile."

"There's all sorts of programs —"

"There's a Warrior camp this weekend."

"There is?" I repeated stupidly.

"This one has a theme, and skills seminars. It's open only to advanced level people."

"I don't know what to say."

"Say yes! You just said if I want anything, it's mine. Well, this is what I want."

I stared into eyes that seemed full of starlight. So much for seven years of sincere repentence. It hurt to know that all my good intentions have only paid interest on that debt. "Yes."

She squeezed my hand. "Thanks. I feel better already," she quipped.

Late Thursday evening found us up in the bedroom, packing for our respective weekends. It was a bittersweet thing to see. On my side of the bed I laid out my boxer shorts, my athletic socks, my white T-shirts. On her side of the bed she laid out her blue bikini briefs, her green socks, her two black full-length leotards. She dropped a hairnet on the leotards. I added a long-billed baseball cap to my pile.

"I've got an extra cap if you want it," I said.

She smiled guiltily. "Well. . . ." She opened a brown paper sack and pulled out a new camouflage fatigue hat, the floppy kind you can cinch under your chin.

"Where'd you get that?"

"Mail order." She tried it on.

"Cute."

So I added my camouflage jumpsuit, my blue sweatshirt, my Thinsulite gloves. And she added her camouflage jumpsuit, a thin black wool pullover, two pairs of black gloves that seemed as light as cellophane. I made a row of items out of my two pairs of

Polarizing sunglasses, Chapstick, zinc oxide, talcum powder, aspirin, Cutter's insect repellent. I looked over at her pile. Cornhusker's lotion, deodorant, Johnson's baby powder, Desenex foot powder, methiolate, antibiotic creme, hydrogen peroxide, rubbing alcohol, maxi pads, Ace bandages, surgical tape, finger splints, a box of Handiwipes.

"Be prepared. Like a Boy Scout," I said.

"Where I'm going there's no pharmacy and no hotel shower."

I drew her close and hugged her to me. "I wish you'd been my den mother when I was a tenderfoot. You could've cooked my weenies for me."

She slipped an arm around my waist. "I'll probably be ready to kill for a hot dog by the end of this weekend. We're supposed to catch our dinners."

"With what?"

"Snares and stuff. I am *not* going to eat bugs."

"I should hope not. Here," and I fished out my cache of granola bars and dropped them on her clothes.

She picked them up, weighed them in her palm, sighed. "No, I can't—really. This is supposed to be as close to the real thing as we can make it."

When we were done, we packed everything in our duffels. I was using my old National Guard bag; she'd gotten a newer but almost identical one by mail.

"You want me to put your name on it in Magic Marker?" I asked.

"No names. We don't want to be traced if we have to leave camp suddenly and can't grab everything."

"Got you. But suppose they do get hold of this, whoever *they* are; what do you think they're gonna make of those maxi pads?"

She pinched the flesh on my back, hard. We tussled a little and pretended to be interested in romance, but in truth we were too tired and keyed up about tomorrow. Both of us would be leaving our jobs early and heading off: Virginia Roy in her El Camino to

Alabama, me in my van to North Carolina. It felt strange, discussing where we'd be and when, like children laying out an afterschool schedule for parents, but I also felt something close to pride at how we were able to work this out so naturally. Both of us were going to get what we wanted. That was the main thing.

It was a long, dirty drive, stuck in the right lane for too many hours, hauling a swaying boat trailer and four thousand pounds of boat. I didn't much like being alone, either, though I had plenty of tapes. Well after dark, I pulled off the interstate and began running along a river road whose curves made my tail-heavy cargo swerve more and more. At least I had company. A regular procession of ruby red taillights and trailer lights filled that country road, round bend after bend, as far as the eye could see.

It was more a question of when, not if, I'd meet up with any of the boys. At a quarter to eight, a familiar six-bar car horn played "Dixie." I looked in my rearview and there was Eddie in "The Talk of the Town," passing a car-and-trailer rig on the wrong side of the road, gaining on me fast. We played tag around the bends, me in front and blocking him by letting my trailer swing out wide, Eddie ducking inside and trying to pass me on the gravel like some kind of stock car lunatic.

We had reservations at a motel by the lake. I backed my boat up to the door of my room and joined Eddie for a drink. Later Cecil came by, and after a while longer we decided to stake out a table at the buffet and let Lucky find us on his own. But first we went back to our rooms and changed.

"This is the moment of truth, I guess," Cecil said, when we gathered again in the parking lot. He smoothed out his camouflage blouse. "Feels kinda funny, to tell the truth."

Eddie said, "This is where it begins, buddy. This is where the rubber meets the road." Eddie wore a dark blue beret with a miniature set of sergeant's stripes sewn on the front. His eyes were shiny and his white skin was stretched taut. "You look good, Gar," he said with a nod. "But where are your second looey's bars?"

"At home. They look too much like a Super-Duper."

"Who cares, as long as they catch fish?"

We pushed through the double doors three abreast, and marched down the uneven carpet to the dining room. It was a wide open Friday night and at first nobody paid us any mind. There were lines of men and women at the buffet, there were other lines at the bar for pitchers; two wide-screens were showing a bass video without sound, not that you could have heard it if they'd had it turned all the way up. The noise was like a dam's spillway discharge: deep, roaring.

Then silence traveled around the room, wiping out entire tables but leaving little pockets of resistance. One by one, the last stragglers took notice and shut up. We didn't try any funny stuff, just walked casually, confidently, to the end of the buffet line. They couldn't take their eyes off of our identical camouflage outfits, our black canvas jungle boots, green web belts and, finally, the red and black insignia of a bass leaping over a skull on our left shoulders.

They stared. We cooled our heels in line. Eddie caught my eye and offered a tight-lipped smile. "It's psychological to strike the first blow."

"No shit," Cec whispered. "Maybe we better go."

The man in front of us in line turned just enough to bring one pale blue eye to bear on us. His woman clutched his elbow and stared rigidly ahead at the steam table heaped with ham, chicken, corn on the cob and mashed potatoes. Just looking at her stiff back made mine ache.

A loud laugh brayed at one end of the room. He was sandy-haired, crew cut, almost fifty, with a weathered face and a drinker's nose. The people at his table grinned as he explained, in a voice that to him probably sounded like a whisper, "Hell, what's the big deal? It's the drill team for the opening ceremonies." He stared over at us and our eyes met. "They must be high school ROTC cadets."

The room broke up in relieved laughter. Score one for the cowboy in the beige shirt with mother-of-pearl buttons, whoever he was.

Lucky finally joined us as we were cleaning up our do-it-yourself ice cream sundaes. His eyes were bloodshot and his hands shook, he was so tired. "Grab a spoon and dig in," Cecil said, offering him half of his dish. Lucky plucked a spoon off an unoccupied table and began to eat bites of strawberry and chocolate ice cream, covered with chocolate syrup, marshmallow creme, walnuts and whipped cream.

We ended back up in my room with Lucky's maps. He had marked the usual promising spots—coves, creek mouths, flooded timber, sandbars, ledges—and had circled some flooded farms in red ink. We divvied up the lake in quarters, marked a few places where there were steep drop-offs. Still, maps don't make the fisherman, although I didn't tell Lucky that. For him, believing he had an edge was the same as having one.

The next morning at six we went in for breakfast as a unit again. The crowd was quiet and nobody paid us any mind.

"Here we go." I checked eyes: Lucky's, bright; Eddie's, intense; Cec's, sleepy. "Remember the drill. We act busy. We don't talk none. No smiles. But not nervous, you understand. Cool. Then at the gun, we go out together, sixty miles an hour for exactly six minutes. Then we scatter."

Eddie gave the table a karate chop. "Like that."

"That ought to get their attention," Lucky said.

There were well over two hundred fifty boats entered, good for an early tournament, but the Bass Commandos drew their share of the crowd. In a mob scene full of flashy orange-and-silver mylar jackets, loud boasting and feverish last-second preparations, we stuck out—quiet behind our dark glasses, uniformed and obviously ready to go.

Instamatics in the hands of fans were popping in our faces during the entire pre-launch ceremony. When the gun went *boom*, our outboards caught on the first push of the starter button and we zoomed ahead of the pack side by side. A helicopter from the local television hovered overhead. I kept my eye on the dashboard timer. At six minutes, the Commandos exploded into action, peeling off to our different sections.

With that psychological stuff out of the way, I tuned into my fishing sense. As my boat skimmed over the smooth water, its speed up to seventy miles an hour, the wind biting my cheeks and flattening my hair, I alternated between watching the flasher depth sounder and tracking the landmarks on shore. A red flash on the screen showed the occasional fish, which I ignored; the only way to win these things is to find a mother lode of bass and stay with it. You do that by testing likely areas—fishing them in the days before the tournament, if you have the time, which we didn't, and then returning to them in the conditions that are best in terms of production. I was going to try to duplicate the process in a few short hours.

This morning was clear, cool and windless. There had been a water release from the dam at four in the morning, creating a current in the lake and an appetite in the bass. Reading Lucky's maps, I was convinced that the current would draw the fish out of cover at the edges of steep drop-offs. Between the map and my flasher, I found and cruised five spots on the one hour run-out. Finally I settled on a small creek outlet where the bottom went from six to thirty feet. I switched over to the electric trolling motor. Noiselessly I crept in, reading the screen, memorizing the ground. Sandbar, dropoff, shoaling creek. A little weed in the creek.

It was time to musk up. I took some Worm Blood and rubbed it all over my hands to disguise my scent. Then I took my Chumm'n

Rub fish attractor, selected the Glitter style, and doped up a four-inch Do-Nothing plastic worm. Using one of the four rods I keep handy—the one rigged for light line—I began my pattern. High lob cast and deep-water doodle, letting the worm twitch slowly, slowly down . . . holding it for twenty seconds before letting it slide some more . . . vibrating the rod tip to give the worm a lively, flipping action. My heart was racing furiously. It always does, on that first cast of a tournament.

After twenty casts, I could feel the panic rising. This is where tournaments are won and lost, in the mind. This lake had one hundred sixty-two miles of shoreline. The temptation was to cut and run, try another spot. That way led to madness. Feeling the tension ebb, I selected a rod rigged with heavier line and clipped on a black Number 1 Uncle Josh pork frog trailer. This time I used the electric motor to head up-creek, because there was a pulsing in my head that told me the bass were preying on the creatures that inhabited the brushy cover along the banks.

I thought like a bass. A nervous, twitchy fellow with a sneer for the little bass and crappie that are hitting on the flies and bugs that have fallen from the brush to the shallows. Unlike them, I'm sitting under a log or a pile of weed. I'm not budging for just any old bite to eat. I want a frog.

I cut the motor at about forty feet. Behind me I heard, briefly, the warbling roar of a bass boat speeding along; when it had faded to silence and I could hear the birds singing, I heaved Uncle Josh right into a bush. Then I waited. A full minute went by. I twitched the line. Uncle Josh moved his fat, plastic frog butt. I teased him along the branches, thinking of puppets with the strings attached.

Uncle Josh hopped into the water. The strike was savage. A largemouth scooped him up, hitting so hard his charge carried him two feet into the air. The bass twisted in mid-arc, spray flying, then belly-flopped, *whop*, into the water. I was ready with a taut line and commanding retrieve, jerking him off balance and away from those weeds he could use to break the line. His adrenaline surged through the monofilament line, through the wildly vibrating rod tip, down my arms and into my shoulders, and I stood up, eyeing the bottom for any structure he might dodge into. It was over in another minute. I netted him with my left hand, carefully removed the hook, weighed him, and put him in the aerated fishwell. A dead fish is penalized two ounces, but that's not why I take extra care. I'll never bring in a dead bass again. Not with the skeletons in my closet.

Three pounds, five ounces is a good-sized largemouth. The rule of thumb is, you can expect "keepers" to congregate—being snobs—in a weight and age group that rarely varies by more than two pounds, plus or minus. The potential for this hole, then, was a high of five and a low of one. But after twenty casts I decided it had been a fluke, not a hole. I glided silently out of there.

I set Uncle Josh aside and clipped on a Whopper Stopper Fliptail lizard. The pork frog had given me ideas. That largemouth had hit at the sound of Uncle Josh meeting the water; why not use something really loud? There was a tree fallen on the opposite bank of the creek, its branches filling the water like a giant tumbleweed. Behind the point where the branches began was a grotto, between the tree trunk and the bank. I musked up with more Worm Blood, then edged up on the enclosure. Whopper Stopper missed on his first try and went over the log. I had to risk a sharp pull to get him out and he went sailing back past my ear with a nasty buzz and into the lake on the other side of the boat. After that disturbance, I benched myself for three minutes before trying again.

Mr. Lizard hit the tree trunk and bounced off into the water. I twitched him lightly. Retrieved a bit. Let him sit for a minute. Twitch, retrieve, twitch. Nada.

Five casts later, I cut it short and checked my watch. Forty minutes into the day and only one bite and one fish. Not propitious signs.

Another noisemaker was needed. I rejected a buzztail, a Rat-

L-Trap and a Heddon Zara Spook. Too artificial. I needed to sneak into this grotto, make friends and influence fish. It was back to basic black, a half-ounce jig well-liquored with a high potency fish attractor, Roe Lube.

Laying the jig in softly with a light underarm cast that I could never have done this early in the season before all the training, I let it rest on the leaves on the bank for thirty seconds, then, before my line had fully laid down on the water, I plopped it into the drink. And let it sink. And sink.

Now the striptease began. Up an inch. Down a half. Dance, jig, dance. Now sleep. I kept my rod tip high and stood on my very toes to get the best attitude as I worked it. Five minutes passed and I figured this was the moment: the lure was crossing out from the shadow layer.

My half-ounce jig suddenly got pounds heavier. There was no surface action. No yank. Just a steady pull.

After four minutes of silent desperation, I had netted another three-pounder. I began working the grotto again, this time laying the jig just back of the shadow line. I had to act fast, because to judge from the way that bass had taken my lure, the fish in the grotto were in a feeding mood, as opposed to that first fish, who'd been provoked into striking. Feeding fish are pure gold in a tournament. Their mood may change in a second, but until it does you can really pack them in. So I stayed there for another forty minutes. In that time I caught six more keepers, all between two and three pounds, and every one struck the jig exactly at the shadow line, at no more than four or five inches from the same spot. I must have tried a hundred casts for the six that hit the bull's-eye. My arms were shaking and eyes were aching by the time the bass suddenly stopped feeding, but it was worth the pain.

At 11:30 A.M. I put my nose toward home. Keeping the speed down, I read the flasher and detoured over interesting structures as they cropped up on the screen. It was all like a dream, to be coming back so early with the biggest string I'd made in years, knowing that tomorrow I had two good holes to return to.

After a long shower and a ham sandwich, I strolled back to the weigh-in center to see how my twenty-one pound, nine ounce string was holding up. The center was this large wraparound wooden deck with a concession stand in the middle. There were tables covered with flags, a Dixieland band sitting on their hands, plenty of moms and dads and grandmoms and granddads, and lots of babies. At the front table a group of men were sitting in front of microphones and electronic scales. There was an easel with a large chalkboard on it, and on the board were results. G. Foote was in first place. L. Bonnard was tenth. The second spot was a guy named Tater.

"Gar, is that you?"

A lanky man in faded blue denim pants and a blue workshirt came up. He wore black plastic glasses over a narrow, deeply tanned face, and though I felt I'd never met him before, he swore we had, shook my hand, and gave me his card. Stu Hollins, it read, Nashville Video Network.

"Can I get you for an interview now, Gar?"

I hesitated. "I was just going to meet my buddies."

His eyebrows scrunched together. "The Commandos? No reason we can't have them along. Good color."

"I'll see if I can round 'em up—Stu."

His anxious smile brightened. "You do that and I'll see that there's something in it for you."

Then this real dude approached. He had bright yellow hair, a pixie's smile and eyes, and his silver and black jacket said "Walter Waltrous" in script across the back. He gave me his card, too, although I didn't need it, thanks to the jacket.

"I saw you talking to Stu. We're old friends, years in the same business. He ask you to be on his show?" I nodded. "Ah-ha. How'd you like to make an easy thirty bucks?"

"What do you call easy?"

"When Stu asks you what your secret is, say a Hornet Hopper lure did the trick."

"What if it ain't true?"

"You want to tell folks your secrets free, be my guest."

"I'll think it over. Thanks."

After Waltrous, I was approached by a man from a boat company, a fellow from a chewing tobacco outfit, two more lure reps, a depth finder rep and a sharp little lady from the steakhouse down the road, who wanted me to plug her place in exchange for two free Porterhouses. I didn't say no to any of them, although I did ask for my money up front.

The boats were coming in droves now. The later you return, the less you have to show generally, but you never know. I didn't crack a smile until it was official that G. Foote was the top weight for Day One. By that time it was clear that the Bass Commandos were going down in the record books, all of us in the top twenty. We stuck to our drill, keeping together, not saying much, although we tried to be gracious and shake every hand and sign every autograph on request.

Stu came up, trailed by a sloppy-looking fat guy whose face was hidden by the black video camera that looked like it was permanently attached to his head. Stu arranged the Commandos and put me in front. A crowd gathered.

"I'll just ask some easy questions to warm you up," he said, "and do a sound and light check. When I hold up my finger, it's for real. Okay?"

I ran through my memorized speech. There were a lot of names to mention and I was beginning to wish I'd written them down.

"Here we are in Tipton, North Carolina, for the opening day of tournament bass fishing, and with us is the first day's leader, Gar Foote, and his buddies. As you can plainly see, these are not your usual fishing costumes. In fact they look more like a bunch of mercenaries, and that's the impression they gave today with a demonstration of pure power fishing that put each one of them in striking distance of the top tournament prize of thirty-two thousand dollars. You call yourselves the Bass Commandos, is that right, Gar?"

"Correct, Stu." I decided to hold off on the names for now.

"Where'd you get that idea?"

"It was a question of dedicating ourselves to excellence. To keep ourselves strong and in good tournament shape, we formed the Commandos."

"With all four of you in the top twenty your method seems to be a success. Now, as you know, there have been complaints that you may have aided each other on the course and acted in collusion, complaints that the committee is looking into as we speak. Any comment?"

I stared into Stu Hollins' sneaky narrow face behind those black-framed glasses. The boys shifted uneasily behind me; I heard Cec whisper, "Shit," and acted to head off the explosion these television lizards surely wanted to film.

"We work out and we train together, but once that gun goes off it's every man for himself. We *certainly* don't need to cheat. Now, if you'll excuse me, Stu," and I turned my back to the camera. "'Bout face, boys." Eddie was bright red, Cec pale and tense, and Lucky just wore the look of a man disappointed yet another time by human nature.

As we turned our backs, the lizard yelled: "If it's *true* that you haven't cheated, how do you explain today's performance after doing nothing for the past seven years?"

"Don't turn around," I whispered to the guys.

"Moon 'im!" Eddie said fiercely.

One look at each other was all we needed. "Ready-y-y."

"Goddammit!" shouted Hollins. The crowd ooohed and roared.

"Time to withdraw," Eddie said.

"Go? I'm having fun." Cec turned his profile to a fifteen-year-old girl in a puffy pink sweater and capris, who was giggling too hard to aim her camera.

"That's my point. Zip it up."

"We have to debrief, Cec," I said. "Come on. Think of all the action you'll get if we do this again tomorrow."

"Forward . . . ho!"

We started for the exit but the crowd suddenly parted for a familiar figure in a beige cowboy shirt with mother-of-pearl snap buttons. It was our friend from the night before.

"I'm Tater," he announced, his sharp blue eyes sweeping our faces. "And you all are the famous Bass Commandos. Which one's Gar Foote?"

"Yo."

That rutted face, it seemed too large for his collar. There were rivulets of sweat in the cracks of his ruined skin, broken capillaries in his nose. But nothing was blurry or bloodshot about those eyes searching me out.

"Yeah, you look about how I'd expect."

People eddied about us, only a few noticing that the smiles were getting forced.

"And how is that . . . Tater? No first name?"

"Ross." He pointedly didn't offer his hand. My heart thudded and, as if he sensed its irregular beat, he was slow in following up: "You look about like someone who would drop a dead fish into his limit. Kinda weak. A pussy-eater."

Eddie sealed off the nearest bystanders on the left, and Cecil did the same on the right. Lucky put a hand on my elbow.

"You came in second today, didn't you, Tater?" I asked. "That's pretty good for someone whose face looks like an alligator's asshole."

Tater looked over Eddie and Cecil's shoulders, which just

happened to close up the space between us. "You're a cheat, Foote," he said. "Before this night is over, everybody in this room is going to know exactly what you did."

"Do you think they care what did or didn't happen seven years ago? I've paid my dues. And I was accused, not convicted."

"Same difference. Anyway, I'm not talking about back then. I'm saying you cheated today." He bared a set of yellowed teeth made the longer by receding gums. "But tomorrow's another day, and I don't want to spoil the committee's surprise."

Eddie bristled. "What surprise is that, you old porker?"

Tater knew he'd scored. He grinned again, deliberately, over Eddie's head. "Have fun tomorrow, Commandos."

The committee waited until twenty minutes before the start. A thin old fellow hooked my arm and escorted me into the concession booth on the deck. There were three of them, all in identical mustard yellow jackets with "Tournament Official" across their hearts.

"Gar, we want to ask a favor of you before today's fishing commences," said the old man. The other two wouldn't even let him finish.

"Professional bass fishing is about to take a leap into the mainstream—"

"The television contracts are being drawn up as we speak. Cable's been a huge success; Ted Turner's network loves us."

"He loves our image, Gar. It's a clean, family-oriented sport we have here."

"So you must understand our reluctance."

"You're exactly the kind of past we don't want to be associated with. It hurts to say that."

"It hurts to hear you say it," I said. "I've known you off and on for ten years, Ben. I don't have to point out to you that an accusation ain't a conviction."

"But look who *was* convicted. And think of the people you—he defrauded. He robbed bass fishing of its most precious commodity: its good name."

"Where is Jerry Roy?" the second old boy said.

"Your guess is as good as mine."

"You're saying, you don't hear from your brother-in-law?"

"That's it. Ben, you're sharp as ever."

"Can the corn. I don't have to tell you, Gar, with this much at stake we can't help taking a hard line."

"Let's hear it."

"You're out of this tournament."

I gazed at the trio. "I've been fishing the circuit for five years now. How come you waited till now to get cold feet?"

"You went high profile on us, boy."

I snorted. "My entry fee looked just fine to you until I had to spoil things by fishing good, huh?"

"From now on, you can save your entry fee. You aren't going to be welcome at our tournaments anymore. It was a mistake to show you compassion. You never learned your lesson."

The funny thing is, we were talking just as calmly and rationally as can be. I suppose that's civilization for you.

"You're wrong about that," I said. "I did learn my lesson. It was about lawyers. Then I didn't have one; now I do. We can injunct your asses anytime we want. I'm sure when the case goes to court, a jury of my peers will look upon my suffering and loss of livelihood with a sympathetic eye."

The three didn't flinch. That impressed me more than anything with how the sport had grown; ten years ago, if you mentioned a lawyer, these people would look at you as if you'd just said you voted for George McGovern.

The thin old fellow was crestfallen. "It would've been so nice if you'd only said yes."

"Pray for me, brother," I said. "And I'll pray for you."

My old former friend Ben gave me a sour look. "Hold your

prayers. And be careful when you fish today; be careful, Gar. Because we are going to be watching you."

When you hit a fish lode like mine, you know where you're going to go first thing the following morning. When the Commandos broke formation, I set my course and scanned my depth sounder. There was a breeze from the south. The surface temperature was cooler. There had been another water release from the dam, same as yesterday.

Wouldn't you know it, when I reached my sweet spot I had company in the form of a bass boat rigged for video production, already sitting not a hundred yards from my grotto. I grunted and shut off my Johnson. But instead of being greeted with peace and quiet, the roar of an outboard gained on me. I whipped around. The guy was on plane, doing seventy, and right on my tail—where he must have been the whole way out, if only I'd bothered to look behind me. As I decelerated, he gunned it and swerved around me. The wake was ferocious. I grabbed the gunwales and hung on, trapping my lure case with my feet just in case we tipped over.

Tater waved as he coasted right in on my grotto. He slowly turned in front of the fallen tree, shifted into neutral, and revved his outboard two and three times, until it literally screamed. I wouldn't have to worry about catching *those* bass for the next day or two.

I knew the video camera was on me, so I kept my lid on and fussed over the depth sounder. Then I picked up my rod and began to cast just any-old-way, waiting on Tater's next move. He began lashing the grotto with casts, as if he were trying to provoke the bass into striking. All he was doing, of course, was spooking them further.

As I figured, Tater left a few minutes later for his own hole. There was no way I could beat him to it, and he probably thought he had destroyed my concentration. When the stink of him had aired out of this cove, I quietly approached the creek where Uncle Josh had worked yesterday.

Something was wrong. The water was too high. The dam release must not have gone on schedule, although surely the committee would have known and announced this. But it was plain that a foot of water now covered the brushy banks of the creek, which would put the bass too deep for a surface-popping lure like a pork frog. I decided to try a worm. Twenty casts later, I switched to a different color worm. Twenty casts after that, I was desperate and went into a five-cast pattern, changing to spinner-baits, to jigs, and finally to poppers. I'd drifted close enough to the bank to use my depth sounder, so I went ahead and pinged the shore. Any number of little inverted *V*'s showed up—bass—for all the comfort that gave me.

I sat back. The video boat, I realized, had been recording my entire freak-out. I thought of the pleasure it would give the committee, Tater, and the rest of them to watch it. They'd probably edit it into the highlights film for a little inside joke at my expense.

Playing defense is demoralizing, but to win at bass you have to stick to your discipline. When all else fails, you turn to junk lures. I picked through the lowest shelf in my box, coming across things the world hadn't seen in years: rusted metal crawdads, polka-dotted hellbenders, the works.

Why had the water risen like that? Why?

Current! If the dam release *had* gone off as scheduled, then there must've been a second influx recently—a big one. My hands were shaking as I got out Lucky's maps. The sky was clear, so a cloudburst wasn't the culprit. There had to be a feeder impound-ment on one of the lake's tributaries. The maps, however, only extended a few hundred yards past the shore; there were at least fifteen creeks feeding in. I studied the bottom contours of each creek, realizing that the steeper the entrance, the more likely it was to be used for runoff.

Three creeks had uncommonly deep mouths, up to thirty feet, with well-defined channels. I made a notation on my plastic dashboard chart, stowed the maps and blasted out of there. It wasn't until I was in mid-lake that I bothered to look back for the video team; they were right there, on my tail.

The first creek was full of boats. My heart stopped. But as I made a cursory pass, I didn't see any action and nobody looked too pleased. On to the second. Sprinting along at seventy, I could feel the sun hot on my forehead and sweat matting my hair close to the scalp. It was midmorning and I hadn't had a strike. In the second cove I found Cecil, who raised a hand and returned to his casting with a furrowed brow. Running on the electric motor, I glided up-creek past two other boats. A vast curtain of willows marked the end of the navigable stream.

When the third creek on my list proved to be a silted-in slough, I knew I'd been whipped. But passing by the first creek, I decided to check it out, crowds and all. Up-creek the banks were bare of cover, never a good sign, and the air was at least ten degrees warmer. But when I dropped a temperature gauge down, I found a real drop between the top and middle layers, which were fairly warm, and the bottom layer, which was five degrees colder. Here was my current—basically, a feeding trough. Now what could I do about it? Stationing the boat in an eddy behind a bend, I rigged a plain red worm with extra weight and began casting across the creek, retrieving as fast as I could the moment the lure hit the surface. I got a tug, missed the hookup, and let the worm sit. When I reeled in some more, the current had moved it fifty feet downstream. It took me twenty casts to figure out just how to fish that current, but then I had my second strike. Yet in that time the sun had gone from directly overhead to over the hill. I had one two-pound fish and thirty minutes.

That's when the big one hit. He sideswiped my bait and I felt it in my knees, the sucker. My hands were shaking as I reeled in and tried to duplicate my cast. I cut each cast short, and then shorter, dropping in on the current instead of dragging across it. The second time, I almost missed him again, my sweaty hand fumbling with the handle on my spinning reel. He jerked around like a man in the electric chair. I fought him up inch by inch, walked him to the deep side of the boat, dropped to my knees with my left arm holding the rod high and rammed my right arm into the icy lake with the fingers outspread. Hooking him under the gills, I pulled the bass up into the air.

"So you really *were* sweating it out, Gar? Looked like Skunk City out there?"

"You bet, Stu. When I realized my hole wasn't producing, I felt like just packing it in. But first I packed my cheek with some Red Man chewing tobacco, while rubbing Andy's Nightcrawler Cologne on my hands and tying a Wobbly Number Five Disco Lady flasher a foot ahead of my lure. Then I decided to cross the lake to a spot I'd reserved for moments like this. But to get there fast, I squirted a jolt of Octo-Jet, the high octane fuel additive, into my Johnson V6. Stu, it was like traveling on the Concorde."

"You sound like a meticulous basser, Gar."

"I am, Stu. I believe in leaving nothing to chance."

"Well, here's the big question I know is on everybody's mind who is watching this live cable feed: How'd you catch the eight pound, four ounce lunker?"

"I used a very hot producer for me, the Zapata Bushwacker, with a Tallahassee Tickle-Tail set ten inches behind it. The pattern was a lob, a one-minute wait, and then a slow crank."

"We thank you for sharing your secrets with us, Gar Foote. And may I ask how you'll celebrate tonight? You'll be out with your buddies, the Bass Commandos, I take it?"

"Unfortunately, my buddies and me all work for a living, unlike you, Stu. So after a short stop at Ethel's Steakhouse, we're going to hit the road and get back to our wives and families."

"But with a thirty-two thousand dollar first prize you can start thinking of the day you'll be able to turn pro. Not to mention the endorsements that may come your way. Am I right?"

"Right you are, Stu. I've already been approached to do some endorsements. Of course, I have my image and the image of the Commandos to think about. It's all for one and one for all, with us."

"Then good luck to all of you, and God bless."

We came along at the birth of bass. If you don't believe me, try to find an old basser. There aren't any. Our generation, Jerry Roy's and mine, took a sleepy ol' thing boys and grandfathers killed time with and, without knowing we were doing it, we changed the face of fishing.

We didn't know how lucky we were. Young, full of sap and ignorance, we made up the rules as we went along. How do you turn a thing as private and syrup-slow as fishing into a professional sport? It isn't easy, or you would've seen duck hunting professionals, raccoon treeing contests, deer stalking leagues, all kinds of events. Compared to fishing rigs, guns are full of possibilities, when you think on it. They make a lot of noise, they're good to look at, and a man feels manly with a gun by his side or on his shoulder. You'd think the television outfits would jump at a pro hunting league, yet it hasn't happened, has it?

Jerry Roy and I kicked a whole ton of ideas around in those summer weeks when he'd come home from SMU in his Hush Puppies and camel's hair blazer, and I'd be pulling a shift at the bottling plant. All we could see was that bass had it, whatever "it" was, and gun sports didn't. Maybe this Weekend Warrior stuff will change everything, but I doubt it. Bassing has classic elements that can't be bought or sold for silver or gold.

A smallmouth bass is born looking mean and hungry, with his lower lip jutting out. He's a complete athlete, all muscle and sinew. He's a streamlined, compact, fighting machine, with a broad tail that can drive him faster than anything else underwater or blast him two feet into the air to get some unsuspecting mayfly. Think on it. You're a mayfly, buzzing along. All you see is a lily pad, the coast is clear. But under that lily pad, in its shadow, *he's* there. He's timing his jump, he's going to make a quick cut with those ventral fins, give a flurry of tail strokes, thrash into the air, twist like a high-diver and—*snap*. Mayfly, you're history. And for what? How much meat is on a mayfly, anyway? You're telling me it's worth the energy expenditure, or is this a case of sport, the art of the water-to-air strike? How many mayflies make lunch, anyway?

Aggression is a God-given talent. So far, the smallmouth has our undivided attention. But ever since I was a boy, I always respected him for his use of territory: the lily pad whose shadow he dogs, the log he creeps under, the rock ledge he patrols. He knows you're there. But he's not going to let that spoil his appetite. The water temperature where he is means that red plastic worm you're using is as dumb-looking as a coonass on the White House lawn. After a minute or two, you switch to a wobbly minnow, only minnows don't like a pH of + .4. He'd rather nibble those larvae hanging off the green weeds and watch you whisper to your buddy. Here comes the fake frog. He's feeling a little sorry for you, so he'll come up and give it a swirl. But he can smell your Skoal Long Cut snuff all over that frog. He gives a sniff and turns tail. You've bored him before, but never has he been this insulted.

The smallmouth, you see, is playing you for *his* sport. Heck, I swear to God that I've seen a bass hit my lure because I finally had it right, the right bait for the time of day, the temperature, the pH, everything. Even if it meant he was committing suicide, he couldn't shake the hook or run the line around a tree stump and break it off. That bass was honor-bound to strike that lure. To do otherwise was unthinkable; I mean how could he live with himself afterwards?

Nothing can compare to hunting a bass with his wits about him. The places I've been and the lakes I've seen, acres of flooded timber, reservoirs caked with milfoil weed, swamp mangrove wearing skirts of lily pads. You bet it's exciting.

And that's why fishermen couldn't resist making a challenge between themselves to see who was best. Jerry Roy and I fished for nickels, dimes, and dollars as we grew up. We fished the Independence Day Chamber of Commerce Bass Derby of 1959, when we were ten years of age. I fished it again last year at age thirty-six. Won it, too. A fifteen-year-old came in second, and don't think he didn't have me scared.

The field was wide open way back then. Anyone who wanted to put up a sign could hold a bass tournament. Everyone anted up and the winner split the pot with the promoter. You backed your boat trailer up to the launching ramp, set the hand brake and threw your stuff aboard. With all the other boats, you'd jostle the starting line until the crew-cut little redneck nephew of the promoter hauled up a shotgun and knocked himself flat by firing both barrels at once. Off you'd go, racing each other to spots you could only guess would be good. Forty miles an hour was fast then.

After a day of fishing, you'd race back against the clock; stopping time was usually 4:00 P.M. Everybody would lay out their strings of fish and weigh 'em on a scale over the dock. There'd be a barbecue smoking up the place, and a keg or two, maybe a band.

There was cheating from the beginning. A man would have four fresh, shiny bass on his string and two blotchy, smelly things a cat wouldn't touch. People would jeer. The man would bristle. Sometimes he'd skulk off, sometimes he'd duke it out with the promoter. And, I don't doubt, sometimes a man would get clean away with it, having kept his fish alive in a hidden tank somewhere on his boat.

In the sixties, all sorts of bass leagues began popping up over the country—in the South, of course, but also in Texas, Florida, Michigan, Nevada, New York. There was money in it now. Manufacturers of engines, boats, fishing rods, lures and fish-finding equipment—that last was a shock when it came around the block—were laying out cash for prizes, gear for qualifying, fees for endorsements. I remember reading about a $50,000 tournament with something like awe, and thinking: If I won that, I'd be set up for life.

When I came back from my tour of duty, two hundred eighty-five days spent pushing piles of red dirt around Cam Ranh Bay in my Caterpillar D-8, there was a job waiting for me at the bottling plant. But first Jerry Roy came by my folks' house. He had long hair, over the ears, and, instead of Hush Puppies, he wore fancy cowboy boots. We sat on the porch and drank beer from long-necked bottles and acted like wise old men who'd seen the world, Jerry at SMU and me in Nam.

Jerry had narrowed his eyes and peered at me. "You give them a startin' date yet at the plant? Because you look like you could do with some kicking around."

Part of me had wanted nothing more than to pick up work exactly where I'd left off, just as soon as I rotated home. But everybody seemed to take it for granted, like Jerry, that I would be in the mood to just lie around, soaking up the R and R.

I said to him, "I sure missed the she-crab soup at the old Celery Top."

"Well, it hasn't changed. But I'm talking about a business proposition. Could be fun."

"Shoot."

"I learned about making money at SMU. Gar, you wouldn't believe how easy it was. I'd never guessed there could be so many people with so much money to burn, and so little sense, as there was at college. Popcorn, holiday hominy, dry cleaning, firecrackers . . . ever hear of a firecracker called an M-80?"

"We used those in rat holes at Cam Ranh Bay."

"Then you know what I'm talking about. More bang for the buck. A big seller. I'd establish the route—frat houses, residence halls—turn it over to some sophomore for a low percentage. Steady money. Just like McDonald's and Colonel Sanders. The key is controlling supply."

"How's this any different than working for the Coca-Cola Company?"

Jerry tilted his beer up at the sky. It was a soft night, thick and dark and friendly. I'd almost forgotten what warm, friendly darkness was all about. A big bowl of she-crab soup, that's what I felt like most—sweet, murky, the spicy crab boil lying under the tongue for hours after. At the Celery Top there was also a jukebox my folks used to dance to, Dad in his blue jeans and khaki shirt with his name over the pocket, Mom in that print dress she called Blue Willow.

He sighed. "I can tell just how far you've been away by how impatient you are, Gar. You used to listen up."

"Ho-kay."

"I'm talking about our one true love now. How'd you like to never work a day in your life again, and get rich off the one thing you love best?" He leaned forward and cracked his knuckles, one after the other. "A couple of fellas and I are putting together a professional bass fishing league."

"That's been done before."

"Not an all-stater. Not as a national event, a world championship circuit. The Bass Bonanza. I took out a trademark on it. And the tour: The Battle of the Bassers, the Bonzai Bass-Off, the Bassa Nova."

"Wait! You're killing me," I pleaded. I was laughing my head off.

Jerry grinned. "Stop laughing, you bastard."

"If I have to listen to any more of your lies, I want to do it at the Celery Top."

Jerry drove a blue T-bird, the pony-sized model, with a ragtop. It was a fraternity boy's car, although I didn't say so, because I knew Jerry had been asked to leave his house over some trumped-up infraction. But Jerry seemed to have read my mind; he suddenly floored it. We left a rubber mark twenty feet long on the highway.

The Celery Top is a low cinder block bungalow. Out front is an oil drum with a flagpole sticking out of it. The only flag that flies on that pole is a blue square of cloth with an orange crab in the middle. That's when the crabs are in. When they aren't, the Celery Top is closed.

We gave our orders at the counter and took a table in the corner. Jerry let me settle in before nodding at the wall. There was a poster: orange and black.

The Biggest Bass Derby of All Time! $64,000 Grand Prize! Ribs, raffle, refreshments. Music by Honest Buck & The Charismatics. Sat. & Sun. March 14-15.
Produced by the Sportfishing Society of the South,
Jerry Roy, B.S., Pres.

"I take it all back."

After letting me eat a little more crow, Jerry ran down the story of how he was driving home from SMU, pockets full of change from his lucrative franchises. In a little town that was nothing more than a crossroads, he came upon a mob of cars gathered along a lake. He almost passed on by, thinking it was just a tent meeting and baptism. But then he saw the boats. He poked around, counted heads, did some arithmetic based on the entry fee, and came away impressed.

Once he had talked a local printer into running off the posters

he needed, the Bass Bonanza was in business. The difference
between it and the local events was that a portion of all Bonanza
entry fees went toward a jackpot at the end of ten tournaments.
The profit came from a rule that said you had to fish five tournaments to be eligible for the championship; it guaranteed repeat
business.

"It sounds good, but what do you need me for?" I finally had to
ask, because Jerry was getting that worn-down, talked-out look he
gets. His eyes had started to dart this way and that, and he kept
wiggling his shoulders inside his shirt like something itched him.

"I want you to fish for me."

"You always used to do all right on your own. College can't
have screwed you up that much."

"Promoters don't fish, chucklehead. Who'll mind the store?
Promoters go fishing when they retire to their big old mansions."
He swatted a crab with a wooden mallet and red-tinged water
shot out the leg joints. "No, I want you to be the house ace. In
return for expenses and a good wage, you agree to sign over any
winnings. I want to make you a star, Gar. The circuit needs name
recognition."

I stirred my soup. "Let me get this straight. You want to make
me a star?"

"Why not? You're damned good, almost as good as me."

"As I recall, I've beaten you more than you've beaten me."

"But I won the Independence Day Derby two years running."

"You were lucky."

"Once, maybe. But *two* times?"

That's how it went for the next week or so, Jerry cajoling me one
moment and needling me the next. I finally figured, what the heck,
everybody wants me to take time off, so why not do it right? There
was also the matter of Virginia Roy. She loves that brother of hers,
even if she doesn't exactly love fishing, and it didn't take me too
long to realize that I'd see a lot more of her if I worked with Jerry,
instead of inside the bottling plant. In fact, our first tournament

was such a successful mess that Jerry talked her into quitting junior college and joining him to help run the show.

And what a show it was. Just like the tent revival preachers, we'd advertise on telephone poles Monday and set up shop on Friday evening. The entries filled up shoe boxes, checks with every one. I was always introduced as The Favorite, and as long as I never won any of the tournaments or even placed particularly high, plenty of folks got the chance to feel proud of themselves.

We made two mistakes, three if you count leaving Jerry in charge. First, we didn't keep receipts. We patterned ourselves on the revival circuit but forgot that they were tax-exempt. Second, we didn't set up anything like a foolproof system against cheating. In the fifth tournament everyone suspected a closemouthed pair of rogue Texans of *something*, but it was like they were daring us to say the word. They were simply too scary. Then *I* won the sixth tournament, and a lot of ugly rumors started to fly, mostly about me, mostly spread in revenge by those same Texans. Jerry started carrying a 12-gauge around after that. We came into the tenth and last tournament on Labor Day, knowing already that something had gone sour and hoping, praying, that we could just get this thing over with. We wanted to go home, relax, and then decide if it was worth fixing up and carrying on into a second season.

By then Virginia Roy and I had set a wedding date for the week following the jackpot tournament. We weren't going to be able to wait much longer than that and still pretend that the baby had come early.

About eleven-thirty the night before the tournament, Jerry hammered on the wall of our trailer. "Come on, Gar, we gotta talk. Virginia Roy, just get your beauty rest."

I pulled on my pants and followed him to his trailer. There was a bottle of I. W. Harper's beside the Coleman lamp. He poured out two slugs. "Drink this," he said, and handed me a glass.

"I believe I'll pass, thanks. Gotta fish tomorrow."

"I said drink it."

"If you insist." He picked up his glass and clinked it hard against mine. Then he drained it before I'd taken a sip. "Are you all right?"

"Won't be until you drink that damn thing up. Now listen," he said as I gulped Mr. Harper's bourbon, "and don't interrupt me. We got a major problem. Two problems. One is money — we can't cover the purse. Don't interrupt. Somehow a lot of money's just gone, we've run up some expenses. That problem is going to work itself out fine. The other problem is those Texans. I think they're planning to cheat. I know they are."

"Can I interrupt now?" He nodded. "First tell me how we ran up expenses."

Jerry pointed both his index fingers at me and slowly brought them together. "We've been getting squeezed."

"You mean . . . ?"

"Every sheriff in every parish, every politician, and not a few men of the cloth. They each come to me for a donation. Hey, you think I'm going to refuse?"

"They asked that much?"

"They also wanted side action. I lost big once. That's all it takes, Jake. At the end of this weekend we're going to have to give someone a check for sixty-four thousand dollars and it ain't there."

I still didn't feel as grim as Jerry did, to judge from his expression. "Well, we can give the winner an IOU for the rest, can't we? We can pay it off after we get jobs." The week Virginia Roy and I got married, I was due to start back at the company.

"Sure. And when we try to run the circuit next year, how many people do you think will sign on? But that's not even the point. The point is, we're liable to be arrested."

The bourbon swam up my throat and burst like a bubble of swamp gas in my nose. My eyes watered. Jerry nodded. "You getting the picture now? Go ahead and cry if it makes you feel better."

"Shut your mouth, Jerry. You messed up here, not me."

"Yeah, like it's my fault you were born stupid. Just look how I got to walk you through this. It tires me out, frankly. Doing all the thinking all the time, while you just sit there making sad old hound-dog eyes at me."

"So where has all your thinking got you?"

"Our only choice is for you to win tomorrow. Then the money stays in the family, don't it?"

"That sounds easy enough."

"It is easy. You're going to win."

"I am?"

"You already have. Two hours ago I planted some nice fat fish in this lake." He reached into his shirt pocket and pulled out a folded square of paper. "The locations are on this map. All you have to do is reach down, find the float and snap on your line."

"I can't do that."

"You will do that."

"No!" I stood up. He leaned back and stared at me over the glass chimney of the Coleman. "You want to land me in jail, when I'm marrying your sister in a week?"

"You rather land her in jail? On paper she's listed as our bookkeeper."

I slumped back against the wall and closed my eyes, feeling the noose tightening. "People just aren't going to buy it."

"They will, because I've hired a lie detector man to test the winner, whoever he may be."

"Well, then he'll find out, won't he?"

"Sure he will. And the sheriff will haul away that Texas fellow, and the number two fisherman, you, will take home all the money." Jerry's grin was tight.

"Won't he test me?"

"Course. We'll attend to that. A man I know taught me how to beat it, and now I'm going to teach you."

I never thought to ask why on earth he would take lessons in beating a polygraph. When it comes to Jerry Roy, I accept that I would rather not know the why or the wherefore of some of the things he does.

Besides, I was slowly getting the picture of what could happen if I didn't win the tournament. If I got in trouble, I might not have a job with Coca-Cola. Virginia Roy's good name would be dragged through the mud. And how's jail for a way to spend a honeymoon?

I said, "Are we going to know how much fish to bring in? I mean, to come in second behind the Texans."

"Now you're thinking!" Jerry folded up the map and passed it to me. He glanced at his watch and reached under the desk for two more shot glasses. "In a few minutes we're going to have visitors."

Being born vicious, the Texans were naturally suspicious. They first assumed, when Jerry laid out the deal, that we planned to trap them. They wouldn't say a thing until Jerry spelled out our troubles and admitted that without their help we were doomed. They liked hearing that. They liked hearing Jerry admit that he'd first wanted to rig it so I won, but that he just couldn't figure out how to make sure they wouldn't top my limit, no matter how much I brought in.

It went smoothly until Jerry came to the part about splitting the winner's check down the middle. They wouldn't hear of anything less than sixty percent. Jerry explained that he needed more to cover ourselves, but they were unsympathetic. So he pulled a long face and we pretended to huddle in a corner while the two Texans helped themselves to the bourbon.

"Okay. You got yourself a deal," Jerry said to them. "Now I want to know how many fish you're bringing in."

"So Gar here can bring back more?"

"I don't need Gar to bring in more, but I do have to have an idea of what it'll take to win. I can't afford mistakes."

Finally he got some kind of estimate out of them. We drank on our deal, but nobody bothered to shake hands. It was a low, mean atmosphere in Jerry's trailer, as ugly as the worst bar I ever peered into from the streets of Saigon, and I hated myself for being involved with men like that.

The first day of fishing saw such large limits of bass that it made headlines. Talk of cheating was on most people's lips when they found that the top five finishers' weights were twice that of the next twenty. Jerry seemed uneasy at this as well. It looked as if there were other cheaters out there, and he didn't have a piece of them. The thing was, I hadn't pulled out a single one of Jerry's planted bass yet and I was good for fifth place. Then it was Sunday morning, the last day. I fished hard, hoping that by some fluke I could pull in enough legal fish that I could forget about the plants. It was hopeless, of course. I had to go through with it.

My heart skipped irregularly and my hands shook so bad, it was all I could do to unfold the map, find my landmarks, look in the water for the submerged bobber and clip on my swivel. Each bass had been securely hooked through the mouth and moored by a spring-release line to a brick on the bottom. They were so fat and so innocent, their gold-edged black scales catching the light as their gills feathered oxygen from the clear water.

I went here and there, pretending to fish, killing time. Near quitting hour I opened up the little blue lure box Jerry had given me and recalled what he'd said.

"Most people think a lie detector test is the same thing as standing before St. Peter on Judgment Day. That isn't the case at all. First they make you nervous by sitting you in a chair and strapping wires all over you. They ask you about a hundred questions, most of them simple: 'Is your name Gar Foote?', 'How old are you?', 'Ever told a lie?' So by the time they get to the big ones, they have a record—sort of like a depth sounder chart—of your nerves. Well, if your nerves are dead, they aren't going to get a rise out of you, are they?"

There were three pills in the box. Valium. I reached in and pinched one between my fingers and laid it on my tongue. It tasted

chalky, bitter, but I let it dissolve a while before swallowing. Next
I reached into my baitwell, pulled out a can of Blue Ribbon and
drank it off in one long, throat-burning gulp. I let the boat go this
way and that in the hot sun, moseying along as I chugged three
more cans of beer. The next time I pulled out the pillbox, it seemed
to take me forever to chase down those rascally little devils as they
rolled about. "Gotcha!" I shouted at last, pinning the last of the
Valium under my thumb. I licked it right off, rid my mouth of that
nasty aftertaste with the last two cans of beer, stood up in the boat,
unzipped my fly, and urinated over the side into my slowly boiling
wake as bits of bright light burst like confetti across my eyeballs.

I wasn't faking my grin as I pulled up. Everytime I closed my
eyes, there was a quiet *zoom* in my bloodstream. Everytime I
opened my eyes, I felt as if someone was tickling me all over with a
feather. I saw Virginia Roy at the official dockside weighing
station and let out a whoop. I shouldn't have opened my mouth; I
couldn't stop. Yodeling as I powered into a slip that was crowded
with other boats, I nearly forgot to slip my Johnson into reverse.
"Whoa boy!" I shouted as I revved loudly backwards in a wild
circle.

After waiting my turn, I plunked down my string of fish onto
the scorer's table. Virginia Roy scowled up at me. "What's got
into you?"

"I just caught more fish than I ever have in my whole life, that's
what's got into me. I just won this tournament."

"Don't be so sure." She looked pale and queasy in the muggy
heat, and her loose white blouse showed sweat patches under the
arms and dark little half-moons under her breasts. She'd been sick
this morning, and now her eyes were ringed with worry. I wished I
could set her mind at rest, but Jerry and I had agreed that she had
to be protected, at all costs, from knowing about our plans. So I
went on with my bragging.

"I must have thirty-five pounds of fish here."

She nodded toward the scoreboard, which showed the fishing

half of the Texan team in front with thirty-seven pounds, ten ounces. Everybody watching must have enjoyed seeing my jaw drop.

At last all the fish were in and weighed. Jerry climbed on top of the makeshift stage and borrowed the country band's microphone to do the honors. First, however, he said he had something to discuss with everyone. Cheating. He had hoped it would not turn out this way, but he couldn't let rumor and innuendo ruin a sport as wonderful as ours. Therefore he had engaged the best polygraph man in Mississippi, a man who did the statehouse regularly, to come out and do all the money finishers of the tournament.

A sharp gasp from the crowd. Jerry went on, sadly, to say that spot testing would be the policy until further notice. Then he called on the two top finishers: "I see one of them is my brother-in-law-to-be, Gar Foote. I just want to say favoritism don't exist to a polygraph expert like we have here."

The polygraphist came up on stage, a short man with a neat black goatee and wearing a blue serge suit, white shirt, white socks and black shoes. He went to the table and sat down behind it, reached into his jacket pocket and pulled out an eyeglass case. After he'd fitted a pair of rimless spectacles on his flat nose, he whisked a tablecloth off his apparatus.

"I, ladies and gentlemen, am Dr. Bocock. I am a scientist of ethical standards. Here before you is an example of the polygraph, or lie detector as it is vulgarly known. Let us begin."

I hadn't seen the Texan yet, but now the crowd began to laugh at something. People gave way before the commotion; then the man was launching himself at the edge of the stage, his whiskered face red and his eyes bulging white as a calf's. Even I could see the drunk upon him from twenty feet away. He fell back into the crowd, who heaved him up again. He got half his body on stage and then got stuck, so he flailed his arms and legs around like he was swimming. Finally, he made it, and collapsed back in an old, wooden high-backed chair on one side of the table.

I was determined not to make the same spectacle of myself and, at a dignified pace, made my way to the steps, up, and across the stage to my chair. Something made me want to look at the crowd as I went to sit down, so I did, with the result that I didn't entirely connect with the chair seat and ended up on the floorboards.

The crowd hooted. Dr. Bocock paid them no mind. He put a bunch of straps on my right arm, took my blood pressure and plugged me in. I looked across the table at the Texan. He glared at me with hate in his eyes. It was enough to sober me up momentarily. I finally realized that what we'd done was tantamount to a declaration of war. Then I asked myself what his being drunk meant, and came to the conclusion that they were on to Jerry's double cross.

There we were, two drunks wired up to a Truth or Consequences machine before a crowd of maybe six hundred rowdy hecklers, all of them having a ball with our answers to the questions Dr. Bocock asked us: Have you ever told a lie? Have you ever driven a car? Have you ever drunk to excess? He worked his way methodically through about fifty questions that had nothing to do with anything. By then the Texan and I were hamming it up, winging it, playing to the crowd, even catching each other's eye and grinning for a moment.

I began looking for Jerry and Virginia Roy. But the evening sun in my eyes made my vision blurry. I kept on rolling my head around on my shoulders, because it just felt so good. Then I'd catch myself and jerk to a stop, and everybody would laugh. The Texan started a wad of tobacco and worked that furiously for a while but, even so, he slowed down and began to doze off between questions. I kept expecting Dr. Bocock to say something; he paid us no mind. His eyes were on the unscrolling chart.

By now the crowd had caught on. Maybe they didn't understand why, but they weren't buying the polygraph demonstration. Hoots, yowls, whistles I was prepared for. When a fat red plastic worm stung my cheek, I began to fear for my safety.

"Are you a high school graduate?" asked Dr. Bocock.

"Yes," I said, feeling my face, half expecting to find a treble hook embedded there.

"No," the Texan said, and then he took a three-ounce lead sinker in the crotch.

I winced, covering my own privates immediately. He'd been sagging down in his chair, but no more. Up he shot and convulsively gulped down his chaw. He came to his senses remarkably quick, considering the variety of sensations he had to cope with, and gagged the wad of tobacco midway down his gullet. It made a bulge in his throat like a rat dinner moving through a bull snake, and the muscles of his thick red neck rippled with the effort of holding it there. Anybody who's ever chewed for any length of time has swallowed a cud. Anybody who's ever swallowed a cud knows what happens after that. The Texan moaned. Those in the front row ducked, those in the second dived on top of the first, but the third row had nowhere to run and so began shoving. Throughout all this Dr. Bocock kept on asking his questions. Perhaps he was aware and didn't care; perhaps he was used to this sort of thing.

"Are all your fish from this lake?" he asked.

"Yes," I said.

"Yeah," grunted the Texan.

"Are your fish all taken legally?"

"Yes."

"*Yuuuuuhhhhh*" and the Texan manfully ejected his chaw onto the floor of the stage. The crowd whistled.

At last Dr. Bocock signalled for quiet by raising one arm and snapping his fingers repeatedly. He peered through his spectacles at the sheet of graph paper rolling out of his machine.

"Ladies and gentlemen, a word before I proceed. The polygraph is not infallible. It measures electricity, not truth. Based on my interviews, I conclude that both of these men had generally uniform electrical levels. Yet both showed a degree of stress on certain questions. Mr. Foote's answers indicate that he did not graduate from high school. Mr. Moxley, I am afraid, has failed a more serious set of questions. Regretfully, I cannot certify him as the winner of this tournament."

"Bullshit!" The Texan tore the electrodes off his arm and threw them at Dr. Bocock. Then he went for me. He bowled my chair over and we began to roll on the floor. Next thing I knew, Jerry had the Texan in a hammerlock and was whaling his ribs with a long leather sap. He left him in a pile and helped me to my feet. He staggered over to the microphone.

"Looks like we got us a winner, am I right?" he shouted hoarsely, raising my fist overhead like a prizefighter's.

Jerry has always claimed that if he had only not made it a question then nothing more would have happened. "I had it all in the palm of my hand," he said to me as we sat in the darkened trailer, hanging on as the crowd outside rocked us back and forth and beat on the aluminum walls with what sounded like two-by-fours. Virginia Roy clung to the sides of the lower bunk bed and listened, white-faced, staring at us in dumb shock.

"Why don't you just go home," Jerry shouted at the walls, but I doubt anyone heard him. "It's too much. I couldn't make that throw again in a hundred years, but I got him! I got him right in the nuts!"

"*You* were the one?"

The trailer tilted slowly, and shelves of papers, books, pots and pans emptied themselves upon our heads. "How soon will the cops get here, do you think?" asked Virginia Roy.

He brushed coffee grounds off his shirt. "Never, I hope." He gave me a warning look. But I was too worried about Virginia Roy and kept on at him. Just when he claimed it was quieting down, the trailer began tilting again. This time it went farther, and farther, until it settled on its side with a soft crunch.

"*Why?* Why are they doing this?" Virginia Roy screamed, thrashing her legs although nothing restrained them. "*What* did you do to them?" she shouted into my face.

I know it sounds crazy, but in the middle of all this I went to sleep. The beer and the pills and the excitement just pooped me out, and right before her eyes I began to nod off. Being flipped on our side had somehow turned off a switch in my brain: *There, that's done it, I give up.*

So I don't know what, or if, Jerry told her after that, although he must've said something for her to think what she's thought all these years. I used to try to get her to discuss it. To her, though, the subject is closed.

Everybody must have slept, eventually. Later on, I halfway opened my eyes in a gray fog of pain and closed them immediately, freezing forever in my mind the sight of Virginia Roy's stark white face pillowed on a stack of posters bound in twine. When I looked in the other direction a minute later, and couldn't find Jerry, I knew he had lit out. I went back to sleep. Much later there were a pair of eyes, staring down at me from a smashed porthole, and a man's whisper. "Hey. Come on, wake up—that's right. Are you all right? Should I call a doctor?"

I licked my lips.

"It's too . . . really, too late," I heard her say. Turning, I saw her wipe her fingers off on her once-white blouse, leaving a dark red handprint over her heart.

"So, are you finally happy?" she asked, smiling at me over a plate of Popeye's chicken, neither of us having had a chance to do any shopping since our weekend away.

"What's that 'finally' supposed to mean?"

She crinkled up her nose. "My, you're all feisty. Am I gonna have to watch myself around here?"

"Yeah. You live with a bass celebrity, you pays the price. The fans seeking autographs. The reporters camped on the lawn."

"The *lawn*."

"The lawn. I expect this place will one day be like Graceland. May as well get used to it. Order a few statues of Garfield to have around the house."

"Gimme that gizzard." She made a stab with her fork. I blocked it with a parry of my cutlass.

"*Garfield* gets the gizzard, you know that." I impaled it on the end of my knife and twirled it slowly. "But he is also very generous, that Mister Garfield." I laid the gizzard down upon her plate. "And I hear some women will do *anything* for Garfield's gizzard."

The phone rang. She didn't bat an eye.

"Telephone," I said.

"Telephone!" she called over her shoulder. After a while, the phone stopped ringing by itself. "I sent the servants home," she whispered, rising and bending forward over the table at the same time. She elbowed her plate of chicken aside and kissed the top of my head; most of the buttons of her peach rayon blouse were undone, and I feasted my eyes on and inhaled the scent of my wife's pale and freckled breasts.

We came back downstairs later because it seemed too early to sleep and she needed to clean up after dinner. I poured myself a Coke and sat at the dining table, going over the bills that had come in since Friday. There was an envelope that had *Department of State* for a return address. It looked like junk mail, but you never know.

"Ha. Get this, honey." I held the letter up. "We've just been asked to contribute to Civilian Military Aid for Nicaraguan freedom fighters. And guess whose name is on the letter?"

"Is it from Rico?"

"How'd you know?"

"I invited him to dinner next week. He's going to hold a fund-raiser at the junior college. I was real surprised to hear about that! Anyway, I hope it's all right."

"Sure." Too much was rolling through my mind at that moment. "So, you talked to him about this at the Weekend Warrior thing?"

"Sort of. He called last week. Remember I told you?"

"No."

"I know I told you, honey. You've just been too busy bassin' to listen to me."

"That's not true." Or was it? When I tried to think about the past two weeks, I drew a lot of blanks. Of course, no man can afford to listen to everything a woman says; I listen at the edges and can generally predict the drift of Virginia Roy's evening speeches by doing a little dead reckoning. "Anyway, he's welcome to stay the night. You told him that, right?"

"Of course not. I wanted to ask you first. But I think he's got to travel on to Birmingham. Say, you know how you could really help?"

"How's that?"

"Introduce him to the Chamber of Commerce Tuesday."

"Good idea." I shoved back my chair and yawned. "You about ready to go up?"

She turned off the water in the sink and wiped her hands on a dish towel. From behind her I thought I could see some tension in her neck, so I spoke up as if the idea had just hit me: "I'm glad somebody in this family has the stomach for politics. You make me proud."

I watched the color tint her cheeks before shouting: "And now it's Scooter Shooter time!" She made a break for the kitchen cupboard the same time I did, and got a leg in there first. She raised her hands, karate-style. I laid my foot in next to hers, feinted with my left and jumped with my right. She whacked me — hard.

"Hey!" I jiggled my arm, numb from the shoulder down. "You hurt me."

"I'm sorry."

"Must've hit a nerve." I cradled my wrist with my other hand until she leaned over and stroked it. Stealthily I reached over her head and took down the bottle of Kahlua. "That's better," I whispered into her ear, and nudged her to one side. Before she knew it, I had the box of Scooter Pies under my arm.

She put her exasperated face on. "Just like a little kid."

We got into our pajamas and turned on the television, skimming the channels before settling on a program. I opened the box. A Scooter Pie is two large cake wheels with a marshmallow filling between them, the whole thing dipped in a dark chocolate shell.

Way back in elementary school I learned that if you bite a hole in the cookie, you could pour your half pint of lunch milk in there and the Pie would hold it like a canteen. Then you'd hold it over your mouth, bite a hole in the bottom, and *whoosh*, the whole thing would sort of gush out and collapse. You had to swallow it all or get messed up.

My little variation was Kahlua and milk. Virginia Roy made disgusting noises as I did my first Scooter Shooter, but she finally caved in and had me make her a short one.

"You are one crazy boy, you know that?"

"Yeah."

The show went into commercials. After an all-American pitch for the latest Japanese pickup truck, a familiar scene unfolded: smoke bombs, laser lights, thumping disco music and our arch rival soda.

"Change the channel, will you?"

"Oh, come on, it's just a commercial."

"That's right. And it's their commercial." I reached for the remote control. While cruising the channels, I tried to get the image of that primping rocker out of my mind.

"He's really good." She leaned back on her pillow and stroked my back. "I'm not saying I like Pepsi, Gar."

"I hope not—look!" One of our latest ads came on. The music sounded slick and powerful, but the lyric was what really sent chills down my spine. "Now *that's* a commercial!"

She sighed. "It's okay, I guess. But it's just a jingle, and he's the real thing."

"Careful how you say that."

"He's just got this innocence about him. It kind of works against his strange side. And you have to admit he dances well, I mean, come on." She tickled me until I squirmed, but my heart wasn't in it, and she sensed it. We stopped.

"His songs don't mean anything," I said, "That was a real message we delivered. He doesn't *say* anything." But it was my turn to know that she wasn't in the mood, my turn to stop. Talk wasn't going to change things. Jingles weren't going to change things, either. Coke needed saving, not from the other side, but from itself.

I went to sleep thinking how a man isn't even safe in his home anymore. Television had brought the cola wars right into my bedroom, and shown me where the battle lines were being drawn. *This* was my fight. I was one of the field officers of the company. But that begged the question: What could I do about it? The answer was a chiller: nothing. Because my leaders weren't even Americans.

The phone rang again as we were sitting down to breakfast. We looked at each other, both thinking the same thing: Who'd call at five-thirty in the morning? We were hardly awake. I picked it up. There was a hollow rushing on the other end, as if the sea were breaking on a deserted beach somewhere far away. Two electric pips and a beep later, a flock of Spanish flew past. "Go ahead," said a woman's tinny, Latin-accented voice.

"Hello? Hello?" a man asked, shouted. "Anybody there?"

"Yes, speaking."

"Anybody there?"

"I'm here. Go ahead. Who is it?"

"Hello, anybody home?" he shouted. "Can you hear me, chucklehead? Shit, I must have a bad connection. Senorita reconnect me, por favor." His voice faded away into a surf of static. There was a click, a buzz. I hung up. Virginia Roy cocked her head at me.

"What was that?"

"A real bad connection. I think . . . it may have been your brother."

A smile lit her face and eyes, the kind of smile any man would like to say he'd brought to a woman. "Really?"

"It sounded like him—somewhere south of the border. I guess he'll call again."

"Gosh, it's been since last Christmas." She stared at the phone, jiggling her foot impatiently. The whole table vibrated, plates rattling forks. "Did he sound all right?"

"Yeah—if it was him." I grinned. "Do you think he really sent those presents, the ones he said he did?"

Virginia Roy pressed her lips tight and gave me a hard look. "If he calls, I'm warning you—don't mention it. I bet the customs grabbed them, or else the post office."

We waited another five minutes, then went our separate ways. We've gotten used to stray calls. Calls from foreign places, calls with no one on the other end, collect calls where the operator asked for names we'd never heard of but that seemed to have some connection to the past—since Jerry fled the trailer that morning, seven years ago, we've gotten more than our share of strange calls. It's tapered off over the last few years. Gone are the days when we'd wait anxiously for an hour on the off chance it was him, calling from a phone booth in Nuevo Laredo or Villa Hermosa or Gatun, speaking with a phony Spanish accent through a handkerchief, pretending that we would understand his fractured messages.

I let Virginia Roy handle the rare straight conversation with Jerry because she misses him so much. He's all the family she has, their mother having passed on while he was hiding from the warrant and the folks from Internal Revenue. I also wasn't sure what I had to say to him. Sure, by running like he did he made it seem as if he'd embezzled the missing bass money, and that took the heat off Virginia Roy and me. Virginia Roy thinks that was plumb noble of him, whereas I now think that he really *did* embezzle the money—the winner's money, *our* money—so he really shouldn't be nominated for any prizes just yet. Try telling that to Virginia Roy, though. She just stared at me the one or two times I was stupid enough to venture my uninformed opinion, and her look said something on the order of: If you know what's best for you, Gar Foote, you'll stop right now this slandering of my brother. The poor, persecuted man, and him having given his life to save yours.

It all goes back, as what doesn't, to childhood. When we were young, well before we had to give a thought to what life had in store for us, Virginia Roy, Jerry and I would spend endless summer evenings down on the old branch of the Okatoma River that had been dammed off in a flood year by a great yellow sand bar. Willows had grown up, closing off the river from view. Pines crept in, encouraged by the leaves and whatnot that covered the sand under the willows. The old branch became a little lake, more properly a pond, always warm and never entirely stagnant, thanks to seepage from the river's underground tributaries. There was a forest of green around the pond, a screen of green that would be stirred, by the slightest breeze, into a sparkling silver. At the water's edge the algae and weed were a bright, fluorescent green, bright as spilled paint. The pond itself was a more mysterious green. I swam across it a million times and always felt a cold nibble at my toes that had nothing to do with temperature, only fear. Of course we tried to scare each other all the time. Sunken tree limbs had snagged and dragged a woman down to her death once, hadn't they? An alligator lived down there, bigger than any ever seen, a relic of the Spanish days.

One thing the pond had, that wasn't the product of our imagination, was bass. We learned to fish there — not by fishing, but by just being there and watching, from sunup to sundown.

Jerry and I were best friends. Virginia Roy, well, she tagged along. She was a pest for years. Dirtier than any child I'd ever seen, and with a bad mouth on her — all the Roys could talk — Virginia Roy, always the two names for some reason even when she was a babe in arms, chased us with the dogged, dumb persistence you'd expect to see rewarded. Only the Lord didn't put anyone in charge except Jerry and me, so she did our bidding and got dirt in the face for it. Naturally she only clung the harder.

I say this because I remember to this day with a guilty conscience the things Jerry and I did to Virginia Roy. They weren't dangerous or ugly things, but just the same we hurt her. I know we did, because we wanted to. We agreed to treat her like a dog one summer. Fine, I said, and called her Mutt Face. Jerry tied a rope to her neck and made her go to the toilet in some bushes while he held on. If she wanted to tag along, we agreed she had to buy us a Coke, even if that meant she couldn't have one herself at the end of a hot day in which she likely carried our lunches and swim trunks.

I ask her about these things. Usually she doesn't recall them. Or she remembers them differently. "You weren't so bad," she says. "I'd not forget *that*." The fact is, she has forgotten. Or else I'm lying, which wouldn't make any sense.

"I was always scared you'd tell me I couldn't come along with you," she'd say. "I was honored. I looked up to Jerry and you so much."

That at least is partly true. She worshipped Jerry and followed us around and endured inhumane treatment, such as eating mashed doody-bug sandwiches, but she did it for his love, not mine. Jerry was fascinated by her ability to grovel and accept the worst he was capable of. "She's a challenge, all right," he once said.

She was. Jerry was forced to think up on a daily basis new torments to visit upon her. I was (not at first but gradually) forced to take a long, hard look at myself, then at this pesky little mutt, and try to make the two extremes balance out.

I never thought I'd marry her. But it fits. I've got to admit that there's a certain logic to it.

Did Jerry also become what he's been accused of, a borderline sociopath, because of her? I'll leave that one alone, thank you. But for sure she tried his patience and his imagination. She stretched him, and once Jerry was stretched he didn't snap back into his old shape.

Everything changed the summer we got ten-speed bikes. She couldn't keep up. Hers was only a three-speed bike. Anytime we wanted to lose her, we'd just head for a steep grade and grind her down until we could look back from the top of the hill and see her struggling, bike stalled sideways to the road, her downhill leg planted and her standing leg on the uphill pedal, as her entire body strained to overcome gravity. Even if I'd wanted to relent, there was Jerry. "We're free as birds," he'd say, and that would be the beginning of a day on the lam. We'd pedal for miles down country roads to see a farm that Jerry had somehow heard about, because a two-headed calf had been born there once, or maybe because someone killed someone there in a knife fight back in 1944. Jerry had a knack for knowing these things.

"Here," he'd say, and we'd dismount and walk up to the farmhouse door. He'd knock and when the lady of the house answered, he'd say, "This is my friend Lister," and my heart would sink. "We're visiting Bible students from Boaz, Alabama, only I think we're lost. Could you direct us to the Interstate?"

And inside of ten minutes we'd be eating berry pie and drinking buttermilk. While our unsuspecting hostess thumbed through the telephone directory, trying to locate the nonexistent church Jerry said we were visiting, he'd wander around and steal things. I didn't catch on the first couple of times. But one day he came visiting and, with this strange-looking smile, gave me a cardboard box tied with string.

"What's this?" I asked.

He shrugged. "It's just a present."

We'd never given each other presents before and I was uncomfortable. But I opened the box. Nestled in pink toilet paper, that he had tried to arrange so it looked like fine tissue, was an antique brass compass and pocket watch set.

I must have put two and two together and said something. It's not anything that I can remember. But I know that a wall went up between us that day. We didn't stop being best friends; if anything, we were even more loco together, in public. Today I know what Jerry gave me: confidence to overcome my shyness, danger to shake my small-town soul. Yet I must have made it clear that I had a limit, because he never pushed too far. Things could get exciting with Jerry, but if there was something else going on, he left me where I wanted to be—in the dark.

Until the Bass Bonanza blew up in our faces, I'd say Jerry and I were even good for each other. I steadied him throughout high school; he taught me about what it meant to be a man. Hey, I know that without Jerry doing the fast talking I'd never have lost my cherry as soon as I did, or as easily, one hot night with two barefoot sisters we met at the fairgrounds.

But how can I forget that Jerry robbed me of the child I might have had, and robbed my wife of a piece of her heart that no amount of time or suasion can restore? And he did it in the worst way: not by being party to it, but by tempting me so that I brought it upon myself.

This is what V.R. will never know, because she'll never want to know it. Virginia Roy thinks whatever Jerry told her before he lammed out is gospel. She's on the inside with him at last, she thinks. And that necessarily leaves me out. It's what she's been waiting for since childhood, and I'm not optimistic on the odds of her ever giving up something she's waited this long to get. It's like she and him are on the ten-speed bikes, and I'm trailing behind on a three-speed.

Trank du Lac brought his breakfast in and joined me in a Coke. "I was reading the newspaper this morning about your victory in the lake. I did not know there was so much money in this bass fishing."

"It was a tidy sum. Course it all goes into the Commando kitty, you know."

"May I see the fish, or have you eaten it?"

"Oh, we let the fish go. It was a live release tournament. You actually lose points if a fish dies."

Trank was quiet after that. He sipped his Coke and ate his sausage and egg on a muffin with a poker face; I felt a kind of sadness about him at that moment. What it must feel like to not know where your family is, or if they're even alive. It occurred to me that he must be lonely. I didn't even know where he lived, except that it must be on the colored side of the tracks, probably directly across from Cecil's scummy place.

"What do you think of that food?" I pointed to the sandwich. He shrugged. "It sure isn't anything like that old fish paste and rice balls you get back home, is it?" Trank had his mouth full and I had mine empty, so I just blundered on: "I bet you miss all that. I know I would."

By now he looked almost alarmed, and swallowed quickly. His black eyes shifted this way and that. "The news on television," he said, and I could feel him gently setting the conversation back on the tracks, "says Coke will change. Why has the company not told us?"

"Because it ain't true." It felt good to deny what I didn't want to believe. I was careful not to glance down at the drawer where the new manual was locked away. "Rumor. Remember when they introduced Cherry?" He nodded, but I could tell he wasn't convinced. "Hey, you know what I'm really shooting for in my fishing? The cap. The Coca-Cola cap. Did anyone ever tell you about it?"

Trank shook his head no. I motioned him closer. "Have you ever noticed how, on television, after some bowling tournament or stock car race, or the Indy 500—or even the Olympics—the winner sometimes is wearing a cap with our logo on it? You've seen that, right? Now let me ask you this: Have you ever seen that exact cap for sale? In a store, a gas station? No, right? You want to know why?"

Trank ran a hand down his black necktie and stared into my eyes, hunching his shoulders and narrowing his face.

"There's a man who works for the company. Nobody knows his schedule or who he takes his orders from, he just shows up wearing that cap, the one with the logo on it. The man with the cap watches the event, and he keeps an eye on the top seeds. He asks around. He observes how they behave at night, in the bar, how they talk. Then, when someone wins, guess who's standing there like he materialized out of thin air, handing him *the cap?* The man. And guess how much he gives you for wearing it? Come on, guess."

Trank screwed up his lips. "A thousand dollars."

"Twenty-five."

"So much!"

"And that's just the beginning. If you have one of those caps, everytime you wear it, and your picture gets taken and published in the paper, or in a magazine, or if you get on television again, a check mysteriously shows up in your mailbox." I leaned back and surveyed the results. Trank was one impressed foreman. There are some things the *Harvard Business Review* can't tell you about the company. "I know if I get good enough, maybe one day I'll see that man with the cap. That's what keeps me bassin', Trank. That's when I'll know I've hit the top."

After completing that little attitude adjustment on Trank du Lac, I had to face up to my own worries. Unfortunately, I wasn't as good at distracting myself. I called Lucky and Cecil, and left a message for Eddie on his machine, just to keep in touch and remind them to put in their hours at the casting pond. Finally there was nothing to do but sit and stew. I wondered why the bottom drawer of every desk I ever had got stuck. I wondered why I was telling Trank the legends but not the whole truth about Coke. I wondered what kind of care my new lawn was going to demand.

I had just decided to devote my entire afternoon to wondering, when the telephone rang. I stared at it, trying to decide from its tone whether this was a friendly intrusion or an incoming round. "Valhalla Bottlers, Foote speaking."

Surf broke in my ear. "Now can you hear me okay?"

"Loud and clear."

"*Que* the hell *paso*, Gar?"

"Not bad. Yourself?"

"You know who this is, don't you?"

"I believe so."

"You don't exactly sound glad to hear my voice."

"Well—is it safe for you to talk?"

"Course it is. Listen to this. Hello, Gar Foote. This is Jerry Roy speaking, do you read me?"

"Loud and clear."

"You mad about something?"

"Naw."

"Shit, boy, then *say* something!"

"Okay." I tried to find common ground. "This is a good connection, isn't it?"

"It should be, the USG paid enough for it."

"The government? Jerry, are you calling from *jail?*"

"Ha. Joke. You're some friend. No, we're talking on a sat-com unit that was just installed last week on my ranch here in Las Mañanas. I can pull in just about every kind of signal you could imagine. I get Russian television, African television, all the regular programs."

"Where's Las Mañanas?"

"Costa Rica. You know, Switzerland with bananas."

"You live there?"

"Yeah. Got a ranch, cattle, peons. And now, TV."

"Sounds like you landed on your feet."

"Indeed. I'd like it if you and the Virgin sister came to visit."

"I can't get over this . . . our talking like this. Are you sure it's safe?"

"I've got no argument with the world."

"No . . . warrant?"

"Oh, *that*. Taken care of. Department of long ago."

"Well, that's news! Virginia Roy's going to be real pleased to hear this. You're a rancher now, is that it?"

"A gentleman rancher, please. We gringos can't set a bad example by working too hard. It's roll out of the hammock, drink a quart of fresh orange juice, have a nice steak, some of the best coffee in the world, finish off with a mango from the backyard. Then maybe ride the palomino or take the boat out for some fishing."

"A man could get fat."

"There are ways to work it off. So tell me when I can expect you."

"You're serious? You know how it is with us, not much free time except for two weeks in summer."

"You're the boss there. Cut yourself some slack."

"No can do."

"What if I was to say there was a bass tournament here you could clean up on?"

I laughed.

"No kidding. Listen to me. Cut it out! That's better, asshole. This is no joke. I'm talking serious championship fishing—the Costa Rican Festival de Bass. It's gonna be an annual thing, draw a lot of heavy-hitters who love side action, if you know what I mean."

"Maybe you haven't heard the news down there."

"What, about the Commandos? The Commandos is what this is all about! I saw it on the Turner Network, the whole thing! You were dynamite! That's what turned on the old light bulb. I said to myself, Gar may not realize it, but the Bass Commandos are a very potent marketing force just waiting to . . . explode." He made a mushy sound like a bomb going off. "You could be as big as Joe Willie Namath, as Billie Jean King, as Magic Johnson, in terms of putting a sport on the map. You think I'm kidding? I've been on the phone ever since, talking about nothing but the Bass Commandos. How does that grab you?"

"Jerry, you know I can't believe a thing you say."

"Don't believe me, then. But buddy-of-mine, you were great on TV. You're a natural. Lots of the big bassers can't talk and the ones that can are too damned expensive. My job is to create a market down here, the government is totally behind this. They see a bass resort, kind of a Club Med thing in this huge, untapped resource of a country they got here. You could be the point man, if you want it." He added slyly, "Unless you're satisfied to bottle Coke till you're sixty-five."

"I can think of worse ways to get by."

"Yeah, I know, you're the last honest man and all that. Must feel pretty good, slaving your life away for a company that's getting ready to dump the good old Number One without even asking your opinion."

"Where'd you hear that?"

"You mean where haven't I heard it? Coke's next to *beisbol* down in these parts. As a bottler, man, they'd treat you like a nuclear physicist, a regular Einstein. But the window of opportunity is now. I'm offering you a celebrity tour, carte blanche, lux accommodations, bar tab. I'm talking publicity."

"It would be a lot easier if you just came up to visit. Or can't you do that?"

"I could be there tomorrow if I wanted to. I took care of those warrants by doing some favors for the USG. And I settled accounts with the IRS, too."

"As soon as your sister hears this, she's gonna want to see you." He sighed. "I know."

"Wait till you see the Jerry Roy Hall of Fame in our front hall."

"Cut it out. Look, ya sure you won't come south?"

"Yup."

"How do you feel about west?"

"How west?"

"Far. I really *was* talking to these TV producers about you. They were down here to shoot the war. Listen to this: A tournament in Las Vegas. Million dollar purse. Live television. Best of all, they roll out the carpet for team fishing. Ya followin' this?"

"Sort of."

"Breaking new ground. Live coverage. Okay, we've seen it before, right? Shot of boats zooming off at the start. Shot of boats coming back seven hours later. Big thrill. But this tournament's different. It's got big money behind it, network money, sponsors. They're getting a section of a lake and grooming it. You know, like a golf course. Swear to God—stop laughing, asshole—ten or twelve artificial fishing holes, ever'body fishing 'em in sequence, in front of live cameras and live studio audiences."

"Ever wonder what a dead studio audience would look like?"

"Wise guy. Let's hear your yucks for the half-mil payout the winning team takes home."

I said nothing. That placated him some.

"You're considering," he said approvingly. "That's good."

"Try to see it my way, Jerry," I said. "I've got my eyes on the prize. Here I've got the Classic in my cross hairs and you want me to uproot and go Hollywood."

"The Classic's not till September. And you still haven't qualified. Think you can fish this hot for four more months? Costs a lot of money just to enter the tournaments."

"There's no fat in our budget, but we can make it."

"Why not have it both ways? TV is the future of fishing and you're getting in on the ground floor. All you have to do is go out to Vegas in May and kick some bass."

"Sorry." I could hear him panting. "Did you run out of breath or just things to say?"

"Look, I'm trying . . . to give you the big picture."

"But what could be bigger than the Classic? That's what I've got my sights on. It's taken me years to get back to the championship level and I'm not about to waste it on a one-shot, fly-by-night tournament nobody's heard of."

"Heard of *yet*. Another thing—"

"My mind's made up."

"A video feature. Cable wants it. I've started a bidding war, without meaning to, just by mentioning the idea to Ted Turner the other day. This is after I'd gotten a go sign from Grimes at ESPN, a handshake deal, with the understanding that, by bearing the production costs, I could slice the pie my way. Plus I'd get an option on a pair of ad spots that I can resell and pocket the difference."

"What *are* you talking about?"

"Money. Fame. Recognition. You name it."

"Same old Jerry."

"Gar, I'm just trying to make you a free agent. What happened happened, I'll not gainsay that. But while you were settling in with a job and Virginia Roy, I was swimming with the sharks and fighting just to survive. Remember, you're talking to a man who couldn't even come home for his mother's funeral."

"So come home now."

"That's not the point. You're refusing to see this as a business proposition. Look, it's a three-hour flight. I'll pick up the tab."

"Jerry, I'm sorry. The answer is no." This time there was no comeback. I'd worn him down at last. "Now. Promise me that as soon as we hang up, you'll give V.R. a buzz at the college? Got her number handy?"

He grunted. This was, I realized, about as close as I'd ever come to derailing a fast freight train. And I'd done it on Jerry's dime, too.

9

"I tell you, there's no sweeter sound than when that four-barrel carburetor stands up on all fours and roars." Eddie's head jerked back, as if slammed by a sudden acceleration, and he tensed his slabby pecs. Taking short breaths he pumped himself up, tightening his T-shirt so that every rib seemed to stand out. His oval face turned brick red.

"Eddie, I swear you're too much," Yvonne said.

"Gross is more like it," Virginia Roy muttered as she passed behind me with a platter of hamburgers for the grill.

"I love my Johnson!" Eddie shouted happily.

"The boy's loco," Lucky sighed. He draped an arm over my shoulder. "He's really bulked up, hasn't he? Do you think it could affect his retrieve?"

"How about it—did you hear that, Eddie?"

For an answer he just reached over and plucked three hard-boiled eggs off the picnic table. He paused, focusing on the space directly in front of him, then began to juggle. The trick wasn't very pretty, but it was better than I could do.

Cecil followed behind me with a platter of sliced onions and tomatoes. He had an absentminded smile on his face.

"I think Cec's got a crush on Virginia Roy," Lucky said, loud enough for him to hear if he'd been paying attention. He wasn't, though. Lucky winked. "Watch out, Gar."

We stood around swatting the bugs while the flames licked the hamburger patties. I carried over V.R.'s iced tea to where she was watching Cecil tend the meat with a spatula in each hand. "We've stopped asking the right questions, it seems to me," she was saying.

"Sure seems that way to me." Cec nodded solemnly.

"What good is a life without meaning and substance?"

"It's no life a-tall."

I handed her the glass of tea. "Thanks, honey," she said. There was a silence.

"You okay, Cec?" I asked, already moving away. Virginia Roy smiled.

"I subscribe to *Soldier of Fortune*," he confided to her after my back was turned. "Do you ever read it?"

I closed my eyes and grinned. Virginia Roy's voice sounded cautious: "Yes, sometimes." I admit I was surprised by that.

"You went to the mercenary school at Dolomite, didn't you? What did you think?"

"It's a solid program."

"I hear they let you shoot machine guns there."

"Really? I didn't see any." She laughed, but her heart wasn't in it. Probably she was staring at my back and wondering how much I was overhearing, so I dropped to one knee and began pushing at the seam of the lawn.

"Look at Gar!" Eddie shouted. "He's lost it over a lawn."

"Did they make you eat cockroaches and stuff like that?"

"What are you talking about, Cecil?"

"A man has certain instincts," Lucky was lecturing Eddie.

"One of them is a desire to own and take care of his own bit of property. You watch, it'll come to you one day. You'll fall for some girl, buy a house, start losing sleep over a lawn. Just like Gar."

"—obstacle courses, orienteering, setting ambushes, laying mines, bivouacing, target practice. But no bug stew or fried snake. Does that disappoint you?"

"Here come the girls, Lucky," Yvonne said. The two Bonnard daughters were walking down the drive. "Why don't you give them some money and send them over to the Sizzle Shack?"

"Oh, there's more than enough here."

"You haven't seen Diane eat."

"Yvonne, I won't hear of it," V.R. said. "Cecil, put two more patties on the fire please."

"Ten-four, Miz Roy."

Both girls wore spring jumpers, and both carried white canvas purses, but even at a distance I had no trouble telling them apart. Diane, the senior, had a full six inches on her sister and was a redhead, with Lucky's black eyebrows and a typically Cajun beaked nose. Dominique, the sophomore, had a short black haircut, a pretty face, and looked like a lark come to sing on somebody's fencepost.

"Hello, Mr. and Mrs. Foote," they called in unison. We all said our hellos and asked them to stay on and eat with us. But no, they were off to a party.

"Can I come along?" Eddie asked.

"Sure," said Diane promptly. Her mother didn't like that, and her father didn't like Eddie asking. But Diane just laughed off the awkward moment. "I've seen your van around," she said mysteriously, and looked at her red-and-white leather shoes.

Eddie tried not to seem too proud. "It's hard to miss."

Diane nodded, deadpan. "Especially parked across from the athletic field every morning during PE."

Dominique giggled and covered her mouth with her hands.

"Uh-oh." Cecil nudged Lucky, who started to say something,

but was cut off by Yvonne telling him to give the girls some money. Eddie beat a retreat, but I noticed that he saved a quick, intrigued glance for Diane.

After we had eaten we had a meeting. Both women took the hint and drifted off to the kitchen while we unrolled Lucky's latest maps. Our target—a reservoir near Tampa. We talked things over.

"This time we won't have the advantage of surprise," Eddie said.

Cecil got all excited over a plan to cover our uniforms in rain ponchos. "Then suddenly, as we're speeding out in formation, we whip them off!" He pretended to pull a poncho over his head, and threw his arms out wide.

"And crash into each other at seventy miles an hour?" Eddie teased.

Cecil raised his right fist into the air. "Then at least let's shoot off a flare!"

"Goddam it, Cec, stop playing soldier." Eddie grimaced.

"Why'd we name it the Commandos, then, huh? Don't lay that vet crap on me."

"Fuckin' 4-F."

"Toilet snake jockey."

"Hog-jumping peacenik."

They went for each other and made a convincing show of it for a few seconds before collapsing on the grass. Lucky and I just looked on, too used to this to react.

"Bring on the bass," Eddie shouted, lying there on the lawn with his chest heaving.

That was Thursday. The following day I pulled my loaded and snugged-down boat trailer into the lot at work at the usual hour, 6:00 A.M., and parked in the usual place. One thing I did that was unusual for me was to listen to the radio. I hate to begin a day with news. All it takes is one sour or cynical comment to spoil my mood. Still, I needed to keep track of the fishing weather. What I got was a call-in show with co-hosts.

"Folks are asking what it means—why announce that you're holding a press conference? Why televise it? What is this 'most significant soft drink marketing development'?"

"Exactly. People are asking: Will they do it? Dare they? I predict a whole lot of people are going to be upset if they do."

"If they aren't going to do it, why announce a press conference that won't be held until next Tuesday? It's a bit of a tease, if you ask me."

"And a press conference in New York City? What does New York have to do with Coke?"

"Everything these days, I guess. We'll take caller number three. Question: Will you drink Coke if they change the formula? The rumor is spreading like wildfire this morning, based upon an announcement this morning, a very unusual announcement, as we've been discussing. Yes, good morning, WKIK drive-*time* talk *radio*. Who am I speaking to?"

"John Pool, Wanilla."

"A new Coke, John? Yes or no."

"Hell, no!"

"Whew, John. Don't mince words none, do you?"

"I could say something stronger."

"Not on the air, please. So this is, in your opinion, a big mistake?"

"It's not a mistake. It's a conspiracy."

"Oh, well . . . thanks, John, for your call."

"WKIK," said the co-host. "Who's this?"

"Katie Lee Henbeck of Purvis."

"Yes or no?"

"I've been a stockholder for years. It's been passed down in the family on my mother's side, and I'm afraid to go outside this morning. How can I face people? What can I say to them? The company didn't ask my opinion, and I'm a stockholder now for forty-nine years. They just did it."

"I take it, ma'am, that you are mildly irritated by the possibility. We should say it's not yet definite."

"It's our Coke. Not theirs to monkey with. Now I can't even face my neighbors for shame."

Trank's rusted-out old Impala hove into view. He braked and a dust cloud engulfed him for a moment. He stepped out and spread a dirty sheet over his windshield, fitting it under the wipers. He was on his way over to the loading dock when he saw me just sitting here. He was slow about coming over, as if he wanted to give me plenty of time to get out of the car. When he was by my door, I rolled down the window and turned up the radio. The host was holding forth.

"—a hundred years old next year, and this is what they do? We're going to pass along something here. It's the annual compensation for the chairman of the company, Mr. Goizueta, who last year made eight hundred ninety-six thousand dollars in salary and an additional million point three in bonuses. Caller number two?"

"I probably make fourteen thousand in a good year and I can tell you in a word, for free, what I think of changing Coke: bullpucky."

"Your name, please?"

"Tommy Hopkins. And another word—un-American."

"Well, you made a good point there. Let's have a little contest here. First caller who can give me the nationality of Coke's president, Mr. Robert Go-ee-zoo-ee-a-ta—I think that's it—first caller to get it right gets a case of the last of the real thing: Coke. You heard right . . ."

Trank crossed his arms on the car window and leaned forward, chin balanced on the crystal of his black digital wristwatch. We listened. Nobody got Goizueta's nationality right.

I turned it off. "Trank, I owe you an apology."

He straightened up and stood in the dusty lot, a morning breeze ruffling his shiny black hair and flipping his black necktie this way and that. He nodded. "I understand, Mr. Foote."

"Let's go inside and plan the day."

The workers wanted to treat this as a holiday; they were overexcited and loud and milled about the punch clock. But we gave them no rest. I said something about making sure the last bottles of the old Coke were the best ever bottled, trying to impress upon them the history they were living through. I do believe it sank in some.

I called an emergency noon meeting of the boys.

When I explained that I wasn't going to fish this weekend, Eddie said flatly, "That's not in the deal."

"We've got the momentum, Gar," Cecil pleaded.

Only Lucky seemed to understand. "Go easy, now," he said. "Give him a chance. This is a pretty big moment, after all. He's got some thinking to do."

Naturally, Eddie had his suspicions. "Virginia Roy put you up to this?"

"She wouldn't do that," Cecil said.

"Thank you, Cec. Took the words right out of my mouth," I said. He blushed, and I felt so sorry for him that I patted him on the back. "Spoken like a gentleman."

Eddie smacked a fist into his palm. "I work for a living, too, and when I fish on a weekend I'm losing money, double-overtime money."

"Yeah, Eddie, but Roto-Rooter isn't Coke," Lucky said. "Gar's got a community position to consider."

"I have a community position, too."

"I'd hate to see it."

Eventually we agreed: if one Commando didn't fish, none would fish. I swore that I would make it up to them.

"It's probably for the best, anyway. You'd have been too squirrely to tournament fish." With that, Eddie offered his hand, and we shook.

On my way home that afternoon, I stopped off at Abe Leonard's drugstore to top off my aspirin supply. It was a half hour before closing and the aisles were full of folks laying in stuff for the weekend. I stood in line behind a woman whose wire shopping basket had what the marketing wizards at the company would call a "personality inventory": calomine lotion, Cornhuskers lotion, Depp hair gel, Clairol Born Blonde Rinse, Johnson & Johnson gauze bandage tape, Ben-Gay, witch hazel, slippery elm lozenges. It didn't take a Sherlock Holmes to figure that she'd be spending her weekend in the garden while her husband was playing in his softball league. And I pictured her, this sandy-haired gal in a jumper full of black-eyed Susans, washing her hair in the sink and setting her curls while Daddy soaked his sore muscles in the tub. A regular Saturday night thing. They'd talk of this and that, aphids and runs batted in, as they dressed to go out to dinner with the other couples in their group. I looked in my basket: aspirin, Midol, fuses. Wasn't hard to tell which couple expected to have fun.

"Can you send a boy around to my car after?" she asked the clerk, a schoolgirl.

The girl nodded, then shouted over her shoulder, "Henry!" She punched up the total on the register. "That'll be one hundred and seven dollars and thirty-seven cents, please."

The woman paid in cash without a word of complaint. I wondered, as I watched the clerk count and flatten the soft, old money, what else she had bought to bring her total up. Maybe some piece of health equipment, like the blood pressure monitor I had to get for Mother after her heart took to skipping. It came to me then that I'd been wrong to envy this woman her seemingly uncomplicated life. I'd just been feeling sorry for myself. It stood me up a little straighter, like a splash of cold water on the face.

"How're ya, Gar?" called Abe Leonard, stepping out from his pharmacist's counter. He gave my hand a flick of his dry old bones, and peered over his rimless spectacles at me. "Had yourself quite a day of fishing, I hear."

"Yeah."

The stock boy wheeled a dolly past. Abe's eyes followed him. "Shirttail in!" he barked. Turning back to me, he smiled at his ferocity. "Gonna turn pro?"

"Thinking on it."

Abe held my eyes. I knew what he was doing. Most of Virginia Roy's medical history has passed through his hands in the form of prescriptions. "Hope you get your wish," he said, finally, and I knew that I'd made the grade.

The boy wheeled his dolly, now stacked high with cardboard cases, out the door to the waiting Chevy pickup. Outside, the sandy-haired gal stood with hands planted on her hips as he loaded the flatbed, then opened her purse, took out some coins, and gave them over.

"That's the last of it," Abe said.

"Of what?"

He checked to see if I was spoofing him. "Coke, of course. Didn't you get my message? We're sold out."

"Everybody is," said a voice behind me, belonging to a stocky young fellow in a madras shirt and blue jeans. "Even the Wal-Mart. Way I hear it, people are hoarding up to sell later."

Abe touched my elbow. "Do me a favor?"

"Sure."

"Get me some supplies for the weekend. It'd do me fine if people knew I had Coke when the Wal-Mart didn't. We're one of your oldest customers. Remember when we had fountain service?"

"Abe, I had my last jerked Coke here in nineteen sixty-nine, just before I went overseas. When I got back the counter was gone."

The man behind me touched my other elbow. "I know a man can get you a sixer for ten bucks."

Abe glared at his customer. "You happen to be talking to a man who bottles the stuff for a living. Gar, here, probably has a warehouse of inventory."

"No kidding! Hey, can I get my hands on some?"

"Sorry. Don't sell retail. Abe, to be honest, well—" I shrugged.

"You mean to say you folks didn't expect something like this?" His lips pinched up. "Or have you got to give what you got to the Wal-Marts first thing? Is that it?"

Brakes squealed outside the drugstore. Leaping out of the cab of a hi-rider, a hairy, shirtless fellow in cutoff shorts and construction boots stomped up to the door, shading his eyes with a hand as he peered from side to side. He spotted Abe in his white pharmacist's coat. "Hey! Got any Coke, man?"

Abe raised his hands. "Sorry."

"Shit!"

"This guy here has a warehouse full," volunteered the customer, pointing to me.

The hairy man glowered. "You selling, man?"

"He's got it wrong. There's no warehouse."

"Stop putting me on!"

"If anybody's putting you on, it's him." I nodded to the young man in madras.

Young madras didn't like that. "Sheee . . ." And the hairy man was moving in, herding nervous customers ahead of him with large, grease-stained hands. I began to back down the makeup aisle, plan my getaway. "Abe, I'll call you." He nodded. Fluttery customers were tittering and thrashing into each other.

Madras began to whine: "Look, I heard the old cooter say that guy was a Coca-Cola bottler. I heard it!"

I slid down the aisle, ducked up another aisle racked high with large plastic clouds of diapers. I whipped around the far corner— and came face to face with *him*. The satin-skinned devil, the he-she prancer with his surgically-altered nose and eyes and lips, the hair pure black oil, the nothing body snugged into persimmon-colored tights and a puffy white shirt open to the hairless chest. He was standing tippy-toe on a stack of cases of Pepsi-Cola, outlined in tiny, winking lights. I raised my fist . . . but this being Abe's store, I controlled myself.

At home there was a strange car in the driveway, a silver Porsche, big and flat as a water bug. I pulled in alongside and found myself looking at Villis Green snoozing in the sports car's reclined seat. Villis slowly lifted his head up and nodded to me. I waved back and walked around to his window.

"Been waitin' long?"

"No matter. It's been peaceful sitting here under the pecan tree." Villis's Porsche sunglasses buried his eyes, but his smile seemed thin.

"Haven't had a chance to tell you. The lawn's a beaut. You go ahead and send along a bill."

"Forget about it. Just wanted to check and see how it came out." He stifled a yawn with the back of his hand. "Keeping busy?"

"Yup. Especially lately."

"So I heard. You'll be sorry to hear Mayor Frears' gallstones are giving him fits."

"I am sorry to hear it."

"So. Any truth to this Coke thing?"

"We'll all be wiser come Tuesday's press conference."

Villis's eyebrows arched over his shades. "You mean they ain't told you either?" I shrugged. "Well, we'll figure out the right way to play it—" He fired up the Porsche. "And while we're at it, maybe put a gazebo over in that north corner there, trim back those weeds, put in a few ornamental peach—unless you prefer fruit-bearing trees? Yes, you probably would." With that the Porsche scurried off to the foot of the drive, then *put-putted* away.

The phone was ringing when I unlocked the door. It was one of my rural distributors wanting more product. No can do, I told him. Hardly had I put down the phone than it rang again; a bigger distributor, which meant a more diplomatic way of saying the same thing. After a while I gave up and just sat by the phone. I didn't even bother turning on the lights.

"What's going on here?" Virginia Roy called as she let herself in. I was listening to a roadhouse mogul do a fair impression of Huey Long as he might have sounded if Coke had cut off *his* supply on a Friday night. Virginia Roy stood there, silhouetted against the pink spring twilight, until she picked me out of the darkness. "You're still here? What about your tournament in Tampa? Why are you sitting in the dark? Are the power lines down again?"

I covered the mouthpiece. "Looks like Coke's going to do it, do the formula switch."

"So? That's what everybody's been saying all along." She kneeled and began sorting the envelopes off the floor. "Why didn't you go fishing?"

"I couldn't agree with you more," I said into the phone. "But my agreeing don't change things in Atlanta." That set off a fresh harangue, and I covered the mouthpiece. "An angry customer. All my customers are angry today. That's why I can't 'just go fishing'. If my customers are stuck, I'm stuck."

"Hang up and leave it off the hook."

"This is my job. It comes with the territory."

"I'd rather see you quit and go fish for a living then spend your days belly-crawling for that company." She struck out down the hall, hitting the lights as she went. I hung up.

It took a minute for her words to sink in. Finally I shouted: "Do you really mean that?" But she had the water running in the kitchen sink and I couldn't make out her reply, if there was one; the phone was ringing again. So I followed her back. She was scrubbing the breakfast dishes.

"V.R." She didn't look up. "Excuse me." She clenched the

sponge in her fist until it bled itself dry. "Can you tell me who pays the mortgage here?"

"I write the checks." She slapped down the sponge.

"With whose money?"

"You want me to say yours?" she asked, all bright-eyed.

"It's not my money. It's Coke's money, same that fed me and clothed me."

"Giving your mama lots of credit, aren't you?"

"She'd say the same."

She raised her soapy hands up and shook them with the fingers pointed downward. Water tattooed the sink. She did it again, then reached for the towel hanging under the cupboard. "What are you going to do about it, then?" she asked softly.

She had me. How well I knew this sinking feeling; Virginia Roy's renowned jujitsu had turned the tables again. I pulled out a chair and sat in it backwards, propping my chin on the wooden back. When I didn't answer directly, she glanced over, found me hound-doggin' it, and began to laugh. "You don't know, do you?"

I puffed out my cheeks.

V.R. slid a fine old knife out of the drawer and leveled it at me. "Start with what's eating you."

"You just don't change Coke. The company's part of what this country's all about. At least it used to be."

"Maybe this country ain't what it used to be."

"What are we supposed to do, then, change the country? No, the company's fine. It's just some people—"

"Who might these people be?"

"The ones runnin' it."

"Naturally." With the flat of her hand, she rolled three carrots into formation, aligned their hairy noses, and began chopping. "Sounds like doing right by Coke isn't the same thing as doing right by the management."

"You said it. But what can I do?"

"You might start by getting rid of the ones running the company." *Chop* went the knife, *tap-tap-tap* went three fresh carrot slices, falling and then rolling every which way.

"I can't just hijack the formula and set up my own company."

"What *can* you do?"

"Complain. Done that already. Guess I bite the bullet."

"Full of that fighting spirit, aren't you?"

I shoved back the chair and gathered my feet under me. She put the knife down, dipped one shoulder, raised both hands. We began to circle. I snatched at her right hand with my left, a feint. She didn't go for it. Our circling carried us to the hallway. With my back to the entry, I took a swipe at her feet with my right leg. She sidestepped it and rushed me. Instead of dropping back into the hallway, like she thought I'd do, I grabbed the doorframe, swung myself up and forward, and clamped her between my legs, right below her shoulders. She wiggled, she strained; she quit.

"Say, don't I know you from somewhere?" I teased. She went limp. I kept my grip on the doorframe, but before I knew it, she was doing the limbo, ducking under, dragging my legs and lower body with her into the hallway. Now I was the one in trouble: hanging on for dear life by my fingertips, facing a six-foot drop. "Okay—hey! Look out!" I released her from my scissors grip. She let go of my feet so I could drop down.

Her lips nibbled at my ear. "Go get 'em. Hit 'em where they live."

"Atlanta?"

"On the television." She prodded me into the kitchen. "Television goes into people's houses, makes things happen. If the TV doesn't show it, how do they know it exists?"

"Seems to me the television *is* the problem. Show some weird sister tap dancing with a can of soda and half the world goes nuts. If you ask me, it was those darn commercials spooked our people—" She poked a finger in my back, steering me in a circle and back down the hallway. "Where you taking me, by the way?"

The finger jabbed. "Okay. Up the stairs we go. TV, huh? You think I ought to learn to moonwalk? *Hey!*"

I landed facedown on the bed with a mouthful of pillow.

She straddled my lower back. Her fingers began to pull and knead my neck muscles. Part of me resisted, but her strong fingers pried up my muscles as if they were old floorboards.

To keep from groaning, I tried to pretend we were having our everyday dinner-hour conversation. "Whole country's going down the"— She gave my shoulder a light judo chop— "tubes. Way I looked at it, Coke . . ." She rode both thumbs up my spine. ". . . would hold the line, *arrgh!*" She'd finally got me. I inhaled, shook my head to clear it. "So I was wrong. They're making it a job, just like yours, like any job."

"It's still a good job, though."

Calm down, I told myself. The girl doesn't really mean it. "But it was . . . more than a job."

How much more I shouldn't have had to explain. We've been man and wife for seven years; she ought to know *something* about me. Coke put beans on the table. Coke put me through school. When I was sitting out in the cab of a D-8 in those hundred-ten degree Vietnam afternoons, what icy, dark thing do you think I thought on? When I hit rock bottom after the Bass Bonanza blew up in our faces, who took a chance on me?

But Virginia Roy said nothing. If I was expecting any sympathy, I was mistaken. "I just don't know if I can stand the change," I said.

"Maybe it's a blessing in disguise. You can put more into your fishing career."

That amazed me as much as anything. Virginia Roy giving the go-ahead to *more* bassing? Not hardly likely, I would have said, before this night.

"Honey, Coke was around long before I ever thought of fishing as more than a diversion. Maybe it's too much to expect you or anybody to understand, unless you've had the good fortune to belong to the Coke family." I reached behind me and grabbed one of her feet.

She leaned into me again, with both hands. This time she was working great sheets of sore flesh around, chasing the tension out in waves. I closed my eyes. *Pop!* like a flashbulb, a bright jolt ran up my neck to my brain, surged back down to tingle the soles of my feet. And exposed in my mind's darkness was a bluish night scene that I seemed to recognize, in which I was a body rolling in the surf of some faraway, tropical sea under fragrant skies, unfamiliar stars.

"Don't fall asleep on me," she warned. I opened my eyes.

"Your turn," I said, and gently unseated her from my back. She sagged onto the bedcovers.

"Go easy on my clothes, now."

The room had darkened gradually to blackness. She lay beside me while I unbuttoned and laid open her blouse and shucked off her skirt. I rubbed my hands over her belly as if warming them before a fire. When I finally launched myself upon her, hardly a ripple was raised on those still waters. Then I knew we were in for a long one, the way we used to make it, back when all our evenings were for love.

But I forgot the cardinal rule: making love to your wife is like bassin' without a depth finder. She's the one person you ought to know best, and she's the most complicated piece of water around. You know what lure works; you know the depth to cast; you observe the precautions with respect to scent and rhythm. And then — she throws the hook with a toss of her head, pushing you off onto your side of the bed, saying, "So my job is 'just a job,' like any other?"

In slow motion we fell away from each other. I was still reaching for her hand.

I said, "You have a very interesting job."

"What's so 'interesting' about it? What do you know about it? Have you ever asked?"

"Seems like every day I ask."

"Want to hear what I did today? Typed and retyped the same letter seven times, all because some twenty-four-year-old seminarian wanted to change the verse in our Bible Business Practices syllabus."

"Sounds like he's a real jerk."

She smacked a fist into a palm. "You could bring them the Book of Revelations written in hellfire and they'd think it was a birthday cake."

I chanced a laugh. It was too dark to see well, but I felt her smile. We were sliding back into our old places now; I knew that in a minute it would be okay if I touched her.

Her warm hand groped for mine, squeezed it, hard. My fierce and beautiful wife; her generous spirit just shames me sometimes.

What a weekend. I couldn't venture outside the house, so Virginia Roy and I pulled the drapes, finally took the phone off the hook, and pulled the plug on the radio and television.

Monday, all my customers, and quite a few townspeople, came by the plant for a piece of my inventory. Tuesday they made the big announcement in New York. The whole shop shut down to watch television on closed-circuit. They all heard the immortal words of our chairman:

"Smoother, uh, uh, rounder, yet, uh, yet, bolder . . . it has a more harmonious flavor."

That did it. Trank and I turned our backs and walked away.

Wednesday morning I took a few calls and prepared for when I would use up the last of the old formula and begin the new. I'd been stalling; I had a surplus of formula on hand, sort of by accident. So, technically, I had been violating orders to switch over for the past day and a half. Today was D-Day, though. The old well had run dry.

After a while I turned the lights off in my office and watched the phone lights blink red, white and yellow in the gray gloom. My mouth had a strange, metal taste, something like what you get after a dentist has been drilling into your molars, raising a lot of white dust and heat. There was a ringing in my ears from all the phone calls, a pulsing like the faraway smiting of an anvil.

Someone knocked at the door and I looked up. There was a shadowy figure on the other side of the frosted glass, behind the old-fashioned original "Coca-Cola Co." stenciled in reverse script. I closed my eyes and rubbed them, saying, in a dead voice, "Come in." While I massaged my eyes I was thinking of how much like green grapes they felt; then there was this soft *click* and a quiet zooming in my bloodstream. The room was full of a presence. But I wouldn't, couldn't, remove my hand from my eyes, nor move my tongue to speak.

I came out of it shivering. Blinking, I rose halfway up in my chair and looked past floating white spots into all the corners. Then a hinge creaked, slightly, enough to remind me of that click I'd heard, and I saw a thin crack of light from the bottling line floor along the edge of the door. It had been opened. Someone had come in, and gone.

I went out and stood in the doorway, overlooking the plant. There was the steady *snick-snick, tap-tap*, sizzling *whoosh* of the bottling machinery, the gray, greased conveyor bearings glinting under the fluorescent tubes. A steady humming in unsteady light. From the cool, dark corners of the forty-foot ceiling hung a single enormous banner with the logo on it, that dwarfed the occasional lone worker going about his duties dressed in the light green overalls and regulation hairnet. I remembered seeing this room twenty-six years ago, being taken to meet the manager of this place where Mom went every day. Where now there were robot cappers and automatic nozzles, then there were scores of women, their hair all gathered in by pale kerchiefs. And one of them stepped away from the long line of women, pressed her thumbs into her lower back, looked up at me: my mother. Our entire fifth-grade class saw. I waved; she smiled and waved back. Of course, I didn't expect to leave the class tour of the plant, and she didn't ask to speak to me. Such a thing would never have occurred to us.

But I had been proud. Darn proud.

Today I heard a voice in the machinery, a voice that spoke of a hundred everyday people, ordinary women, who'd come here because there was no place else to go. Times were hard. Men had the better jobs, higher up in the machinery, fixing things. Women like my mother filled the bottles, capped the bottles, packed the bottles on pallets for the forklift drivers. Where now there were robots, women had fed entire families on a dollar-forty an hour per twelve-hour shift. No overtime. No benefits.

This system is what I had trained for all those years and now had run for even more years. Mom was proud of me when she died. But now there was no one left to please, unless you counted the ghosts where the robots stood, and I was feeling too torn up to want to stay and watch them change the formula.

I went back into the office and picked up the phone, placed a call to the local television station, and got through to somebody important enough to sound irritated. "This is Gar Foote, general manager of the Coca-Cola bottling plant in Valhalla. I'm going to make a statement."

"Be my guest," said the man at the other end.

I peered down at what I'd written yesterday evening. "As an upholder of the public trust that is, or should I say was, Coca-Cola, I feel unable to take part in the betrayal being carried out by the present management of this hallowed company. Time will prove them cowards who fled the ramparts at the first rattle of arms. But for now, Garfield Foote of Valhalla Bottlers will allow no Coke but the old Coke to be bottled so long as he is general manager." I sighed. "That's it." There was a long crackling silence. "Hello?"

Click. Dial tone. Just my luck, a bad connection. I dialed again, and talked my way to the same fellow. "We got cut off," I said. "What do you think?"

"Boring." He yawned. "Can't use it."

"It isn't news when a general manager of Coca-Cola . . . You're putting me on, right?"

"Listen, Jack, I got people busting cases of Coke with sledge-hammers, I got people burnin' effigies of Coke's president — and you want to make a statement."

"But those are crazies. I'm a general manager."

"I know — at Coca-Cola. Congratulations." He sighed. "Those 'crazies' know more about the tube than you do. They're vidiots, they speak the language. You have to think visually. Props. Symbols."

"We have a carrying capacity of four hundred seventy-five thousand gallons a week. Stopping my plant's production of New Coke should send quite a message to headquarters."

"Fine. But my job is reaching people, millions of 'em. I got a red-hot blonde reporter costs me seventy grand a year. She needs face time the way you and I need meat. Can't you think of something? Stopping production — it's just not visual."

"What if I pour some New Coke down the drain?"

"Better if you dump all of it."

"All four hundred seventy-five thousand gallons? Right."

"Well, at least say you might. Make 'em think you're a desper-ate man — 'Top of the world, Ma' — that kind of thing."

I didn't respond. How much was this worth to me?

"We can have a camera crew there," he said casually. "This seems to be a slow day, news-wise. You could lead off the five o'clock feed."

I thought of the old man, Mr. Woodruff, and the company he'd built up, and the public relations man he'd paid to keep his name *out* of the newspapers. Not dead a month, and headquarters doing this to him.

"You don't mess with the sublimated essence of America."

"I beg your pardon?" His voice quickened. "Wait. Let me get the wire on." There was a crackling on the line. "Go ahead."

"You just don't monkey around with Coke. This is America, not some Communist country. So I'm going to show the bosses in Atlanta and New York City what a Coke man, born and bred on Coca-Cola, will do. I'm going to pour the new stuff down the drain. And I want everyone out there to join me. Just pour it down the drain."

"Now *that* should pull in an audience," the man said. "We can run parts as newsbreaks throughout the day, build up to five o'clock. See you around four-thirty, champ."

At a quarter to four, I got on the loudspeaker and told everybody to go home. Didn't say why. A few minutes later I went to the door and stepped out onto the loading dock. The parking lot was emptying out, horns blaring, cars and pickups heading home, down the employees' dirt road. A pinkish cloud of dust hung in the air, and above that, like a black mechanical vulture, hovered a helicopter against the blinding red orb of the sun.

"They want the old drink," said a weathered gentleman I hadn't noticed before. "That's all they want."

I stepped out from under the eaves of the roof into the hot dusty air. About a dozen people were sitting under the lip of the loading dock, some on barrels, others on stacks of lumber, some old, some just babes in arms. They were dressed in faded calico or butternut or patched blue jeans. There was enough family resemblance to figure they were the old man's kinfolk. They looked tired, mostly, as if they'd walked for miles on a dusty country road; they squinted against the sun and looked up at me. I went back inside and got out a couple of sixes of cold Coke. When I returned, Trank du Lac was there to help hand them out. I looked at him. "You know what you're doing?"

"No deals," he said. "This time, we fight. No deals."

"What's he mean, 'this time'?" the old man asked.

"Time to make the evening news," I said, slapping Trank on

the back. He looked up at me with dust-reddened eyes set in those black plastic frames, and I could see his faith in America crumbling. "Come stand by me, Mr. du Lac. Be my witness."

A van, with a cone poking out of the roof, pulled up the road, bouncing along in the ditch to avoid the cars leaving the plant. It swung right up in front of me, and two burly men were out before it stopped. They slipped on power packs and cameras, while a third member of the team, a young woman with long blond curls, began climbing the ladder up to the dock. She accepted my hand up.

"Mr. Foote? Delilah Jones. I'll be doing the interview."

"Five minutes, Delilah," said one of the technicians, helping himself to a Coke and lighting a cigarette.

Delilah looked around. "Boys, we'll shoot with those big double doors to his back." She turned to me. "Do you have a bathroom handy?"

"Sure. Follow me." I walked up to the side door and went inside. "Watch your step—"

Two grim fellows, wearing dark suits and Old Spice, grabbed me from behind. My arms were twisted firmly behind my back. There was a tug at my skin, the quiet snick of a lock: cold steel clamping my wrists.

"Gar Foote?"

A man in a dark blue suit stood by the tanks. My clipboard was in his hand. He had a tie on of the brightest yellow, a shirt of the richest stuff. Even his skin seemed unnaturally healthy and as evenly tanned as a ham.

He smiled. "Your butt is mine."

10

A guard came and unlocked the cell door. "Howdy, Gar," he said. "Remember me? Lance Crowfoot."

"Sure I do." We shook hands. Lance had been to high school with me. He had put on weight since then, I noticed.

"Well, you're on your way home," he said heartily. "Sorry we couldn't see more of you."

We went through a couple of doors. Just before a third, we paused at a window. A white-haired woman in a blue uniform passed me a manila envelope and a clipboard with a sheet of paper on it. I signed without opening the envelope.

The door swung open. Virginia Roy looked up from a wooden bench, and put aside the magazine she'd been reading. Her eyes were bloodshot.

"Guess I blew it big-time, huh?"

She threw her arms around me and hugged me. "I love you, honey." I buried my face in her sweet-smelling curls; she was warm all over, and when I closed my eyes it was as if none of this had happened. "I'm so proud of you."

But when I opened my eyes again, a gray mood engulfed me like a fog. "Shall we get out of here?"

She nodded. As she turned back to the bench to collect her purse and magazine, I had a thought. I went back to window and knocked to get the policewoman's attention.

"The gentleman with me, do you know what happened to him?"

She just looked blank. "Don't recall no gentleman."

"Mr. Trank du Lac."

"What about him?"

"Is he still here?"

"Yup."

"Anybody go his bail yet?"

"Nope."

"How much is the bond?" I turned back to Virginia Roy. "Did you bring the checkbook?"

We got Trank sprung from there in under a half hour. He came out waxy and pale green, as if he'd been in solitary for ten years. It shocked me, and I wondered if that was what I looked like to V.R. Between us we bundled him into the car and headed for home. We made only one stop, a quick one at McDonald's for Virginia Roy to run in and pick up some dinner.

When she got back in with three cartons of food, I said what I'd been thinking the last five hours. "Pretty stupid of me not to know who owned that TV station, huh?"

She checked the rearview mirror as if expecting to see someone following us. "They set you up to shut you up."

Nobody said anything else. We drove the deserted roads, skimming through patches of midnight fog, our headlights picking up the red points of animal eyes in the ditches. The sweet fried onion and ripe beef-fat smell made the car seem a warm and cozy place, especially after the piss and Pine-Sol perfume of the jailhouse.

The live oak that marked the turn-in for our driveway loomed.

Virginia Roy braked sharply. I thought the tree was on fire, but they weren't flames. The trunk was consumed by fluttering yellow ribbons tied in big loopy bows.

"Ahhhh," said Virginia Roy. "Look what somebody's gone and done."

She slowed up and passed the tree. WELCOME HOME GAR said a cardboard sign, DOWN WITH COKE said another. As we crept down the drive, I could see yellow ribbons—well, toilet paper actually—tied to every tree, and lights on at the house, and cars in the turnaround, and—

For a moment we just sat there. The porch was packed with folks. They were waving flashlights and shouting out.

Virginia Roy leaned over and kissed me, then grabbed my arm. "Come on, hero. This is no time to be shy."

I walked slowly up the walk, V.R. on my arm, du Lac trailing behind. I had to keep looking back and waving him forward. The gang launched into "For He's A Jolly Good Fellow," led by the Commandos, and ended with a lot of applause. Next, two young girls stepped out carrying guitars, and began strumming and singing in sweet, lilting voices. After a moment I recognized Diane and Dominique Bonnard.

Someone handed me a glass and I sipped it: bourbon. I coughed and gasped, and it seemed like ten people jumped to swat me on the back; one of the hazards of popularity, I guess.

Arms around each other's waists, V.R. and I swayed through the crowd. Some were eating off a full buffet—Yvonne Bonnard's doing, with her signature touches of okra pickles trimmed to look like bass and yam pirogues filled with red beans and rice—while others were socializing under the party streamers. I didn't recognize the place, it had been so long since we'd had a blowout this size. I nodded to people here and there, smiling, feeling like an imposter. My heart was still fogged in.

"Gar, you remember Rico Octoponte," Virginia Roy said, squeezing my arm.

I sipped my bourbon, wondering whether I'd entered a lost episode of *This Is Your Life*.

"Sure do. Welcome to my funeral."

He puffed on his cigarette and then jutted out his bearded chin. "Not funeral. Baptism—your baptism." He grasped my hand and began shaking it. "I must apologize for intruding. Believe me, I have no idea you would be staging your own *revolu-cion* on the day I am passing through to my fund-raiser." He held out his arms. "Which I tonight learn is cancelled. Very sad."

Octoponte was wearing about the only unwrinkled linen suit I had ever seen; I couldn't take my eyes off it. "I'm sorry to hear that. That's sure a nice suit you're wearing."

"Thank you." He eyed me, blowing smoke down his nostrils into his beard like the twin exhausts on my outboard on a cool morning. "You and I, we should talk, I think. When you've had some rest. We have much to say to each other."

"You bet." I began to edge away. There's nothing more boring than a couple of grown men on their best behavior. "So enjoy yourself. You have the run of the house."

"Thank you. But I feel I must say one thing," he added. I waited expectantly; he moved closer. Suddenly he grasped my head in his hands and stared into my eyes. "Coca-Cola abandoned you. They abandoned you the same way this country abandoned Cuba." He crushed his beard into my cheek, then snapped me back at arm's length. "For you, the struggle is just beginning. For me, the struggle never ends."

He was right about that, at least. The party was one long struggle. It wasn't until 3 A.M. that we walked the last guests out to their pickups and tucked them in for a snooze or the drive home, their choice. The last to go was my old classmate Lance Crowfoot, who had invited himself over, in uniform, just as soon as his shift at the jail ended. "I just feel terrible, Gar, terrible," he kept saying, knocking back the beer and eating off the plates of food that were lying around the house and porch. "It's always this way. I've met more people from the class of '66 in that jail than at our ten-year reunion. And nobody is ever happy to see me."

After Lance headed down the steps with a paper plate of brownies and ice cream to tide him home, V.R. and I put everything perishable away that would fit into the fridge. I said, "Stuff's gonna spoil. There's too much here."

"People care."

"But a whole turkey? It ain't even been touched."

"It'll get eaten up. We've got houseguests, don't forget."

"Trank doesn't eat much."

"Neither does Rico."

"How come he's staying here?"

"You told me to ask him to, remember?" She looked at me with exasperation, then bent down to wrest more space from the refrigerator shelf.

"I thought you said he had to travel."

"Look, you shouldn't have said it if you didn't mean it."

"I meant it. But things have changed. I mean, there's a Holiday Inn five minutes from here."

"This is a man who spends probably two hundred-fifty days a year on the road in places like the Holiday Inn." She looked up from where she was kneeling in front of the fridge. "Anyway, your friend Trank is here, and he even has his own apartment."

She had me there, of course. "We're just destined to be one big, happy family, I guess."

She was squeezing a baggie of chicken drumsticks into the butter shelf. I watched her profile, saw her smile into that crammed ice box, bountiful as a cornucopia, an avalanche of food our troubles had dislodged and sent roaring into our house.

"Maybe so," she said in a small voice. She shook herself then and rose, ligaments cracking. "I hope so."

I slept the rest of the night and well into the morning. Laying there in the bedroom with the warm spring breeze shifting the treetops back and forth outside the window, I listened to footsteps and creaking floorboards, cabinets opening and closing, the buzz of the phone, and I gradually understood that this day was mine, and the next, and the one after that. Nobody was going to bother me, nobody was going to disturb me up here.

Yet the longer I stayed up here, the more I felt the weight. It sat on my limbs as I dozed, making me feel as though I were slowly crushing the bedsprings to the floor. I dreamed I was a spread-eagled man falling through clouds. I heard a faraway ringing, and smelled white-hot iron curling under hammer blows. Car doors opened and shut. Voices loud in the yard were swallowed by the house, then returned at the foot of the stairs to be told to go away.

I put on an old shirt and a pair of dungarees. I couldn't stand it any longer—I craved a Coke. I hadn't gone so long without one in ten years.

The long table in the cool dark kitchen was bare except for a basket of tiger lilies and a stack of newspapers. I took my drink and stood there, leafing through the news. The screen door slammed, and Trank paused in the little mud room with the laundry tubs, vacuum cleaner and years of living.

"Hey, Trank. How you doing?"

"Okay, I guess, Boss."

"She put you in the rumpus room?" He looked blank. "I hope the aquarium pump didn't keep you awake."

"No. I think I will be going now . . . Boss."

It seemed to strike both of us at the same moment. "That's the last time you'll ever say that." He nodded, staring into space. "From now on, it's Gar. Got it?" He shifted his weight from one foot to the other. "What will you do now?" I said.

Trank nodded yes.

"What's that supposed to mean?" He shrugged. I pulled out a chair from the table. "Sit down. Come on, sit."

We faced each other and, not without nervousness, began to dismantle the habits of the past five years. For the first time we were outside the chain of command, marching without a tune. We drank a lot of Coke that afternoon. Chiefly I found out that Trank believes his family—some of them, anyway—are still alive back in Vietnam. But he can't go back, and the money he sends just disappears, and now there was no more money. He didn't think he would stay in bottling.

"It's a skill. You can go anywhere," I argued.

"To work for a company, when a company can do what it did to you?" He drummed his fingers on his can, then popped in the sides so that it chirped like a tin cricket. "For me, the feeling is like Americans leaving Vietnam. They promised to stay, and they left. Now I know, living here, Americans always leave . . . forget the good son's promise to the father, break the vows with wife. And now Coca-Cola? This feeling never more again. I will work for Trank du Lac."

I mulled that over. "What will you do, then?"

"Go fishing."

"Come again?"

"Go shrimping." He gave me a sly smile. "There is gold not only in bass, Boss."

"You forget you can't use that word anymore."

"I don't forget."

The afternoon sun was level with the windows and flooded the kitchen with the same orange-red light of the tiger lilies on the table. At some point Rico Octoponte showed his face. He'd been walking out in the yard, and not sticking to the path judging from the briars and stickers snagged on his pants. It surprised me to hear myself asking him to pull up a chair and offering him his choice of Coke—diet or regular. But it seemed that all bitterness had been leached out of me. This strange, endless day had filled my bones with dull warmth and my head with cloudlike wisps from my lately departed life.

Rico fluffed out his beard with his fingers and sat with his chubby legs sprawled out. "This reminds me of my years as a little boy on the island, when days were lazy and full of comradeship and laughter." Rico closed his eyes and spread his arms wide and I swear I could see his island, a hazy, bright place with sugarcane plantations and a church with a bell-tower. It was just a way he had of making his face follow the words he spoke. "We thought it would never change! Life was slow and ripe. Cuba was a flawed beauty, perhaps, but there were always guitars, always a song. And such women! Beauties, with spirit to set a man's soul on fire."

He slowly raised a hand to his lips and kissed its bunched fingers, then blew on them until, like a dandelion, they flew apart. "All gone now. *Mi vida y su vida.*"

I looked at him. He nodded, and I felt a tightness in my chest. "Go on," I said.

He brought his face close to mine. "Now, with Castro, the woman she is a Soviet whore, her children monstrous. Slowly they strangle the romance out of a country of guitars and song." He took a tiger lily and twisted its stalk and, when it didn't snap, tied it in a knot. "To my father, who never quite believed that he could be mistaken for one of the enemies of the people, Fidel was always 'coming to his senses'. Papa didn't outlive his delusions — Fidel's secret police saw to that. When they ordered him to appear, it is said my father put on a white straw hat and his best suit . . . that he stopped on the way down the steps to pluck a rose for his lapel. 'You see,' he said. 'Castro has come to his senses'."

I noticed Trank was staring, too. I think, like me, he was hypnotized by Octoponte and his hoarse grandeur.

Virginia Roy joined us at dusk, throwing a few pots of leftovers on the stove and then leaning against the fridge behind me. Occasionally she'd trail her fingers through my hair or rub my shoulders. It was strange listening to Rico tell the worst night-mares of his life as if they were so many shaggy-dog stories. He told them one after the other, like jokes, but without the pause for laughter. And all the "jokes" were on his family, his sisters when they were forced to do the laundry of prostitutes in Miami, his mother for spending the laundry money on palm readers, on his uncles for believing John Fitzgerald Kennedy and landing at the Bay of Pigs with the 2506th Brigade.

Then Eddie and Cecil showed up, and we had to drag out the folding chairs to accommodate everybody.

"Eddie Bucci, Cecil George, this is Rico," I said. "I don't know if you met him last night. He's a professional anti-Communist. These guys are Commandos, Rico."

"What's a professional anti-Communist do?" Eddie asked.

Rico fixed him with his fisheye. "The same as an amateur. Just better. We track the enemy and identify where his poison has been introduced. We mobilize to counter the threat."

"What'd'ya use?" Eddie snapped a wad of gum in his cheek.

Rico stroked his beard. "That depends on the problem. A textbook assigned to a high school, a book that steals the soul of children with subversive, corrosive, secular humanist morals — that is a kind of poison. And Marxist-Leninist despots taking over a Central American country is another."

Cecil cleared his throat. "Do you ever use . . . mercenaries?"

Eddie shot him a disgusted look. "There you go again."

"Shut up, Eddie. I just asked a question."

"Yeah, but we all know where it's leading."

Rico looked slightly confused, and glanced at me for help. Before I could say anything, though, Virginia Roy spoke from behind my back:

"Eddie, I don't understand what was so wrong with Cecil's question."

Cecil colored and quickly looked down at his pack of cigarettes. Taken aback, Eddie checked faces and chose his words carefully. "Cec thinks too much about it, that's all."

"About what?"

"Playing soldier."

"Is that what Rico's doing?"

It was Eddie's turn to color. Myself, I was surprised at V.R. launching such a sucker punch — and at one of the boys.

Rico held up a hand for silence. He gestured at Eddie and said, "You served your country, yes? I thought so. Like Gar here?"

"Trank, too," I said.

"Yes, of course," said Rico with a courtly nod to Trank.

Cecil interrupted: "I tried to enlist, but I failed the physical." Cecil's eyes couldn't quite choose where to settle down. I felt for him, having his sore spot banged on, over and over.

Rico nodded. "I thought it would be something like that. Anyway, no matter. One day you will be called and you will be brave, eh?" He wagged a finger at Eddie. "And as for you, my proud friend, tell me this—if there is a snake in the path, is it better for the man who has never killed a snake to try to kill it? Or should the man who tried and failed to kill the snake receive another chance?"

Eddie leaned quietly on his elbows until the table creaked. "I'm not sure I get your drift."

"At least Cecil has an opinion on something that doesn't eat worms and swim in a lake," said V.R.

I whistled. "Whoa there—"

She yanked playfully at my hair. I yelped, and raised my hands in surrender.

Eddie took my cue and laughed. "Well, if I was getting on you, Cec, you know I don't mean it." Eddie rolled his eyes. "God strike me dead."

"Gar is one man here who has stood up for his beliefs," Cecil said. You could tell he was embarrassed by V.R.'s compliment and was trying to make up for it.

Virginia Roy took the can out of my hand. "And look what he's still drinking."

Eddie said, "I'd switch to Pepsi if I were in your shoes."

"Why? Coke's still the best." I took the can back from V.R. "Besides, this is the old stuff. Once it's gone, maybe I *will* change—drink Dr. Pepper or something. But never Pepsi."

It was the first time I could ever remember saying the other side's name.

153

"A loyal man. And we see where it got him." Rico made a fist and softly thumped the table.

"Rico, I been meaning to ask you something," I said.

"What's that?"

"What do you make of the fact that Coke's president is Cuban?"

Everybody kind of looked away, except Rico. He looked into my eyes. "There is absolutely no proof to what you are thinking."

"That's it? Just a big coincidence?"

Rico nodded. "Something like that. Until we know more, that is all anyone can say." He made a helpless gesture with his hands. "My friend, if what you imply is right, we must go after the source."

Eddie shook his head. "What do you suggest—we nuke Atlanta?"

I got up. Nobody said anything as I went out the door. As I climbed the stairs, I could hear them inventing various tortures and punishments for the chief executives of the company. Some of them were quite original, but none could come close to producing the pain I was feeling at that moment.

Another morning without work. Virginia Roy made sure I was awake by the time she left but I still didn't make it downstairs until two o'clock. That same aching took over. I just lay there on the bedspread and stared at the treetops, until a wild thirst finally got me to dress myself.

The kitchen was cool and gloomy, like yesterday, but the table was cluttered with ashtrays, empty bottles and a big stack of mail. I picked up the top letter and saw it was the mortgage. Under it was the phone bill. Under that were the gas and water bills, the electric bill and two credit card statements.

"There you are!" Rico called through the screen door as he scraped his feet on the mat. "Feeling better now, yes?" He pushed his way in and waved at the woods. "There are so many edible plants out there, a man could live off the land."

I shrugged. "It may come to that."

He looked puzzled. Then a slow glow came over his ruddy face. "It would be nice, yes? To go back into the field one more time, to see if the old skills are still there—the woodcraft, the stalk, the kill."

"Doesn't that Weekend Warrior stuff do the trick?"

Rico's eyes were shining bright as buttons, but at this his chin jutted up and his eyelids drooped down. "You are joking me. Octoponte does not play at war."

"I'm not saying you all don't take it seriously. Virginia Roy, for instance."

"Now there is a woman. Mr. Foote, she is never satisfied unless she wins, never. We do not yet know what her destiny is, but she is certain to reach it." Rico crossed his arms upon his chest and stared at me defiantly, as if daring me to disagree.

And I was in just the mood to take him on. "As a hobby, fine. As a destiny, well . . ."

A six-note car horn sounded faintly out in front. Rico unlocked his stare and his arms. I walked to the porch window while he opened the fridge and rummaged around. I heard footsteps on the gravel out back.

"Hey! Gar!"

I went to the screen door and saw Eddie, dressed in his work clothes and carrying two of his rigs. He jerked his head toward the pond. "C'mon, dude. Time to practice."

"Maybe later."

"Done your reps for today?" He gave me a searching look. "I won't even ask about yesterday. No? Yes? We are fishing this weekend, you know."

"I know. Believe me, I know."

"Gonna be ready?"

"I'll be there."

"I didn't ask if you'll be *there*, I asked if you'll be *ready*." Eddie glared at me, then waved a hand across his face and bent to pick up his tackle cases. "You know something? You're behaving like a total *amateur.*"

He tramped off into the woods. After he was gone I began to grin. Not for Eddie the kid gloves treatment, and who was to say I didn't deserve a whipping? Out loud I said: "Eddie, you're such a pissant."

It put me in mind to do something, so I decided to face up to the bills, even though that was Virginia Roy's chore. Taking the day's mail up to our bedroom, I sat at the little cherry-wood table, the only piece of furniture that had escaped those Roy aunties who "sat" at V.R. and Jerry's mama's deathbed. Mama Roy never gave away anything in her life until her last day, but she sure made up for it then, if you believe those aunties.

I opened the top drawer and took out the checkbook in its Indian bead covering. The payment entries were in neat red pencil, the deposits in blue; everything was organized, as tight as V.R.'s curly hair. Here was my paycheck—no more of those. Here was hers—after five years, they still weren't paying her beans. It hadn't bothered me when I had a job, but now it jumped out at me. There was the three hundred-dollar registration fee for that first Weekend Warrior; here, my four-fifty entry fee for the last bass tournament.

For a second I fantasized what it would've looked like: the $32,000 first prize written in blue. But it had gone into a special Commando account, of course, and we'd already paid out expenses and a couple of thousand on non-refundable entry fees for the tournaments leading up to the Classic, the ones that sell out early because they're the last chance to pick up a few qualifying points. Part of the reason I'd never made the cut was never having that kind of financial foresight, but Lucky had pointed it out right away. Just making that commitment had turned the Commandos into a true team. Eddie had worked with me on my frog technique; Lucky visited state archives and county seats to dig up ancient ordinance maps that showed hidden fish structures — the towns and farms and buildings and topography submerged by the creation of an impoundment thirty years before — that on a modern map were a featureless plain. Nothing on earth could move me to ask for that money back from Eddie or Lucky. And I certainly could never ask Cecil, who needed the Commandos so badly and whose loyalty was so unshakeable that it kept the rest of us in line. We'd made that money as a team, and it was taking us to the Bass Classic in September. If I could just make it to the Classic . . .

I could close my eyes and see the revenue stream pouring down like a waterfall after a cloudburst: tackle endorsements, bassin' seminars, store appearances, free equipment and boats, even clothes — all for the asking, if I qualified for the Classic.

I opened the mortgage envelope, wrote a check, then worked my way through the others, subtracting from our balance on the little photovoltaic calculator Coke gave us for Christmas last year. The phone bill was last. We were just going to make it.

"Sweet Jesus!" I was looking at a total figure so askew that it jumbled my head like an upended tackle box. I flipped through the bill items. "International operator, Costa Rica." It cropped up two, three times a day.

Can't blame the girl, I guess. He *is* her brother. But we were now running in the red. Running a finger up the check register, I ticked off unnecessary expenses: hairdresser, cable TV, aerobics classes, shooting range, tai-kwan-do dojo, K-bar knife . . . *K-bar knife?* Firing range? I almost smashed the calculator flat. Was V.R. intentionally trying to bankrupt us? What woman needs to visit a shooting range? Let her thin out the local rabbit population, if she wants to shoot; that's what we keep the .22 for, and the lettuce in the garden would surely appreciate it.

Even as I let my grievances build up, a nagging voice asked, What about that battery recharger for the Minn Kota trolling unit? What about the soldering guns and electric bench tester for the depth sounding equipment? Those were big-ticket items. Hey, with lures at five dollars a pop, nothing about modern bassin' was cheap.

Except maybe me. Hell, I didn't need to cut our expenses; I needed a job. Getting up from the table, I wandered over to the window and peered down at the yard. The sun poured bright and brave upon the lawn.

I suppose that it was in the back of my mind all this time, only I just didn't want to face up to it: I could have a job, a big one, just for the asking. A leadership position. Maybe it wasn't coming to me strictly on the up-and-up, but I would deal with that when the time came, after first making my name as an upholder of old-fashioned American values. Hadn't I already taken the first, giant step in that direction by saying no to New Coke? Once I was in office, there wasn't a thing Villis or Woody could do to me.

If that young grass down there was to grow, someone had to take care of it. Same as if this town was to grow. Someone would have to lead it, an individual who could stand up to events — even if it meant taking his lumps — and do right by his people. Now *that* was a job.

I snatched the closet door open. Back in a plastic bag was my pale blue Botany 500 suit, the one that Bob Griese, the Miami Dolphin quarterback, wore in this commercial where he ran and passed all over the Orange Bowl. I bet a lot of guys bought that suit in '72, the year the Dolphins won the Super Bowl, only to discover, the way I did, that it was like wearing a polyester shower curtain.

I squeezed into it and fished out my brown wingtips. Villis and Woody were going to beg this boy to be their mayor. Then I heard the truck. It was shifting into a lower gear to handle the driveway grade, and the driver had to double-pump and grind some. I went downstairs and stood in the living room as it pulled into the turnaround. There were four colored guys in green coveralls riding on the back, and they jumped off before it even came to a halt. Two of them grabbed shovels and the other two, hoes.

I opened the door and stepped onto the porch. A fellow with a clipboard got out on the passenger side of the cab and waved the colored guys down to the treeline. He gave me a sidelong glance.

The workers pried and pulled at the edge of the grass. They stuck their shovels in and wiggled them around, moving up the seams a lot faster than I would have thought possible.

"Hey! Just what the fuck are you doing?" Eddie called.

The supervisor stepped back behind the cab and stared into the backyard, where Eddie's voice had come from.

"Hey, you! Yeah, I'm talking to you! Git on out here and tell those boys to stop."

Eddie came boiling around the side of the house. He saw me, and flung an arm at the truck. "Can you fuckin' believe it, Gar? I caught these guys stealing your lawn!"

"I've got a work order." The supervisor had the cab door open and one foot on the running board. He was looking at me.

The workers began rolling up a strip of lawn just like it was a carpet. Eddie stared from me to them, and back.

"It's all right," I said.

"It *is*?" Eddie clenched his fists. When I didn't say anything more, he started to shake with the effort of holding back. Finally he nodded to himself, and settled in to watch. He crossed his arms akimbo and set a stern look on his face. One leg kept jiggling, though.

The lawn didn't take long; in a way it was instructive to watch these fellows work. They were fast and well-trained, and didn't have to talk much. They knew each other's moves. They were a bit like commandos.

As the truck backed up to turn around, its warning bells chiming, someone coughed politely at my back. I looked over. Rico stood in the doorway.

"They can do this to you?" he asked, seeming both shocked and fascinated. "In America?" Then he noticed my suit.

I waited till he stepped aside, and went in.

Later that afternoon there was a scream of what sounded like pain: "The lawn! Somebody's stolen *the lawn!*"

I looked out the window. Virginia Roy stood, hands spread wide, beside her red El Camino in the drive, a torn brown grocery bag spilling cans and boxes at her feet. She turned this way and that, staring at the bare dirt field surrounding our house. Then a force just seemed to draw her gaze up to the window. We just looked at each other through the screen.

She turned back to her pickup and hefted a sack of goods. Then she went up the porch steps. I listened to her footsteps without stirring.

"You know something about this?" she said before she was even through the door.

"Something, yeah. I'm sorry, darling."

"Did you forget to pay for it or something?"

"That's about the size of it."

She stared at me with a sour twist in her face. "It's not the lawn, it's getting our butt kicked in public that I care about. What's wrong with you, honey? You stood up to Coke. Can't you stand up to some gardeners?"

"It was theirs. I'm not a thief."

"Well, then, what are you?"

When a beautiful woman who's your wife says that to you, I believe things are supposed to happen to your blood. I just felt like I was shot full of novocaine.

Finally, I said, "A man with a wife, a mortgage and no job. A man confused." I winced. "A man with no lawn."

"Gar, you're under some kind of misconception if you think I, or anybody who knows you, thinks the worst of you. I mean, you're a hero. One of these days, people will pay just to have their picture taken with you." As she spoke, Virginia Roy lost her angry color. Her freckles paled, she began fanning her hands with enthusiasm.

"I guess I'm feeling sorry for myself."

"Well, go right ahead. Tomorrow we'll see if things don't improve some."

"Think we can make next month's mortgage?"

She nodded.

"I'll look into finding work."

"Gar, honey." She took my arm and laced hers with it, then squared off and faced me. We looked at each other. "Don't you *want* to fish? This is your chance."

"It's too big a risk."

"Seems a little late to worry about that."

"I wanted to work into it carefully. Make the transition."

"Seems like you already made the transition. Now you got to go for it."

I took her hand and kneaded it into a ball, then pried the fingers loose and matched them with mine. "Bass fishing is all about confidence. Mine's about a quart low right now. I'm scared to go out there and disgrace myself. It would wreck the Commandos."

"They're nothing without you. You're ten times better than any of the other guys."

"Don't say that."

"Why? It's true. Isn't it? Jerry says you're capable of blowing anyone off the water on any given day."

"Well, that's Jerry for you."

"Pretty generous of him, don't you think? After all, he's given up a lot to protect you."

"Is that what he did? Protect me?"

She sucked in her cheeks but something checked her. The air whistled out of her mouth slowly. "You—"

"I'm sorry. My big mouth and all that. So. Been talking a lot to Jerry lately, haven't you? Is he president of that country yet?"

She was silent while she registered my knowing about her phone calls and, I hoped, my good-natured acceptance of them. Looking me straight in the eye, she asked, "Why didn't you tell me about his tournament?"

"That's not a tournament. That's a fish story." I reached out a hand and, feeling clumsy as a teenager, took a handful of her blouse and pulled her toward me. She resisted, swaying. "If Jerry was Jonah," I said, "he'd tell everyone he just missed catching that whale."

We smooched a while.

She sighed. "Gotta fix dinner."

"Let 'em eat leftovers." From somewhere deep inside me my infinite capacity for wit and tact surfaced: "Rico could stand to lose some weight."

"I don't know what your problem is, Gar Foote, but from now on, if you have to say something nasty and uncalled-for about my brother or Rico or anybody, I don't want to hear it." The whole time she was saying this, Virginia Roy was disengaging herself from her clothes.

There was a knock on the door to my room. "Come in," I said, and Lucky poked his beaked nose inside.

"Don't be afraid. The moon ain't full yet," I said.

"Then I'll check back in an hour." He winked. As he shut the door behind him, I saw that he was wearing a Walkman on his white patent-leather belt. He pulled up the cane-bottomed chair across from the bed where I lay.

"Lucky, I'm not going to apologize for being such a slob."

"Nothing to apologize for. You're just taking it hard, is all." He reached out a hand and patted my shoulder. "It can't be easy, what you're going through."

"How would you like it if you woke up one morning and your job wasn't there?"

Lucky stared at me. "I'm sorry about the lawn, too."

"I'm not. I was going to dread mowing that sucker."

"Gar," he said. That was all. I felt the bile and the backchat subside. When I finally looked back at him, I was almost ashamed to meet his eyes.

"Go ahead, I'm here."

"Do you remember, Gar, when I was working with the state on the road crew? That was my daddy's job that was waiting for me after I graduated high school. Taking turns driving around and cooking hot asphalt and filling potholes."

"When you weren't sleeping off a drunk on some back road, you mean."

He nodded. "Or worse. And I was there for six years. Did you ever think on how I got out of that rut?"

"Well—you got taken on at the realty, as I recall."

"Why did they take me? Me, the son of a no-good, Cajun, alcoholic featherbedder. No college, no special smarts. A honky-tonking fellow. Did you ever wonder why?"

"Because you're Lucky, I guess."

He shook his head without cracking a smile. "One man made a difference—a man I met on the road with a flat. I fixed his tire for him."

"That was nice of you."

"He only had one arm."

"Oh."

"But he had the biggest Lincoln Continental I'd ever seen, Gar, and it had antennas and upholstery like you wouldn't believe. This man wore a suit that caught the sun like a crystal chandelier. I finally had to ask, 'Who are you, sir?' And he looked at me for a long, long time. 'A salesman, son.' And I thought about that and asked, 'What do you sell?' 'Anything,' he said. 'Everything. What I sell the people want; they want me to sell them something.' And I said, 'You must be pretty good, then?' And he said, 'Yes, but the greatest salesman who ever lived was Jesus.' And then he asked me what he owed me, and I said nothing. 'Then let me sell you something,' he said, and he opened up this sample case in the trunk of his car. I could see that, inside, it held boxes of shirts from the French cleaners, and there were neat packets of braces and shoelaces and an alligator belt. He picked up a book and handed it to me. 'How much is it worth to you, to have what I have, to know what I know? I'm talking about the keys to unlock and control the power of your mind.' And I looked into those eyes, Gar, and gave him my last ten-dollar bill."

Lucky put his hands together and clamped them between his knees. He hunched his shoulders and stared without blinking into my eyes. "That book changed my life."

"It did."

"And now I'm going to change yours. You are going to listen to a tape. It's one I listen to every morning, the first thing when I get up. Yvonne does, too. This tape is the distillation of everything that book told me and more. It is the state-of-the-art in the field of positive thinking, or psycho-cybernetics."

"Say what, Lucky?" I laughed nervously.

"You are still in shock, Gar. You've lost your job and your lawn and your confidence. This tape is going to teach you how to get it back."

He took the lightweight headphones from around his neck and beckoned me forward with them. I bowed my head, and let him fit the foam earpieces on. He punched a button on his Walkman, then unhooked it from his belt and put it in my hand.

"Where are you going?"

"Home. Talk to me tomorrow morning, before I leave for work." He paused in the doorway. "After you listen to the tape, that is."

Some music came on and I must have blinked, because Lucky was gone when I looked back up. A man with a deep, resonant voice came on: "I am the most creative being in the universe. I am filled with immense power. All sights, sounds, and sensations are channeled through me and shaped by my great will. Who am I? I am your subconscious mind . . ."

I snapped: "And you should be embarrassed." My voice sounded muffled coming from outside the headphones, but I kept them on and tried, for Lucky's sake, to give it an honest ear. But then Mr. Sincerity started in on how important it was to have subliminal success messages piped into your brain. He recommended tapes while you were sleeping, tapes when you drove, tapes while you worked. And guess who just happened to have the appropriate tapes for sale! Wasn't that gosh-darn wonderful?

So I took off the headphones and sat cross-legged on the floor of the bedroom. I was picturing the two sweetest, most solid people I knew, Lucky and Yvonne, listening to this day and night with none of us the wiser. The worst of it was I'd actually been hoping for some kind of a boost, and now I felt like I'd been caught peeping through a keyhole.

The thing is, I can still see the skinny, slouchy Lucky of nineteen lurking inside today's thoroughly professional realtor, scientific basser and loving father. It *has* always seemed a bit of a miracle that he'd turned his life around. I'd chalked it up to the example of his father's sad final days, but nope, these are modern times, got to be up-to-date, worship at the electronic altar. So it's a tape and a Walkman and another faith born as another huckster fleeces the flock.

It was hard to say what I was angriest about, Lucky being such a dupe or having his fake faith work as well or better than a true one. Or maybe I was angry at having a friend's weakness betrayed to me this way—just when I needed all the support I could get. All I knew was, I'd had it with true believers, myself included.

11

When it comes to lawyers in Valhalla, it's said that you go to Luke Fontaine when you're angry about something and to Charlie Hood when someone's angry at you. My problem really needed both men, but practicality won over the emotions, this once. I went to Charlie Hood. His office is across the square, in the Big Clock Building, a brick blockhouse with two flagstaffs at port arms flanking the entrance. It's the building for businesses that need to impress people: Villis and Woody hang their shingle on the second floor, as does the local A. L. Williams insurance agent, the chiropractor and the interior decorator wife of our mayor, T. O. M. Frears.

A round face with Ben Franklin spectacles, Charlie Hood's, peered up at me when I came in his office. "Well, well," he said, rising from the sighing leather cushions of his captain's chair to offer me a hand soft and pink as a Casaba melon. "I wondered which one of us you'd choose."

He walked me through the events leading up to my arrest, helped me relive the moment I'd rather forget, then relieved me of a check for two-fifty as a retainer. I asked him where he thought I stood.

"Too early to say, until I contact the other counsel." Charlie put his left pinkie in the corner of his mouth and delicately nibbled at its cuticle while giving me a squint. "They might want to dismiss to avoid negative publicity. On the other hand, they may go for the extortion charge to reap maximum publicity and discourage others. It's iffy." He wrenched his head slightly to one side; the little finger followed with a jerk, as if it was on a leash.

"What happens if they go for the maximum?"

"Suspended sentence, three years probation. Maybe some community service, or a fine." He pushed his glasses up his nose. "Found a job yet?"

"It's been ten years since I last looked for one."

"You're lucky. These are boom times. Get your real estate license. Try the insurance field." He winked. "Send a resume to Pepsi—can't hurt none."

I shook my head.

Charlie walked the fingers of his right hand across his desk to his calendar. "I'm not just being polite. This may be a very costly time for you. This—" He touched the check I'd given him. "—is muchly appreciated, but if the company wants to make an example of you, you will need many more of these."

It sounded to me as if this prospect didn't entirely displease Charlie. But before saying anything, I concentrated on unclenching the cold knot in my guts. "Maybe we can sue them right back. Shake them up a little, right?"

He gave me a shocked look. "Gar, if that's the kind of representation you desire, I suggest you take yourself across the square to that patron saint of lost causes, Luke Fontaine. He'll be glad to sue Coke for you. He sues them once a year anyway, on principle."

With that woodshedding freshly applied and still smarting, I started down the old wrought iron circular staircase. A door swung open when my head was on the level with the second floor, and a small stampede of three pairs of shoes and legs spilled out. I looked up at the railing, at the startled faces of Villis Green and Woody Thuper.

Nobody wanted a long silence; we all spoke at once. "Howdy." "Morning." "Say, Gar."

"Sorry to hear about your trouble," Woody said.

"Can't figure what got into Coke," Villis added.

I stared at the third pair of feet and wondered who the scuffed red and white saddle shoes belonged to—the owner was hidden behind the two developers in their identical fawn-colored sheep-skin coats.

"Greed," I said. "That's what got into Coke. It gets into us all. Even me." I turned and stared down the staircase's descending iron spiral, thinking: Whew, Gar, where do you come by such talk?

Woody's lip curled. "You don't like greed, try livin' in a Communist country."

"Ah, Woody, leave him be." Villis took off his Porsche sun-glasses from where they were hanging from the neck of his open-collar shirt. "What did you think you were doing, Gar?" He snapped open the sunglasses, then popped them closed. "We had an agreement." *Snap.* "You were supposed to be acting leaderly." *Pop.*

"What was I supposed to do, ignore the suffering Coke was causing innocent consumers?"

"Nobody suffers the loss of a soft drink, Gar."

"This nobody did." I had to bite back on a yawn; suddenly all I wanted was to take a nap. "Well, gotta go. Thanks for lending me the lawn."

Villis and Woody were still standing shoulder-to-shoulder in glowing tan sheepskin, the nappy white fleece of their outturned lapels as rich-looking as a field of cotton. But then, wiggling furiously as earthworms after a rain, fingers squirmed between them and forced the two pals apart and I was staring at the splotchy red face of the mayor, blue eyes bugged out, tongue gliding along the top row of his scraggly yellow teeth.

"Howdy T.O.M. How you feeling?"

He shook his head from side to side. "Feeling much better, thanks to you," he said in a strangled voice. "Doing much worse, overall."

He put his hands on the shoulders of Villis and Woody and, just as if he was banging closed a great big pair of double doors, yanked them back together. The red saddle shoes spun around and marched their owner back inside the office.

Woody's chins tripled as he struggled to hold in his laughter. "Guess he sure enough had his mind set on The Estates at Frears Farm."

Villis cocked his head at me. "It's a setback to the community, and Mayor Frears *is* feeling poorly, but his sense of civic duty may hold him in his chair for yet another term. I hope you don't end up having him on your conscience."

The coolness of these two, shuffling and dealing the lives of a mayor and a (former) leading citizen, no longer entertained me as before. I'll take the cardsharps that haunt old Luther Hebert's hardware store, any day. At least they tell stories while they cheat you.

I waved. "Better him than me, boys. See you later on."

Driving back to the house, I rolled events around in my head. When I just couldn't handle the wheel anymore, I pulled onto the shoulder.

"Time to face the facts," I muttered, embarrassed to be addressing myself in this manner. "No money. No job. Time to fish. Time to *win*." Brave words, but my voice sounded thin.

Six notes from a tuned car horn blared out "Wish-I-Was-In-Dixie." Eddie's chocolate brown van hurtled over the double yellow to come to a rattling stop, his tinted front window six inches from mine, his glaring eyes and inflated mastoid muscles pulsing.

We got out, stretched and stood in the tiger lilies, facing the woods of Norfolk pine. Eddie put a cigarette in his mouth but made no move to light it. "Got a call from Adele," he said.

"Oh? How's the kid?"

"She says he's got chicken pox and is asking when I'll come to give him a present. Two-faced bitch."

I gave Eddie a quick glance. The muscles were crowding out of him more and more each day, sprouting as if they were another kind of pox, beyond his control. His forehead had a deep *V* crease. It occurred to me that I wasn't the only one sucking air. All of us were. Cecil on his temperance tightrope, Eddie on the edge of black despair. Even Lucky, wired for success as he was to the world's finest positive thinkers. Even Virginia Roy.

I punched him on the bicep. "Come on, Bucci-boy. I know just the trick." He grimaced at my cheery tone. "We're going to buy that boy of yours a present he won't forget."

We caravanned to the mall outside Tara Towne and hoofed it inside. Eddie pulled up at the Walgreens. "They got toys here," he said.

I took his arm. "Nothing doing. How old is he? Four? Let's try out that fancy yuppie toy bo-tik."

The boutique looked like a kid's version of *The Lifestyles of the Rich and Famous,* with giant inflated blimps and shiny, plastic kites, an electric train set running everywhere with flashing signal lights, one wall solid with glamorous gal dolls. The employees were dressed like elves. A covey of pretty State College coeds, in leotards and velour jackets studded with bells, surrounded us, chirping and laughing, enthusiastically singing along to the tape-recorded children's songs that seemed to come from everywhere. I caught Eddie's eye; his deep *V* crease vanished in a loud laugh.

"Look at this." Eddie pointed at a foot-tall man walking, stopping and saying, "Greetings. I am your robot friend. How may I assist you?" Robot friend bumped into a squat turtle that reacted by flashing its red eyes, extending its beak and snapping hungrily. I stayed to watch while Eddie wandered off. I could remember when toys didn't have batteries, much less 5-byte microprocessors.

"Neat, huh?" An elf in a page boy bent at my feet to straighten some boxes. "How old is he—or she?"

"Beg pardon?"

"The child you're buying a present for." She glanced up. "Or are you just shopping for yourself?" she teased.

"What do seven year olds like these days?" As soon as the words were out of my mouth, I almost died. But to her it seemed a normal request and she led me over to a section of planes and tanks and cars.

"It is a boy, isn't it?" she asked, suddenly afraid she'd done me a discourtesy.

I nodded. That's what the doctor said it was, after.

She left me to help another customer. I stood before the colorful shelves. Just looking at these treasures seemed wrong. I didn't want to connect the dots . . . So I busied myself noticing how many of the figures came in sets, gangs or squads, whether of soldiers or Superheroes or (this is surely new, I thought) rock 'n roll groups. Boys are always going around in gangs, I guess. Only the Rambo figure didn't seem to have any friends, maybe because he'd taken so many steroids he didn't need any help.

Suddenly I wasn't just thinking of what he might have been like—my child—but who his friends might have been, the games they would've played, the toys he would've wheedled out of Virginia Roy and me.

The air in the boutique got warm and close, while the music faded away. I was feeling my way up a dark stair into some old and musty part of myself, a place I hadn't visited in years. A room in my head to retreat to, the sort of place I figure V.R. had been going to for so long. Now I had my hand on the doorknob, and I knew who would be inside: the little one who has always been there, keeping pace with me, a questioning smile on his lips as if he were asking, Would I be like this, do you think, Daddy?

"This one's very popular in Japan," said a sales elf to a young boy with a skateboard tucked under his arm. "It has a 10-K memory chip." With that, she activated a six-inch dinosaur that commenced stalking through the shelf, pausing only to flash its red eyes, throw back its scaly head and roar.

"Gar, I think I found just the thing." Eddie beckoned me over to a corner. Over I went, still watching that dinosaur out of the corner of my eye, shaken and chilled.

Leave it to Eddie to find a scale model bass boat with trailer and 4×4 Grand Wagoneer. We gave it the Commando Laboratory test—practiced haul-outs and backing, checked the authenticity of the deck layout. Then Eddie's beeper went off. He swore, looked around. "Gotta find me a phone."

"It'll just take a second to pay for this."

"Nah." He was starting to twitch. "If I don't call right back, the bitch dispatcher'll give the job to somebody else." He reached into his hip pocket and pulled out his wallet. "Here," he said, stuffing a twenty into my hands, "I'll pick it up at the house tonight, okay? Thanks."

After he was gone, I gathered up the toy. The girl at the register smiled as she it rang up. "Your friend with the beeper a doctor?"

After parking in the shade of the pecan tree, I tucked the toy bass boat, trailer and four-wheeler under my arm and headed up the path between the two halves of the rowboat to the house. My foot was on the first step when I saw the man, in a blue workshirt, faded jeans and cowboy boots, leaning on a cane and watching me from the porch.

For a minute we just stood there. Then he gave a familiar shrug of his bony shoulders and tossed back his hair with a shake of his head. Seeing that old move again, I had to grin.

But when he started to smile, I stopped. "Well, amigo," he said, "*que* the hell *pasa?*"

My feelings got blurry. Part of me wanted to welcome my best friend back to civilization and part of me wanted to kick his ass back to Costa Rica, where it belonged.

"When you get in?" I asked.

"While ago. Helped myself to a cola." He nodded to a glass balanced on the porch rail, then parked his eyes looking outward. "So. Place looks the same. Though I must say, even knowing you as I do, Gar, that this lawn situation is a disgrace."

After this promising start the conversation slowed. We sat down in silence. Jerry shot me quizzical looks from under his cliffy pale eyebrows, tugged on his long sunburned nose. He pointed at the box in my lap.

"What's that?"

Without a word I handed him Eddie's gift to his boy. Jerry studied the bass boat and trailer rig through the clear plastic wrap.

"You decided what you're going to do with me?" he asked, as he pushed the plastic with a forefinger.

"Careful. It's a gift."

He grinned sourly. "V.R.'s gonna love it." Handing it back to me, he raised his eyebrows. "Well?"

"Doesn't matter what I decide, as long as you're Virginia Roy's big brother."

"It matters, bub. Life's complicated enough as it is without having people hate you. I'd just as soon leave if that's the case here." He opened his hands, and spread them palms up. He stared down at them. "Have you tried to have another baby?"

"Every month."

He took a long breath, then let it out slowly. "And it never takes, does it?"

"No."

Jerry had clutched his knee and begun rubbing it smartly between both hands, like a shoeshine boy who'd passed the shoe and just kept going. "*Ahhh!*" he cried, through gritted teeth.

"Where'd you get the knee?"

"Jumping out a two story window." He swore. "And that's all I'm going to say about it."

"I thought you always landed on your feet."

He laughed and shrugged his shoulders three times, quickly, like a swimmer loosening up for the start of a race. "Oh, I get a kick out of watching you, Gar. You think I'm out to screw you over. Is that nice? Is that fair?" He propped his chin on the end of his cane and waited for my answer.

I pretended to think, but my brain had been stuck in first gear all day. "I guess seven years is long enough." As soon as I said it, I thought: Never's not too long for you.

"I'll always owe you. That I know. But you won't regret this." He reached out and snapped his fingers. "Com'ere, give me your hand." I stuck out my right. "The other one."

I stuck out my left, and he unhooked my Casio digital sports watch that cost me $29.95 at Walgreens. Then he held up his left arm and shook the shirt cuff down, exposing this mighty chunk of gold with a silver and gold-filled expansion bracelet.

"This, my man, is a Rolex. It's no ordinary Rolex, either. It's the President model; been with me on all my biggest deals. I've used it as a cash reserve in poker games. I've even made a down payment on a fishing boat with it. And now, my bass brother, it's going to be yours."

He slid it over my hand. Lord, it was heavy. He snapped the bracelet and it just fit. We'd take the same size handcuffs, Jerry and I. "You didn't have to do that, Jer. This must cost a fortune."

"Maybe it did. It's solid gold." He pushed himself upright in his seat, and gripped the porch rail. "Maybe I took it off a dead man just before pitching his body to the sharks."

"Say what?"

"Gold's magic. Gold makes liars of us all." He winked. "Just you watch, in five years that watch will have more tall tales stuck to it than dogs to a bitch in heat."

He grabbed the cane and started hopping down the steps. "Come on, Gar. We're going to visit V.R."

On the road to Palestine College, Jerry pitched a few questions at me, about what Virginia Roy did at her job, who she worked with and so on. I kept my answers short. If Jerry thought I was being rude, too bad.

The fact is, I didn't have any answers. We never had much reason to drop in on each other's offices, and the sad truth was I'd never gone beyond the driveway. There it was — a horseshoe drive of pitted asphalt, a circle of grass around a brick pedestal with a statute on top, then a maze of tan one-story temporary buildings that had been rendered permanent by sidewalks and trellises drooping with wisteria. Jerry and I got out. Immediately he seemed to freeze up. Then he hoisted his cane and pointed at the statue. It took me a moment to understand that the figure was one of those colored jockeys that stand, ring in hand, on certain curbs in Valhalla. Only this chap had been given white skin, a preacher's collar, a string tie and a black suit. In his outstretched hand he held a large key instead of a ring. An inscription below his boots read: "Helping Him To Unlock Heaven's Highest Gates."

Jerry growled something. Then he stalked away, casually employing the cane to rap down dandelions and pulverize toadstools in his path. Inside the administration building, we came upon a long open room with offices along the walls. Virginia Roy sat upright at the center desk as she typed on a huge gray IBM typewriter. Her fingers were fairly flying, her eyes fixed on the paper held by a wire rack. Then I noticed the strangest thing — a row of sunburned young men in short-sleeved white shirts and black neckties, standing behind her and reading what she was typing so earnestly.

She finished, sat back, rolled out the sheet and, without bothering to look, handed it back over her shoulder. An eager hand took it; V.R. was already rolling in a fresh sheet and preparing to begin again.

175

Jerry rapped on the counter top with the end of his cane. The baby preachers jumped. "Can't you see we're busy?" one of them said.

"I see one busy woman and seven idle gents."

"Ignore him, Geoffrey," another urged. "This letter must go out."

But one of the preachers detached himself and sidled up to the counter, his hands clasped over his tummy. "How may I serve you, brother."

"Ain't your brother. I'm hers. Hey! V.R."

She turned, saw me first and her expression didn't change, a waxwork figure with a Peter Pan collar and a floppy red bow at her neck. Then her eyes lit up, and she melted.

"Jerry!" she shouted, standing straight up in her seat. "Jerry?" she asked, low and husky. "You're home? It's you?"

Jerry Roy opened his stance and spread his arms wide. "Where's my hug?"

It was a good thing the preachers parted ranks, because V.R. blew across that room and through the half door. Just before she arrived, Jerry tossed the cane to me and braced himself. She hit him like an Alabama linebacker, wrapped him up, lifted him off his feet and plunked him down with a fierce *huhhhnnnn!* He got his hug and more.

A look of terror crossed her glowing face and she let go with a howl that would've done a wolf proud. She started sobbing great lungfuls of air, torn out of her heaving body.

Standing there, I felt tired and old. Who could match this? When had I ever merited such an outburst? It probably would've scared me to death to be on the receiving end, but that felt like my fault, too.

My wife's tears darkened the shoulder of Jerry's blue workshirt, her fists hammering his back. Behind her the seven seminarians covered their mouths with their hands and *tsk-tsked* amongst themselves, checking their wristwatches, then clucking some more.

"I think, Ginny, you should pull yourself together now," suggested the fellow who'd approached us before. "It's almost four. Last mail is at four-thirty. Only four more letters to go."

She pulled away from Jerry, blinking, and blotted her tears with the back of both hands. "I—I'll be right with you—Jer, soon as I finish. You can wait, can't you?"

Jerry stuck out his right hand. The seminarian took it. "Jerry Roy, V.R.'s brother. How d'ya do?" Jerry kept shaking and shaking. "I've been away a spell. Well, more than a spell, actually. Seven years, in fact, most of it in Central America. Finally got a place, a mango plantation—do you like mangos? It's in Costa Rica. Been in a lot of rougher places, you know, Salvador, Honduras. Got your death squads, your drug smugglers, basically army brats in charge. Always lots of work for missionaries, right? Isn't that one way of looking at it? I always hated it when the army trucks came by at night, always at night. Never knew what I'd find under the mango trees next day—lot of squashed fruit, a man, sometimes a woman or a kid. Once a priest— The collar—you know. So. Seven years is a long time, a long time."

The seminarian was staring at Jerry's hand as it moved up and down, up and down. "I see. I think I understand . . . Jerry. May I call you Jerry?"

Jerry dropped his hand just like that. He gave me a flat look. Then he edged up close, the toes of his cowboy boots touching the other man's French Shriners.

"You may call me Jerry. You may also call me Beelzebub. I don't rightly care. But don't let me ever hear you calling my sister *Ginny*. Do you hear?"

The seminarian clutched his hand. "I . . . hear."

"Now sister," said Jerry conversationally, turning to us, "If it suits you, you just do these letters tomorrow."

With Virginia Roy on his arm he marched out the door while I brought up the rear holding his cane. He didn't need it anymore, now that he had V.R.

Jerry took the wheel on the way home. "American highways!" he cried, rolling down the windows. He stopped at a package store for a half-gallon of I. W. Harpers, at a Popeye's for fried chicken, and he couldn't wait to get home before tearing into either one. "American chicken!" And he ripped open a drumstick, filling the van with its fatty perfume. "*Ahhh!*" He inhaled the bourbon's nose-wrinkling fire. "Ah, America the beautiful."

"Open up," V.R. said, holding aloft a fried ball. "I know just what else you want, too." She dangled it over his open mouth as we roared down the roadway. He snapped it from her fingers, gulped it down.

"Good gizzard," he remarked. And she clapped.

I felt like a man clinging to a rope as it parted, strand by strand. "I hear gizzards give you heart disease," I said.

"If you're a laboratory rat." Jerry sniffed. "And I don't care how many white rats get heart attacks, because I only know one way to live—the Jerry Roy way."

Virginia Roy tilted the half-gallon bottle up and took a hefty swig. I closed my eyes. Bite your tongue, Gar Foote. When I opened my eyes, thank God, the driveway was in sight.

"Pass that jug back here, will you?" As I reached up, Virginia Roy saw the Rolex on my wrist.

"Where did you ever—"

"It's Jerry's."

"Yours," he corrected.

"But it looks like gold."

"Baby, it *is*." He killed the engine and let us coast down the drive.

I wanted to tell him about the power steering—about how it would now freeze, and we'd veer off into a tree—but it was a no-win situation. Put another way, it was worth racking up a $15,000 Ford van to cast any amount of doubt on Jerry Roy.

"Bush pilots wear that gold as an insurance policy with the natives. See—" The steering froze; we rocked sharply left. Jerry just reached down and flicked on the ignition, straightened the wheel, and turned it right off. "You never know when you're going to have to put down, or where."

We were home.

Around quitting time the boys rolled in for afternoon practice and came face-to-face with the skeleton in my closet.

"Grats, men, on your showing in Carolina," Jerry Roy said.

The boys allowed their hands to be shook, but they weren't taken in by him a bit. They remembered Jerry. They knew he was involved somehow in the old scandal. They wanted to stand behind me. But they didn't know where I stood because I had to stand by Virginia Roy.

"Let's show Jerry some action," I said, casually. Lucky's chin jerked up and he caught Eddie's eye. Cecil drummed his fists on his thighs, then vaulted the porch rail to the dirt, shouting, "To the pond!"

We scorched the practice lanes for Jerry's enlightenment. First came long casting on heavy and medium reels, followed by short slip-casting for accuracy under brushy banks. Sitting in an aluminum deck chair, Jerry just smiled like he'd seen it all before.

"Spoons!" someone shouted. In an instant, everybody reeled in and switched to spoons.

"Sidearm left!" barked Eddie like the sergeant he'd once been. "Sidearm right!"

"Frogs!" We dropped to our knees along the muddy banks of my bass range and unclipped the spoons, clipped on frogs.

"Musk up!" I shouted, fumbling for the Worm Blood and coating my fingers. We threw the frogs and practiced retrieves.

"Structure!" Lucky stepped to the large waterproof flip chartnailed to a tree stump. He flipped to a blow up of a flasher chart showing a ledge at twenty feet, dropping away steeply.

"Cecil, it's seventy-two degrees up top, water surface fifty-two degrees, a front blew through three days ago. Where do you fish and what are you using?"

"Sir, I-am-fishing-at-the-thermocline-using-worms-sir!"

"Worms? Just worms?"

"Sir, I-mean-Purple-Twisters-or-Ditto-Gator-Tails, nine-inch-yellow-or-black." Cecil stopped, panting. He hesitated and then shouted, "Not musked!"

"Why not?" fired Lucky.

"Because . . . because the front blew them in from a creek. They're colder—they're dead."

Lucky nodded approvingly. I snuck a look at Jerry; he was leaning forward, lips pursed, eyes hooded in thought.

"Bass attack!" shouted Eddie. We spun in our tracks and paused over our quivers of rods, waiting for the next command. Eddie filled his lungs. "Spring spawn. It's late April. Big females full of roe are moving to their beds to spawn. Lucky, what water temperature?"

"Sixty-five is optimum."

"Gar, what do you say to that?"

"Lucky's right about it being optimum, but the best time to fish is pre-spawn. Say, fifty-eight degrees. Course, you want the warmest part of the water, the north bank."

"Thank you, professor," Eddie said. "Lucky, what bait?"

Lucky looked blank. Then a light filled his eyes. "Jig-and-Eel or Rebel Crawdad."

"Then let's hit it!" Eddie barked. "Twenty yards."

We snatched at our long rods and heavy reels, clipped on the right lure or a close match and began to fire at the Clorox bottles in the middle distance. Lures splashed close, closer—by the third or fourth cast, hollow *thunks!*, direct hits, were sounding. And Jerry was moved to his first comment: "Nice."

Now Cecil stepped up with a quiz on weeds, current and holes, interrupted by an equipment breakdown—"Strip your reels!"—and two sets of push-ups.

Gasping, muddy-nosed, but proud, I turned to get Jerry's reaction. His chair was empty.

The boys didn't linger after practice; they knew V.R. and Jerry had some catching up to do. And, although I wished I could go with them, I stayed.

We ate a dinner of pork chops in gravy, then trooped onto the porch to talk and sip bourbon. They talked, I sipped. Jerry told story after story of narrow escapes and clever deals.

A hangover kicked me out of bed earlier than usual the next morning. V.R.'s side of the bed was cold, empty. She had never come upstairs. I went down to the kitchen for some water and found Jerry lying on the sofa and V.R. on a bed of cushions off the two living room chairs. But they weren't asleep.

"Morning, bub," said Jerry.

V.R. jumped up. "I'm making breakfast."

"Been thinking about you," Jerry said as soon as she'd gone. "About your tournament this weekend."

I looked at the Rolex: 5:10 A.M. There were at least seventeen hours to go before I could sleep again, seventeen hours of Jerry Roy in my hair, in my ear, in my face.

He said, "You're on the right track. You're defining a true Commando style. We'll work up some new routines. The idea is, each guy has his own quirk, his own personal thing. We market the group *as a concept*."

I didn't answer.

He said, "Anything the matter?"

"All this 'we' stuff."

He rolled on his side and flung one arm over the back of the sofa. "Still bitter?" He stared at me until I looked away. "You sorry dog, you. I'm only trying to help you out of the sizeable hole you've dug for yourself."

Trank du Lac came out of the guest bedroom, smoothing down his shiny black hair with both hands. He stopped at the sight of us. "Excuse me. I did not know."

"Makes two of us." Jerry yawned.

I made introductions and said, "That slugabed Rico still asleep back there?

Trank shook his head. "He left yesterday, for Birmingham." Trank must have seen my hopes rising, because he quickly added, "He is coming back today, I understand."

Turning to Jerry, I tried to explain Rico Octoponte: "He's part of this war thing V.R.'s kinda into."

"V.R.'s into war, you say?"

"It's a game." This led to an explanation of skirmish contests and Weekend Warrior, but Jerry wasn't having any of it.

"You just let her go off and do this shit? Man, you out of your mind or something?"

"V.R.'s a grown-up. This is important to her."

"She's a woman. You got to ride herd on her." His eyes brightened, and he waved. "Hey, Sis, when's breakfast?"

Virginia Roy, leaning in the door frame in order to watch us, waved back with a long wooden spoon. "One minute. You want OJ or V-8 juice?"

"I got my friend here." He patted the nearly empty half-gallon of bourbon on the coffee table.

She sauntered in, a bemused smile playing over her lips, deftly speared the built-in handle on the bottle with her spoon and hoisted it out of her brother's reach. "Last night was an exception. From now on we're in training."

"What'd'ya mean, 'we'?"

"You'll see." She gave her brother that dark look of hers. Then a smile lightened her face. "Let's eat. Gar, Trank."

After breakfast, my favorite scrapple and scrambled eggs, V.R. sat down and poured herself a second cup of tea.

"Shouldn't you be getting dressed for work?" I asked.

She shook her head, stirred honey into her camomile. "I'm not going back. Be pointless after yesterday."

"Surely if you explain that that was your brother—"

"Your evil brother." Jerry smiled.

"Oh, they might buy that. If I crawled on my belly." She was quietly focused, which is Virginia Roy at her most decisive. "But I can't stomach *them*."

She looked straight at me.

"What'll we do?" I asked. From two incomes to no incomes, real fast, couldn't help but worry me.

"What we do best. You'll fish tournaments. And I will organize. And train. And try to develop myself as a combat artist."

"Organize what? Train for what?" I wasn't about to dignify "combat artist" by saying it. But I did give Jerry a sidelong look, which he refused to meet, the coward.

Virginia Roy folded her hands on the table. "Rico has offered me a position in his organization." Again, it was like she was daring me to attack. "He's already decided to make his national base in the South. I said, 'Why not here?' We can get in a couple of computers. While Rico travels, I'll hold down the fort."

I nodded, then said, "Excuse my ignorance, but just what is Rico's *business?*"

"He has three." She got up and pulled something out of the porcelain water pitcher on the sideboard. *Slap, slap, slap.* I was staring at three business cards on the coffee table, all in the name of Dr. Ricardo U. Octoponte, Lt. Col., ret.; Bachelor of Science, Tulane University; D.D.S., Salvatierra Universidad. He was chairman of the MANO Foundation ("Mutual Assistance Networking Organization"), president of Combat Consulting, Inc. "Incorporated on Grand Cayman Island, Bahamas" and publisher and editor-in-chief of *Combat Artist* ("Serving The Inner Warrior").

I fiddled with the cards' edges for a while, then said, "Must be tricky wearing three hats." Virginia Roy took a breath, but I forged on. "He paying you three salaries?"

She scooped up the cards. "I'm working for MANO. The

others already have their own offices and staff. I'll be the coordinator of fund-raising for the south-central USA."

Jerry slapped her on the shoulder. "Won't that look fine on a business card? Way to go, Sis." He looked at me and shook his head in awe. "Mom always said V.R. was the brains of the outfit."

I stood up and stretched. "Why don't you mosey out to the bass pond, Jerry."

"Oh, too early for me." He laughed.

"Then take a bath or something."

He raised his hands and backed out of the kitchen. I turned, stood over her, put my hands on her shoulders. She didn't look up. For a second I was stumped. I didn't want to start a war, I wanted to start a conversation. But talking to the top of somebody's head isn't any way to get down. Suddenly, Virginia Roy looked up at me.

"Hi, there," I said.

"Hello."

"Just thought I'd check in, see how things are. Uh, anything you want to say to me?"

"No."

"I mean, you holding anything back about this Rico deal? I want to get it all at once, if you don't mind."

"You're not mad?"

"I like to be in on things. I don't like surprises, just like anyone else. But not mad, no."

Her eyes smiled.

Jerry slapped the tabletop. "Now *that's* the sister I know! We Roys just aren't meant to take orders. Our ancestors would rather be hung for cattle thieves than serve in the King's pay. You know, V.R., I'm something of an expert in home offices; you ought to see my ranch setup. Maybe I can advise you and your, ah, partner."

Turning a dish towel inside a casserole pot, Virginia Roy smiled. "Maybe you can."

"I can get you a good deal on computers, office equipment, the works."

"Maybe you and Gar can introduce Rico around at the Chamber of Commerce and the Rotary. I'd do it myself, only—" She left unsaid the obvious, that no women are allowed at these meets.

"Heck, no problem. Right, Gar?"

"Sure thing."

It was like old times again. The three of us back in the saddle, planning the next event as if the seven years in between hadn't happened.

I stood by the stove top, dipping plastic worms. It's tricky. You take the worm by the head, dip it quick in boiling water, then roll it in scent formulation, before tossing it into a freezer bag for tournament action. The hot water makes that rubber soft and fleshy, the scent lubricates and tenderizes it, and even provides in-the-water bubble discharge to drive the largemouth mad with lust.

The steps outside the back screen door creaked. We all turned our heads at the sound. A bright orange dot glowed momentarily, then faded. Then, materializing through the screen, came an enormous blue smoke ring.

"*Buenas noches,*" crooned Rico, poking his face up close into the light.

From the moment they laid eyes on each other, Rico and Jerry were on their toes. Baring their teeth in bright, almost identical grins, they turned tight verbal circles around each other:

"You live in Costa Rica?"

"Las Mañanas. Know the place?"

"Oh, I know it well. In fact, how do I not know you?"

"Maybe you haven't been there recently."

"And you have?"

"Ask my buddies. Lou Trumpy, the USAID man. Or Palourdes, the man we call 'Mister Coffee'."

"I will. Palourdes, of course, has often been a guest at my lectures."

"Oh, yeah," Jerry nodded. "He's big on charitable causes. Lately it's the rain forest. Let me guess—you're a save the rain forest type, right?"

V.R. laughed and punched his bicep. "Jerry, cut it out."

Rico ashed his cigar into his palm, closed his fist, grinned. "Let's say I save the *animales* in the rain forest. The big cats, the quiet killers. The panthers."

The tension changed then to a lower key, but I still had the sense of two heavyweights sizing each up on the prefight scales. Rico accepted a cafe espresso, something V.R. had learned to make since his arrival on the scene. And Jerry poured himself a tot of bourbon, despite V.R.'s disapproving vibes. After draining their glasses and smacking their lips, they started right in on each other again. But now it was sharply focused on one issue.

"I hear you like war and all that? Well, I want to know—since my sister is involved—if there's any money in it."

"Not war, freedom. I, personally, despise war. But freedom is too precious . . . you should know that."

"Why is that?"

"Excuse me if I am uninformed, but were you not dispossessed of your own freedom for a time—in Honduras?"

"Must've been some other Roy. I've paid my dues, but not that way. And, bye-the-bye, I thought you said you'd never heard of me?"

"Well, obviously, I haven't—because you aren't the person in Honduras of whom I speak."

"And close only counts in horseshoes?" Jerry said.

"Excuse me?"

"So is there money in it, this MANO?"

"We are successful at fund-raising."

"What's your cut?"

"I take no salary."

"How do you eat, then?"

"The generosity of friends who accept the morality of our mission. Like your sister."

V.R. set out plates of shortcake with the first strawberries: tiny things, floating on lakes of clotted cream. Jerry and Rico ate heartily. Rico drew out a pair of cigars, handed one to Jerry. Each had a penknife on his keychain and began assiduously trimming the point on his stogy while continuing the duel.

"Now, I'm worried about my sister working for a man who admits he isn't in it for the money. Where does that leave her, I ask you?"

"She is knowing the joy of service. And, of course, we are offering her a salary."

"Grandpa Roy always said, 'Never hire the fool who says he works for the love of it. There's no way you'll ever be rid of him'."

"You must understand about your sister, she is rare, the kind we call 'La Apassionata' and recognize as our moral superior. It is something lost on you gringos, you with your Teflon religions."

"Nothing wrong with Teflon," Jerry observed. "You use it, don't you, Sis?"

V.R. wiped her hands on the dish towel. "I'm going to bed. Got to get up early."

Rico held up a hand like a stop sign and reached with the other into his leather shoulder bag. "I saw something I thought you would like." He caught my eye, winked. "She is a big reader of books, yes?"

Out of his bag came a large coffee-table book with a bright blue photographic cover of a dark-skinned, sloe-eyed beauty in dusty fatigues, her tan breasts and slim hips slung with web belts, ammo pouches, grenades, an M-79 launcher and a FAL Belgian assault rifle. The title glowered above her in clouds of battle red: SABRA WOMEN AT WAR.

Caught by surprise, V.R. reached for the book impulsively, then hauled it in close to her chest. "Gosh, Rico—thanks. It's really neat." She glanced up, smiled merrily at us. "Night all." To me she added, "You come to bed soon, hear?"

Not hard to figure, that Virginia Roy. Give her a cause and she operates on all cylinders, flat out. It's the only way she knows. And it's a trait that Jerry always exploited, one I consistently underestimated and which Rico had obviously discovered on his own.

12

By the end of the week Rico and Jerry were as thick as thieves, God was in heaven, and the Bass Commandos were off and running again. Our house echoed with Jerry's blustering voice as he made call after call from the kitchen—and I'll be the first to admit that he was amazing. Not only did he not care if we stood around listening, he seemed to feed on it. He called all the major rod and reel manufacturers, one after the other, hitting them up for equipment—"and Fed Ex it, please." He did the same with the lure makers and the line makers, the Johnson and Evinrude outboard motor people, the electronic water surveillance manufacturers. To all and sundry he sold the same lie:

"That's right, the television special is on the newest stars. No, not those guys—they're not fishermen, they're fish wrappers, yesterday's newspaper. You have to understand, this is national TV, not local. They want state of the art, they want young, they want crossover. That's the Bass Commandos. Look, I got to take another call." Jerry would cover the mouthpiece and shout, "Who?" Then he'd name the rival of the company he was talking to. "Sorry. Let me get back to you while you think it over. Oh?

You've decided? Hey, you guys call your own shots, don't you? Not like some other places I could name—some of them your competitors—where even a vice president has to ask permission to fill a single order. Pathetic, ain't it? Let me give you my Fed Ex number . . . Why, that's very kind of you. We got to have a beer sometime, you and me. We think alike. We can shoot the shit and talk tie-ins and special promotions. Sure, after the special. The special comes first."

If that weren't enough, he and Rico were having a kind of contest. It would start early in the day, around when I'd just be propping my eyes open with a cup of coffee—something I just couldn't get used to, after a lifetime of Coke. In would stroll Rico, cordless phone in hand, waving to us like some famous singer on stage at the Opry. "Hello, is this Mrs. Boynton? *Ahhh . . .*" and off he'd go, crooning and stroking and massaging the money out of the purse, into the hand, the envelope into the mailbox. Then Rico would grin and wink at Jerry. And Jerry would call some poor unsuspecting lure manufacturer and do it to him. And when he was done, he'd hang up, make a little *o* of his mouth and punch his fists low and fast like a boxer in the clinch.

After a couple of scores each, they'd break for cigars and espresso, Jerry sweetening his from a boot bottle. "Now that was a neat little twist on a Puppydog Close," Jerry might say. "I'm surprised you didn't ask them to adopt a Contra for the Easter Holiday." And Rico would tease Jerry about his call, and after a bit more of this they'd both leap back on the phones.

Along about noon, though, they got to arguing over which was the harder sell, fishing or war.

"All *you* got to do is bang the drum and play the fife," Jerry scoffed. "War's a done deal, way I figure it. No way I can wrap the flag around a fish."

Rico pointed out that Jerry was selling fishing as war, which I thought was pretty deep. Dead wrong, but deep. In war, you hate the enemy because he can take your life. In bass fishing, we love our quarry, even as we pursue him with every bit of technology and cunning. When we capture a fish, all our attention shifts to keeping him alive, to preserving him for the tournament scales, so that he may live to fight again. That's not war — that's a game, like Weekend Warrior. If you ask me, what Rico and Jerry were doing was more like real war — making cold and calculated use of other folks' lives. They kept what they caught.

Finally, Rico dared Jerry to make one of *his* calls. Jerry just laughed. "Punch up a number and watch me work," he said. When Rico handed him a hot phone he didn't flinch. He just dove right in, the only difference being that he spoke much more slowly, almost haltingly. "We're talking about a chance, perhaps the very last chance to stop the rowdies and Communists in this hemisphere before they reach our doorstep. These are brave men. I've been down there myself, and the — the suffering, it's heartbreaking. These men, they're not alone, you see. They have their . . . their families with them, sharing the danger, the . . . the hunger. It's inspiring. Your tax-deductible contribution of office equipment gives this fine group, this low-overhead organization, which the White House has singled out for high, high honors, the ability to put that money to work on the front lines of freedom."

And when he hung up, he challenged Rico: "Now let's see you bring in Lure Menu. That's a software program that reads out water temperature, pH factor, water clarity, trolling speed, thermocline depth and fish presence, into a color guide display for lures. Retails for about a grand. Think you can get it for free?"

Rico stared at the phone Jerry was offering. He raised his hands: "*No mas.*"

After we quit laughing, he added, "This bass fishing that you do, it is not the old sport. It is rocket science, yes?"

"That's right!" Jerry rapped the table with his cane. "You got more electronics crammed into the modern bass tournament boat then was in all the B-29s flown in World War II put together."

I turned to Jerry. "Lure Menu's a deep-water tool. It wouldn't be much help. Except maybe on a big desert impoundment." I waited.

"Such as Lake Mead in Las Vegas?" Jerry shrugged, then smiled.

I nodded. "Just noticing. The way I notice how good you are on the phone. Been growing telephone wire on that farm of yours in Costa Rica?"

"Hey dude, for most of seven years I couldn't leave that farm," he growled. "You're damn right I know how to use a phone. Like a friend of mine said, 'Next to the accordion the telephone is the world's most underrated musical instrument.'"

During those weeks, the UPS and FedEx drivers became familiar faces around the house and boxes cluttered the living room, porch and basement. And day and night now the boys were apt to be on the pond, rigging out the new gear, bench-testing the electronics. For V.R. and me, privacy was impossible. Even when we went up to the bedroom at night we could hear the house stirring.

She brought her work up with her, anyway. We flopped out under the ceiling fan, the television on at the foot of the four-poster. I took my eyes off her for a second and the next time I looked she was scribbling in a notebook again.

She said, "You'll make sure Rico has a spot at Rotary next Tuesday, the Chamber on Wednesday."

"Already done it. Called it in."

"How much are they good for?"

"How do I know? Maybe two hundred."

"We can double it. Why don't you call a couple of the guys you know and have them promise to kick off with fifty bucks each, right at the beginning. Shame the rest."

"Rico learn you that trick?" I said. She nodded. "I don't hear much about your weekend war games anymore."

"Don't tell me you miss it, 'cause I know that just isn't true." She made eyes at me.

"Well, you're right. But what I mean is, you could do one of those Weekend Warrior things while I'm off fishing this weekend. You know, the way we did before."

"I guess I've outgrown it." She dropped a hand onto the stack of books on the night table: *SAS Survival Handbook*. *The Israeli Army, 1969–73. Air America. Secret Armies. The Journal of Counterintelligence. Mercs. With the Contras.*

Lying beside me on the bed, she looked blankly up at the ceiling as if trying to remember what, indeed, had happened. Then she began a recitation: "Armies are expensive to raise, expensive to train and maintain. Soldiers need beans, blankets and bullets. The first duty of the general is to the troops."

I wondered if that meant Rico would be helping us with the mortgage. It was a measure of my new attitude that I kept my mouth shut.

On Thursday, at noon, the Commandos assembled at the pond. Their attitudes had changed, too, from being wary of Jerry to a kind of peculiar pleasure in being bullshitted by a true expert. It's the old tent preacher thing. Nobody'd think of throwing money at a parish padre, but let some pale-skinned, snake-thin fellow roll in and lookout, Baby Jane, silver dollars fallin' down like rain.

"We don't have enough time to mount all the new stuff, much less dial it in," Jerry said, lecturing from his aluminum deck chair. He waved his cane at us. "What we can do is mount a display of such power, of such skill, that, before the tournament begins, the other fishermen are psyched out."

It had been one of my secret fears all along that Jerry would turn out to know what he was doing. As he went on, I could feel my fears come true.

After he was done, Lucky stood up and gave a short laugh. "You are a slippery one, though," he said, as Jerry smiled and tossed his head back. "I almost feel sorry for those boys tomorrow." Lucky turned around and faced me directly as if reading my startled mind. He lifted his palms to the sky. "What can I say, Gar? The man's a salesman."

At 4:30 the next morning I backed the van up to the boathouse, unlocked the two Yale padlocks and swung the doors wide. There she was, snugged-down and ready to roll. I picked up the end of the trailer tongue and pulled the hitch up to the ball joint on the van's rear bumper, snapping in the cables for the trailer's taillights. All over Valhalla at that moment, Commandos were going through the same drill.

Jerry hopped into the passenger seat and laid his cane between us. V.R. leaned in to kiss my cheek and pressed something heavy into my hands—the Fuzzbuster. "Tally-ho, amigos," Jerry cried into our CB, and a chorus of clicks and fuzzy cries told us the Commandos were airborne.

Eddie and Lucky were waiting at the deserted Red Lion parking lot. "So where's Cecil?" Lucky asked me.

"Probably trying to decide which set of camouflage to bring." Eddie himself wore a black crew sweater over his fatigues, a black beret on his head.

We heard a rattling and a backfiring, and turned to look toward town center. "Trank," I said. "Know that muffler anywhere."

Eddie pointed: "Here comes the Cecilmobile." We saw a blaze of sparks on a dark side street, then heard a grinding; finally, we saw a truck speeding without headlights. "Draggin' tail, ain't he?"

"Won't make Georgia at that rate." Lucky looked over at Yvonne. She smiled up at him, and wrinkled her long nose. "Time to set up the video."

Yvonne went back to the Land Cruiser and began to assemble the tripod and camera. Cecil and Trank pulled in and bailed out almost at the same instant, and walked fast toward us.

"Check it out."

"Who-eee."

Cecil wore a beautifully tailored camo suit with epaulets; his red beret was pulled through one set of shoulder boards. His black boots were gleaming. A K-Bar knife in its scabbard adorned his right ankle. He wore his Commando baseball cap, and over the other shoulder had slung a glossy black nylon jacket with our bright red embroidered insignia: a bass jumping over a skull.

Trank had put up fierce resistance to Jerry before finally agreeing, this once, to wear the baggy black pajama trousers and blouse of Victor Charlie. Instead of an Kalashnikov, he carried something just as deadly, in its way—a Daiwa 7.1:1 baitcasting reel mounted on a carbon graphite blank trimmed with Fuji grips.

We waited for Yvonne to give the high sign. She peered through the 35 mm camera and raised her hand. The four original Commandos formed a circle and stuck their fists into the middle.

"Let's go!"

"It all starts now," said Lucky.

"Take your arrows in the forehead."

Everybody looked at Cecil for an explanation of this remark. He blushed.

"That's from the Japanese code of the *wabi*—warrior."

"Sounds good, whatever it is," said Eddie. Cecil looked relieved.

Jerry strolled up behind Lucky and said something. Lucky nodded, reached into his shoulder bag and handed out cassette tapes. "Bass Commando Audio Program. BASSCAP for short," he said for the benefit of the recording camera. "There's nothing on them," he whispered, "but later we can say there was."

"Another fine Commando product," said Eddie.

"This is a dry run." Jerry slapped Eddie on the back. "Think categories, think merchandising."

"Okay," called Yvonne, and we were all at ease.

"Hit the road, Jack. Monitor channel six-niner, talk on one-one."

"Gar and Jerry, drive point for the first fifty miles."

"Good-bye, Daddy." Yvonne kissed Lucky once, twice, three and finally four times. "Don't bring home any fish, okay?"

Driving in the pre-dawn darkness, with Jerry smoking silently beside me, it was too easy to pretend nothing had changed in seven years.

"So," I said, to establish who had the upper hand in this thing, "What's on your mind?"

"Silkscreened T-shirts."

"Uh-huh."

"It's a question of price points. Cotton versus cotton-poly, the depth of color, how many colors."

I glanced over at him. His lean, sunburned face held no surprises for me, but still it was mesmerizing, like one of those clocks in a Plexiglas box with the gears exposed.

But I was committed to showing him how indifferent I was, so I said, "Don't think I'll be able to stay awake much longer if you don't change the subject."

He twisted around in his seat so he could lean against his door and stare at me. "How about this, then: In roughly ten days you are going to be making history on a lake in Lake Vegas before twenty-five hundred spectators and a live camera, with the chance to take home half a million."

"In ten days we'll miss our first house payment. This van will be repossessed. V.R. can hang onto her El Camino, it's paid for."

"Win or show. That's all it takes."

"By hook or by crook?"

He knew what I meant. He said, "A man couldn't cheat now, not with these new rules and tests." He rubbed the bridge of his nose between his fingers and smiled. "I've given it some thought, of course. In another few years, this microchip business will give us stuff we never could've imagined. Maybe by then . . ."

We surged along the highway, the van straining against the trailer.

I finished the sentence for him: "Maybe by then you can work up the courage to tell your sister the truth."

To my surprise, he didn't get angry. Nodding, he French-inhaled his cigarette until his features seemed to be lying under a waterfall of smoke. "I almost did. Came close this week, again. She stopped me, though."

"V.R.?"

"The way she looked, everything about her said, 'Don't take anything from me unless you can be sure of replacing it.' She's the one who really lost out, remember."

"You're telling me?" I said.

"She doesn't want to know. When I look at her I see a sign like the one in the china shop: You Break, You Pay."

I glanced at him. "She's tougher than that. She's a country girl."

"She knows I'm it, bub—her only family. Don't forget she's a female, full of hormones and squishy things. Not rational like us." He peered at me as I drove.

I didn't want to believe him. But he'd insinuated just the right doubt.

And he could tell. "Hell, just look at the difference here. You and me, we know we're playing a game, a big and complicated one, sure, but we know where to draw the line. It's still just fishing. But this warrior thing . . . Does she know where her line is? Ask her and she'd probably say, 'What line?' Do you think she knows where she's going?"

"It's getting ridiculous, that's for sure."

I had hopes that maybe Jerry would decide Rico wasn't worth the trouble he caused and would get tired of having him around. Easing Rico out couldn't seem to be my idea; Virginia Roy wouldn't listen if it were.

Lake Seminole is a big bass lake, with two hundred-fifty miles of shoreline, acres of stumps, deep river channels. We knew we were in for a stiff fight. The two hundred or so boats entered were the latest and finest designs. The fishermen were the type to spend the off-season studying bulletins from the department of Fish and Game and taking night school courses in wild fisheries management. You wouldn't think that having the Commandos materialize on the starting line would throw these canny veterans one bit. And you would be right, ninety-nine percent of the time.

"So where were you guys the last few weekends?" a well-known bass journalist asked me during check in.

"Around."

"You had every tournament boss in the entire country sweatin' that you'd pick his event. You know that, don't you?"

When I didn't say anything, he nodded and turned a page of his narrow notebook. "A war of nerves. Okay—anything else you can tell me?"

"Watch our dust."

"They're not through with you, you know. Today's plan is to pretend you guys don't exist. They figure, no publicity, no Commandos. Y'know: if a bear shits in the woods and nobody hears it . . ."

I laughed, and he looked pleased with himself. I thought of all the tournaments where I'd seen this particular journalist hanging out with the stars, passing around the Red Man, swapping lies, his little notebook sticking out of his hip pocket. He was known as the Walter Winchell of bass. It felt good to be on the inside

"Well, if that's the case, I can tell you strictly off the record that we were putting in a few wrinkles." Taking a deep breath, I buried my chin in my chest and stared at him. "Some of it's software—the tactics and training. Some of it's hardware. The electronics boys have been mighty helpful, particularly in the stealth department."

"Stealth department?" He quieted down and maneuvered closer, getting me all to himself. "What are we talking here? Fishfinders? Multi-screen probes?"

"That's old hat. Look, I can't spell it out for you, understand? I signed some pretty formal documents." I looked about casually. "But I can help point you. What do jet fighter pilots train on, for instance, besides airplanes?"

He looked stricken. "Uh . . . flight simulators?"

I nodded approvingly. "Okay. Now imagine a *bass* simulator that puts you on the lake of your choice and allows you to fish it in real time. That's one wrinkle."

"There's more?" His writing hand was jerking to keep up, his shorthand zigzags looked like a graph chart depth sounder running over a bed of stumps.

"We've got a direct feed from COM-CON/SAT-NAV, the spy satellite lofted last October? Well, imagine the resolution of that camera. It's the one that photographed a mosquito on Castro's ass, remember? Imagine it coupled with thermal imaging to penetrate any kind of cover: clouds, forests . . . water."

"Water." His face had turned ash-white, his eyelids twitching; he licked the back of his Bic pen after every word like a deer glued to a salt lick. And I was the hunter who had him in my sights. Exhale softly, pull the trigger.

"We know where the bass are. Right now. If they move, we'll move with them. If they dive, we'll know how deep. You see, we have already acquired our targets for tomorrow."

He moved his shaggy head from side to side. "Nobody can compete with that." He sighed. He searched my face for some sign of compassion and found only "the mask of dominance," the expression that Jerry had had us practice in front of the video camera.

"There's something else, isn't there?" he said.

The whole crowd of anglers, who had already been watching, stopped pretending to be doing anything else. The great wordsmith of the waters, the man with the power to make or break bassers, to start or stop a career, plucked at the pocket of my flotation vest and peered up into my face.

"Why, I already told you," I said pleasantly, with a puzzled shake of my head. "Stealth lures, of course. Got a number where I can reach you?" While he dug in his pockets for a card, I recited the teaser we'd worked out the previous afternoon as we rested up around my old bass pond. "The Commandos aren't about fishing as we know it. We're an A-Team, parapiscine strike unit engaged in global bass suppression. In our charter we have latitude to flex our fishing muscles just about wherever we please. In that capacity, then, the government will be employing us in various ways that must, for the forseeable time, remain classified."

The journalist scribbled furiously, flipping pages like a man dealing blackjack. I patted him on the shoulder. "Gotta go fish."

There were twenty minutes to go. Two hundred nervous bassers gathered on the shore directly in front of the starter's tower. The sun still hadn't poked through the fog. A blast of weird electronic howls came from my van, which had sprouted antennae and small satellite dishes overnight. Standing apart, the Commandos finished suiting up, each of us sliding a Plexiglas visor and lightweight headset over his head.

"Hut!" Cecil rapped. We snapped to. "Twenty jacks!"

We gave him twenty jumping jacks, then jogged in place while Trank, in the role of Victor Charlie, circled us doing this tai chi'i stuff with his Daiwa-Fuji master-basser fishing rig. Trank tossed a ball at the ground; pink smoke billowed up. The fishermen could hardly take their eyes off us. When Cec barked, "At ease!" they came up like puppies begging to be petted. Trank distributed our BASSCAP tapes to us.

"What's on the tape, my man?" asked a lanky fellow.

Cecil frowned as he adjusted his earphones. "Fish programming."

"How's it work?"

"Interfaces with the electronics."

"Huh." The man couldn't think of anymore questions, and stepped back to his fellows. "It hooks into your fishfinder," he explained. "He wasn't talking, but I eyeballed the setup. It gives you the casting pattern. Like a computer."

If only that were the case. The tapes were blank, but I made a note to myself about what these boys thought they ought to have on them.

The five-minute warning horn sounded. For all our bragging and boasting, we still fish had to catch. Everyone was lined up.

The starting gun popped and boats blasted out to coves and holes their captains had plotted on the huge lake. Some cut their speed and trolled about, searching for pockets of fish, and everybody kept polite casting distance. Nobody talked loud. The fog lifted slowly on a mean, hot sun.

As I passed by boats and coves, heads lifted forlornly for a moment above slumped shoulders; eyes lingered on me, empty of hope. Talk about your slough of despond: nobody was catching fish. If ever proof was needed of how much fishing is about confidence, then this was it.

Problem was, my mental attitude wasn't in tip-top shape, either. Right from the start, I wasn't myself. On the way to a deep-water bar I'd picked for my first stop, I saw a creekmouth and decided to test it. As soon as I'd cast a plug, though, I wanted to crank it in and race off. My fish sense and my fish science weren't in synch. Trying to link the two together, I took a hard line. I would stay put. An hour passed, my discipline was impressive. Pity I didn't have any fish to show for it. I started up the engine.

My next stop was the deep-water bar in the middle of Lake Seminole, a mile from any land. But I was late. There were twenty boats floating silently, the only sound the *zzzzzzzzzzz-plop* of the lures being cast. I circled on electric, looking for a toehold of shoal in my flasher. Hopeless. Worse, I saw people catching fish. That could've been me.

In this heat, the fish that didn't soon go deep would be too sleepy to eat. I cut my engines and unfolded Lucky's chart. The lake was huge, with a reputation for choking weed in the shallows. But in hot weather, that's where the catchable bass would be.

So I went and found the biggest, thickest, slimiest square mile of weed and began to work my way into it, inching forward with the trolling motor, unclogging the props every few minutes. I took an hour to get two hundred yards. By then my arms and face were wet with the blood of mashed bugs and some of my own mixed in, compliments of a cloud of mosquitos. I wrapped my head in a towel and slapped on as much Cutter's as I had with me.

The fish must have been laughing themselves sick.

We took stock that evening. For all our bluster, the Commandos hadn't done anything spectacular, except everyone else had done worse. It was the first tournament in memory where not one stringer topped ten pounds.

"What's the matter with you guys?" Jerry asked in the motel suite, where he'd set up headquarters. "Afraid to win?" He laughed, then waved his hand in front of his face as if brushing aside a mosquito. "I know that's not true. In fact, I'm not worried at all. Your competition is already washed out."

I wondered about that as I went out to the local steakhouse with the boys. Was it just my imagination, or was the dining room quieter, the bar deader, the motel pool, when we got back, emptier. The official tournament square dance was an unnatural disaster. Was it just me, or was everybody in a zombie trance? This was our doing, I sensed. We'd taken the spirit out of the competition, as surely as if we'd detonated a neutron bomb.

Down by the lakeside, where the elevated boardwalk ended and weeds and brambles began, I put my back against a piling. The far reaches of the parking lot petered out behind me; the only car for a hundred yards was a decrepit Ford Fury, its back bumper long gone and replaced by a series of Confederate flag stickers placed end to end: the typical Southern approach to guarding your rear.

Footsteps squished through the lot's clayey mud. Muffled voices, one raised in anger: "No point in sticking around for tomorrow. I'm gone!"

A lower voice murmured in response, soothing—to no avail: "Sure, they're just toying with us. So they didn't catch much today. You think, that with all that equipment, they'll strike out tomorrow?

Suck, suck, went the shoes. The talkers went away, into the cicada backwash.

I stared out over the inky water, smelling the sulphuric taint of a rich, fecund bassbed pumping out nutrients. The stars rippled in the lake. My tired body told me to go back to the motel. But I stayed. I breathed. The lake lapped at the shore under the boardwalk. Frogs *larrupped* and flung themselves at each other like professional wrestlers.

"Son."

The lake had spoken. No, there was a low, black prow edging out from under the boardwalk. I sensed, not saw, a paddle change sides. The pirogue glided in a slow turn until a crescent of light from the faraway motel lit a whittled-away forehead, nose and chin. An older man. A man with a wiry body and an ancient face, stringy and tremulous.

"I've never seen fishermen like this," he said. "Is there some trouble? Because the fish are there, eh? In all these years I never seen so many fish — right here." He splashed the surface with his paddle. "Under the dock, around the pilings. Also on the lake. But nobody catching."

I crossed my legs. "Maybe you ought to enter."

He looked at me — or I should say, the dark hollows under his eyebrows pointed in my direction. "You are a great fisherman. Seen you. Nineteen seventy-two."

"You're mistaken. Never fished here before in my life."

"Didn't see you here." He stuck his paddle in the water and without seeming to move a muscle turned the pirogue about-face. "You didn't use all the electric doohickeys back then. What happened, lose your nerve?"

He dipped the paddle as he moved away along the brushy shore. The rumpled water he left behind dimpled and swirled as night-feeding bass came to investigate.

. . .

The tournament leader was a fellow who'd collected nine pounds of fish. The Commandos were in mid-pack, ranging from Cecil's high of six pounds to my one-pound, two-ounce keeper.

"Well," Eddie said, "at least you did better than eighty-seven others."

"Thank you for pointing it out, Eddie."

Cecil said, "Gar ought not wander too close to any barbecues with his face looking like that. Somebody's liable to take it for a hamburger and throw him on the grill."

Trank hunkered down against the wall with a chart in front of him, marking down the day's weather prediction. "What do you think, Victor Charlie?" asked Jerry. Trank gave a little shrug.

"That's what I think, too," Jerry said. "Today's the day we either make good on our promises or else crawl back to Valhalla on our bellies. I can't fish for you, boys, and I won't pray for you. But I can promise to cut off your balls with a hacksaw if one of you doesn't bring in a big string."

Twenty minutes later I faked a stallout and let the two hundred boats roar off at seventy miles an hour. After the wakes died away, I went for a shoreline cruise, back to where I'd been sitting last night. I visited the boardwalk, the boathouse and a pier with a restaurant on it, both in plain sight of the tent and banners. All proved to have quite a sizeable underwater clientele. They kept my Wiggle Worm right busy. I must've caught twenty fish, and by culling out and releasing the smaller ones, I ended up with a respectable string.

Unavoidably, everybody in the restaurant could watch. Pretty soon word got out and media crews appeared and began filming, probably not realizing who I was at first. When I decided to call it a morning, there was a round of applause. "Come here," some people yelled from the restaurant's pier, so I trolled over, and they tossed me a cold one.

I one-handed it, and stared down at the label of my old friend.

A bitter feeling came over me. I wanted to throw that can of Coke as far out into Lake Seminole as I could, right in front of the cameras, and be done with it. But I reconsidered. "For old time's sake, then," I mumbled and took a sip of the sweet black essence, the bubbles burning up into my nose.

I lay out by the pool until four, then went down to the dock. The last fishermen were just trickling in, including the other Commandos, faces puffy and red with insect bites. It had been a slow, hot day out there in the weeds.

Eddie hauled his fishbox up and slammed it on the dock. "I shouldn't even bother to weigh in."

"Skunked?" Lucky asked me, taking in the bathing suit and pink sunburn.

"Look at the big board."

My combined weight was first by three pounds.

In an hour it was all over. They hailed me up on the weighing scale platform and presented me with the keys to a brand-new Chevy 4×4 pickup hooked to a Ranger bass boat with all the trimmings. "A thirty-six thousand-dollar value," the tournament chief said, looking just sick about it.

Cornered by television cameras and boom microphones, I fielded the first questions while watching Jerry squirm his way through the crowd. When he couldn't get any closer, he frowned for a moment, then gave me the high sign. He lifted his cane up and over the heads and shoulders of the reporters. An envelope was hooked to the rubber tip by a lure. He thrust it within my reach.

I opened it and found a list of product endorsements. Also a plug for the Commandos written by Jerry. Thinking of the mortgage payments and other bills to pay, I rattled off the product names with great enthusiasm.

A somber TV reporter said, "Gar, Turner Network. Where'd you get the seemingly nutty idea to fish the boardwalk and the restaurant dock? It's a place that's congested, noisy, hardly conducive to tournament action. And yet you scored, scored big."

I paused. Here was where Jerry's plug fitted into the Big Picture, but it didn't fit nearly as well into my conscience. I can tell a stretcher when the situation calls for it, but this was different. That old man. I felt I owed him the truth, that old-fashioned bassing had won the day. Yet that wouldn't go down too well with the sponsors. It wouldn't even interest the fishermen, who had come to expect flash and special effects and high technology. A man, a worm and a tip from an old-timer? Who cared about that? There wasn't anything in it that you could sell and buy or that would let you think you, too, could win a big tournament.

I fingered the card. "Commando intelligence had tracked several schools moving out of the sun into deep cover. After that target acquisition, the outcome was no longer in question. Commando mental performance products, Commando simulation software and, as always, the bedrock of Commando training—a grueling physical and mental regimen—won out. I didn't win this tournament; the Commando system did."

Then it was time to go inside the tent for the awards banquet. On all four walls there were wide-screens showing my restaurant performance. It felt funny sitting there, watching myself fish.

"You just don't see stuff like this," I heard the tournament chairman say, tinkling his glass of Jack Daniel's. "Maybe there's something to this talk about putting cameras and all on board."

I put down my ribs and looked across the smoky tent. Folks were smiling as they watched, nudging their neighbors, grunting as yet another silvery bass was boated. The buzz was back in the air, the pall had lifted. I was seeing the future, and it was me.

We decided against a Sunday evening departure—too many long neck-drinking fools on the highway—but our plans to slip away early Monday were upset by a gang of people who spotted us from the motel restaurant windows. There we were, six-thirty in the morning, surrounded by fans waving twenty-dollar bills in our faces, asking for Commando products that didn't exist yet.

Eddie grabbed my elbow in a vise-like grip. "Cecil actually went and *sold* his audiotape!"

"He *what?*" I stared across the parking lot, past the people, the video kiosks, the showroom bass boat mounted on a twenty foot-high revolving table. Cecil was up beside a flasher fishfinder getting his picture taken. "He couldn't be that stupid, Eddie."

We started for him. Before we could get there, a wiry fellow in a blue flotation vest came bounding up, a cassette tape in his fist.

"What the hell's going on? You sold me a blank! I want the fish program. That's what I paid for!"

Cecil stood with his mouth open, eyes vacant.

"Mister, what's your beef?" I asked.

The guy whirled around. He stuck the tape under my nose. "Ain't nothing on it. It's a gyp!"

I took it and examined it. "This is the real thing all right. You wanted a souvenir, that's what you got—a piece of the Commandos."

He puzzled over that. "A blank tape? I wanted that fish program."

"Cec, didn't you *explain* it?" I hollered. Then I looked at the man and laid a hand on his shoulder. "These tapes are set to self-erase upon playing. It's the only way to keep them from falling into . . . other hands."

He stared into my eyes. You could see for miles inside that sunbaked head.

"Tell you what," I smiled. "Cec will autograph this for you. Right, Cec?" And I tossed him the tape. He woke up in time and made an impressive grab with those quick hands of his, plucked a pen out of his shirt pocket, and scribbled a signature. Then he fireballed it back to me.

I gave it to the fellow, who handled it as gently as a robin's egg and said, "God bless you."

13

We made good time and reached the county line at high noon.

Jerry was asleep when I made the turn down the drive and nosed the van toward home. He woke fast when I stabbed the brakes and gave a shout. Eyes still too startled to see, he twisted his head around, while his hands scrabbled frantically over his shirt, patting at his pants pockets, as if looking for something. Finally, he slumped back in his seat.

"Jesus, bub. What's wrong with you?"

"It ain't me. It's the lawn."

"You don't have a lawn. Remember?" He shaded his eyes and peered through the windshield.

At that exact moment there was a whistling sound and a bright crack, accompanied by a wink of white light. A fountain of magenta smoke billowed skyward from the middle of where the lawn had been. Two figures rose up from the red dirt and rushed a rustic palisade of logs topped by barbed wire, then across a deep trench, under planks suspended two feet off the ground, then through a hog wallow.

Semiautomatic weapon fire sputtered out from a long bunker at the back of the property. Two men threw themselves face down in the hog wallow and burrowed in deep, sparing only their weapons from the mud bath.

I looked at Jerry. He looked at me. "Did you make a wrong turn while I was sleeping?" he said.

"Somebody did." Switching off the engine, I hopped out. We made our way toward the house, sniffing the acrid aroma of cordite. Cadres in camouflage thrashed through the woods to our right.

A figure in black, sporting olive-dappled makeup, popped out of the driveway culvert, trained his weapon on us, silently hosed it back and forth, barked "Road kill!" and rolled back down into the ditch.

We pressed on. Trenches, barbed wire, foxholes, pillboxes, sandbagged emplacements—my home was surrounded. Thankfully the path to the porch was clear, even freshly swept, and the primaveras and black-eyed Susans in the rowboat planters were blooming. As Jerry and I reached the top step, we heard a voice hail us from the field.

"Fellas!"

"Virginia Roy," Jerry yelled, laughing. "Is that you playing in the mud?"

She lay on her belly under a knapsack, the only clean thing about her the flash of her white teeth. There was a shrill blast of a whistle. She held her helmet down snug and rose to her knees, then her feet. Staggering under the pack weight, she negotiated a maze of five-foot-high posts.

I felt a presence on the porch and turned. Crisp in a starched blue jumpsuit, Rico Octoponte surveyed his little Camp Lejeune, his Disney Dien Bien Phu, impassive except for a smug waggle of the Creme de Havana in his lips.

"Mr. Foote, I totally admire your wife," he said.

"Yeah, well, just don't admire her too much."

Jerry reared back theatrically. "Whoa, dude. Don't go ballistic on poor Richard here. You know, other women get the urge to

Spring-clean. V.R., she just has to get down and dirty." He laughed and pointed with the cane at his sister scaling the wall of the blockhouse. "Always in the thick of the fray, that girl."

Rico patted my elbow. "It is true, what he says. Never have I had such a student. The way she strips—" He paused to suavely eject a shred of tobacco from his teeth with a thumbnail. "—her weapon. Ah, it gives such pleasure to an old soldier."

Jerry snapped his fingers under Rico's nose. "Got another stogy, Rick?" He kept watching his sister, who was hanging one-armed from the lip of the blockhouse while cocking the other arm to toss a grenade. *Flip* went the grenade. She unslung her shorty M-16. A ominous *thud*—dust and particles went flying off the log wall, dust everywhere except where Virginia Roy clung, dust outlining her body, dust and smoke.

"That was live, wasn't it?"

"That's how she wants it." Rico gave me a troubled look. "Mr. Foote, believe me, I most earnestly desire the women to stay home with the children. But in history there are always exceptions— certain women, chosen by circumstances, who reluctantly pick up arms in the struggle. Let us not denigrate their efforts, nor deny one such woman her destiny."

Jerry snorted. "You're such a feminist, Rico."

She levered herself up to the lip of the blockhouse, tipped the muzzle of her weapon over, and squeezed off a blind burst.

"Firing on auto, too, I see." I cleared my throat. "That's against the law."

Jerry nodded. "Better cool it before we all end up in the hoosegow."

"The more it is uncertain, the better the training." Rico shrugged. "Jail is nothing compared to what they'd face in a real action."

But he reached inside the neck of his jumpsuit and fetched out a whistle on a lanyard. He gave three sharp blasts, then put the whistle back. "How was your weekend?"

"Everything went according to plan." Jerry thumped his cane on the porch. "How's about a drink, boys?" He bumped his way inside.

I waved a hand at the defoliated back yard. "Who arranged all this?"

"My students." Rico caught my surprised look. "Oh, yes, they paid for the privilege, and paid well. First they build the obstacle course, then they destroy it. It is very satisfying to them."

A black woman I knew from town poked her head out of the door. She wore big gold hoop earrings, an LSU T-shirt and blue can't-bust-'ems. "Dinner in a half hour." She paused, nodded to me. "Afternoon, Mr. Foote."

"Hello, Juney. Glad you could lend a hand."

I wasn't about to let on that I wasn't boss of my own homestead. The town already had enough to gossip about.

We ate out back at a pair of picnic tables that had been set up under a canvas fly. Juney put out chicken and gravy, potato salad, succotash, white bread and butter, and pitchers of Kool-Aid and Wyler's iced tea. For a couple of minutes Jerry, Rico and I had the shade to ourselves, before the guests started to trickle up from the long green canvas barrier set up by the pond's wellhead. I had expected a salty bunch of guys, but the way they ambled up — wet behind the ears, hair slicked down, in what probably was their one clean set of camouflage clothes — softened my heart somewhat. One big old boy sweetly volunteered to say grace.

V.R. eyed me worriedly. If she was waiting for me to say something about the yard, I certainly wasn't going to oblige. Surrounded by two such slick talkers as Jerry and Rico, I'd vowed to hold my tongue from now till nevermore.

It was hard, and I was rather glad we weren't alone. The things I wanted to tell her weren't going to make her happy. Nor would I enjoy saying them. I didn't marry V.R. expecting to play the protective husband.

But who else was going to point out that she'd gone too far. That her desire to test herself was being exploited. What complicated everything was that there were *two* of them turning her head. So far, I'd fared poorly going up against either individually, let alone both together. It was a problem, all right. I needed a plan, I needed time, had neither, only the feeling of hanging on for dear life.

Our lunch guests were your basic dog-shotgun-pickup fellows, but the instructors cut wilder figures. In the first place, they couldn't have regular names but called themselves Mota, Kraut, Indio, O'Shaunnessey and Laertes. They looked the part, too. I counted one shiny bald head, two Fu Manchus, a nose stud and one earring, lots of tattoos. They ate and talked among themselves, probably to keep from getting too buddy-buddy with people whose asses they'd be dogging all week.

"Anybody here going to the Soldier of Fortune convention next week?" asked a skinny student, looking pointedly at the instructors. "Going to Las Vegas?"

This proved to be a lucky shot. The bald one with the Fu Manchu grunted. It seemed to be an affirmative-type grunt.

The skinny student glowed with success. He pressed his luck. "They'll be signing up mercs for the contras, I guess."

Mr. Fu Manchu belched. "Nice cherry like you do real well down South. They're real short of women, I hear."

Oh, but this made the boy's day. "All I know is, I'd pay for the chance to pop some caps at the Sandinistas."

"I bet you would."

"So, are you going?" His knee jiggled nervously; he really had lost his cool. "To the convention?"

"Yeah, I'm going to the convention." Fu shoved his chair back and limped down the hill, cursing.

"How about you?" the boy asked V.R.

Jerry boomed, "Gar would never let her go to Las Vegas all by herself." Now he was using his sister to get me to Lake Mead.

V.R. looked over at me. I smiled at her. One thing was for sure. I wasn't going to give Jerry the satisfaction of knowing he'd started a fight between us.

After a sweet potato pie that seemed to sink right through my belly like a pound of lead, it was past time for Gar Foote to nap. I caught V.R.'s eye. "Want to step upstairs for a spell?"

Uneasy smile. "Can't." Jerk of the head at the other instructors, who were leaning back in their folding chairs, clicking Zippos and lighting Tiparillos. "Have to stay alert. But I heard the tournament went real well for you."

"After a brush with disaster, yeah."

"See?" Full smile. Blue-gray eyes dead on, chin lifted slightly.

"See what?"

"It's working out. For both of us."

I looked around me, at the table, the war zone. "You mean this is your regular line of work now?"

"I *warned* you to take better care of the yard," she teased. Her smile softened, and I realized that she was, indeed, happy. "We're just here this once. Rico likes to take his recruits—"

"Recruits?"

"Well, that's what we call them, it's more authentic to *them*, you see." She heard herself getting carried away and paused, slightly breathless and looking at me. She flushed prettily.

I leaned across the table. It was too wide and only our hands could meet.

"All right, everybody," drawled O'Shaunnessey. "Time for a little contest. I want to see everybody's weapon field-stripped in five minutes. Last one done takes a four-mile jog with forty-five-pound pack."

The recruits exploded out of their seats. The table rocked this way and that, knocking glasses of Kool-Aid over. She smiled at me, still holding my hand.

"Hadn't you better go?" When she didn't respond, I said, "Come on, you're making me nervous. You don't want to be the one to have to run, do you?"

"It's worth it." Slowly she rose from her seat, bent forward, kissed me. "Now watch this."

With a sweep of her arm she dumped our paper plates, plastic silverware and cups, napkins and whatnot onto the grass. From under the table she pulled out a folded poncho and spread it open, revealing a folding-stock M-16. She removed the magazine, cleared the action, ejected the chambered round. Then she tore it apart. It was as Rico said: the girl could strip.

It is impossible to nap with small arms fire crackling in your backyard. I lay on the bed and plotted. Told myself: You *did* just win your second tournament. First place finishes are rare; two are rarer still. But two wins so close together is altogether unheard of, and if you just finish respectably in a few more tournaments, then your spot at the Bass Classic will be assured. The other Commandos were within striking distance as well. The time had come to dump Jerry.

He'd nearly wormed his way into the Commandos. I had to admit that his psych-job on the Lake Seminole competitors had been masterful. Another week and it would be too late; the boys would grow accustomed to his sneaky face. I didn't have to wait another week. I could rip his suckers off us tonight, and I would, before he steered the boys too far off the path. Because I knew what he wanted—nothing less than control of the Commandos.

It was doable. Once I claimed my prize and sold it, my share could tide me over well into June. I could now afford the luxury of telling Jerry where he could stuff his Vegas tournament. It sounded cheap and glitzy, like Jerry. It was honky-tonk fishing. To the purist, the Classic was all that mattered. Just to be among the top forty-one would be an honor. And it meant serious income, too.

"Do it now," I said out loud, and sat up on the edge of the bed. Jerry was a bad habit that had to be kicked. I knew it, but the Commandos didn't. They were enjoying the bad-boy glamour. They liked thinking it gave them an edge in competition. But they couldn't see where it would lead. Only I knew the depths to which Jerry could rise, the slimy bottom feeder.

The phone rang.

I stared at it. Incoming. Definitely incoming. Don't pick it up. I picked it up.

"Gar? Charlie Hood. Good news on my end. The legal is coming along nicely. Coke's team and I had a nice meeting. I turned myself inside out for them, made a trip to Atlanta, bought lunch for the whole team at the airport tower restaurant. The bottom line is, they're going to be nice guys."

"That's a first."

"Here's the deal. They'll drop all charges. You'll sign an agreement not to speak out about Coca-Cola, the company or its product. Everybody gets what they want, right?"

"It'll be a pleasure to never speak the name again."

"Right. Now, they originally asked for a two hundred thousand dollar bond, but I've got them down to fifty thousand." He cleared his throat. "I know that sounds like a lot."

"I don't have fifty thousand dollars. I hardly have anything."

"Well, you can raise it with a second mortgage. If we back off now, they'll start playing hardball again. That'll mean months of litigation you can't afford."

"Tell me about it."

"While we're on the subject, I need a check for four thousand from you by Friday. That covers my hours so far, plus the trip to Atlanta."

"Charlie . . ."

"Did I tell you they saw you drinking the product on television after you won your tournament? That helped, believe it or not."

"They were watching?"

"Apparently."

"About your fee. Can you bear with me for a while?"

"Come, come." Charlie ladled the honey into his voice. "With a nice new car and boat, you can't be hurting too bad."

After hanging up, I lay back down on the bed and stared at the ceiling. But the handwriting wasn't on the wall. It was in the checkbook. The pleasure of getting rid of Jerry would have to wait.

A promise is a promise. I was to introduce Rico to the Chamber of Commerce, so that's where I headed the next morning. Jerry had backed out, naturally. But I'd humbled myself by phoning Lucky to make sure he was coming, then further lowered myself by begging him to throw away fifty bucks on an early pledge. Nobody in the Chamber would be fooled, of course, but it would establish a bench mark of sorts.

The Red Lion must've had a convention or a religious meet going on, because it took me five minutes to find a parking space. Rico and I had to hoof it across a half mile of asphalt, then squeeze through a lobby packed with folks. "Strange," I said.

"What's that?" he asked, smiling.

"Haven't seen so many local people here since my high school's twentieth reunion."

Despite the crowd, we found good seats inside the dining room. I ordered up breakfast and, after a long hesitation, substituted iced tea for my usual Coke. I felt unduly sensitive, as if my every move was being watched.

Sure enough, when I surveyed the room I noticed there was a stranger present, fellow in a white shirt, dark tie, blue sport coat with a breast pocket full of colored pens. I caught him staring right at me; he looked away quickly.

That's how I knew. Coke's new man. He'd be expected to join all the local clubs. A new man for the New Coke.

The meeting started with a prayer and the Pledge. Old business, new business, fines. "Gar Foote, the Master of Arms shall collect the five-dollar fine for missing a meeting."

"More!" someone shouted. The president held up his fist, extended one finger. "Ten?" Booing. Two fingers, more boos. All the way up to five fingers and twenty-five dollars.

Wincing, I dug out my wallet and passed the money up to the front.

"And for winning another fish tournament, the Master of Arms shall collect from Gar another five—"

"More!"

And there went twenty-five more dollars. It was starting to hurt, now. These fellows had jobs, they could shell out a few dollars without wondering where the next installment would come from. I couldn't help feeling bitter. They thought it was only funny. The stranger was smiling a tight smile.

Further humiliation awaited; it was time to introduce Rico. I clumped up to the podium and tapped the mike. As I began, I was surprised to see Jerry Roy standing at the back of the room. It touched me. He'd come after all. So I got to feeling better and gave Rico a rave-up he probably didn't deserve—or expect.

Taking my place, he spread his arms wide and gripped the edges of the podium. Then he grinned. Somehow, without him saying a word, we were laughing.

"Friends. Amigos. Mr. Foote has already said enough today to embarrass me and, in his customary modesty, has refrained from saying anything about himself. Allow me to make humble restitution for his gracious hospitality. Normally, my job is to travel around this and other countries soliciting funds for the men and women on the front lines of democracy. I tell my audiences of the heroes of freedom whose names are still unsung. Today, however, I give you a man you know, who himself has fought bare-handed against oppressive forces many times his size." Rico closed his eyes and gripped the podium again. "As you know, he did not win."

His eyes flared wide. "But he has not been defeated. In fact, as you also know, because you love him as your own flesh and blood, this man has gone on to perform impossible feats of an athletic nature.

"Now he has come to his Rubicon. He has debts — as who does not? — and he has no other job. Caution tells us he must put away childish things. Reason tells us he must leave this lovely town in search of a job.

"But what does the heart, *el corazon*, say?" Rico thumped his chest twice, then raised his fist slowly up as if it held the organ itself, pumping away.

"Doesn't the heart say this must not be? That this shall not come to pass? Doesn't the heart say no, it would rather die than be defeated again?

"Here is Gar's heart." He shook his fist at the crowd, his beard jutting out. Then he swung his arm in a wide arc until it was pointing at the wall behind him. "*There* is the hope that can save this man's heart." He looked down at the podium and read off a three-by-five card. "The first Monster Bass Shootout in Las Vegas, Nevada. A totally unique event that Gar and his friends the famous Bass Commandos can enter as a team and win five hundred thousand dollars. That's right. Half a million. I must confess, I do not know one thing about catching these fishes, but tomorrow I will begin to learn, yes?"

That drew a good laugh. I just sat there, wondering when the fox would emerge from the underbrush and make his move.

"But somebody here today does know more — a man who you all know. He is returned from a long stay down in Honduras and Costa Rica where he performed valorously in the service of your government." Rico paused to sweep the crowd with a stern glance, quelling any would-be spoilers. "I give you Jerry Roy."

Now this was interesting. Jerry gimped up to the podium, shook Rico's hand and turned to the crowd.

"Televised bass fishing," he said, leaning heavily on his cane.

"The first-ever to go live, the first to use a prepared patch of water. It's the start, make no mistake, of the sport of the future. And there's one man and one team who's gonna bring this tournament to its knees—Gar Foote and the Bass Commandos."

Well, I was sitting in shock. As Jerry Roy was talking, Rico had reached up to the presentation easel behind the podium and flipped over the covering sheet of paper, revealing a sign which read:

LIMITED OFFERING SHARES
BASS COMMANDOS, INC.
PRESIDENT GAR FOOTE,
CHAIRMAN JERRY ROY

"Now here is something I bet you never knew," Jerry said after the murmuring died down. "Any company can offer insider shares in the state in which it is incorporated without going through any federal folderol. They're only redeemable upon the company's sale or liquidation. You can't trade 'em or tell the board of directors, the Commandos, what to do. What we're proposing today is to sell a limited number of these shares to the community, to let Valhalla show the world that it has the best *damn* fishermen anywhere, anytime, anyplace. Let's send Gar and the Commandos to Las Vegas next week. *Whad'ya say?*" He raised both hands in the referee's traditional touchdown sign.

One man clapped; then ten clapped in rhythm. The entire room applauded, whistled, stomped. Silverware jumped around on the tables.

Rico stepped up to the mike with a sheaf of paper. He held the first sheet aloft. "What am I bid for share number one?"

"Fifty dollars!" Lucky popped up, waving a hand. I closed my eyes to keep from laughing at my old friend's faux pas, but I ended up keeping them closed—they'd filled with sudden tears at Lucky's blind loyalty. It was just like the noble Cajun.

The room of Chamberites loved this. They wouldn't let go of that first share. Up it went, dollar by dollar, then by fives, tens.

A dark, commanding voice cut through the hubbub. "*One thousand and one dollars.*"

I turned. Villis Green was on his feet at the back of the room, holding his sunglasses over his belly in both hands. He saw me looking and nodded to me once. In the hush everybody was thinking the same thought: When was the last time Villis did anything without a profit in mind?

"Sold! Now . . . share number two."

Rico knew his business. The shares moved briskly and sold out in less than forty-five minutes. None of the rest went for more than two hundred dollars, but not too many sold for below a hundred, either. Everybody was buying: friends, acquaintances, people I hadn't spoken to in a year. Lucky's customers were falling over themselves to get a piece of their favorite realtor. It was an altogether humbling experience, to be clutched to the bosom of my community with scant hope or means of ever repaying them for their kindness. It was hard to abandon that prickly armor of pride each of us carries around him, the belief that we are self-sufficient, beholden to no one and no thing.

But this was bigger than just me. These folks were rallying around the idea of themselves, their way of life. I think they saw what happened to me as a test case — the real world getting its foot in the door. There are none of us self-sufficient anymore; no community is safe from the dangers outside. What happened to me could happen to them.

Instead of cutting me loose as a poor investment, Valhalla was raising me up as its standard-bearer. In the eyes of my community, I was no longer Gar Foote, the Coca-Cola man; I was the soul of an entire town sent to do battle. There was no chance for me to say no. With Rico's help, Jerry Roy had done it again.

Valhalla versus Las Vegas. On live television. Tell the world.

14

The morning we staged the boats to the hauling company that would truck them to Nevada, V.R. and I sat in the van waiting our turn. It was just daybreak. The rest of the Commandos were hitching up around us in the parking lot; Yvonne was teaching Trank videocam operation; Lucky's daughters were packing up their musical instruments after serenading us with a pretty collection of Cajun tunes.

A sweet sort of sweat came over me. V.R. smiled. "Nervous, honey?"

"Yeah. But I wouldn't trade places with nobody, not now."

She slipped her arm around my neck. "Me neither."

Jerry came out of the freight office. He'd talked them into donating the trucks; we only had to pay the drivers.

"I don't know how he does it." I said, "Look—" I pointed. Behind one eighteen-wheeler, Diane Bonnard and Eddie were breaking off a long kiss. "Cute."

"He's more than twice her age," she said.

"But he's been lonely since Adele took the kid."

"Then he should've paid more attention to her when she was his. Instead of playing Romeo Rooter."

"Is that what they call him around town?"

She nodded and put us in gear.

"One second," I said. She touched the brakes. "Thank you for agreeing to this."

She half turned with a surprised smile. "Don't thank me. I'm happy to be going to the SOF convention. Thank your buddies. They're the ones giving up their vacations and their paychecks."

"Yeah. They're good buddies." I thought of Eddie ceremoniously taking out his Roto-Rooter beeper and tossing it in the training pond—a gesture no woman could understand.

She looked down at her lap. "I guess that's love for you." A quick cat grin crossed her lips.

"What?"

"Oh, just remembering. This is kinda how our honeymoon was supposed to be."

Once V.R. brought it up, of course, there was no escaping the memory of *that* charming fiasco. We'd been driving and weeping and fighting and falling stony silent for three days since V.R. left the hospital. She kept saying I was off the hook, and I kept begging her to marry me anyway. Then she called a friend in Valhalla.

When she came walking back from the drugstore phone, I knew something had changed. "We're getting married," she said, simply.

"Well, of course we are."

She glanced at me. "The police have been sniffing around the house."

I winced. "Uh-oh." Jerry had chosen our final tournament site carefully, on a lake that straddled three separate town jurisdictions. It'd been fairly easy for me to creep away while the three sheriffs sorted themselves out. I'd followed V.R. to the hospital, and had even congratulated myself on getting her discharged without attracting any attention.

"Let's find the courthouse."

"Here?"

"If we're married to each other, we can't be made to testify against each other," she explained, talking extra slow, the way you would to a retard.

"But what about the wedding that's set for Valhalla?"

"We can go ahead with it, if you like."

"Well, it's supposed to be for *you*," I retorted.

"Every girl's dream," she said. "Who cares?"

"I do. I loved you before. I love you now."

She began to cry then, as she stood in that drugstore, in a strange town, in front of strangers, her wrist still sporting a hospital bracelet.

She put on a lacey blouse and a flowered skirt, her face all puffy, her breasts the color of ripe peaches, all swollen for the life that would never be. We drove to a local Justice of the Peace. For a witness we had a strawhatted geezer yanked away from a traffic violation trial next door to the JP's, and given half a dollar for his trouble. Jerry had flown the coop, by then, naturally. And after the wedding, we drove into Valhalla and the arms of the law. There was no honeymoon, unless you count the hours we spent in the sheriff's office trying to explain the absolute disappearance of all our financial records, our prize money and our partner, Jerry Roy. The funny thing was, they knew about our scheduled wedding and were quite solicitous about it. I even remember being offered a choice of serving alternate weekends, starting the one after we were supposedly going to be hitched. But, as it turned out, we never had to bring out the certificate; Jerry Roy's absence explained everything.

I looked at her, now, and realized that after all these years she'd actually gotten over it. She was sitting there, just smiling at the memory. I had to smile, too, finally.

. . .

Landing in Las Vegas in the middle of the night after a long flight, we formed ourselves a fast taxi caravan and plunged into that carnival city of pulsing electrical displays that hung in the air without visible means of support. Maybe there were buildings there, I don't know. To me we seemed to have entered the liquid crystal heart of the world's largest fishfinder. There were no boundaries, no right angles. Everywhere colored lights waved and bounced and doppled. My eyes couldn't take it in, my head swam.

"Silver Stirrup's a nice place," our driver said. He'd already introduced himself as a member of the Mormon faith and a graduate of Brigham Young University.

"You must meet some interesting people in this job," I said.

He twisted around and looked at me. He wore dark glasses, the old-fashioned Ray Ban kind, despite or perhaps because of the neon waterfalls cascading around us.

"This isn't a job. This is my ministry." He smiled humorlessly. "Most people don't give me a second glance on their way in. I do my best work on the way out of town."

The Silver Stirrup was on the outer limits of the city. This pleased me, actually. I had no doubts of my ability to focus on the fishing, but I couldn't be so sure of the other Commandos. While Lucky was solid as ever, Eddie and Cecil had both shown signs of feeling the pressure.

Eddie and Cecil were talking about the attractions of Vegas. "All night action. Slots, Keno. The Mustang Ranch," Eddie said. "Got to see if making it legal takes the fun out of fallen women. And you're coming with me, Cec."

Cec cast an embarrassed glance in V.R.'s direction. "Probably not, Eddie. That's not my idea of fun."

"What is your idea of fun, exactly?"

Cecil said, "I'd like to shoot a machine gun." He saw Eddie's double take. "Well, as long as we're in Las Vegas, I thought I'd spend some time at the convention."

Cecil pointed at the Silver Stirrup's marquee.

GREETINGS SOLDIERS OF FORTUNE
CONVENTION ENJOY YOUR STAY
WE SALUTE YOU
LOCAL CHAPTER NATIONAL
RIFLE ASSOCIATION

The Stirrup looked like a twenty-story cowboy boot, with the office in the heel and the low-roofed restaurant occupying the toe. The taxi stopped. I paid the Mormon driver his thirty dollars. He looked at my camouflage suit and up at the marquee. "One of them, huh?"

I pretended to be busy with the baggage. The Mormon watched the others getting out of their taxis. He turned to me and thoughtfully removed his Ray Bans. I flinched; his eyes were pink.

"Don't worry," he said, with a laugh. "I'm a downwind baby."

"Downwind what?"

He put the glasses back on. "The nuke tests. You'd be surprised at how many of us there are."

"Uh-huh. Well, see you."

"Here's my card. Remember: I can take you home by way of heaven."

We checked in. V.R. and I said our good-nights in the lobby, half asleep on our feet, and took an elevator up to our floor. Our room had a terrace overlooking the desert to the south, where Lake Mead lay. I shoved the sliding glass door open and shut off the air conditioning.

"Smell that."

Desert air rushed in, warm but drier than the wet cotton we breathe in Valhalla. V.R. came up beside me.

"Smell what?" she asked. "There's no smell at all."

"You know why? There's no mud. Can you imagine a Mississippi Spring night without the smell of mud?"

"No." She gave my shoulder a shove. "But that doesn't mean we can't wallow over here on the bed."

We lay in the dark on top of the covers, dizzy with traveling, but not too tired for a little light messing around.

"Let's see," she said. "Have we ever stayed this high up in a hotel before?"

"Fourteen floors up. It's gotta be a record," I said.

"That one in Atlanta, we were on six. Right?"

"And the rest were motels." As I said it, I wished I could take it back. The motels belonged to the doomed bass circuit of years back.

She hummed a bar of something and sang:

Who knows . . . that to-morrow may find me-e-e-e . . . in some hole in the ground.

"What's that? A song?" I laughed nervously. "Cheerful."

"It's pretty," she said, sounding defensive. "A soldier's ballad."

"No soldier I ever knew would sing a pretty song."

She laid a hand on my belly. "It's hard to remember, sometimes, that you were ever in the army."

"That's no loss."

"I wasn't very . . . much help to you, when you came back. Because I didn't understand then what I do now."

This conversation was making me itchy. I sighed. "You mean how I really wanted to go loco and shoot a whole bunch of folks at some mall?"

She didn't say anything, but from the way her hand jerked on my belly I knew I'd hurt her feelings—as usual whenever I tried to get smart.

"Sorry," I said. "I guess I'm tired of hearing about these television vets, these talk show types."

"You're just afraid to admit you do have some unfinished business."

I held my tongue. As the Lord is my witness, I held it until it rattled. "Oh?"

She rolled over on top of me, pinning me with her arms and pressing her forehead on mine. I could see the whites of her eyes, wide and fierce.

"Listen," she hissed. "You don't have to tell me about it. It's your private thing. But let me tell you about it, about how I remember you when you first got home. The first thing you did was take a skiff out in the lake and fish. I watched you sitting there, shoulders stiff and hunched up peculiar, baseball cap on your head, staring down where your line dropped straight into the depths. You didn't catch anything; you didn't seem to want to. After a week, it was like you woke up — you started to try casting and different lures and so on. A week later and you were a demon, absolutely possessed. Too intense. I had to stop watching. Now I think I know what you were feeling. It was like there was a big hole in your life and then along came this passion you could pour into everything. You couldn't relax a moment until that hole was filled, until it was a memory, till you'd burned grooves into your fingertips and blistered your hands and sweated out every last drop of that dead feeling." Her face rose an inch; her teeth shone. "A dead feeling — like the one in me that I just got to get rid of."

"Gar!"

Zeeeeeeeee. I peered through a crust of sleep. No reason to get excited. *Zeeeeeee.*

"Gar! Wake up! Somebody's trying to break in!"

Lurching upright in bed, I looked at the door.

"The balcony," she whispered, clutching a pillow over her belly and a room service menu over her breasts, while trying to clamp a phone receiver between her jaw and bare freckled shoulder.

I followed her eyes. A thin black line was swaying slowly back and forth across the terrace, twitching now and then. Suddenly it snapped taut. A black figure dropped from the sky, feet tucked, then using them as shock absorbers when he swung into our terrace railing and paused.

He wore a black Balaclava down over his face, black bodysuit, gloves, black sneakers. A black web belt was crammed with pouches and metal rings yet he seemed weightless. Our eyes met. *Zeeeeeeeeeeeeee*. Down he went, out of sight.

"What in the hell?"

We ran to the railing, covering ourselves with sheets. Trailing all over the hotel like vines were long, black lines and over a dozen rappelling figures, some above us, more below. Other guests were on their balconies. Across the parking lot, movement atop another hotel tower caught my eye. As I pointed, a triangular drogue chute blossomed against the face of the tower, another, and another: men parasailing off the twenty-story building in close formation. As they spiraled down to the parking lot, a knot of men burst out of God knows where and raced over the tarmac. They stopped and set off a fierce clatter accompanied by firecracker-red flashes far below . . . automatic weapons. Two loud pops, a shockwave. Black smoke swallowed the men on the ground. The parasailers went into a long glide out across the field, firing their own weapons, and landed at a dead run.

I winced at a high-pitched squawk from a public address system and looked at V.R. Her bare shoulders were dimpled with chickenskin, but it wasn't at all cold out. Though the desert floor rippled with golden light streaked by the city's shadows, she only had eyes for the show downstairs.

"Gar! Virginia Roy! Over here!"

I spotted them, two men in jockey briefs and black socks, several balconies to our left. Cecil and Eddie. We waved, made a date for breakfast and went back in and pulled the drapes. Good morning, Las Vegas.

. . .

Jerry rubbed his knee briskly, as if putting a Sunday school shine on it.

"Every move we make from here on is tightly choreographed, got it?"

He pushed himself out of his chair, hands smoothing down his gold herringbone sport coat. He paused to perch a pair of dark glasses on top of his head and admire himself in the suite's full-length, three-panel mirror. Satisfied, he grunted and snapped the dark glasses down over his eyes.

"Trank down there with the camera?" he asked. "Okay, the limo's at the door. Let me look at you guys."

We formed a ragged line and he walked it, strutting like a brigadier.

"Cecil, your belt missed a loop in back. Eddie, you look very crisp." He reached out and ran a finger along the crease of Eddie's sleeve. His other hand unsheathed Eddie's Buck fishknife. "Too crisp."

Slash. The sleeve hung off Eddie's rock-hard bicep. Eddie stood stock-still, veins bulging. *Slash.* A triangular patch, including a breast pocket, fell like a flap, exposing a slabby pectoral muscle and an indented nipple ringed by black curly hair. Jerry handed Eddie back his knife with a curt nod.

"Do your own leg, below the knee," he said.

Jerry moved on to Lucky and paused. "Consider getting a Mohawk. Don't answer. Think on it." He gave me a cursory glance. "Let's hit it, gang. Act One, The Bass Commandos do Vegas."

We observed recon rules—silence, hand signals—down the long carpeted hall and onto the elevator for the endless ride. As we stopped at floor after floor, more and more people got on. The first bunch was elderly, next were honeymooners. The stares were gratifying. On the seventh floor though, the doors opened on a hall filled with men in camouflage. They stared at us. We stared at them. They nodded at us, we nodded back. A couple of them squeezed in, excusing themselves politely. The doors closed.

"Hey," said one to Cecil. "Where you from?"

Cecil appealed to Jerry, who nodded. Cecil turned back to the man. "Valhalla."

"No shit." He glanced at the elderly couple. "Pardon me." He squinted back at Cecil and softly said, ""Where the fuck's that?"

"Mississippi. How about you?"

"The Aryan Nation, man. What ZOG calls Idaho. Terminator City for mongrel Communists." He jerked his head around and glared at the honeymooners as if they'd contradicted him. The bride blushed and looked down at her bare knees. "Having a nice time?" he asked loudly.

The groom gave a slow, toothy grin and nodded. "You bet."

"I bet, too." Mr. Aryan tugged on his earlobe, which had a rude cross crudely tattooed into it. "That's a joke. This is Vegas. You said you bet, I said I bet. Get it?"

"That's pretty good," the groom said, carefully.

"Are you Jewish?"

"Yes, actually." For the first time, the groom lost his smile. But his nerve didn't desert him. "Why, are you?"

The elevator shuddered to a halt on the lobby level and everyone stepped off and scattered.

We piled into a white stretch limousine out front. Jerry removed his dark glasses and surveyed our blank faces.

"Shake it off. This town has its share of creeps. That's all there is to it."

The limo slid away.

The Monster Bass Hospitality Pavilion had been set up in the lobby of one of the smaller casinos. A swarm of swimsuit queens greeted us curbside, and a camera crew bored in behind them, shooting through the bare bellies and jiggling boobs that seemed to engulf us. We burst past the first circle and ran the gauntlet. As we entered, a blare of music greeted us, and the MC's voice boomed through the loudspeaker: "You can swim but you can't hide. They know where to go. You can't fight, don't even try. Here come the Bass Commandos!"

Jerry caught my eye and gave me the high sign. This was it, he seemed to be saying. We've really arrived. As I looked about me, I thought he might well be right. Dead center on a semitractor-trailer flatbed done up in red and blue bunting was a gigantic bass carved out of ice, forty feet long and ten high, a neon treble hook flashing on and off in front of its pugnacious nose. To the left was a stage with cranes and light standards hovering over it. On the main stage were three separate little islands of furniture and potted plants, each isle with its own inhabitants. To the right was the MC on his own separate platform, surrounded by banners of the various boat manufacturers and sponsors. Eddie pointed up to the ceiling. Hanging from a steel hook was a clear glass globe filled with bricks of hundred dollar bills, and a banner that read: $500,000 GRAND PRIZE $500,000 TEAM PRIZE.

There were security guards in every corner of the room. Babes in bass costumes circulated, shaking flippers. Flashbulbs popped; television lamps bathed broadcast-handsome faces in intense light. The fishermen themselves seemed rather underdressed in this sea of tuxedos and sequined swimsuits.

Eddie gave me a clenched fist. We clapped our hands in unison, once. Stomped the floor with our combat boots in 4-4 time, then upped the speed, chanting, "Huh!" Legs spread slightly, hands locked behind our backs, eyes front.

Having first given way, the crowd now pressed close. Eddie's right arm flew to Cecil's shoulder, Cec's right flew straight out to touch Lucky, who did the same to me.

"Yo, give and go, lock and load," Cec sang.

Our left arms thumped diagonally across our chests. "Huh!"

"Commannnn—do! Your left, your right, your left . . . We marched in place to Cecil's cadence. "For-wardddd ho!"

Four abreast, we advanced on the packed crowd. It was touch

and go for an instant. They almost panicked, and a stampede would not have been pretty. But a path cleared to the stage and we marched into the massed floodlights of every major television network in America, chanting in unison.

"Who will go where no one goes?
        Commandos!
Who's a friend when all are foes?
        Commandos!
Who fishes to win and not for show?"
        Commandos! Commandos! Commandos!"

Later, back in Jerry's suite, we settled back to enjoy our performance on tape.

"God, here it comes again . . . wait, slow it down, dammit, Cec."

"Look at their faces!"

"Slow it down!"

"Back it up! I got to see that Hollywood reporter get that poleaxed look. Come on, Cec, one more time. Yeah."

"Here it is, here it is. Stop. Give me that thing, Cec. Think you never saw a TV before, can't even get the hang of a G.D. remote control—"

"Back it up! There!"

"Here it is. Look, she's perfect. Check it out. She's doing Lucky. *Shhhh.*"

". . . Mr. Bonnard, I understand you are quite a student of this wily fish. Tell me, what does the bass make of all this attention, the electronic equipment that looks like something out of Star Wars, the incredibly fast boats. What's a poor bass to do, that's what I want to know?"

"Here it comes!"

"*Shhh!*"

". . . no doubt it's an unfair contest. We're no match for this heavily-armored submarine dreadnought. The bass, ma'am, is the *Red October* of fish. All that equipment you see hanging off our boats just helps to level the playing field."

"Here it comes . . ."

"Speaking of equipment hanging off things, Mr. Ed Bucci. You seem to have had a run-in on the way here. Ah, your 'look' is quite fashion-forward for this kind of crowd, isn't it?"

"Look at her. Definitely hot for your bod, Eddie."

"Look at that tongue! The way she's licking her lips — looking straight at that rip over your titty."

"Hot. Definitely hot."

"*Shhh.*"

". . . Gettin' through that crowd of wimmen was rougher than anything I faced outside the wire in Vietnam. Jeez, somebody ought to feed them once in a while."

"Hooeee!" We roared ourselves silly for the third time.

"Enough," Jerry said. "Why don't you all get lunch poolside while you can, then assemble here at oh-thirteen hundred for our skull session."

The boys trooped out in short order, leaving me behind. After the door closed, Jerry sank into a chair and splayed out his long legs. He stared at the silently running television replay, then grunted.

"Trank's a good cameraman."

"You're an expert at that, too?" I said.

"Have to be. Leave nothing to chance. Especially the image you project."

The telephone rang. Jerry picked it up. "Roy . . . Uh-huh. Right. Be pleased to discuss it. No, not at liberty to disclose that. It varies . . . Okay."

While he talked, I watched the silent screen. A commotion was convulsing the crowd at the Hospitality Pavilion and Trank was running out his cartridge filming it. People were pushing Trank, the picture was jittery. The tape went black.

"—it isn't that we don't support charities such as your own, Reverend, it's just that we can't possibly accept every invitation we get or else we'd never have time to fish. Yes, I understand, Olivia Newton-John is a perfect choice for a co-host. No. No. Let me say it again: The Commandos are not modern dancers. Okay? But I'll consider it, Reverend." He hung up and puffed out his cheeks. "Where were we?"

"Something about fishing, I believe."

"Well, tournament's tomorrow. Got any ideas?"

"We've got the best equipment snake oil can provide. This here Lake Mead is a tough nut, for sure, but that's nothing new."

"Ever fished in front of this big an audience before?" Jerry reached into his jacket for a cigar. "I don't worry about you. But are your boys tough enough?"

"Plenty. Though we're all curious about this 'next level' you've been talking about."

"Well, it's not like last tournament. That was a one-time backwoods deal. If we tried a psych-job like that here, we'd be lucky to catch the next bus out of town. You saw some of the names up there, right? All the big boys. Real tournament fishermen. Hell, you got half your Bass Classic winners here. So much for your talk of purity and class. Money talks, bullshit walks."

"Okay, okay. I'll admit I was wrong, if that will help us win this tournament."

Jerry smiled. "I don't think there's any way you can win this tournament."

I couldn't have heard him right. "Come again?"

"You guys are out of your league. This is a top-heavy field." He wasn't even bothering to look at me as he spoke. He twirled the unlit cigar between his fingers and stared out the window of his hundred and fifty-eight dollar suite, paid for by the good people of Valhalla.

"Excuse my ignorance, but why are we here then?"

"Marketing. The team thing is new to fishing. Let me tell you, the TV producers I talked to were going crazy at the thought of showing six hours of a bunch of rednecks fishing. They don't know fishing; they just know good TV, and that don't cut it. So we got to discussing what would liven up the show. And guess whose names came up?"

"The Commandos."

"Correct. It doesn't really matter if you guys catch fish. What does matter is that the camera has something guaranteed to be interesting to cut away to when folks have had enough of watching some guy spit tobacco juice in a pail while jerking off a fiberglass stick. Don't think fishing, think visual impact."

I felt the wallpaper, the light fixtures, the very oxygen in the room — everything — sag, and then come down on my shoulders. Jerry Roy had done it again.

"I think you underestimate us," I said.

He pretended to misunderstand. "Oh, no. Today's press conference went right off the charts. You guys are a wonderful bunch of entertainers."

"What exactly do you have in mind? We take our fishing pretty seriously."

"Let's save it until the others are here." He stood up and limped over to the complimentary fruit and champagne basket on the dresser, picked up the remote control and zapped the television. The regular channel came on and guess whose pout was puckered up against a cold, sweating can of Pepsi? The Anti-Coke, the he-she with the swivel hips and lustrous black tresses, plucked eyebrows and hairless chest.

"Now *there's* an entertainer," Jerry said.

In the lobby a crowd of conventioneers bobbed and surged around me like an olive-brown sea. Yet it didn't feel the same as being in the Army; nobody wore any insignia, nobody was in charge. These were bodies milling about, men with fantasies, men without leaders. And some weren't even men.

I couldn't locate V.R. It was my own fault for agreeing to stay here, at the same hotel where the Soldiers of Fortune Convention was bivouacked. At the time, it seemed like an even trade, my tournament for her convention. Now, I had my doubts.

I did manage to get my hands on a convention program and step outside to read it in the peace of the parking lot. But here again, a crowd of camouflaged conventioneers had taken over. In the center of a wide circle of spectators was a monster Ford truck, its high-lifter hydraulics fully extended so that the chassis floated high above the eight-foot tall knobby tires. No big deal, I thought, even after I saw the fellow trying to pull the Monster Ford by a rope held in his teeth.

"I can take it. Hurry up and pull!" shouted a man lying on the ground with the front tire of the Ford resting on his chest. "Do it!"

Gutty little guy. I walked around to the pool, reading the program. There were manufacturer seminars on scores of weapons, everything from "Plastic Pistols" to "Sound Suppressors," and a panel on "Night Vision Systems."

A thump and a grunt of pain. I looked up in time to see a body splash, fully clothed, into the pool. Above the water, on a thin beam that spanned the pool's width, was a large man holding a quarterstaff, ends tipped with large foam balls. "Who's next?" he bellowed at a knot of men, openly gloating.

Cecil stepped forward. Before he could get into real trouble, I made a megaphone of the program. "Form up, Commandos. On the double!"

The boys reacted instantaneously, lining up and staring in my direction, obedient as bird dogs. Unfortunately, so did pretty much all the other hundred or so men in fatigues or camo, as well as a couple dozen in swim trunks hanging around the pool. They all snapped to attention, or something close to it, and every last one of them stared straight at me.

The giant with the staff broke the silence. "Who're you to give orders to me?"

"Sorry. Have to muster up the Valhalla Commandos. Every-body else, carry on."

I led the boys to a table under a palm tree. "Let's not forget why we're here, okay?" Cec frowned, but he didn't speak.

There was a roar. Out on the balance beam, a new king of the quarterstaves trumpeted his challenge. Cec shook his head.

"See? That could've been me."

I checked the time: it was running out. Let them find out about Jerry's new plans in the strategy meeting.

I shepherded the guys upstairs and into the suite where Jerry was waiting. First we would make our reports. Lucky was first up with a bassologist's overview.

"Lake Mead is an extremely deep and clear impoundment of the Colorado River created by Hoover Dam. Unlike most of the water where we've been fishing, it has no tree or brush on its steep walls and banks, relatively little weed on top, no bottom structure, and almost no feeder currents. In sum: twitchy bass at maximum depths make this a tough nut to crack. For the Monster Bass Shootout, however, twenty fish structures were installed two months ago in a vertical position. Starting at thirty feet, going as deep as a hundred, the structures look like tall, bare trees, upside down. Fish scientists call them 'Christmas trees' on account of all the colorful blips that show up like ornaments on their branches during a sonar scan. Each blip, of course, equals one fish."

Lucky took his bows and yielded the floor to me. I tapped my ladder chart.

"The Monster Bass Shootout is a departure from a typical tournament in ways other than fish structure. On Day One the field of one hundred twenty-five anglers will fish whatever Christmas trees they please. Then the field will be trimmed down to sixty individuals, including the top five four-man teams. On Day Two these individuals will fish assigned trees and rotate every hour or two—three men to each tree, a unique face-off.'"

Jerry spoke up: "Do I have to add that this is potential TV dynamite?"

"We'll be under intense pressure here. And that's before we consider the audience factor. Jerry?"

He swung around to face the boys. "Each hole can accommodate up to three anchored bleacher barges, as well as two VIP pontoon boats for celebrities and members of the press. I understand Wayne Newton has reserved an entire boat for the first day."

Cecil whistled. "Never fished before no celebrity before."

Eddie raised a hand. "Won't all this spook the fish?"

"That's why they chose this lake. These fish are so deep, applause won't carry."

I kept waiting for him to tell the boys what he'd told me, but Jerry held his tongue. Finally, after we'd heard from Crankmaster Cecil and Drill Sergeant Eddie, Jerry took the floor. He dragged over a cardboard shipping carton, took out a padded envelope and gently removed a multi-hued and segmented metal-flake minnow, with an extra long lip jutting out.

"This is one of the latest deep-diving lures from the laboratory of a major manufacturer. We're getting first crack at them. That's all we'll need for Day One."

"That's all?" asked Cecil.

"We don't need gimmicks to win," I said. Cecil shot me a look.

Jerry reached deeper into the carton. "On Day Two, we hit them with the heavy artillery." He winked at Cecil. "Got to have something in reserve, right?" The box he brought out was sealed with orange duct tape. "The contents of this are so special you won't believe it. No one will believe it. It's your ace in the hole. All I can tell you is it involves a two eighty-six microprocessor. It'll leave the biggest bass weak with desire."

Signs of approval floated around the room. I couldn't figure Jerry out, though; one moment telling me we were outclassed, the next proffering secret weapons of this caliber. This new lure had to

be something on the order of the world's first computerized lure.
He couldn't have located that in the last hour.

I reached out for the sealed box, eager for a peek inside. Jerry
shook his head no.

"The deal with the company on this is that we unveil it on
camera."

"Seems like of risky, right out of the box. What if it doesn't
work?" I frowned.

"It'll work. I've seen it. But we only get to use it if we do it their
way."

Nobody argued with that, which bothered me, but I had to let it
slide in the interests of solidarity. The meeting adjourned. We
filed out together and waited for the elevator to our rooms. I
cracked a joke to break the tension:

"Does it seem like the only one not catching fish here is living
highest on the hog?"

Eddie grunted agreement.

"I think he's worth it." Lucky rode out my surprised look. "He's
coming through with the equipment. And he's dealing with the real
world stuff none of us wants to touch—yourself included, Gar."

"You got me there." When your most main man sends a signal
that strong, you respect it. I'd lay off knocking Jerry Roy tonight.

Besides, I had V.R. to worry about. All I knew was that she
and Rico were out in the desert with ten thousand desperados at a
place called the Bush Facility. I headed out there on a shuttle bus.
The bus was pleasantly empty, except for a talkative group of
Georgians. One slightly-built fellow was explaining to the others:
"I'm a collector of Eastern Bloc arms. This is where I meet with all
my best dealers at one time, buy them drinks, break bread with
them."

Stroking a walrus mustache, a portly passenger shifted his
weight. "I'm a salesman. To effectively market our new lines of
ammunition, I have to know what's happening on the cutting edge.
And these men here are the industry trend-setters."

Trim and athletic in a shiny Mylar running suit, a graying crew-cut father patted his son's Mohawk haircut. "We just can't get our fill of all the guns. And then there's the chance to rub shoulders with the world's great adventurers." He gave the Mohawk a fast knuckle burn. "Though Bill Jr., here, really likes looking for the baddies."

His son beamed a look of love into his father's face, and I felt a pang of envy.

This bus ride in daylight was my first serious look at the town. The late afternoon sun slanted through the side streets, ricocheting in an arcade of mirror glass and temporarily comatose neon displays. Then we were in a outlying block of trailer courts and, after that, islands of convenience stores surrounded by hard packed dirt. Just as some real desert began, we arrived at the Bush Facility.

I coughed up the six-dollar admission, and just stood there. I had thought the Monster Bass Pavilion was something else, but this Soldier of Fortune Convention Center was another country. First, the entrances were obscured in banana leaves and palm fronds. Camouflage netting covered the outer walls. A pair of quad 20-mm AA guns flanked the main door, along with a SAM-7 ground-to-air missile on a pedestal. And that was just the outside.

Inside, you walked into deepest rain forest. Right there stood a big Asian elephant with saddlebags strapped on its sides. First I thought it was a mock-up. Then its trunk curled up and scratched an ear, and I realized it was a clever robot, probably on loan from Disneyland.

It took a half-step, and I saw the chain running from its foot to a steel clamp set in concrete. That elephant was *real*.

Lashed over the saddlebags were rocket launchers for those 137-mm NVA specials that used to whoosh in on us at Cam Ranh now and then. Crouching in the foliage nearby were NVA regulars. Actually, they were dummies from department stores, with slanted eyes painted on. They were pointing into the air; I looked up and saw, suspended on a wire, a two and half ton bomb, and above that, hanging from the ceiling, a model of a B-52. Talk about detail!

After that little scene, I passed into a more-or-less normal convention hall, if maybe a bit louder than usual, and smokier. There was an immense indoor area hung with barrage balloons, and to the back an even larger outdoor section under canvas roofing.

The site was a rabbit warren of high earthen banks, bunkers, trenches, spider holes and refreshment stands. Lines of adventurers, waiting their turn to run the various courses, passed the time by watching the action inside on video monitors. The hazy air popped and hammered with firing weapons; I could taste cordite. Moving quickly, I dropped in on the Machine Gun Bar. Sheets of fire, gobbets of flame, geysers of smoke downrange, blizzards of empties glittering in the sun. Old guns and new clattered in joyous unrestraint. But no V.R.

There was no MANO to be found in the program, either. I cursed Rico out for a big-talking no-account who didn't even have the wherewithal to open a booth. Then I checked out some attractions: "Bunker Busting," "Nest of Snipers," "House Calls, a one-man course in house assault," "Charlie Mike, a goal-oriented game of attrition for teams. Object: continue the mission despite losses and against mounting odds."

A crowd of bodies around a row of card tables caught my eye. A sign floated above, obscured by heads and shoulders. FRIENDSHIP FOR was all I could make out. Pushing closer, I spotted V.R. through a gap. She was sitting behind the table, handing out packets with one hand, waving a clipboard with the other. I got in line and waited my turn.

"Hi there."

She didn't look up. "What's your pleasure, soldier?" She gestured at the piles of pamphlets under signs labeled Afghanistan, Angola, El Salvador, Guatamala, Honduras/Nicaragua, Philippines, South Africa, Other. "If you can't make up your mind about which Friendship Force you'd care to join, there's an evening briefing at the Silver Stirrup at 8:30 P.M. tomorrow night."

I tapped her wrist. Her head snapped back and for an instant I saw her fighting side. But as soon as she recognized me, she patted an empty chair. "Come around and sit with me."

"You look busy enough as it is," I said, feeling the crowd of mercenaries pressing at my back. "Can I take a brochure?"

She reached out, paused, selected Honduras/Nicaragua and El Salvador. "I worked on these. Are you going to stick around?" She checked her watch. "I'm getting off at four to run the three gun tactical match."

Our eyes met. Then the mercs surged in and she had her hands full.

I stepped away and read the brochures the way a betting man might read a racing form, turning the words every which way to find a particle of guidance. The Friendship Forces, "a division of MANO," offered "adventure travel with a twist," a chance to visit a foreign country and put "much-needed paramilitary skills to work in defense of freedom. Enjoy military hospitality, crosstrain with unusual weapons/tactics, refresh your resume. MAKE YOUR NEXT VACATION A REAL TOUR DE FORCE. Ask your accountant which portion of your expenses can be deducted as a charitable contribution."

I had to hand it to Rico. There must be thousands upon thousands of Americans with military skills and no place to use them. All Rico had to do was play matchmaker for the most attractive countries in terms of mercenary action.

After passing the next half hour marvelling at the wonders on view, I turned up for the "3-Gun Tactical Match." What kind of husband would miss his wife competing in a thing like that?

. . .

Under the blue desert sky a video projection screen fluttered in a light breeze. I rounded a corner and found a crowd of men sitting cross-legged on the ground like recruits watching propaganda films. I edged around for a look.

On the screen was a grainy, wide-angle view of an empty street lined with the facades of houses.

"Contestant twenty," a loudspeaker announced quietly. "Last call. Contestant twenty."

A man walked into the foreground, his back to us. A cutout appeared in a window and he drew. The cutout shook violently; a faint *pop-pop.*

"Scratch one gardener," said the man to my left.

Indeed, the cutout was of a crude slant-eyed figure holding a rake. With a shrug, the gunman replaced his pistol in its holster and continued on his Gary Cooper ramble.

V.R. was waving at me. As soon as I saw her, she turned back to the screen. I tiptoed through the crowd, sank down beside her.

"He's going too slowly, he's running out of time," she said.

The fellow pulled on a dog taking a leak and the crowd roared. He shot a wicked-looking grandmother. "Go, go, go!" chanted the crowd. He went berserk, running down the street, taking potshots at anything that moved.

"Whew. Total panic. He'll lose a lot of points for that," she said.

"Just like in real life."

"Giving me lip, Foote?"

"Nah."

She clasped her ankles and arched her back, closing her eyes and breathing in and out deeply and rhythmically. "I'm doing my relaxation exercises now."

She stayed in a trance until they called her number, then rose, joints cracking. Just before she ducked into the entrance, Rico appeared to give her a swat on the back and a few words of encouragement.

When she stepped onto the screen, she stood ten feet tall.

"A true Valkyrie from Valhalla, eh?" asked Rico, sliding in next to me. "Most women, and many men, would use a lighter gun than the nine-millimeter Parabellum. But not our Virginia Roy."

She walked with loose arms and straight shoulders. A cutout popped up in a car window, one hand holding a cellular phone. She didn't shoot.

Pop—almost as soon as it appeared, she dropped a cutout of a shotgun-toting bandit

Pop—a cutout of a Doberman. She held her fire on the human handler. After a pause—and no buzzer from the trial judge—a murmur of appreciation rose in the air.

Rico slapped my knee. "You see, it is the clarity of her choices. So compelling. Now that she has the judges seeing through her eyes, she can control the scoring."

She glided through another setup. Suddenly cutouts were popping up all over—behind a mailbox, out of a bank, from the back of a motorcycle. V.R. dropped flat on her belly, elbows wide, her gun in a two-handed grip. *Pop*—the bank robber. *Pop*—the getaway motorcyclist. She held her fire on the black teenager behind the mailbox and rolled to the cover of a planter box.

She crawled along until she reached a store window, peered through it, drew a bead on the figure. *Pop*—the teenager's head tore in half.

"Good penetration, good ammo," Rico said.

She reloaded, checked her watch, rose, and began to trot. A cutout of a policeman escaped unharmed. She held her fire in a tricky hostage situation.

A baby carriage rolled into the street, pushed by a heavyset woman balancing a shotgun across the pram handles.

V.R. drew smoothly, then hesitated. Hesitated. A buzzer sounded. The crowd heaved a collective sigh.

Rico looked puzzled. "She had the shot."

15

A pale green star wavered over the low line of chalk-white mountains. Blinking, as a pink cotton ball patted my forehead, I focused on Venus as she faded into day. The makeup artist breathed in my ear. "You really should wear sunblock when you're out-of-doors," she said.

"Eyes front, Mr. Foote," called another girl. "Let's hear you read this."

Words marched past on a large white stand-up screen. I recited them: "I—only—know—"

"Speed it up."

The words crawled faster: "One-way-to-fish . . . and-that's-all-out." Venus winked and vanished. The copper-green sky was suddenly flushed with billowy pink particles . . . a cloud of my makeup getting trapped in my eyelashes. A pair of scissors snipped the hair over my right ear as a pair of hands fitted an earpiece to my left.

A small voice said in my head, "Gar, I'm the segment producer. If you can hear me, lift your left hand. Okay."

"Three minutes," someone announced.

"We're ready," said the makeup lady.

"Clear the set."

The shaggy-headed talk show host eased himself into his chair.

"In honor of the location, I'm wearing this string tie," he said, tapping the dark yellow stone at his throat. "The crew gave it to me. It's a lizard's dick preserved in fossil amber."

The lights went on. "Five-four-three . . ." said the tiny-voiced producer in my ear. Then everything disappeared, except for the host's wide and direct eyes staring at the prompter behind my head, and his warm, wonderfully sympathetic voice. The minute I heard it I felt I could trust him with my life.

We were in the midst of a talk about the virtues of plastic worms versus spoons when the voice piped up in my ear: "That's fine."

The host smiled strongly into the camera. The shooting lights went off. Eager hands removed the earpiece, assisted me out of my chair, off the stage.

"You did great, guy," said a bulky cameraman in white shorts.

I wandered down to the Commandos on the pebbly shore. Lucky peered close. "Gar, you look pale as a sheet."

"It's the makeup."

"How'd it go?"

"Okay, I guess. Felt strange, though. Me, on *Good Morning America.*"

I stared out at the featureless gray plain of water that was Lake Mead. In less than two hours the curtain would go up on the next act of my life. I could forget all the distractions, the hype, the sponsor decals that seamstresses were feverishly sewing onto our flotation vests this very minute, and just concentrate on the fish.

Just me and the fish. I could hardly wait. The purity of pursuit, the adrenaline of attack, the serenity of self-mastery—it seemed an age since I'd been able to seek repose in such simple pleasures.

The start of the tournament was heralded by the twanging of the One Hundred Banjo Band from Santa Cruz, California. We went down to the waterside—one hundred and twenty-five of us game enough to cough up the $2,000 entry fee—and we started our engines. The sound of so many big hogs spitting, sputtering, roaring to life, echoed off the desert canyon walls and made my insides tremble with the vibrations.

We waited for a hovering helicopter to drop the signal flare, then charged down the flooded valley, turning tightly around the sculpted sandstone bend, each boat pushing for the lead. I kept an eye on the flasher and steered wide on the inside turns, not wanting to risk a dinged prop so soon. Choppers raced over our heads, the downdraft of their propwash adding to the furiously churning brown water.

Emerging from the canyon, I angled for the outer reef—a picket line of submerged Christmas trees. On the surface, nothing marked their presence, but colorful shapes were rising on my flash-forward sonar.

A low-flying chopper gained on my left and a video cameraman hung out the Bell JetRanger's door, feet on the struts, tracking a target. I checked out the boat next to me and saw the great one himself, Marty Kershaw, his silver mane of hair flowing over his blue metal-flake jacket embroidered with white stars, each one signifying a tournament win or a trophy of some kind. A living legend.

Marty glanced over and flicked me a salute. I returned it, dry-mouthed, though I doubt he actually saw it. Maybe later, when he reviewed the videotape.

I thought of what Jerry had said about our being outclassed. What a sorry attitude that was. Jerry just didn't understand how battle-proud we were. Though we might be outfished individually on any given day, as a team we would never let down. Most of the other teams had been thrown together at the last second on the beach by individual entrants thinking they would hedge their bets. But they still viewed each other as competitors and wouldn't be caught dead sharing information, equipment and encouragement as the tournament hotted up. These teams of convenience would fall apart late today or tomorrow. They'd lose confidence, while we'd only be gaining it. All our Commando routines would drive home the point.

Boats peeled off right and left as we entered the field of sunken structures. I held my line, the sun at my back. The way I had it figured, the bass would be huddling close to the structure. Because bass can see five times better when their eyes are shaded, only the ones with their backs to the sun would be active. I was aiming for the outermost structures, to cut interference from noise, but also to get a fix on other spots I might want to hit on my travels. Finally I pulled up and went to my electric unit, gliding in while I musked up and lowered my probes for deep-water pH and temperature readouts.

First I fished some bogies at thirty feet in a thin band of warmer water, using a HooDoo Love Worm. My line trembled as several bass took it in the mouth but refused to bite, fondling the fleshy tail with aggravating caution. I kept my head and didn't try to foul-hook them with a sudden sharp pull. Instead, for the next hour I worked systematically through my worm kit and scent formulations, testing and teasing those finicky eaters with a Sunday buffet of stinkbait. Then I sat still for a quarter hour. A portrait of Mr. Lake Mead Big Shot Bass was forming in my mind.

Reared in the wide open spaces of the West, last month he'd suddenly found a roof over his head with abundant shadow and cover. The only thing was, the Christmas tree had made him lazy. He didn't care about TV, and he didn't know Wayne Newton from a fig. But this tournament had fattened him up too safely and too soon. He was bored. He was edgy. He craved excitement the way only a spoiled fighter can.

So all my tastefully prepared worms were as nothing to him. *Micropterus salmoides*, Mr. Las Vegas Largemouth, a rake and a dandy, a duelling roué with a jingle in his pocket and a diamond on his pinkie. A big-time bass, he sneered at worms.

Instead of trying to blend into his natural diet, my next lure had to be pure entertainment. A sucker bait. I hadn't decided about where or when or even if I'd be using Jerry's secret deep-diving minnow. Basically I'd been hoping conditions wouldn't call for it. But now I took it out and laid the sparkling metallic thing athwart the seat. Somebody knew his business: it looked as jazzed-up as a Wurlitzer jukebox. A hot bar of sunlight pressed on the back of my neck. The air had mud in it. Wavelets lapped against the side of the hull.

I thought how contrary the world was, how the natural and the unnatural were partners in the game. Here I was fishing. And down there was a fish. Simple. Here was a lake — except it was an impoundment, created by a dam. Artificial. The bass needed shade or they wouldn't actively feed. Simple. So underneath this placid, unruffled brown-green fake lake was an elaborate sixty-foot metal and wood jungle gym put here to create prime habitat. Artificial. But it's real, too. What catches fish after all but something artificial, tarted up, like a lure? Sure, it's a lie. But we use the lie to catch the true thing.

Where would it all end? Already I was seeing a fish course, groomed like a golf course. To hunt fish we were using electronics fancier than any I'd seen used in Vietnam to hunt men. And of course we needed a quiver of rods to handle all contingencies, a suitcase of lures and a library of piscatorial knowledge. Still it wasn't enough. We had to have competition, and more of it. Once we'd tilted the scales in our favor, we had to make it more challenging. It had to be tight and tough. A ladder of play-offs would cover the country, so that no fisherman went untested, unranked. Soon there wouldn't be a fisherman alive who didn't know his place, who didn't know who his heroes were supposed to be. And still it wouldn't be enough. We had to have what other sports had — television. We had to have it. We couldn't be satisfied unless we had taken this solitary and slow pastime of ours and calibrated it with championships and modernized it and dressed it up to suit the networks and made it more theatrical for the average

Joe watching it on the sofa so the advertisers could sell him more pickup trucks and beer. And soft drinks. Can't forget them.

The only thing we hadn't engineered so far was the fish. But who's to say we won't? Who knew what kind of genetically designed lunker was swimming up to spawn in which laboratory?

I gazed across monotonous miles of blank water dotted with our low-slung boats. On each bar stool swivel seat in the bow of every boat there sat a man like me, doing his level best to outthink a close relative of the first creature to ever set foot on land.

There were one hundred and twenty-five of us out here, roughly the same in age, in equipment, experience, desire. The pioneers of a new frontier. But only four of us had this multihued segmented metal-flake minnow, a deep-diver direct from the laboratory of a major manufacturer. How could we fail?

While we waited for the results, timed to make the five o'clock network news feed, we decided to drop in on the Bush Facility. I wanted to catch V.R.'s second round in the 3-Gun Tactical Match. The boys were all for following Cecil's lead and blowing up a few magazines at the Machine Gun Bar.

We hopped in the white limo Jerry insisted we use. Trank drove it two blocks, parked it just inside the fence surrounding the Convention Center lot, and we flagged down the shuttle bus to take us the rest of the way.

When we arrived at the dirt-floored waiting area, the big video screen was blank, the crowd buzzing in anticipation. V.R. was sitting over in a corner getting a pep talk from Rico; I got as close as I could without pushing, and resigned myself to a long-distance connection.

Rico was addressing a circle of recruits, his hands in his pants pockets, pacing forward and back. "—nervous? Don't be. You think you're nervous now, wait until is somebody shooting back at you, shooting to *kill*. That's nervous. Any other questions?" He braced his hands on his hips and rolled his butt around, loosening up. He looked like he was doing the hula.

A spectacled boy with the baby fat still on him raised a hand. "How good a score do I need, if I'm not a veteran but I've engaged in a lot of paramilitary behavior?"

Rico clenched his teeth and visibly steamed. "I have said this — too much already. Forget the score! I am not looking at the score here. This is not the same as live combat. Nothing is. No man can know how he will react until live rounds come singing in."

A darkly-tanned man spoke irritably. "You mean I can ace this thing and you still might say I can't enlist?"

"Everybody can sign on with a Friendship Force. But not everybody is combat-ready. Not you, not me." He slapped his belly. "Look, hombres, I've seen very able men, tough, top physical specimens, excellent marksmen, who just freeze under fire. They can't help it. The oldest question a man asks himself is still whether or not he is coward."

That stunned them. "Now." Rico grinned. "Think of me as a headhunter. My job is to send good recruits. You. I send too many men don't work out, pretty soon I need a new job, right?"

"What if you say no?" asked the dark man.

"We offer a certificated three-week session at an accredited War College that has placed its graduates in many of the top conflicts and police actions around the world." Rico nodded to my wife. "Commander Toro here has done the course two times."

Commander Toro? I smiled. But the others were looking at V.R. with respect. Smart man, that Rico. Now all these men would be wondering what the course would do for them if it could produce a warrior like V.R. Of course, only V.R. produced V.R., but they wouldn't know that.

"Okay?" Rico surveyed his recruits. "We go in five minutes. If your weapon isn't clean and your bowels aren't clear, then do it now."

I checked my watch against the overhead clock. Darn Rolex

was running slow. Then I ambled up to V.R. "Good luck, Miz Roy." She broke into a full-freckled grin. When we hugged, I could feel the muscles trembling all down her back. "See you after?"

She tightened her grip around my neck, burying her nose in my hair. "I'll just die if I screw up like yesterday."

I patted her rump. "You did fine yesterday, and you'll do even better today. And one thing Rico said I know for a fact: it ain't nothing like the real thing, so relax."

She was pulling her socks up, but this stopped her. She peered at me. "How'd you know? You never said you saw action over there."

"Well, not officially."

"But you did?"

"Once or twice, yeah, they'd airlift a bunch of us 'dozer drivers out to build a firebase or something. We'd get a taste of it, then air cav'd come take us home for our suppers. Those D-8s were too valuable to lose in a firefight."

Moving up close, she stared into my face. "Just answer the question. Did you shoot?"

"Did you ever look at how high off the ground a bulldozer seat is? Like a throne. Guy designed it just so every G for a mile around can take target practice at you. Of course I did."

"You never— How come?"

"Nothing to tell." She was getting her teeth way too deep into this. "How come you haven't asked me how we did today?"

"Well, how'd you do?"

"Don't know yet. They post the results at five." I laughed and tickled her, turned her so she faced the entrance and gave her shoulders a gentle tap. "Now go get 'em."

The course selected for automatic rifle was a classic obstacle scenario with a few wrinkles thrown in. V.R. rumbled through the mud firing from the hip; walked the balance beam snapping off rounds at snipers; made a hand-over-hand ladder crossing under fire. She did good. But she had the usual difficulties a woman would have, mostly in the upper body strength area; I held my breath on one twenty-foot wall climb, sure she'd fall. But she finished up nice, jogging up an embankment while laying down an impressive suppressing fire. She looked no worse than a lot of the men. That said, I have to admit that most men just seemed more natural out there. Some of them, great hulking physical specimens in service tank tops, carved the course in big bold sweeps as if they were wearing ice skates. They squeezed every obstacle of every drop of drama and suspense. They made soldiering look like a thing of beauty, when it's really the sloppiest, scariest thing around.

I went around to the exit and waited for her to come out. After a few minutes passed, I started to go in. A security guard stepped forward. "Wrong door, bud."

"I'm going to see a contestant."

"Rules is rules. Sorry."

"But it's my wife."

"I'm sorry about that, too."

Then I saw her. Rico was with her, supporting her with an arm around her waist as she limped. Her face was bright red, so inflamed her freckles looked white as stars.

The guard never laid a hand on me as I rushed past. "What happened?"

"What does it look like?"

"But I didn't see anything."

"I sprained it stepping down, after I finished." She grimaced. "Just like a woman."

Rico shrugged at me: a bearded ox yoked under her arm.

"I might as well wear high heels for the finale tomorrow." Now she glared at me. "You happy?"

Taken aback, I said nothing.

"You got what you wanted, right? I've got to scratch. Now I can go back to being your little woman."

"In the first place, I didn't want this. And in the second, you've never been my or anybody's little woman and I wouldn't expect you to start now."

"You'll come around. You think I haven't seen all the big bassers and their slavey wives?"

Rico gave me a look of sympathy. Ducking his head, he let V.R. loose. "Wrap the ankle up tight," he said, fleeing.

"V.R., you're hurting and hot as a hornet in frying oil. But none of it's my fault."

"You would just have to tell me about your combat experience right before I did the course. It just destroyed my concentration."

I blinked. "But I said that to help you relax. You know, how it really didn't matter so much."

"The way nothing I do ever matters."

V.R. leaned on me as we hobbled out into the main concourse—two well-camouflaged commandos having a lover's quarrel in public.

"Edged weapons seminar, plenty of seats still available," yelled a barker in a kiosk as we slowly passed by. He casually flipped a knife into a wooden target ten feet away.

"Everything you do matters to me."

"You sure pick funny ways to show it. You ought to leave me, find yourself a woman to have children with."

"I love *you*, baby."

"You're just staying around out of guilt. I don't want that."

"I love what we have."

"Well, I need something more."

Of course she and I were still yoked together, arms around necks, so she wasn't going anywhere this minute. But her words struck my insides hard, like a clapper in a big church bell.

"Look, this stuff is old. We've outgrown it."

"Maybe you have." She wasn't yelling anymore; she just sounded tired. "You got over it the next day, I recall."

"I was trying to keep us out of jail—if you recall."

"And whose fault was that?" She sighed. "I just feel we've never been out from under a dark cloud since before we were married. Face it: we're doomed."

"You aren't looking at things from a positive side. Look around you—we're on the verge of breaking through here, if we just stick with it. *Can't* never did, remember."

"Neither did a sprained ankle." She squeezed my head closer to hers. "Okay, I'll forgive you one more time. But I warn you, I'm never ever going to be your Miss Magnolia Blossom."

"Deal." I kissed her sweaty hair. "Where now, ma'am?"

"Help me find the combat medicine seminar." She gave a grim laugh. "Maybe the first casualty of the day gets a discount."

I looked at my watch, shook my wrist. "And maybe they fix Rolexes, too."

I hooked up with the boys outside the Machine Gun Bar. They looked shell-shocked and sandblasted, but happy. We watched a few of the combat videos on continuous loop that were scattered around the facility. Cecil pulled me aside and flashed what seemed to be a business card: "The bearer is a member of MAC-SOG. Do Not Detain or Question Him. He is authorized to wear civilian clothes, carry unusual weapons, pass into restricted areas, requisition equipment of all kinds."

Cec smiled. "Bet you remember this from Nam."

"I don't, actually."

"The original CIA operative's 'Get Out of Jail' card?" He rubbed it gently between finger and thumb. "All the PsyOps and Specials carried 'em."

"Well, I drove a bulldozer. What'd it cost you?"

"Ten bucks. Can't wait to try it out."

"Cecil."

He flinched. "I'm not gonna use it for real, you know. Maybe try it on girls or something."

"Or something."

It was time to head back to the pond. Feeling good, we formed up and double-timed across the parking lot, goofing at cadences. The shuttle came and hauled us to where we'd left the white limousine. There was Trank stretched out in back, reading a magazine and watching the television, waiting for the results of the day's fishing to be broadcast on the sports cable network. We crowded in to look.

A flashy scramble of still photos of Monster Bass Shootout action zoomed by to a throbbing disco beat. We were in several of the shots. Then the camera did a close-up of the revolving neon scoreboard back at the Hospitality Pavilion, a turntable in the shape of a huge bass boat, occupied by a bevy of bathing suit models. First we saw the individual leaders. Then the camera slowly panned the list of the teams.

We had done pretty well, we thought, and yet we were in ninth place. Only one spot away from elimination—but alive. I had fared poorly, the others only slightly better. Eddie was our leader, with nine pounds.

For a moment no one said anything. "Well, at least we made the cut for tomorrow." Lucky reached for the on-off knob.

"Wait," I said. "Turn it up."

"—ended up doing quite well on his home lake, leading his team, let me be careful how I say this, the Bloody Bassters—to first place on opening day. Tell me, given your kinky tastes and style, whatever drew you to bass fishing?" And then we saw this creature from the Black Lagoon, this weird sister in a punk-rock kind of outfit, with long tousled hair, fake black eyelashes and bright violet mascara.

A subtitle flashed underneath. *Bass Akvaards, Team Leader.* He licked his crimson lips with a large and muscular tongue. Shrugged. "Not much to do growing up in Las Vegas, you know, except watch the grannies hit the slots and play dress-up with Mommy's clothes. My mates and me, we didn't want to start a rock 'n roll band like everybody else. I guess what got me going was hearing somebody call professional bass fishing a cult sport.

We were all really into cults anyway — and fishing, too, 'cause of the lake. It just clicked."

I twisted the knob. The screen went black. Everybody looked at me, surprised. "Let's get back to the hotel," I growled.

Trank laid down his magazine, *American Film Quarterly*, put on his chauffeur's cap and took the limo's wheel. As he drove, sandhills streamed by our windows, veined rocks in near-human shapes reared up unexpectedly.

Eddie broke the spell. "Well, at least we know we got a secret weapon for tomorrow."

"That's right." Cecil smacked his fist in his palm. "It was a good thing Jerry gave us that special deep-diver today or we'd be out on the street right now."

"You don't know that." My voice had much too sharp an edge to it. "Seems to me we did all right before he took over."

Nobody said a thing. They were all too embarrassed for me. Cec turned the TV back on to find close-ups of the day's bass heroes in action. Our natural curiosity in watching our competitors at work soon outlasted any lingering uneasiness. My outburst was forgiven, if not forgotten.

After eating a ridiculously cheap steak dinner at one of the casino buffets, with twice-baked cheddar cheese potatoes, Roquefort salad, and New York Style cheesecake, we went right to work, pooling information on the day's best tactics, inputting weather and water data into our tables for tomorrow's fishing and entering waypoints into our Loran-C sets so that we could find the hot Christmas trees with pinpoint accuracy. After a short prayer — Lucky's idea, led by Cecil — we split up for the night, the boys to some much-needed and hard-earned R and R, me to a rendezvous upstairs.

A serious party was in progress when I walked into Jerry's suite. The men were in fuzzy peach sweaters or baggy charcoal suits; the women in tight black dresses with pearls, glittering gold pantsuits, or something in a modified Western style. Jerry grabbed me by the arm and right away marched me up to this woman, Shearlean James, who had on a fringed buckskin mini-dress with the face of Geronimo painted across her bosom. A room service dining cart was piled with fruit baskets, a ham, a turkey, a smoked salmon, and assorted things to go with them. There was a drink cart, and a dessert cart with fresh strawberry pie and a colossal chocolate cake.

Virginia Roy sat by the door, behind a card table covered with name tags. "Welcome to Open House," she said.

"How's the ankle?" I could see her foot propped on a cushion.

"It's going to be fine—sorry I blew my stack like that."

"Who are all these people?"

V.R. watched Shearlean James throw her hair around and laugh. "*She* brought them. Friend of Jerry's. A society reporter, knows everyone in Hollywood and TV, she says."

"But what do they have to do with Rico's outfit?"

She cocked her head at me, smiling. "This party is for *you*. Well, for your company. To promote it."

"Funny *we* weren't invited," I said.

But V.R. didn't hear me. Jerry was in the center of an uproar, circling Shearlean with a sappy grin on his face and a drink parasol in each hand. "Geronimo!" he shouted, and made to plant the parasols on the Chief's eyes. Shearlean shied away, under-standably nervous: the Chief's eyebrows were arched over her nipples. She slid by Jerry, and he seemed satisfied to get a piece of her bare shoulders.

"Forty-five-year-old women shouldn't wear their hair long," said V.R. under her breath, blind as usual to her brother's true nature.

At eight o'clock the room emptied out as if somebody had pulled a drain plug. Nobody wanted to miss the one really indispensable shindig, the one the Bloody Bassters were throwing. Even Jerry let it be known, as he went waltzing out the door — with Miss Geronimo on his arm — that he was planning on dropping by.

I didn't know how I was supposed to feel about that. Hurt, I guess. But the more I thought about it, the more I hoped everybody had a wonderful time and stayed out too late, danced and drank too much — with that Mr. Bass Akvaards leading the pack. Because tomorrow we were going to whip his pale, pimpled, hung over ass all over the lake.

Rico made an appearance while we were straightening up the mess. "You are ready?" he asked V.R. Putting his weight behind the service cart that carried the food, he began to push it through the door that led to his room. "Having yourself a little late night snack?" I asked.

"*My* guests, they arrive at eight-thirty." He bent over the cart as he pushed and nipped a maraschino cherry right off the ham with his teeth.

"We're interviewing recruits," V.R. explained. She smiled before following Rico next door.

I walked down the hall to the elevator, but going down I decided to take a stroll and think about tomorrow. Out in the night air the scent of sage wafted over the exhaust fumes. Lines of cars cruised, bright red taillights rippling in a long chain reaction, on and off, on and off, soothing me. Just when I was feeling ready for sleep, I checked my watch. Dead. I stood there, cursing Jerry. I started downtown at a fast clip, hoping to find a drugstore that was still open to sell me a timepiece. Soon I'd found the heart of the place, people eddying about aimlessly under ledges of fluorescent tubes and steeples of neon. In the midst of these daydreaming herds slinked the coyotes, sharp-faced fellows in plaid sport coats or tight, leather jackets, sniffing and searching. I thought of Jerry Roy, his dud Rolex, his trick lures, and four trusting souls — well, three — and asked myself what I really intended to do about it.

The electronics store's window, a solid wall of television sets tuned to the same channel, pulsed with some nasty teenagers dancing to the noise of a V-8 throwing a rod. I went in and found myself in front of a twenty-foot counter of watches. Good. Take your problems one at a time.

A black counterman stood across from me. I unhooked the Rolex and handed it to him. He flipped it over, took a slim tool out of his shirt pocket; the back was off in seconds.

"How much you pay for it?"

"It was a gift."

"You still was robbed. Counterfeit junk."

"Got a good digital under thirty bucks?"

He glided along the counter.

It was the money, I realized. Jerry always had control of the money.

"Tell you what. This is a nice band you got here. I'll put the works of this Seiko inside. You still got your Rolex, and nobody know the difference." He paused, and smiled slightly. "Specially the ladies. Can't disappoint them. And maybe tomorrow you get the real Rolex out of pawn."

I considered it. I liked it. While he worked on the Rolex, I watched the news on a tiny television no bigger than a camera. There was an outdoor barbecue scene from the Soldier of Fortune convention. They showed the rappelling ninjas and a close-up of a muscle-bound hunk licking an ice cream cone. Then it was back to the barbecue and—*hello*. A barrage balloon in the shape of a human figure was floating into the night sky, illuminated by spotlights. It was like Macy's Thanksgiving Parade, except I couldn't recognize the balloon.

The counterman did. "Hey, Hanoi Jane, you flying now."

That's when they opened fire. The sky filled with streams of tracers; the camera cut to close-ups of an honor guard blazing away, then back to the balloon. Hanoi Jane was leaking, losing it fast, her nose and eye swelling up huge and strange as the last gas bubbled up into her rubber head chamber.

They cut to two laughing news anchors, a man and a woman. Then it was the fishing tournament, a scramble of boats, shots of bass being netted.

I paid the counterman. He drifted away. There was a close-up of a man in a boat hunkered over his depth finder, reaching into his tackle box for his lures. I waited around, hoping to see what he would choose, but the news ended.

Looking at that cute little television set, I thought of V.R. laid up with a bad foot. Wouldn't it be nice if she could sprawl out by the pool tomorrow and just watch her favorite shows? I took out my wallet again; the old girl needed cheering up, and if she used the TV to also cheer on her favorite fisherman tomorrow, well, I wouldn't complain.

I started back to the hotel. But before I could sleep there was one more task: it was time to confront Jerry, if he didn't have Shearlean in his room. Maybe even if he did.

"You want what?" he laughed, standing in the door in a hotel bathrobe, a water glass of bourbon in his hand.

"To see exactly how much of the Valhalla money we got left, and what it's being spent on."

His sandy eyebrows pressed downward, hooding his angry black eyes. I let him see that I was not impressed. His jawbone jutted up with a quick jerk; I tried not to flinch as his big chin moved close. He hesitated. "Well, old buddy, you have selected an inauspicious time for doing the books." He lowered his voice. "Fact is, I've got company."

"She can stay. I don't mind." When Jerry just stared, I threw down the gauntlet. "Or we can go next door and do it there. V.R. is always happy to see her brother."

He sighed, looked over his shoulder into the room, sipped his bourbon. He glanced down at his blue-veined bare feet, shook his head and leveled a 12-gauge glare at me. "You asked for it, you

got it. I don't have to show you nothin'. You are only an officer of
this corporation. I'm the chairman. If you look close at that paper
you all signed, you'll find that only one person has a claim on the
Bass Commando name. Only one. *Me.* You and your friends
serve at the pleasure of the chairman—and the chairman is mighty
displeased at this moment. He isn't going to be opening his books
for you, tonight or any night. He may just decide to hire some other
foursome to be his Commandos."

"Kinda late notice for this tournament, isn't it?"

He shrugged. "I'm not going to have to do it, am I? So what's
the difference—as long as you know I can."

I stood there, letting the jelly-like feeling in my legs and gut
curdle into a cold, hard, black solid. When it had set, I knew I
would be able to walk away in a straight line. But I had one
question: "Why did you tell me, yesterday, that you didn't think
we had a chance? And then give us those special lures?"

Up went the eyebrows, back went the bourbon glass. He
smacked his lips. "That's for me to know . . . And you know
something? You'll thank me tomorrow, too."

Wandering back to the room with V.R.'s little gift under my
arm, I tested out my options. Not much in this hand I'd been dealt.
If we didn't fish tomorrow, our names would be ruined—half the
public bathrooms in Mississippi would bear witness to our shame.
If we did fish, Jerry won. Unless *we* won so decisively that we
became personally, individually indispensable. But the odds were
stacked against that happening at this late stage of the game.

16

Light. The good light of the desert sunrise soaked into my face as my bass boat made the turn out of the shadowed, echoing canyon. Land and water spread out before my eyes, going on forever and ever, a horizon you could get lost in. Sandstone the color of a Coppertone billboard, hills the shape of women sleeping by the pool. Water bright, brittle, blue. I stared into the black hole of my depth sounder, followed the subterranean ridge that pointed true to my assigned fishing station. Plenty of bogies were coming up on my screen, but were they hungry?

The shadow of a helicopter crossed my foredeck. I raised a hand in case they were filming. That's all. Commando discipline.

The previous day we'd been allowed to fish at will. Today we would fish given sites. Two different tests of skill, one of hunting, the other of gathering. Tough bassing anytime, but especially now, with spectator boats floating close by and the TV eye everywhere.

Before departing, Jerry had handed us each a schedule—our TV time. As each of us went on camera, we were to unwrap the last, special, secret lures. And fish the hell out of them.

Cutting my big guns, I coasted in on Christmas tree No. 17.

Our trimmed-down field meant just three of us would fish each structure. Getting there first, I'd have my pick of where to start. I laid alongside the underwater habitat, dropped my probe and started my scanning. Bogies in bunches. Breakfast bogies, just waiting for a wake-up worm and a glass of fresh-squeezed scent formulation.

I musked up and moved to the bow, took the bar stool chair, put my toe on the electric trolling unit's floor pedal. A second bow depth flasher kept me on station while I began my worm's slow and seductive stroll. "Bite me, baby," I whispered, counting off the feet until enough line had paid out. Drift and tumble. Turn and twitch.

The second and third boats were just gliding in when I netted my first bass. A faint smatter of applause reached me from the spectator boat. In an hour's time my fishwell had three keepers in it, cooling their heels. But the day's heat was driving the fish deeper, and they'd stopped feeding.

The morning had gone well for me. It backed up last night's decision, which was based on the three stages of fishing: feeding, transition and defense. You can be red-hot on one, like I was this morning, but stone-cold on the other two. Most times, most tournaments, a streak a day will do you. But not for me, not with so much riding on it.

It was time. I unbuttoned my shirt and fetched out the remote control unit hanging from a lanyard around my neck. Power on, volume up: the backup fishfinder at the bow began to glow. But instead of a green cathode screen cut with a grid and a scattering of bright targets, I was looking at a color television picture.

The five-inch by four-inch TV screen came into focus. The counterman at the electronic store was right about the reception being excellent. I slipped the single earplug in, bent over to where the other end of the cord came out of my pant leg and hooked that into the jack-and-cord I'd laid under a strip of duct tape early this morning.

Then I settled back to watch my own tournament.

The challenge of bassing is matching up your fish sense with the conditions and the contents of your tackle box. It's not spying on your fellow competitor. But that's what I was going to do. Ordinarily, it wouldn't be worth the effort to peek over another man's shoulder; you'd be too far away to see. Having a televised tournament, however, changed things. I'd already seen zoom shots that let me count the feathers on a Peavey Popper, a lure that imitates two copulating mayflies. If I'd been a bass, I'd have busted my nose on the glass trying to get to it.

It still wouldn't be that useful to see what a man was fishing, however, unless you could see it while he was fishing it. Knowing what somebody is fishing in real time, I can duplicate his lure, cast, and pattern. Live TV could give me that. And my shopping at the electronics store would make sure it did.

Now, keeping an eye on the screen, I fished my defensive lures. The two other boats on this structure were doing the same. The three of us were like some fast-motion picture, reeling in, casting, unhooking one lure and hooking another on. The TV sportcasters commented in low, urgent voices as the screen showed boat after boat. They cut away regularly, to capsule biographies, shots from the previous day's fishing, commercials. After ten minutes of absolutely dead action, a man boated a fish. There was a reaction shot of the man's wife in the pontoon boat, clutching a handkerchief and chewing on its embroidered borders. She'd gotten lipstick all over it. The thought of V.R. acting that way crossed my mind, and I gave a snort of laughter. Then a zoom of him unhooking the fish and slipping it into the fishwell showed me what I needed to know: Pisces Perpetrator, a stock jigging lure in everybody's box. But of all the fishermen, only I knew that. And the sportcaster came on to give me the depth at which the bass had struck. Thanks, Brent.

I unhooked myself and went back to my tackle box and found a P-Perp. For a moment I stared at Jerry's handwritten schedule.

As I plugged myself back in, the sportcasters were filling some dead air time with a discussion of fishing's greatest champs. They showed the usual shots of Bud Mobley, "Heck" Heckleberger and Ted Williams. Then they started in on the eccentrics, and talked the standard line about Ernest Hemingway and Moby Dick, which everyone down at the lake is so sick of hearing about. Only when the face of Bass Akvaards filled the little screen did I pay close attention.

I slid the Perp into the water and ranged the bogies on the screen. Bass on. Just like that. Unhooking the television cord, I fought the bass, a nice one, to the back of the boat and into the fishwell. When I got back, Cecil's head was filling the TV screen. I checked my watch against Jerry's schedule: right on time.

As I watched, Cecil opened Jerry's secret package but, before touching the lure inside, he grabbed an aerosol can of Turtle Musk No. 9 and gummed up his baiting hand. I was as curious as anybody what Jerry had come up with, but even so, I complimented Cec's discipline. He'd come a long way in such a short time.

Now he reached inside the package and removed the instructions. Reading, he felt around and pulled out a paper-wrapped object. The sportcasters were playing the suspense for all it was worth.

"Let me tell you about these guys. Call themselves the Bass Commandos. Bunch of country boys. And they're fishing their cotton-picking hearts out."

Cecil's eyes were big, almost popping with the strain of straight money fishing with a television chaser. To my mind, he looked the way the thoroughly modern basser of the future will—swift, strong and handsome, yet as innocent and clean-limbed as a Boy Scout—and I was pleased to see him finally getting his due. Watching him now, you couldn't have guessed the trouble he'd seen, the battle for his confidence and against the bottle. You wouldn't know that there was literally no one else in Cecil's life except the Commandos. He didn't have anyone to tell him that there were other, more important things in life if he failed. Maybe because, for Cecil, there weren't.

He stripped off the outer wrapping of a long narrow box and stared at the bright red carton of Marlboro cigarettes he held in his hand.

One sportscaster chuckled. "Yeah, they don't make 'em like this anymore. He's the old-fashioned kind. He'll take his own sweet time, rely on his own homegrown skills and bait. All over America you can meet his kin at the local feed store — talking big on Friday, walking tall come Monday morning."

The other sportscaster asked: "And in between? During the actual tournament?"

"During the tournament? Well, he's overmatched. There's no way he can compete against the high tech sophistication the big bassers have."

I snorted. "Make him *eat* those words, Cecil baby. Go fish."

But Cecil apparently had other things to do first. Reading from Jerry's script, he shook out a pack of Marlboros, opened it and lit one up.

Looking a little impatient, he shook the carton again. Something dark and slender, wrapped in cellophane, fell out. It looked like it could be a lure. My spirits rose. Cecil held the wrapper to the sunlight and the camera: "Slim Jim Pepperoni Stick." Dutifully he opened it and took a bite. I could see his eyes following the script. I could see it was driving him crazy.

"I see what you mean. He's a throwback, isn't he?"

"This is the way it used to be, Brent. In the old days, a slower-paced life-style let plenty of characters like this Cecil George approach tournaments in a leisurely fashion. Now I'm not putting down his skills, you understand. He wouldn't be here if he hadn't kicked the heck out of some very big bassers. Somehow."

"Got lucky, in other words."

"Goddammit!" I kicked the thwarts of my boat.

By the time they'd finished laughing at their sophisticated wit, Cecil had hit the jackpot: a Red Man chewing tobacco can pierced by nail holes. It was filled with loose, moist dirt and—night crawlers.

"What a hoot. Imagine—real worms. Who'd a thunk it? In this day and age—I mean, *real* worms."

"Colorful. Colorful guy. A museum piece."

"Now it's interesting you should say that. This is great for the new viewers, those we're trying to reach. They can see how far the sport has come, all by watching this boy George from Mississippi."

Cecil hefted the can of worms in one hand and Jerry's script in the other.

"He's straight outa 'Hee Haw', ain't he? The Grand Ol' Opry, the whole nine yards."

Cecil held up a worm. The camera left him.

It took me a few minutes to recover. Then, snapping to, I fumbled for Jerry's schedule. Yes, Eddie was next, then, fifteen minutes later, Lucky. Jerry had saved my humiliation for last.

So this was Jerry's setup. We were the cracker cousins, the hillbillies, the Minnie Pearl-Homer-and-Jethro butts of the joke. I stared across the lake. It was a lost cause—I couldn't save my friends. I could only save myself.

The TV had mercifully gone back to the fishing. I did, too, taking a second keeper on the Perp. They cut to one of the legends of bass. If a Shagnasty Grandaddy jig was good enough for him, it was for me, too.

A voice was eating at me, telling me to stop this—that I didn't need to cheat, now. But a desperate man doesn't listen to reason. I'd led the boys to this pass. I had to catch enough fish to carry us all to victory.

Eddie was next. He could hardly wait to open the package. He knew he was on the tube. He kept his biceps rock-hard and his neck muscles bulging, which made his face flush some and a blue vein pulse across his forehead.

Here was a *man*—with all that entailed. That his married life had come apart last year there was no doubt, but Eddie hadn't called it quits. In training he'd held our feet to the fire. He'd made me a better basser.

Now he unwrapped his box and arrayed his treasures on the console before him: a blue carton of Hercules Nutrition System All-Power Diet Milk Shake, a baseball cap and a comic book. The cap's logo was for a national quick-oil change franchise. The comic was *The Incredible Hulk*. And, in its own plastic dish with a Kraft label, an assortment of tiny colored marshmallows and bait hooks.

"Shucks, I remember using marshmallows once, when I was just a tadpole," said one sportcaster.

"I'd try anything once," allowed the other one. "But not *that*. I mean, a man's gotta face himself in the mirror every morning. Marshmallows for bait is just pitiful."

Slowly, painfully, Eddie made his body obey his mind. He'd made his deal. He wouldn't back down. His movements stiff and undoubtedly crampy from an excess of lactic acid in his turbocharged muscles, he forced himself to rig that bait. He'd do this for *us*.

I knew what it was worth, this self-abasement, and it struck at my heart with chopping blows. The fact was, we were Jerry's puppets. We'd traded in our identity and our good name and our fish sense—for some advertising dollars. For product placement. Oh, yeah, we were celebrities now. This was the American Dream, now. When they say it's a machine, they aren't kidding.

Then it was back to the fishing tournament. I wasn't letting down. I was on automatic pilot. Screw them all. Did somebody nail a nice piece of bass on a Sweedish Pimples spoon? So would I. I had no pride.

But when the camera zeroed in on Lucky, a man with more natural dignity than anyone I know, I put down my rod and cried.

His noble Cajun brow wrinkled in thought, Lucien Bonnard unwrapped his package and beheld a glittering, rhinestone-studded, sequin-sewn white jacket with tassels along the yoke and arms. On the back bold letters commended our souls to Graceland, home of the King. Simultaneously on the TV screen an 800 number flashed in red along the bottom, telling us where to call to buy that jacket, although the sportcasters pretended not to notice, marvelling as they were over Lucky's resemblance to Elvis in his Vegas days.

In a second box, shining wet and invitingly, was a bottle of Yoo Hoo and a jar of bright orange Balls O' Fire salmon egg bait. It was a hat trick from hell: Lucky despised all Elvis impersonators, feeling that they were responsible for the cheapening of the man's reputation; Lucky certainly would never touch a chocolate soda, since like most Cajuns he has a soft spot for Dr. Pepper; and, of course, Lucky was in no way, shape or form a bait man. With all the years of bassin' science under his belt, the idea that he would resort to salmon eggs was like catching Albert Einstein counting on his fingers and toes under the table. It's something that a reputation just doesn't recover from overnight.

But Lucky gritted his teeth and flung the jacket over his shoulders like a cape. He uncapped the Yoo Hoo and pretended to take a sip; he even forced a smile. But those Balls O' Fire were making him sick just to look at.

The camera crew must've picked up on Lucky's discomfort, because as the sportcasters launched into a rendition of "Love Me Tender" the view on the tube switched to the broad, brown wasteland of the desert lake.

Well, no way I was going to get caught with my pants down. I picked up Jerry's package and started to heave it overboard, before recalling the rules. The bass world is so image conscious that littering can cost you a two-ounce penalty at weigh-in. I stuck the sack under my seat. But then I hauled it back out and peered inside. I'm sure Jerry put a lot of thought into the contents — yes, he must have licked his chops in anticipation of crucifying me on national TV. There was a pack of Black Jack gum. A sack of Cheez Doodles. And a can of Pepsi-Cola.

I don't know how long I sat there. Finally a cool breeze reached me, and my sweaty skin jumped, and the trance was broken. Within ten minutes I had another fish in the well and was just beginning to wonder if perhaps the Bass Commandos could mount a comeback and take this meet after all. Then the camera cut to a boat far away on the copper-colored lake, came closer to show a man's back, zoomed in tighter and tighter, until with a sudden leap the man spun around on his swivel seat and tore off his hat. We were staring at the freak face of Bass Akvaards, his volcano of hair erupting as he pranced around the boat. He looked like a slimy lizard in a tattered, black fishnet shirt; there were leather lily pads sewn over his chest, and a white plastic skeleton of a fish entangled in the net. He put down his rod and picked up a small electric piano keyboard. There was a close-up of his sweaty face streaked with violet mascara, then, with a quick spin, we were staring at a tattoo of a spider on the bare cheek of his G-string covered ass. He spun around again and thrust his pelvis into the camera eye for all to see. Rearing up in my face was a horrible thing, rising from a thick coil of viscera that bulged out of a tear in his guts . . . a kind of mutant codpiece, tapering upward into a grotesquely veined and skinless beast, half-serpent, half-rat, covered with scales, fangs bared and oozing blood. A vestigial tail ran out between Bass Akvaards' legs.

"Wouldn't want to meet him in a dark alley, now, would we, Brent?"

"Nooooo, but I have a teenage daughter who would. And that's what this sport needs, young blood."

"And more of the kind of intense rivalry we're seeing here between Bass Akvaards and the leader of the Bass Commandos . . ."

The screen showed a solitary boat. The camera began rushing up on it, skimming over the waves like a bird and I just sat there watching a man, in camouflage, hunkered over his swivel bowseat, peering into his fishfinder which was showing . . . which was showing . . . In a panic, I felt for the remote control unit inside my shirt and pushed, hoping to hit a button, any button . . . I thumped my chest, and prayed.

Jerry answered my knock. His face crinkled up in disgust. "What do you want *now?*"

"Looking for Virginia Roy."

"You may regret it when you find her. Bub, you blew it big-time."

"She's not here?"

"I am not my sister's keeper, is the saying, I believe. As pissed as she was last I saw her, you and I won't be related too much longer." He sounded flat and matter-of-fact, like he'd recently had the wind knocked out of him. "She's not sure she likes being married to the village idiot."

I nearly jumped him for that. But as he was only telling the truth, I uncocked my fist. He waited until I was through, my blood pressure sinking, before slipping in one last lick of sugarcoated venom. "We had it in the bag, Gar. Please try to understand. It was all there for the asking—plenty of endorsements, major media coverage, the works. You guys were going to have a steady gig, thanks to me."

I stepped back from the door. She might still be at the outdoor facility.

I started on my way, and he called out after me: "Wait a sec, there's something else we got to discuss." I just kept walking.

He finally caught up with me at the elevator, out of breath, clutching a paper. He thrust it at me. It was the incorporation agreement for the Bass Commandos.

"I'll sign it all over to you, just wash my hands of it. That's what you want, right?"

The elevator doors opened. I looked inside, looked at him. "Big gesture, but a day late. Why?"

He shrugged.

"The Commandos are yours. After I set it up so carefully, how could you guys give that interview trashing every single product you'd just endorsed? How could you do that to *me*?" The elevator door started to close; I stopped it with my hand, and stepped inside the car. Jerry blocked the door with his foot and, pressing the contract against the hall wall, began writing on it.

He thrust the now rumpled sheet of paper at me.

I ducked, saying, "You called the tune, now you pay the bills."

When I didn't take it, he let it drop to the elevator floor. A buzzer began to protest. Slowly Jerry reached into his pocket and pulled out his money clip. He peeled off the outer hundred, another, a third. When I didn't move, he threw them on the floor, cursed, and flung the money clip after them.

He ran a hand through his hair. "Now you got to give me something. For consideration."

I took my finger off the elevator's DOOR OPEN button. The door started to close. Jerry stopped it. "Seriously, for this to stand up in court. You got to give me cash, a check, something."

Pulling a crumpled bill out of my pocket, I handed it to him. He looked at it — a dollar. Looked at the floor littered with the faces of the presidents. Ground his teeth, and said, "Congratulations. Your ass is in a sling now, sucker. You're in hock to your eyeballs. You'll be paying off lawyers in the year two thousand—"

The door closed. I bent down to pick up the money and the

contract, the proud owner of all the liabilities, present and future, to be attached to our disgraced name. I wondered if this would be the last nail in my coffin. Probably, but I liked having our name back just the same.

For the third time in an hour, I stopped at our room. When I pushed open the door, the chain rattled. I waited. "V.R.?"

"Go away."

I put my back against the wall. "I just want to apologize."

"It's quite all right. You did what you had to do."

"Nobody *has* to watch the Flintstones. Particularly not on a boat in the middle of a lake." By listening sharp, I heard her stifled laugh. "But after using live worms, salmon eggs and marshmallows for bait—we *had* to clear our good name. Now I'm done raising Cain for the day. Now I'm just a fool who wants some company."

The chain rattled. She peered at me, a mystified smile on her so-serious face. She sniffed carefully as a hound dog inspecting a skunk. "Come in, then, and get dressed. The banquet's at seven."

Everybody should have a wife like mine. She'd laid my one non-camouflage outfit out on the bed: jeans and a polo shirt. There was a pack of Black Jack gum on the bedstand. "What's in here?" I picked up a brown paper sack. "Scooter Pies!"

"Though you don't deserve it." She adjusted the big floppy bow at her collar. Reaching for a short-waisted green jacket, she grunted, froze, and rubbed her lower back with both hands. I slid over on the bed and joined in on the massage. She dropped her hands and just stood there, let me work solo on her.

Now I felt shy again. "Soldiering is hard work, isn't it?"

"Hard, yes, but in a good cause."

"Know exactly what you mean, ma'am. Right now I'm working extremely hard on this massage. There's nothing more important to me on earth."

"Well, there ought to be. Something. Something you don't just throw away—" Perhaps she heard her voice starting to shake, or else she couldn't go on. But she stopped there.

We went to the banquet. Let me tell you something. As banquets go, that one was good. In my mood, the usual Vegas floor show would've seemed like torture. But these soldier of fortune guys weren't to be denied their time in the spotlight. At one point, when about a dozen chorus girls were doing the old Andrews Sisters number about "The Bugle Boy in Company C," a gang of happy dogfaces just hopped up and joined them. And the side action wasn't to be believed: I'd glance down, under my tablecloth, and there would be some Special Forces graybeard on his belly, a bowl of jello in his hand, slithering toward an unsuspecting crony at another table. Then there was the big showstopper, a number that began with a dozen GIs on patrol by a tree. Well, it wasn't a tree at all; when the leaves fell off, it was a girl, and her outfit was booby-trapped with wires. When a GI tripped on one, boom, off came a piece of her clothing with a realistic puff of smoke. The finale nearly brought down the house.

We were enjoying ourselves, V.R. and Rico and I. It was good, clean, all-American fun, in contrast to the sick scene at the tournament, where Bass Akvaards and his scrofulous crew of winners were undoubtedly still the center of attention. We'd pulled out early. There was nothing to be gained by hanging around.

The guest speakers tonight were a mixed bag of adventurers, but they had tales to tell—of war in Afghanistan, of dirty ops in Laos, of hot times in Angola, and strolls down memory lane in Rhodesia and the Congo.

"There's a lot of pride in this room," one soldier said. "We're part of that elite who know what it's like to face the adversary, to stare him down. We know what it feels like to bluff past a roadblock with an ID so fake they were using it for toilet paper in the last village. And it's great for the bird-watchers and tree-huggers among us. After all, we know the quiet meadows and tall mountains only guerillas get to see."

Rico nodded and leaned forward to V.R. He muttered a name, pointed at the speaker. She stared, wide-eyed.

The man bowed his head and pointed to the bald spot surfacing through his graying crew cut. "Now, like so many warriors who get to my age, I'm getting sentimental. Looking at so many fine, young men out here tonight, and on the courses during the day, I get an itch to see the old places once more before I pack my kit bag for good." His voice became deep and melancholic. "And when I hear news of an old friend fallen to the foe, I know being sentimental has nothing to do with it — that I am needed out there, on freedom's front lines, even if I'm not as quick or as strong or as smart."

Through the loudspeaker came an old familiar strain of music. At first I thought it was a foul-up on the part of the sound crew. Then I heard the words about putting silver wings on a brave boy's chest.

"Bad news tonight, just in. Could you all rise, please, and observe a moment of silence for the soul of Barry Sadler, who has drawn his last rations with us of the brotherhood of Mars."

We stood in silence through the entire "Ballad of the Green Berets."

When it was over, the sound of chairs creaking and men coughing filled the room. "He always said he never had it so good as when he was in-country. I think a lot of us here would agree."

A waiter bent over Rico's shoulder, spoke to him, handed him a slip of paper. He arched his eyebrows at our curiosity and unfolded the note. The good humor faded from his face, the lines deepening between nose and mouth as his lips turned down. One hand came up and began combing his beard. "*Ay-ay-ay,*" he said softly.

He turned to Virginia Roy. "I must go." He gave me a curt nod. "I am sorry. Please stay and enjoy the evening."

V.R. reached under the table and brought out her handbag. She looked over her shoulder at me, nodded. "Ready?"

Rico held out his hands, motioning for us to seat ourselves again. But we were right with him.

As we waited for a taxi, Rico handed V.R. the paper. It was a telegram. There was a lot of gibberish, alphabet soup, that I took to be the initials of various military or government groups. In the end I let V.R. do the reading. It was tame stuff, about a somebody who wanted a spokesman to deliver a briefing to a subcommittee in Washington, D.C., at such and such a date and time . . .

"This is the one you were hoping for," V.R. said as we rode in the cab back to the Silver Stirrup.

Rico, riding in front, peered anxiously out the window as if looking for the constellation of casinos that would lead us to the hotel. "The timing is so bad. To have to leave for Washington now. Forgive me."

Up in his suite, Rico unlocked the porta-safe in the closet, pulled an address book out of his briefcase and made some fast phone calls. But even when he could manage to get through, he didn't seem to obtain any satisfaction from the party at the other end. He paced from the front door to the terrace, eating grapes from the room service cart. There were several boxes tied with twine in large white shopping bags between the twin beds. With nothing better to do, I snooped and read the labels: Banana Republic.

Rico went to use the fax downstairs. We stayed put, manning the crisis center, I guess. I kicked off my shoes and put on a baseball game.

A knock at the connecting door. Before we could say *boo*, it opened on my former business partner. Jerry froze at the sight of me. Virginia Roy he merely eyed with disapproval.

He looked around the room. "Where's Rico? I gotta talk to him."

"Something's come up. Good news, really: the Senate wants him to testify on Central America."

"He told me to drop by around about now." Jerry checked his Rolex. "I need to get . . ." His eyes brightened. "Ah, there it is." He crossed the room in a bound.

That nagged me, the easy way Jerry moved without a cane. Rico's aluminum briefcase was in his lap, his thumbs were under the latches, the top was lifting, before I could say anything about it. Then V.R. beat me to the punch: "What do you think you're doing?"

"Huh?" Jerry's eyebrows went up and down, three big reps. "Making a withdrawal. What else?"

V.R. stood, feet wide, arms crossed under her breasts, like a sumo wrestler. "That isn't your money, Jerry Roy."

I looked at her. I looked at the brown paper packets that filled the briefcase from corner to corner. "Is all that really money?" I asked.

Jerry ignored me. "Sis, I cleared it with Rico. Swear. It's a temporary loan to cover a temporary—" He ground his teeth and made it quite clear who he was thinking of. "—cash flow problem."

Now, V.R. knew who he meant and what he meant, but she just kept her head low and her eye on the ball. "You're going to pay that back, and soon."

"Of course. What do you take me for? Look, Rico said to be here at 8:30 sharp. If you like, I'll wait for him." He sat down heavily on the edge of the bed and crossed his ankles.

"By soon I mean in twenty-four hours," she said.

The whole thing had interesting potential, I thought, for a seriously overdue sibling spat. There was so much at stake for me, in fact, that I willingly put aside a second thing that puzzled me, something that had popped up in Jerry's remarks. Why would Rico tell Jerry to come by now, at eight-thirty, when the banquet wasn't scheduled to be over before ten o'clock? If not for Rico's telegram, Jerry would have missed us completely.

"Will do, Sis. You know you can trust me for it."

He helped himself to a brown packet, ripped a corner open, thumbed the bills once and slipped the whole thing into his gold carpskin jacket.

After he left us, I sat tight and managed not to comment. No, I'd learned my lesson; if those two were ever going to get sick of each other, it wouldn't be because of anything I said.

"Honey?"

"Hmmm?"

Just a stare, but she gave me a soul full. It wasn't that kind of look, though, so I stayed put.

"You seem kinda relieved," she said. "At peace. I wouldn't have thought it."

"It's over. We gave it a shot. It was like having a fever, and now the fever has burned out."

"Then maybe there's hope for me," she said.

"I've always thought so," I said stoutly. "You do anything enough, you burn out. Even war."

"Well, I haven't done *that* yet." She spoke so fast she clipped her words. "I haven't even started."

"It's one experience you can miss. Believe me."

"That's like saying life is something you can miss." She smiled quickly at her tone. "It's just that I feel—more alive—the more, the closer I get. The more real it gets—the more real I feel."

She meant it. And that's where we left it. Rico returned, shook his head in response to our looks. "It is intentional," he declared. "They know, these cowards in Congress, that I am on my way to bring sustenance to our boys." He pointed a stern finger at the aluminum briefcase on the bed. "But they force me to fly to them instead, while the muchachos who sleep under a rubber poncho must count their bullets and dream of victory on an empty stomach." He stared around him with wide eyes, fists balled at his waist, as if searching for someone or something to fight.

"Richard." V.R. interrupted gently. "Don't worry. I'll go."

"It is me the bureaucrats want, I'm afraid. My eyewitness testimony."

"I mean, I'll go to Honduras."

He dismissed her with a wave. "Someday you shall go, but not this time."

"Why not? Don't they need the money to buy food and medicine, and bullets?" She made it sound simple, like the commonsense thing to do. Betty Crocker's Contra recipe.

"This is not a game we are playing," he warned.

"I'll never know that unless I go."

"There is a point of no return."

"I know that."

"A place where you draw the line."

"Yes. I'm drawing it here. Now."

Rico turned and faced me. He said nothing, but it was clear that he expected me to object. And I would've, too. I had no lack of ways to start, from the sensible stuff about where will she stay and who will meet her at the airport, to the nitpicky stuff about what to wear and the right shoes, to the subversive questions, like what's the right antidiarrhetic and how big are the mosquitos? They would all lead up to the one true question.

But I didn't see how I could stop her. She'd as much as warned me, a few minutes ago, that her time was coming. She'd tried to prepare the ground. And I think I got the message—she had a need. And this was what would fill it, she thought.

I leaned back on my elbows and glanced from him to her. Didn't say word one.

Rico hesitated, opened his mouth to speak, thought better of it. "Tomorrow evening it will be."

Virginia Roy stood there and let the realization sweep over her. Her tight smile faded. With a move of a hand, she pushed her curls back off her forehead and held them there. She could have been standing on the edge of the ocean, searching the horizon for a ship that was due in.

I felt a hand on my shoulder. "Go to your rooms, now, my friends. This is your Uncle Rico speaking."

We shuffled to the door. V.R. turned. "We have to talk about where I'll stay and who will meet me at the airport—"

"Plenty of time. Go."

She stopped again as we stood in the hallway. "I almost forgot. Jerry borrowed one pack of fifties, he said you'd okayed it."

"That's right, I did," Rico agreed, but a twitch of his nostrils put me in mind of a horse about to kick.

V.R.'s forehead wrinkled anxiously. "He'll pay it back tomorrow, but shouldn't I enter it in the books? I'd better do it tonight."

Rico closed his eyes and shook his head, making soothing sounds. "No, no, no. Tomorrow will be fine."

We walked to the elevators holding hands, and rode down to our floor without breaking the spell. In the room V.R. pointed at the flashing light on the phone. "Shall I check our messages?"

"No. And take it off the hook." I patted the bed next to me. She sat on the edge, then leaned back into my arms, sighing. We lay there, huddled together, until we drifted off to sleep for a second, just long enough to snap us both back into awareness when our heads jerked up. Then we got up and took our time about undressing and getting under the covers. The room had been shut all day and the air conditioning chill had gotten in under the blankets. We rubbed our legs together, making a bigger fuss over the cold than it deserved, grateful for the excuse. Gradually the spark caught and we started making some good old motel love, the kind where the strangeness of where we are makes us newer and shinier to each other. Even so, this was much hotter, much more intense. But then I don't think we'd ever been in a stranger place than here, on this last night in Las Vegas.

18

We met out by the pool, on a concrete pad with an unused barbecue, toward sundown. Looking to Las Vegas over the peeling iron rail that was blockaded by a drift of tumbleweeds, I could see the office towers of the city, made of modern reflecting glass, catch the sun like pillars of fire, rising up between and outshining the casinos. As I watched, a jolting, hopping ball of dust came out of the desert and ran up against its tumbleweed brethren at the fence.

There were fourteen recruits. All were in civilian clothes, but no other effort was made to disguise them. Their duffel bags, for instance, were identical. So were their boots. Rico had them pull the pool furniture in a circle and then ordered each man to hand in his wallet. With Virginia Roy at his side, he leafed through and picked out all driver's licenses, social security cards and other forms of identification. These went into individual manila envelopes, which went into a bag at V.R.'s feet. The wallets went back to their owners.

Rico looked over at me. "I don't see yours here."

"Didn't know it was needed. Sorry." I handed it over. He had recovered nicely from my bombshell announcement that I was going; more gracefully than my wife, who seemed to feel this was my way of denying her the true flavor of the war experience.

Everybody checked each other out, as new people will, but some seemed more interested than others. A man I thought of as Joe Cool was putting on the slack-jawed, gum-cracking James Dean act for V.R.'s sake. A young fellow, who reminded me of Cecil, only had eyes for Rico. Then there was one with a tattooed ear, who I could swear I'd seen before. But he wasn't looking at anybody, just squatting with his hands clasped between his knees, staring at the ground.

I didn't hear the command, but suddenly they rose and hefted their duffels. Out the back gate were four taxi-vans. We got into the lead van, only to find Jerry waiting for us next to the driver.

We headed out of town on a narrow ribbon of road, buffeted by gusts of wind that rocked the van off plumb and forced the driver to oversteer. It would be challenging weather in a boat on the lake, blowing tackle and gear overboard, raising gas consumption, risking the chance of the boat kiting and flipping if it took a wave too fast. V.R. sat with her chest restraint on and the aluminum briefcase between her knees. She wasn't interested in talking to me, so I closed my eyes rather than risk being talked to by Rico.

I felt myself slipping off, and fought it. Seems like sleep, the Great Healer, always comes over me after a big tournament, but this was one time I needed to be alert.

The most likely troublemaker would be Tattooed Ear. The way I had it figured, there'd be a bad time when we landed and another one when we transferred the money and then a day or two of keeping our guard up while we moved in-country. The only question remaining would be when Virginia Roy was willing to come on home.

I didn't have an answer for that. I don't believe she did, either. But I'd seen her eyes, blue-gray and direct, as she took in the poolside conversation before Rico called us to order. A stringbean-lean Texan had been joshing a youngster in time-honored fashion. "Oh, I do this strictly as a gut check," he was saying. "I'm drawing a twenty-year pension. With PX privileges, that goes a long way, especially if you hunt and put up your own venison and game.

"But every so often I catch myself going on in the roadhouse, usually to my buddies or the barkeep, and I think, Jesus Christ, Harry, you're turning into a honky-tonk hero just like your old man. That's when I go find me a bit of action.

"You see, to be a player in this game means that sooner or later you gotta go South, chamber a real bullet, get a man in your sights, and squeeze the trigger. Only then will you know if you're playing a game, or if the game is playing you."

The van stopped with a jerk. With a *whoosh* the sliding door flew open and a gust of grit filled my mouth. I hung in my chest restraint, blinking on dust, drool on my sleeve. V.R.'s butt was in my face as she exited, then Rico's. Hitting the release button, I lurched out into the gray murk of posttwilight in canyonland.

The airstrip ran the length of a shallow valley. A twin-engined Dakota, the old war bird, sat facing the wind, wing tips snugged down on either side to fifty-gallon fuel drums. A gust blowing through just then showed how necessary these wind anchors were.

A burly man in jeans, down jacket and cowboy boots stepped out from behind the cinder block hut. When he saw Rico, he turned and walked to the plane's rear ramp and disappeared inside. Rico herded the recruits to the Dakota and hustled them aboard, then trotted down the ramp and up to us. He waved at the oil drums anchoring the plane. "Jerry and I, we'll untie the ropes after you're aboard."

There was an awkward pause.

Jerry grimaced. "Let's make this brief." He hugged V.R. and stepped away. "See you back at the ranch, I guess."

He glanced at me and looked over his shoulder at the taxi. "Meter's running."

Virginia Roy shifted the briefcase from one hand to the other. She stared pointedly at Jerry. "Aren't you forgetting something?"

He scuffed his toe in the dust. "Maybe I was, and maybe I wasn't." Straightening up, he offered me his hand. "But I can't harbor no grudge against my boy Gar."

"I meant the money."

We both turned. V.R. had her look. Jerry snorted in disbelief. He arched his cliffy eyebrows. He smiled.

"Let's have it, Jerry. You heard me say it had to be paid back."

"Did I?" He feigne l confusion.

"Don't play games with *me*." V.R. set the aluminum case down between her booted feet. She rubbed her hands briskly together.

Behind us, there was a *brraaap!* and a puff of black exhaust from one of the Dakota's engines. A second *brraaap!* followed immediately. The sand on the hard-packed earth began to slide and roll in a low tidal surge along the ground, coming upon us from the backwash of the propellors.

"A packet of fifties," she said. "We're not going without it."

Rico gave her a troubled look. "Virginia Roy, he is your brother. We can trust him for it, no?"

"I'm not sure we can. You were doing a lot of shopping while you were here, Jerry. For you and that woman. Not to mention the gambling."

"What I do with my money is my business."

"But it wasn't yours, was it?" She smacked her hands together. "Come on, Jerry, where is it? I want it now."

The wind blew his hair to one side. He tried to brush it back, gave up. "Hell, who bought dinner the other night? You think that Crystal Palace floor show came cheap?"

"That is correct," Rico said, in a deep, serious voice. "I have allowed you to pay far more than your share. The catering for the Open House, now that I remember it . . . ."

"That wasn't his money, that was *ours*," I said.

"What are you gonna do about it?" Jerry waved his cane in the air. "Gonna take me with you if I don't pay up?"

"You'll pay up. I'm going to see that every cent goes where it rightfully belongs." She leaned forward and stuck her nose right up to his. "With the people who depend on it for their lives. I *don't* want to see it buying lingerie for your cheap Hollywood women."

"You're the cheap one! Christ, you think Rico's not taking his cut, his twenty percent? That's show business, babe, and you're just a sucker if you aren't in line for a taste." He gripped the cane below its crooked handle and brought it up under the point of her chin. Slowly he exerted upward pressure, lifting her chin against her will. He stared down into her eyes. "So don't you come chasing after brother Jer for—"

She thrust the cane into his belly and he folded up like an umbrella. "Let's have it," she said.

The money began to emerge. First, he pulled a sheaf of bills out of his wallet, still crisp from the packet. He took an envelope from his jacket and found some there. His new money clip produced more. A wad in his jeans pocket finished him off.

"You're still short a hundred-fifty."

He just stared. "You're a ball-breaker, you know that. You break Gar's, now you want mine. Well, that's it."

She hesitated, and I honestly thought she was going to wade in and knock him around. But she didn't.

"Please." Rico was watching the plane, the road, the hills growing darker. "This is foolish. Go, now."

She kneeled on the ground, the money in both her hands. Tipping the briefcase on its side, she jammed the cash under one knee, trapped some in her armpit and held the rest between her teeth. Her hands free, she sprung the locks. The case opened. The gusting wind scooped at the brown paper packets. She closed the case a bit, then tried opening it again.

The inside latch must have snagged an edge of the paper,

because as she lifted the lid a brown packet came sailing with it, as if hooked. Virginia Roy made a grab for it. The paper tore. Grayish white rectangles of paper blew all over the place, plastering Rico and Jerry, vanishing upward into a passing dust devil, dancing downwind.

Virginia Roy held one of the paper rectangles. She flipped it over. "Rico?"

He turned, and the white rectangles slipped off his body. It was as if he'd turned into darkness. But he was really only running for the plane.

19

My last sales call was so far into the Natatoches Parish that even with a radar detector I couldn't get back to Valhalla before dark fell. Driving too fast, I brodied the turn to the driveway, but even as I straightened out the wheels I saw that I'd missed V.R. Her El Camino was gone.

She must've just left, switching on the porch light as she went out the door, because the house was filled with signs of her. The long conference table in the old living room was stacked with reports in file folders, yellow sticky notes, empty soft drink cans and three pizza cartons. I guessed the neighborhood boys had talked her into a free lunch again.

Out the window the woods were fading into twilight. Summer had burned itself out like a fireball last week, taking the treetops with it. Their leaves looked brown and dry. I unbuttoned my shirt and stripped off my tie, squeezing a stain that looked like brown sauce between my fingers. At the rate I was running through ties, I'd have to stop having gravy. Or maybe I should cut out the business lunches, as Virginia Roy has been suggesting, and try to get some exercise, lose five pounds.

In the end I'd just buy some new ties. Pouring myself a Dr. Pepper, I kicked off my shoes and tugged at my sweaty socks, throwing them down the basement stairs. From a basket of fresh, unfolded laundry I pulled on a pair of gym shorts, covered my nakedness and finally planted myself in a wicker chair by an open window with a fan and a good, mosquito-proof screen on it.

Staring at the sales chart on the wall opposite me, I mentally filled in today's report. A month back I'd moved some merchandise into two stores that I'd been aiming at. It wasn't the Wal-Mart, but it was another step in the right direction. Well, today both stores reported sales that almost made my monthly targets. We're starting to get a feel for our market.

Next to the chart she'd hung a picture of the boys and me, taken just after our arrival in Las Vegas. The portrait seems old and remote, from a bygone era—just last spring. Life has gotten so much busier. I can't recall my last complete day off. Haven't touched a fishing rod since that tournament. My van needs a complete overhaul, and my body feels like it does, too. Owning your own business isn't all it's cracked up to be. But, as they say, nobody can take it away from you, even if sometimes you wish they would.

I stretched my legs, almost knocking over a pile of cartons ready to be taped up and left out for the UPS man. Can't even find a place to sit in this house anymore. Everywhere I walk, I'm stepping over stuff. This is what happens when your dreams come true: they take over your life.

After Rico went south, Jerry swore he had no idea that Rico had been looting the treasury. I didn't believe him then, but I guess even a con man can get fooled, and Rico's con was the slickest kind—the one a man pulls over on himself. He'd spent years being what he said he was, a man dedicated to a cause, years when he didn't have two dimes to rub together. Then the boom in Latin anti-Communism struck. Suddenly he was wallowing in dollars.

Nobody, not even the government, questioned what he did with the money. Bit by bit, it began to stick to his fingers.

He'd made it through the lean times, only to self-destruct in the time of plenty.

As for Jerry, well, we get phone calls. He's in Hollywood, he says. He's written a screenplay, he says. Taking acting lessons. Doesn't say how he pays for anything, and we don't ask.

Before getting onto the computer and working on the spread-sheet, I decided to put some music on the hi-fi. Then I saw V.R. out the window, walking up the driveway. She was wearing a full track suit striped with reflecting tape.

"What happened to the car?" I asked when she came through the door.

"It needed a tune-up. I dropped it off and ran back." Her cheeks were flushed, and when I tried to kiss her, she turned her head aside. "Please."

"That's nearly six miles."

"Six point two on the odometer." She peeled off her top as she went up the stairs. She turned on the water in the shower.

While I waited, I poured her a glass of water and checked the refrigerator. There was a packet of sliced turkey, a loaf of whole wheat: sandwiches for dinner. I set out an assembly line on the kitchen table. It reminded me of how we put together the first Commando products—the Bass Exerciser pole, to strengthen your wrists. We did it right here on this very kitchen table. Sold about two, and ended up refunding the money on one.

That led to the Commando Mental Studies course, which attracted a handful of enrollees. The only one to stick it through a full six weeks was this convict at the Angola State Farm. Then there was, let's see, Commando Strike Lures and The Amazing Commando Worm.

We'd just about resigned ourselves to hanging up the rods and looking for other work when one of V.R.'s neighborhood buddies brought over a set of action figure toys. She happened to catch her son putting a GI Joe behind the wheel of a boat and pretending he was a Bass Commando. When V.R. told us the story later on, Eddie and I just looked at each other. We knew.

So now we've got a full lineup of the Bass Commando Force— *As seen on national television from Lake Mead, Nevada!*—each of us represented by his own individualized action figure. Mine wears a red cap, and if you squint it sort of resembles *the* cap. The Coke cap.

Now I'm trying to build up sales myself until one of the national outfits agrees to take us on. We've had offers to buy the company, but we're holding out. We own our name, and we like it that way.

"Can you drop me at the station?" V.R. called from the top of the stairs.

"Sure. Made you a sandwich."

"Thanks." She stood in the dark, tucking herself in with many a jingle and jangle. "The focus group says they think the Eddie doll needs a bigger physique."

"What do a bunch of ten-year-olds know?"

"They're the customers."

She began clumping down the stairs in those awful black shoes, keys and danglers jingling like a tambourine.

"They're going to give Eddie a swelled head."

She stopped at the bottom, gave her belt a last cinching, checked to see her revolver was securely buttoned down in its holster. "Seen my hat?" she asked, and kissed me.

"It's on your head, Officer Foote."

"So it is," she said, reaching up to check. "So it is."